A Fallen Sparrow

A Novel of the American Revolution

LYNNE BASHAM TAGAWA

A Fallen Sparrow: A Novel of the American Revolution

Blue Rock Press

5606 Onyx Way

San Antonio, Texas 78222

ISBN (paperback): 978-1-7325739-4-9

ISBN (ebook): 978-1-7325739-5-6

Library of Congress Control Number: 2022939897

Cover photo courtesy of Minatoishi Photography, San Antonio, Texas.

Cover design by JD Smith Design

Are not two sparrows sold for a farthing? and one of them shall not fall on the ground without your Father.

—*Matthew 10:29*

PROLOGUE

Yea, in the shadow of thy wings,
My refuge I have plac'd,
Until these sore calamities
Shall quite be over past.
—*Psalm 57:1,* The Bay Psalm Book, *1640*

March 1770

Ruth Haynes scrambled for the first word, the first phrase, but first sentences were always the hardest to write.

She leaned back in the governor's darkened carriage, the silk upholstery soft as a cloud. The middle of the essay was straightforward in her mind, and the ending obvious, but the beginning eluded her.

"I know that face. You're writing." The moonlight reflecting off the snow outside made Sarah Hutchinson's complexion glow like a pearl.

"Thanks to you and your family, I have everything I need." Including a list documenting every penny spent to repair the governor's home. The people ought to know the cost of Samuel Adams's intrigues.

Thinking of the list, Ruth thrust her hand in her pocket where it met with the soft bulge of stockings she'd knitted for one of the wharf boys. She quickly realized her mistake and laid a hand on her bodice, a tiny rustle assuring her that the piece of rag paper was secure.

"I worry about you," Sarah said. "That night haunts me. The violence."

Five years ago, the Stamp Act had stirred the colonies, and Ruth had agreed with the principal complaints. But debates in taverns were one thing. Mobs had spilled out into the streets of Boston and destroyed several homes, including Governor Hutchinson's. Tensions had ebbed since, but now there were soldiers stationed here, and the town was strung as tight as the lines of a tops'l in a gale.

"Papa never writes anything offensive and always casts an eye over anything I contribute. We shall not be in danger." Ruth rarely saw her friend nowadays and had enjoyed the chance to visit, even if it was for an article for the *Observer*. She looked beyond Sarah's features to her own ghostly reflection in the carriage window. Dark eyes in a pale face. Beyond, night-shrouded Boston slid by, the snow brilliant under the light of a waxing moon, illuminating the buildings along the street. It was late. Hopefully Papa wouldn't be worried.

She went back to her composing. The details of the damage would lead to her true message—rebellion against the King was wrong. Papa had given her permission to write such a commentary, but she needed a pen name. *Honorius? Or Honoria?* Should she present herself as a man, or—

Unexpectedly, the vehicle slowed and came to a creaking stop.

"Wait here, Sarah." Before her friend could protest, Ruth slipped out of the carriage onto the running board. Her shoes were undoubtedly sturdier than whatever the governor's daughter was wearing. Without waiting for the footman's help, she stepped into the snow.

Under the yellow glow of the carriage lamps, the coachman was standing with one of the horses' hooves on his knee and a hoof pick in his hands. He looked up at her. "Snowball."

Another delay in getting home.

Ruth tugged her cloak close and scanned the street. Even her mild-mannered papa would scold her for this; no excuse would suffice for arriving home at nine, not with scalawags and soldiers about. It used to be that the only ones swarming the streets were young men who met in groups for friendly bouts of fisticuffs to burn off their energy.

No, the fisticuffs were serious now. Bitter stevedores and tradesmen arrayed themselves against the "lobsters," as the red-coated soldiers were known. Only two days before, a serious fight had broken out at the rope maker's.

The Boston of her childhood was gone, replaced by a town full of anger and suspicious looks.

Exchange Street was empty except for a single man, striding along, greatcoat flapping. Going home, she supposed. The coachman resumed his seat, and Ruth laid her hand on the polished carriage door latch.

Then she heard a sound, the murmur of voices. A boy's shout.

Up ahead the man slowed and turned his head, listening, and she recognized him with a sigh of relief. It was her friend Henry Knox. He resumed his quick strides in the direction of the customhouse.

Sarah's face was pale in the moonlight. "Is there a disturbance?"

Ruth's pulse quickened. She needed to know the news. "Ask your driver to take us to King Street." Where Henry was headed.

"Hop in, my father would want to know if there's trouble."

The coachman urged the horses, and over the crunch and squeak of their motion on the snow the sound of shouting grew louder. At the intersection the vehicle stopped, and Ruth opened the door. Cautiously, this time.

Dong … dong … dong. A church bell reverberated, an alarming sound at this time of night. A fire?

She stepped out of the carriage. Men and boys gathered before the red brick state house, which also served as the customhouse. A boy was taunting the red-coated sentry guarding the building. A few other boys joined in.

Ding … ding … ding. A second set of bells pealed a mad cacophony.

She drew nearer. Was there no fire?

Ice splattered the soldier's uniform. The boy jeered and scooped up more snow.

"Ruth, come away. 'Tis dangerous." Sarah's voice was tight.

Ruth turned. "Stay there, Sarah. Henry Knox is here."

The beleaguered sentry backed up onto the customhouse steps. Henry appeared to be speaking to him. Henry was only nineteen, but he was a sturdy young man, both physically and otherwise. Surely he'd be able to defuse the situation. What had started it Ruth couldn't imagine. The sentry was only doing his job.

People entered the square, pouring in from the surrounding streets. She recognized Patrick Carr, an indentured leatherworker. Many carried leather fire buckets, probably hearing the church bells and looking for a fire.

Others seemed intent on mischief. Young boys threw snowballs as they mocked the sentry. Older lads brandished sticks and clubs. A few sailors and dock workers peppered the crowd, joining in the harassment.

With jerky movements the sentry loaded and primed his musket, sending a shock wave through the crowd that even Ruth could feel.

"The lobster is going to fire!" shouted a boy.

No, Lord, surely …

Henry continued to speak to the soldier, probably trying to calm him, but she couldn't make out the words.

The mob surged forward, sticks visible. Ruth stepped back, her pulse thundering in her ears.

There was no way to stop a mob.

Sweat glinting on his forehead, the sentry lowered his weapon, the bayonet silver in the moonlight. "If they touch me I'll fire!"

Someone was going to be killed.

Ruth retreated to the carriage. Behind her the sentry shouted for reinforcements.

"We need to leave!" Sarah urged.

"Go tell your father. Mr. Knox will escort me home, I'm sure." She needed the story for the *Observer*. Her father struggled to stay solvent.

"Jem!" Sarah's voice was shrill. "Stay here with Miss Haynes. I'll return with my father!"

The footman joined Ruth, and the Hutchinsons' carriage pulled away.

The cold was numbing Ruth's fingers even through her gloves, and she pulled her cloak closer. More soldiers arrived and formed a defensive line before the sentry, their ghostly reflections in the large windows behind them seeming to double their number.

Townspeople filled the streets as far as she could see. Henry strode up to a soldier in a crimson coat brighter than the others', a metal device glittering below his stock. An officer.

Fearful but curious, she drew nearer, careful to stay out of the line of fire.

"Take your men back again." Henry laid hold of the officer's lapels. "If they fire, your life must answer for the consequences."

"I know what I am about," spat the officer, twisting away.

The new soldiers loaded their muskets as taunts flew thick from the crowd.

"Lay aside your guns, and we are ready for you," shouted one. "Come on, you rascals, you bloody backs, you lobster scoundrels, fire, if you dare. We know you dare not."

The British officer clenched his jaw. "Disperse!"

The mob pressed forward, and the scene descended into chaos. A soldier slipped on the ice and fell.

A shot was fired. *Pop!*

Another soldier went down, and more shots were fired.

Henry!

Ruth retreated against the customhouse wall, heart hammering. She finally spotted Henry, standing a little apart from the soldiers. He looked as horrified as she felt.

Then she saw the blood on the snow. And the bodies. Heedless, she rushed forward—were they dead, or wounded?

Patrick Carr. *No, no, no.* The Irish indenture was lying on his back in the snow, blood on the front of his coat. Was he still alive?

She knelt, the cold seeping through her skirt. "Mr. Carr?"

He blinked up at her. "What happened?"

She yanked her kerchief from her bodice, disregarding the paper—the list of expenses—that fluttered to the snow, and folded the length of cloth. She loosened Mr. Carr's coat and placed the makeshift bandage over his hip. She pressed gently and the man winced.

The footman squatted nearby.

"Jem," she said, "he needs a physician. Go to his master's house." She gave him directions.

"I should stay with you."

Henry hurried to join her, his face sweaty despite the cold. "Ruth—Miss Haynes—" He turned to the footman. "I'll escort her home."

Jem left, and Henry knelt. He folded his scarf and placed it under Mr. Carr's head. Folks milled about, helping the injured, sending messages.

The red-coated soldiers retreated, their expressions horrified or confused.

Shaking, Ruth stood, willing herself not to look at the others lying on the snow. This was all the *Boston Gazette*'s fault. Ever since the Stamp Act, irresponsible men had sought to inflame the town against their God-given government.

Henry rose and took her trembling hands in his. "'Tis the shock." He guided her away.

"The musket ball didn't strike his head or his heart. Perhaps Mr. Carr will recover."

He shook his head, his normally jovial face shadowed.

In her mind's eye Ruth saw the stack of books Henry read when the shop lacked customers. Military books, all. He probably knew more about armaments and military protocol than the officer he'd been arguing with.

And he probably knew more about injuries. "Is there any hope?"

"Perhaps."

Not much. Her eyes filled with tears. This was all Samuel Adams' fault. "Henry, what is happening to Boston?"

His jaw worked as his gaze took in the square. "I'll see you home."

Her article … she needed to write about this.

But all she could think of was the blood on the snow.

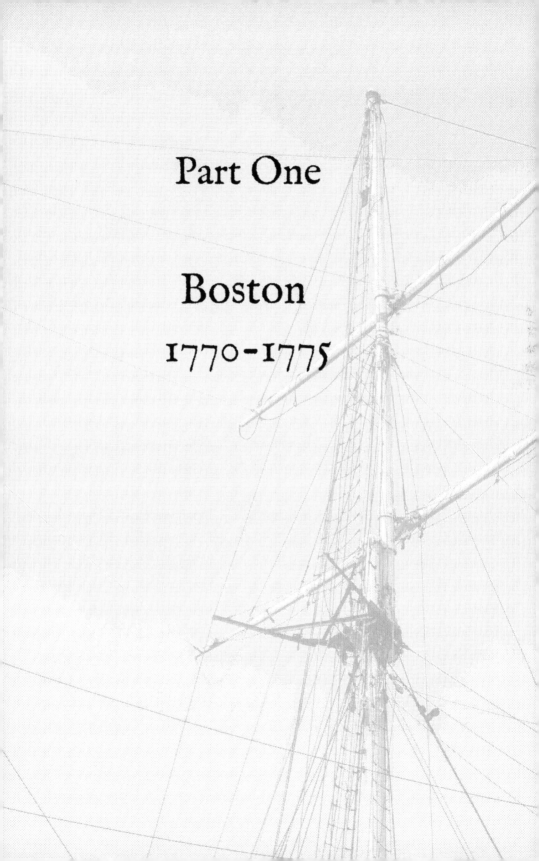

Part One

Boston
1770-1775

1

I go to a rest prepared; my sun has arisen and by aid from Heaven has given light to many. It is now about to set—no, it is about to rise to the zenith of eternal glory.

—George Whitefield, last sermon, September 29, 1770

September 1770

Morning sunlight gilded the New England countryside and spangled the grassy verge with starry dew drops. Tidy homesteads lay peacefully along either side of the road.

Jonathan Russell felt like a stranger.

For one thing, his clothing. He, his father, and his brother Nathan all wore their usual leather hunting jackets while traveling. At least Jonathan had stashed his tomahawk below the wagon seat. It drew stares.

"How far is Newburyport?" he asked his father on the wagon seat beside him. Jonathan ran his hand through his hair, snagging yet another wisp of hay. He didn't usually mind sleeping in a barn, but not on a day like this. He wasn't normally fussy about his appearance, but going to hear a preacher—wasn't that like going to meeting?

"A wee bit farther up the coast." His father twitched the reins, and the sturdy Conestoga mares swiveled their ears and picked up the pace.

Jonathan finger-combed his hair and tied it back as neatly as he could. In the half-empty wagon bed behind them, Nathan made a sighing sound in his sleep. They'd left the tavern's barn when it was still dark, as Da was eager to find the parsonage where George Whitefield was staying. Travelers filled the Ipswich tavern's rooms, hoping to hear the famous preacher, and the owner had only been able to offer the Russells the hayloft.

They'd traveled all the way from the Shenandoah Valley to sell goods and buy supplies. By a wonderful providence the preacher was in Massachusetts.

There was no discussion. They were going to hear him. All his life, Jonathan had heard of this man, read his sermons.

"It smells like salt." Nathan's sleepy voice intruded. His red-gold hair stuck up in every direction.

"Ye're smelling the ocean. I'll take ye to see it before we head to Boston." Da tightened the reins slightly as the road veered to the left. The horses' long shadows bounced over the track ahead of them. "I dinna think it's much farther."

Nathan rummaged in a sack and handed out bread.

Jonathan grunted his thanks. He wished he knew his mind as well as his brother did. As unlikely as it seemed, Nathan had decided to haul freight for a living. Jonathan wasn't sure of his own trade. He knew farming, knew horses, but his hands loved to make things. And the restlessness he felt, the loneliness that hit at odd moments. Nathan had nailed it just last night, in the loft.

"Ye need to marry, Jonnie. It's not good for a man to be alone, the scripture says."

Well, maybe. Eventually.

They washed down their breakfast with ale from their flasks and admired the neat stone walls along the road, so different from the rough-hewn rail fencing of home. The scent of apple trees heavy with fruit sweetened the misty morning. The road turned north again, and they came to a river. The horses' hooves clattered over the stone bridge, and the smell became marshy.

Whitewashed homes clustered closer. They were coming up on a town.

"Newbury," Da said. "It won't be long now."

Jonathan's jacket suddenly felt too warm despite the chilly morning. He ran a finger under the kerchief around his neck. Whitefield was reputed to be cross-eyed, but ministers had an uncanny knack of turning to that verse you didn't want to hear.

Would this man expose him somehow? Expose his heart?

Behind him, his brother brushed hay and breadcrumbs from his clothing and tied his hair back indifferently.

"We're looking for Federal Street." Da's gaze took in the buildings and narrow alleyways.

A bell tower rose above the top of the other structures, leading them to a fine brick meetinghouse, flanked by a smaller structure. Presumably, the parsonage.

Da had just halted the mares when a man burst out of the parsonage door, tears on his face. Had he been affected by a sermon? Jonathan had heard tales of men breaking down and weeping over their sins.

The fellow spotted them. He stepped closer but did not speak. Was something wrong?

"Might I help ye?" His father slid off his seat and hopped to the ground.

The man took a gasping breath and said, "Mr. Whitefield is no more. He has gone … to glory."

No—no, it couldn't be.

How could this man die? The very sunlight seemed to dim.

SEVERAL HOURS LATER, Jonathan staggered to the wagon and clambered onto the seat, still in shock. How could Whitefield be dead?

He barely noticed when Nathan took his place beside him and clucked at the horses. As they left Newburyport, Da settled back in the wagon bed, his hat over his eyes. The bright midday sun had chased away the September chill but failed to cheer Jonathan.

He thought back over the scene they'd witnessed inside the parsonage. Weeping and praying had filled the house. He'd felt strangely shaken, as if the very ground had shifted under his feet.

Finally Whitefield's assistant had gone off into a corner with the parson to discuss arrangements. At that point his father had decided they should leave.

Jonathan's stomach complained, but it was the Sabbath. Taverns were closed. He wondered vaguely where they'd eat.

"Rein left at the fork," Da's voice rumbled from behind him. So he wasn't sleeping. Probably praying or thinking. Or both.

The road to the left dwindled to a mere track. The salt smell grew stronger. Coarse grass rose over lonely sandy hills. Then Jonathan glimpsed a shimmer.

"Da!" He straightened. "The ocean?"

The horses plodded on until finally the gleaming water stretched across the horizon. Nathan pulled up the horses and slid off the wagon seat. He went to the near mare's side, laying his hands on her neck and bridle as if the animal would be startled by the sight.

Jonathan joined him, marveling at the stretch of undulating water, gentle swells extending to a limitless distance. The waves sighed as they flowed up the beach. Dark rocks peppered the smooth sand.

"We'll spend our Sabbath here," Da said simply.

Jonathan's lips parted. He wished his sister Hannah could see this.

"It's so big." Nathan spread his arms as if to embrace the sight. "I never imagined the ocean was like this."

They unharnessed the horses and tethered them to graze on the rough grass.

Nathan pulled out the food, beef pies and Connecticut cheese. They settled on a grassy dune above the beach and ate silently.

The waves mesmerized Jonathan, teasing, testing, challenging. Challenging him. *What have you done?* The dark memory intruded at the oddest times.

"Nathan, what are you doing?"

His brother was removing his shoes. He trotted down the slope and onto the sand. In a moment he was in the water. "It's cold!" He ran back and forth, splashing in the foam, whooping and laughing like a lad.

His father chuckled. "I'm glad he can play, despite his age. Despite …"

Jonathan took a deep breath. It would take a lot more than water and salt air to dispel his gloom. Nothing was right. "Why, Da, why?"

"Whitefield wanted to 'wear out, not rust out.' His own words. He finished his course well."

Every parish, every town, had its own minister, but Whitefield was the preacher they all knew and loved. He was irreplaceable. And it wasn't just that.

Jonathan picked up an apple and studied it. The oppressive acts of Parliament. Then the shooting in Boston. His own dark secret.

His world was upside down. Once, the peaceful rhythms of the Shenandoah Valley had seemed inviolate, his own path clear. He'd follow in his father's footsteps, farming, breeding horses. Finding a woman to spend his life with. But even the valley's peace was disturbed by the Stamp Act, and even though it had been repealed, the passage of the Townshend Acts meant that Parliament was set on a tyrannical course.

He examined the rocks standing sentinel on either side of the cove. They'd be dangerous to a boat. The Townshend Acts were like those rocks, dangerous to American liberty.

Jonathan put the untouched apple in his haversack and pulled off his shoes. He stepped gingerly down the dune and onto the beach, the sand squelching cold between his toes. "Nathan, what would Whitefield say about the Townshend Acts?"

His brother frowned and studied the horizon. The salt breeze nearly swallowed his words when they finally came. "We have the right to defend ourselves."

Defend—what was he saying?

Surely—hopefully—it wouldn't come to fighting.

IT WAS the next day before Jonathan realized his father hadn't fully answered his question about Mr. Whitefield's death. Perhaps *why* questions couldn't be answered. He tugged at his old waistcoat, deciding to leave the top two buttons unfastened. "Who invented these things, anyway?"

Beside him, reins in his hands, Nathan glanced at him.

It was hard to hide his moods from his brother.

They'd left the beach at dawn and made good time, the mares trotting briskly after devouring a bucket of feed each. An hour ago, they'd stopped on the outskirts of Cambridge to water the horses. They'd also changed from their usual garb into something suitable for Boston shops. His brother looked neat, for once, his old blue coat and tricorne clean.

Cheerful yellow leaves flashed now and again from the deep green of the trees. It was a beautiful time of year. Maybe he'd buy a new waistcoat. If he had to suffer the thing, might as well get one that fit.

"You asked the Wards to order knife blanks for me?" Jonathan asked his father. He'd never met this branch of the family.

"Aye."

The Wards and the Haynes were kin, but not blood kin—relations of his mother by marriage.

"The Wards' dispensary is next to her brother's shop. Gideon Haynes is a printer." Da pointed to his left. "The Charles River. Before us is the Boston Neck."

Beyond the trees, a broad expanse of water shimmered in the midday sun. Apparently, Boston was located on a peninsula. Connected to the mainland by a very skinny neck of land, it was almost an island. Suddenly it seemed like a vulnerable place to live.

"Da, when is the trial?" Nathan asked.

"Any day now."

The shooting had ripped off the scab that had formed after the Townshend Acts. Folks had been settling down, starting to order British goods again after the boycott, and now this. "Da, was it truly the redcoats' fault?" The soldiers could be hung if convicted. Probably would be.

"If I build a fire, and you put your powder horn next to it, whose fault is it if there's an accident?"

An accident. But it was hard to think of a shooting as an accident.

The mares slowed to a walk as they passed through a cluster of homes and entered the Neck. To their left, the honks of water birds floated over a reedy swamp; to their right, a few weathered scows nestled along a ramshackle pier.

Ahead was a gate and a guardhouse to the side. Several men poured out of the building. They wore red uniforms.

Redcoats.

Jonathan's hands curled into fists.

2

Send a heavy heart up to Christ, it shall be welcome.
  —Samuel Rutherford (1600-1661)

*R*uth nudged the soap with a kidskin-gloved finger. The three lone bars of French milled soap were now perfectly equidistant on the dispensary counter.

George Whitefield was dead—the news had flown through Boston like a sudden nor'easter. Papa would need an article for the paper, but right now they knew little. Not the kind of news she wanted to write about, anyway. Her heart floundered. Whitefield was a national treasure, now suddenly taken away.

And what would happen to the orphanage he supported in Georgia?

Ruth pushed the thoughts away and tried to focus on the task before her. She straightened and examined the counter again. Aunt Betsy claimed another shipment of soap was coming. Ruth hoped so.

Her aunt and uncle Ward had participated in the recent boycotts, and their stocks of foreign goods were still thin. Most medicinals her uncle needed for his dispensary were available locally, and many of her aunt's scents were too. But fine soap was quite another thing.

French soap was especially problematic, as it was expensive. They couldn't get it directly from France, for that was illegal. All such goods had to be shipped on British merchantmen. The Wards didn't make money on it.

Ruth frowned at the lovely lavender bars. The soap maker three blocks away made a decent enough product, but no one in the colonies produced anything like this. And it was too bad, because ever since her uncle had ceased making house calls, they were depending more and more on the sales of incidentals. Her father's print shop made little.

"Anything else, Aunt Betsy?" Ruth asked. With no apprentice, Papa needed help in the afternoons. Ruth tugged at her gloves to remove them, needing them only here in the dispensary where ink-stained fingers could be a problem.

The door opened and a tall man stepped into the shop. He removed his hat to reveal silver temples. Not a young man, but his vigorous presence filled the room.

"Aunt Betsy." The man addressed her aunt, nodding at them both in greeting.

"John Russell! Is that you?" Aunt Betsy's plump form rounded the counter.

Was this man their relation from the Shenandoah Valley? Ruth struggled to recall the connection.

The door creaked again. Two more men came inside.

The first was almost a mirror image of his father—for he had to be his son. Same height, stance, chestnut hair. His blue gaze wandered all over the shop, settled on Aunt Betsy briefly, then on her.

Ruth twisted the gloves in her hands. The man wore a waistcoat that was too tight across his chest, and indeed, he seemed uncomfortable standing there, like a boy who'd been forced into his Sunday clothes. She found herself staring.

Aunt Betsy's voice penetrated. "—and this is Ruth, Gideon's daughter."

"I heard about your loss—" Russell's voice was warm.

"Yes, we lost her mother to smallpox in sixty-four," her aunt affirmed.

Ruth's cheeks warmed, but not just with embarrassment. She disliked being talked about that way.

The second man stepped out from behind the first. A brother? Same height but poured into a more graceful mold—lighter hair, a striking reddish blond that resisted its bonds, and fine features. A slight smile played at his lips.

A veritable Adonis.

John Russell was still talking to Aunt Betsy. "We went to hear Mr. Whitefield—"

"Did you hear the news?" Her aunt interrupted.

"We arrived just after he passed."

They were all silent a few moments. It seemed unthinkable to ask for details for the paper.

Ruth cleared her throat. "It has been a difficult year."

They all looked at her. The elder Russell said, "Forgive me, this is Jonathan, my eldest son, and Nathan."

Jonathan was almost as tall as Henry Knox, but leaner. Ruggedly handsome.

"Welcome. My uncle is ill, he's upstairs," she said.

Yes, he was handsome, but there were questions behind his eyes.

JONATHAN SPOTTED her almost as soon as he entered.

He'd followed his father into the dim dispensary, which took up half of an ancient house; a print shop occupied the rest of the ground floor. As Jonathan's eyes adjusted to the light, he noticed a large mortar and pestle dominating an apothecary's bench; a cabinet with tiny drawers stood behind it. A multitude of glass bottles marched along shelving above. On his left a myriad of ready-made medicines and other products swam in his vision: James's fever powder, elixirs of every kind, tooth powder, herbs—some he recognized—and scents. A few lonely bars of soap held pride of place on a counter.

And two women, an older and a younger. His father greeted the older as "Aunt Betsy."

The younger was dressed in an ink-splattered apron over what Mother would describe as a Sabbath gown. A quilted silk petticoat peeped out over sturdy, no-nonsense shoes. But then, Mother was often the same. She dressed in decent clothing but was constantly working, either inside or out in her herb garden, and her apron took the brunt of the damage.

He shifted his gaze quickly, not wishing to stare, but he'd already noticed dark eyes in a heart-shaped face. A pretty face.

He caught her name. Ruth.

It was not surprising they'd heard the news about the minister. A fast rider could have arrived yesterday. And everyone loved Whitefield, or at least respected him. Certainly, all the inhabitants of Boston would know of his death by sundown.

A man came in the back door of the shop, round-faced with spectacles.

"My brother Gideon Haynes," Aunt Betsy announced. "Owns the print shop next door." Jonathan reviewed the family connection. The young woman in the silk petticoat was his cousin. But no blood relation. For some reason he was glad.

"I'll get the soap," Nathan said.

"Soap?" Ruth's expressive face lit up.

Nathan went out for the boxes, and Mr. Haynes started asking questions.

"How did Mr. Whitefield die? Can you give me any details?"

It sounded morbid, but glancing at Ruth's ink-spotted apron, Jonathan wondered if Mr. Haynes published a newspaper.

"Gideon—wait until supper." Then Aunt Betsy addressed Da. "Will you eat with us? Stay for the night?"

"Aye, thank ye kindly."

Nathan came in carrying a crate. "Where should I put these?"

Aunt Betsy cleared a space on the counter, moving aside shaving supplies.

"What do you have?" Ruth asked.

Jonathan joined his brother and pried the top off with his case knife. "My sister Hannah makes fine soap, best in the valley." He felt unaccountably nervous under Ruth's watchful gaze.

A woodsy odor greeted him. The box was filled with brown and green bars, representing the labor of an entire winter. But was it good enough for a Boston shop?

Ruth removed several and placed them on the counter.

Aunt Betsy lifted one to her nose. "What scent is this?"

"Birch," Nathan said. "The brown ones are cloves and orange. Underneath is lavender and marigold."

Ruth continued to remove them from the crate, and the shop was filled with fragrance.

"Thank you. Very nice." Her face bloomed with a warm smile.

His midsection warmed.

JONATHAN FOLLOWED THE OTHERS UPSTAIRS. Chairs and other furniture of various age and provenance crowded the small spaces in the Wards' living quarters. He saw his father squint in appreciation at a cherry occasional table. They entered a small, fragrant room with bread, beans, and other steaming foods on an ancient sideboard.

The long, narrow table was smaller than their own on Russell's Ridge, but somehow they all managed to fit, and a woman with brown skin served them from the sideboard with a flourish.

After grace was said, Jonathan tore a hunk from a loaf and spread it with creamy yellow butter, as good as his mother's. Then he scooped a piece of the sauce-covered cod on his fork and tasted it. Pleasant and tangy, but different from his mother's chowder or pan-fried fish, the only way he'd ever eaten seafood.

Across from him Mr. Haynes asked Da a question about Mr. Whitefield. Ruth said nothing, but her expression revealed her interest. Periodically her fork paused and hung suspended above her pewter plate.

Light glinted off the printer's spectacles. "It is a sorry event for our country, to lose such a bright and shining light."

Ruth's fork hovered, her face troubled. "Might we print some of his sermons?"

Her father smiled sadly. "That sounds much more enjoyable than the political wrangling we must report." He looked to Da. "I print the *Boston Observer* weekly."

The silence was interrupted only by the sound of cutlery for several moments.

"We went to the beach," Nathan said. "The ocean is grand."

Ruth lifted an eyebrow. Her eyes were a beautiful shade of clear brown, like the finest tea.

Jonathan returned his attention to his plate, scolding himself for admiring his cousin. He mopped up his remaining gravy with a piece of brown bread.

"Have you never seen it?" Aunt Betsy asked. She addressed Da. "But you hail from Ireland, do you not? You have seen the ocean."

"Aye, I was a lad when we crossed," Da said, gesturing with his fork. "An adventure, to be sure. But my own children were born here. They've never seen the ocean."

Mr. Haynes seated his spectacles more firmly on his nose. "Why did your family emigrate? I have heard some of the reasons, but it must have been a serious matter for thousands of folks to leave their homeland."

Da laid down his fork. "We Scots had moved to Ireland for various reasons, partly for freedom of worship. But several laws were passed that made life difficult for us."

A line appeared between Aunt Betsy's brows. Jonathan wondered what the members of his Boston family thought of the Townshend Acts.

"Ye ken," Da continued, "most of us were Presbyterians, and only members of the Church of England were allowed to have a voice in lawmaking. And the laws became oppressive. We could no longer afford to feed our families."

Ruth's gaze was fixed on his father, but Jonathan couldn't read her expression.

Mr. Haynes frowned. "That seems unjust."

"Like the Acts Parliament has passed," Jonathan said.

"You disagree with the Townshend Acts?" Ruth asked.

"Of course," Jonathan said. "The revenues raised are meant to pay loyal officials, to guarantee their loyalty to the Crown. We have no say in these laws, no representation, so no true means of redress."

A tiny smile appeared on Aunt Betsy's face, while Dr. Ward scowled. Clearly, not everyone at this table was agreed.

"Granting your thesis, what would you propose to do about it?" Ruth's gaze bored into his.

Do? Jonathan opened his mouth, but nothing came out.

"How goes the trial?" Da asked.

Jonathan took a deep breath, thankful his father had turned the conversation.

"Starts soon." In contrast to his plump wife, Dr. Ward was withered like a stick, his lined face sallow. "Can't be over soon enough, if you ask me."

"The governor waited for tempers to settle," Mr. Haynes said. "As it is, there is a good chance the soldiers will hang."

"I hear a man named Adams is involved," Da said. "Samuel Adams?"

Jonathan continued to observe Ruth's expression as he buttered another piece of bread. At the mention of Samuel Adams her lips pursed disapprovingly.

"Nay. John Adams. A lawyer and honorable man. He's been threatened because of his willingness to defend the soldiers, who, needless to say, are very unpopular."

"Someone needs to," Nathan ventured.

Ruth's eyes rounded. She seemed to agree.

"Well, if only to be fair," Jonathan agreed. "Without a trial it's naught but a lynching."

Ruth's gaze narrowed. "You think the verdict is a forgone conclusion?"

He blinked. "They shot those people, didn't they?" He didn't know how, but he'd lost his footing again.

Mr. Haynes intervened. "The question is whether it was murder. Was it murder or manslaughter?"

"Ruth was there." Aunt Betsy said.

Dr. Ward cleared his throat in a disapproving harrumph.

"'Twas chaotic," Ruth said. "The crowd was loud and threatening. The soldiers were nervous. I believe Captain Preston did his best."

"Too bad ye canna testify," Jonathan said dryly.

"Mr. Knox can and will." Her face softened. "And poor Patrick Carr's words will be brought before the court by his physician."

"Who is he?" Nathan asked.

Mr. Haynes patted his mouth with his napkin. "An Irish leatherworker who happened to be on the scene. He was shot and later died of his injuries. But he maintained that the soldiers acted with restraint, and they fired in self-defense."

"I hear half the soldiers have been withdrawn as a result," Da said. "Seems like a good thing."

"There are mobs in Boston stirring up trouble." Ruth folded her napkin with sure motions. "Inspired by Samuel Adams. He's the cause of it all. He uses the label of patriot to excuse sedition."

"Ye sound like an Englishwoman," Jonathan blurted.

She stared. "I am."

He opened his mouth and closed it again. God help the man she married.

3

Let me observe, how fatal are the effects, of posting a standing army among a free people!
    —Samuel Adams, December 10, 1770

July 1771

The sun beat down on the back of his regimental uniform as Lieutenant Robert Shirley approached Ashby Castle, his mare trotting smoothly beneath him despite the long hours on the road. She had proven to be a good mount, worth every penny he'd paid Richard Tattersall.

Leicestershire was square in the middle of nowhere, but it was a beautiful nowhere. Lambs gamboled near their dams on green rolling hills; stands of oak and beech marked gurgling streams. It was the place of his youth. And it was the Shirley family seat, and no matter how the Shirleys might be whispered about in London, this place was still home.

His godmother had summoned him, and he had no idea why. Especially since his commanding officer had given him extended leave as a result. It was unheard of. The Countess of Huntingdon had a certain fame, but only in religious circles. How she could influence a colonel he had no clue.

The castle ruins loomed before him, and Robert guided his horse around the skeleton of the tower, slowing her to a walk. Beside his commission, the mare was the only property he had left; he would not push her past her limits.

Ashby Place came into view, a picturesque manor, the only part of the estate that had been maintained—and that just barely. Ivy crawled over weathered gray stone, and several rose bushes extended unpruned branches in riotous color.

A groom emerged from the stable. Robert dismounted and entrusted the mare to the young man before climbing the steps. Almost before he'd finished knocking, Grayson opened the door.

The butler looked the same every time he came, though today, as Robert followed the man through the hall, the butler's gait seemed slower than before, his stride more halting.

Robert glanced to the left, where a double door opened upon a large drawing room.

It was empty, which seemed strangely incongruous. The last time he'd been there, three years before, Mr. Whitefield had preached to a packed room.

The preacher's strange squinty eyes and humble dress had faded away before the dramatic force of his words. Standing against the wall listening, Robert began to understand the drawing power of the minister. And he believed the stories of huge crowds gathering in open fields to hear him speak.

But the magnetic voice left no lasting impression on him. Robert had been baptized in the Church of England and attended services occasionally, as all gentlemen did. That was certainly sufficient for his soul, though if others were benefited by this man's preaching, he welcomed it.

Grayson led him to the back parlor. Sunlight filtered in from a large window framed by aging green drapes; the familiar furnishings were worn but tasteful. A man sat with the countess, a tea table between them. The man wore no wig, but his cravat was fine and edged with lace. Robert stiffened to attention as the butler announced him.

"Come join us, Robert." His godmother's angular face retained a mature beauty, like the charm of the manor itself, ancient and settled. She addressed her companion. "Lord Dartmouth, may I present my godson, who is also a relation on my mother's side. Lieutenant Robert Shirley, the Earl of Dartmouth."

The man's dress, subdued in color but expensive, had already signaled his rank. Robert bowed. "I am honored."

The Earl of Dartmouth possessed warm hazel eyes and a lively mouth. "The biscuits are quite good."

He'd heard of this man, a devout "Methodist," a follower of Whitefield and the other new preachers. Once he'd heard the moniker Psalm Singer applied to him in mockery.

"Sit, Robert," his godmother commanded.

He perched on a faded settee and waited while the countess poured him tea, wondering again why he'd been summoned. His neck was abominably hot underneath his military stock.

She handed him a cup and he took it carefully.

"Countess, what news from Georgia?" The earl asked.

They ignored Robert as he sipped his tea, a strong Bohea. They seemed to be discussing George Whitefield's orphanage.

"The new caretakers have arrived," the countess said.

Listening, Robert gathered that Whitefield's orphanage had been left in his godmother's care. Not a surprise—she'd supported the minister financially while he lived. It seemed her religious work continued after the man's death, both across the Atlantic and in various other places, including a college for ministers. He focused on the tea tray, where biscuits crowded pastries and scones.

His stomach rumbled.

His godmother's dark gaze shifted to him. "Eat, Robert."

"My lady." He snagged a scone and nibbled at it. The house might look neglected, but his godmother had a fine cook. The flaky treat melted in his mouth, a far cry from anything the army had to offer.

He was on a second cup of tea when the conversation turned to him.

"Robert, Lord Dartmouth has a proposal for you."

"My lord?" He hoped he had no crumbs on his face.

Dartmouth put down his cup with a clink. "You have no doubt heard of the unrest in the colonies. And most recently, the unfortunate incident in Boston."

Robert replaced his cup. "The officers of my regiment took note of Captain Preston's situation." The earl's open expression encouraged him to continue. "Of course, there was great sympathy, and some confusion over the legalities."

"Oh?"

"The colonel of my regiment said the man ought to have been tried by a military court," Robert said.

"The colonel is right. But there were political realities to consider," the earl said.

Robert wasn't sure why this was important. In London, unrest was periodically put down, a few lives always lost in the process. Regrettable, but it was life. Peace and order must be maintained. In any case, no harm was done—the Boston court had cleared Preston of murder.

Robert studied the earl's face, remembering that he was Lord North's stepbrother. And a very important man in his own right—he held some kind of ministry post. Why would he take note of a mere lieutenant?

"Political realities are important," the earl continued. "We erred by passing the Stamp Act when we had no idea of how it would affect the common man."

Robert frowned. The citizens of Great Britain were routinely taxed; why the colonies refused a small contribution was beyond him. "My lord."

"I began to cultivate sources of information beside the usual channels. A sea captain, for instance, has regularly supplied me with intelligence."

Intelligence. Belly tensing, Robert nodded in response.

"Your godmother trusts you, and that is why we have summoned you today. You would report only to me."

"My lord—but—"

""I have contacted your commanding officer. Your commission is now inactive. You are no longer under oath until such time as we deem it best to reinstate you."

We deem it best … He had no choice. "A spy? I will spy for you?" It was horrifying. Spying was dirty work. He was a gentleman. Granted, he had no title, but still.

The man's hazel gaze turned no-nonsense and penetrating. "We are not at war with a foreign power. Our troops merely keep the King's peace." The earl reached for a pastry. "Therefore, you will not be a spy, only an observer. Still, there are several reasons for removing you from active duty." He took a bite, chewed, and swallowed. "For one thing, you will be able to move about without suspicion. We may ask for information leading to the arrest of a ringleader. If you are able to insert yourself into their number, all the better."

Robert's mind whirled. He was being ripped from his duty here with the Fifth Regiment and inserted into the melee of Boston political intrigue, a totally unknown world. The parlor itself seemed to waver. "But General Gage? Does he have his own sp—sources?"

Dartmouth paused while the countess handed him another cup of tea. "General Gage uses his own judgment. We have given him considerable leeway in his command. After all, we are three thousand miles away. But consider this, lieutenant. It is clear the inhabitants of Boston hate the soldiers stationed there. How is Gage to gather intelligence? How is he to discover the thinking of the ordinary man? Worse, he will have difficulties discovering the plots of the rebels."

Discovering the plots of the rebels. This was a serious task. He had only one more card to play, a weak one. "I have a cousin who might be willing to serve in this capacity."

Lord Dartmouth studied him.

His godmother arched an eyebrow. "Nonsense. Lord Rawdon is too young." Her voice dripped with what she would not say, that her grandson's character was deficient. Robert's cousin was a scapegrace and a follower of the rakehell Banastre Tarleton. Both had been behind him several years at both Harrow and Oxford, and they were notorious for bullying the youngest students. Rawdon's father had washed his hands of him, and his uncle had purchased him a commission.

She was right. There was no escape. "My lord, I am honored to serve King and country."

"Your country thanks you," the earl said dryly, "even if the King remains ignorant of your service. Your godmother brings a quiet honor to the Shirley name—"

Of course, the Earl of Dartmouth knew the ignominious elements of the family history. He'd been at the trial.

"—and you will receive a reward. You will receive your officer's half pay plus a generous stipend. And,"—his face turned friendly again—"I hear you have a mare with good bloodlines."

Robert wrinkled his brow. Horses didn't do well on Atlantic crossings. "Yes, she is a sweet goer. Good disposition."

"Statecraft stands at stud in my stables. I'll house her, and if you wish, breed her while you're away."

Despite Dartmouth's religious interests and modest clothing, he was a wealthy man, and it would not surprise Robert if he bred blooded horses.

"I'd be honored, my lord. I won't need a mount?"

The earl's mouth twitched. "Perhaps, but men are judged by their horses, and your mare will shout that you are not a humble bookbinder."

Robert's mouth fell open. "Bookbinder?" Gentlemen did not labor with their hands.

His godmother had a twinkle in her eye. *She knew?*

"I have arranged it. A discreet master bookbinder at Longman and Sons will teach you the trade, and you'll be ready to depart for Boston early next year."

Robert blinked. "Yes, my lord." What else could he say?

4

———

Guide me, O thou great Jehovah,
pilgrim through this barren land.
I am weak, but thou art mighty;
Hold me with thy powerful hand.
—William Williams (1717-1791)

March 1772

*I*cy wind needled Robert's face as he clung to the rail. Most of the passengers had been ill during the storm; thankfully, he had suffered only a vague nausea that came and went. But what had convinced him that a February crossing was advisable? The North Atlantic was fiercely cold in winter, and he rarely braved the open deck. The tradesman's garb he wore lacked the weight of the regimental broadcloth, and the greatcoat did not keep out the chill fingers of the wind.

But the sun was out today, and he had to see Boston. They were approaching the harbor, and Robert knew the joy of a convict released from his bonds. A little discomfort was unimportant.

In the distance a glittering white shoreline slowly grew more distinct. It was March. Perhaps the storm that had buffeted the ship last night had dumped a late snow on land.

Jesus, lover of my soul, let me to thy bosom fly...

Charles Wesley's hymn sprang unexpectedly to mind. The journey had been tedious in the extreme, and he had space for few books. He wondered if the bookshop to which he was headed carried much in the way of history. After Oxford, he'd managed to collect a few history books, but they lay undisturbed in his room at his uncle's manor. Only two volumes fit in his sea chest: Marcus Aurelius's *Meditations,* and the hymn book his godmother had presented him.

After re-reading *Meditations,* he'd memorized a stanza or two of one of Charles Wesley's songs out of boredom. He'd met the man once at Ashby Place, and the poetry was tolerable.

But Robert identified more with Aurelius. A quote sprang readily to mind.

Of my grandfather Verus I have learned to be gentle and meek, and to refrain from all anger and passion.

Roman ideas of virtue he understood. Religious enthusiasm confused him.

The ship passed several small islands, and Robert examined the harbor entrance. What did he know of Boston, beside rebels and Samuel Adams?

During his apprenticeship, he scanned the London papers assiduously, searching for information, but little was to be had. Seemingly, things had quieted. Two years had passed since the unfortunate shooting involving Captain Preston. There were few speeches in Parliament about the colonies and very little in the way of news.

By chance, he'd stumbled upon a pamphlet written by a man named Benjamin Franklin. The man's view of the Crown's authority over the colonies was dangerous. Franklin believed that Parliament had no jurisdiction over the colonies because they had no representative there.

Robert tightened his grip on the rail. How many of the inhabitants of Boston agreed with this position? Surely only a few. He couldn't imagine the goodwives of Massachusetts parsing the constitutionality of Parliament's actions in the markets.

Empty masts like sticks cluttered the harbor ahead. A proud naval frigate dominated one dock, weathered fishing boats berthed on either side like donkeys beside a stallion.

The bosun's whistle shrilled, and the crew darted about. Robert went below to get out of the way.

The earl's letter flashed into his mind, the words burned into his memory. After all, he'd had all month to consider them, old-fashioned capitals and all.

Codes are cumbersome and often unnecessary. You will simply write to your uncle William in care of your Godmother. Couch your Observations as a naive Bookbinder would. Open and close with the Weather and Trivialities.

My Replies will be written in the same Vein. I will certainly provide News of your Mare, as a good Uncle should.

Do not, I urge you, let your presence be known to General Gage or to the men there. Destroy this letter.

And so he had, tossing its fragments overboard one windy evening.

"Look lively now!" Shouts from above penetrated his musings.

Soon the ship was moored, his long journey over.

Robert waited until the others had disembarked. He wanted no confusion over his cargo, the crates of books for Mr. Knox's bookshop. He hoisted his chest of personal belongings on his shoulder and went to find the supercargo, and soon the straw-packed boxes were on deck.

"Here's a feller who'll deliver it." The supercargo pointed to a dock worker with a gap-toothed grin.

The chest digging into his shoulder, Robert walked down the gangplank to the bustling dock and greeted the man. "Are you acquainted with Henry Knox's bookshop?"

The dock worker's explanation was lost, a nasal accent tumbling the words into obscurity.

Another dockhand joined him, and they hoisted the crates and took off. Robert shifted his chest to the other shoulder and followed through snowy streets. Thankfully, there was a clear path, beaten by scores of feet. To either side the white drifts approached three feet in places.

Soon the smell of manure, chamber pots, and woodsmoke cloaked the fishy odor of the wharf. A savory aroma flooded out the open door of a tavern, and his stomach contracted, the ship's biscuit at dawn a distant memory.

Tradesmen, sailors, and a few ruffled gentlemen made their way along the narrow street. Robert felt naked, exposed, as if his task were obvious, then his trepidation was replaced by curiosity. The number of people on the street was growing, not just men but sometimes whole families, all going one direction, as if for church.

Was it Sunday? The days had blurred together on board ship, but he counted back to the last day the captain had led prayers. No, today was Thursday, the fifth of March.

The dockhands halted at a shop, and once inside, the warm air restored circulation to his face. "Hail, shopkeep." The place seemed empty.

The men deposited the crates and left.

From the depths of the shop a large man emerged, thrusting his arms into the sleeves of a greatcoat. "Might I help you?" The tall ruddy man before Robert projected health and strength, not at all what he imagined a bookshop owner to look like.

"Robert Shirley, at your service." There was no need to use an alias. *Tell the truth as far as possible.* The earl's final instructions. "I trust you received my letter?"

"Henry Knox." He extended a hand. "Yes, welcome! You're the book-binder? So glad to meet you. We can use your help. These crates from Long-man? No, never mind, we'll see to them later. I'm closing the shop for the noon hour—come with me to the anniversary meeting—Dr. Warren is speaking. Have you heard of Dr. Joseph Warren?"

Robert shook his head. "Anniversary?"

Knox buttoned his coat. "Have you heard of the Boston Massacre?"

"An unfortunate shooting, I believe." They were going to celebrate a shooting? No, that didn't make sense.

It was hard to read Knox's expression. "More than a shooting."

A chill ran up Robert's spine. Questions threatened to spill from his lips, but he held his peace, resolving to observe. It was what he was there to do.

Soon they were on the street, and in a matter of minutes they arrived at a large red brick church that dwarfed the structures around it. Robert stayed close to Knox, who frequently exchanged greetings with townsfolk of all kinds, even young ladies. The bookshop owner was clearly well liked. Once inside, they ended up standing against a wall. Hundreds filled the pews, hundreds more the aisles and gallery.

Black cloth shrouded the pulpit, confirming his fears. The "Boston Massacre" had scarred the minds of the entire town.

A young man about his own age mounted the pulpit steps, introduced as Dr. Joseph Warren, wearing a wig and fine waistcoat. Tall, fair, and dark-eyed, he addressed the crowd with a hearty fervor, yet his speech was clearly educated.

Was this a rebel? Dr. Warren's genteel appearance instantly destroyed every preconceived notion Robert had of the infamous traitors—that of poorly dressed tradesmen and ne'er-do-wells skulking in dark taverns.

The man began speaking.

Robert was mesmerized by his eloquence. A brilliant sketch of the history of New England soon gave way to political argument.

"...for if they may be taxed without their consent even the smallest trifle, they may also without their consent be deprived of everything they possess."

Murmurs of approval swelled and echoed against the high ceilings.

Dr. Warren testified of seeing the bodies of the dead and treating the wounded. The descriptions were riveting. "Our streets were stained with the blood of our brethren."

Despite his better judgment, sympathy for these people welled in Robert's heart, and he fought to stay sober minded, rational. He needed to make a useful report.

The tenor of the oration intensified. "If we complain our complaints are treated with contempt; if we assert our rights, that assertion is deemed insolence; if we humbly submit the matter to the impartial decision of reason the *sword* is judged the most proper argument to silence our murmurs!"

Rumbles of affirmation swelled at these words, and Robert swallowed, his hunger forgotten. Dr. Warren continued speaking, and though he did not command the inhabitants of Boston to take up arms, the implication was there.

It was a brilliant speech, and all the more dangerous for that. Mentally Robert began to compose a letter to the earl.

Then he wondered. What about his genial employer, Henry Knox. Was he a rebel too?

THE WOMAN next to Ruth on the hard pew smelled faintly of sour milk, but that was understandable given the cluster of young children at her feet. The church was packed, and Ruth was glad to get a seat. Usually, Papa went to important events like this, but at the moment he was printing a handbill, and they couldn't afford to turn down a job. Ruth enjoyed gathering information for the newspaper, often in the company of her aunt. But her uncle had taken a turn for the worse, and Aunt Betsy's every spare moment was spent with her husband. Today Ruth found a family to sit with in lieu of a chaperone.

A man ascended the platform, and her heart plunged. It was Dr. Warren. How could he?

Sam Adams, a man she knew only by sight on the streets, was one thing. But the beloved doctor a rebel? It was unthinkable.

She opened the commonplace book she used to take notes. She'd never heard him speak before. Perhaps his speech would be conciliatory.

As she jotted down shorthand of his opening words, she was hopeful. But then he turned to a description of that awful night, and Ruth's pulse began to race.

The blood on the snow.

He was bringing it to life, but he did not stop there. He used it as an excuse for promoting discord—for rebellion.

Dr. Warren's words rang out, sure and reasoned, and her face warmed with anger. Today's speech and the precious memories she had of him from sixty-five clashed in her heart.

His dark eyes and expressive mouth were etched in her memories. His kind face hovering in her fever-warped vision, gentle hands placing a cool cloth on her forehead, a murmuring voice asking Papa questions. They'd both been inoculated with smallpox after Mama died of the dread disease, along with hundreds of other fearful Boston residents. Papa recovered after several days, but she became quite sick, with pustules breaking out in multiple places. Dr. Lloyd and Dr. Warren paced the rickety building tirelessly, tending to all, rich and poor. They lost only one to the speckled monster.

Dr. Joseph Warren was the beloved physician of Boston, and now his words choked her.

"Use every method in your power to secure your rights—"

What did he mean by *every* method?

"…with united zeal and fortitude, oppose the torrent of oppression."

Applause erupted all around her. Shouts of approval battered her, pressed her down.

Like a worm in a shiny apple, sedition had found its way into the best and brightest of Boston.

SUN on the snow momentarily blinded Robert as he emerged from the meetinghouse. Some men walked briskly away while others lingered and conversed. Boys dodged about, throwing snowballs.

The crowd ebbed and flowed around Henry Knox, who gaily greeted friends, colleagues, and even one fellow Robert suspected was an off-duty soldier.

A tall, dark-haired young woman bounded up. "Henry! Introduce me to your friend." She was well dressed, a fur muff covering her hands.

"Miss Flucker, meet Robert Shirley, my new assistant. A bookbinder."

She nodded her greeting. "Wonderful. Mr. Knox is overworked. The shop is thriving, and only his brother William helps him."

"Where are your parents?" Knox asked.

"Oh, fie! They stormed out. I've never seen Papa so angry. The Olivers will take me home."

Robert absorbed her words with interest. Clearly not everyone was thrilled by Warren's speech.

"You're welcome to come by the shop at any time." Knox's face flushed slightly.

She curtseyed prettily and departed.

The bookshop owner beckoned to someone else in the crowd. "Miss Haynes!"

Another young woman turned their way. She was a comely brunette with a heart-shaped face, but her expression was pinched and unhappy. She wore a decent cloak but her plain, sturdy shoes reminded him of a Quaker Robert had once known.

"Henry," she said, "tell me it's all a bad dream and I'll wake up."

HENRY KNOX'S large frame appeared before Ruth like a safe haven. Surely Henry wasn't one of the rebels. Red-coated officers frequented his shop, and

Lucy, the young woman he courted, was a member of a respectable and loyal family.

Ruth blurted out his Christian name before realizing that he wasn't alone. A young man stood beside him. The stranger wasn't as tall as Henry, but then no one topped Henry's height. Still, compared to most men, the newcomer would be considered tall and well-made. His hooded eyes were light brown, almost amber, his posture and bearing like a soldier. Even his skin resembled that of the men who drilled on the Common, tanned from frequent exercise.

"Ruth Haynes, may I present Robert Shirley?"

"Pleased. A soldier?"

Mr. Shirley's brows jerked, then his expression shuttered. He bowed. "At one time, Miss Haynes. You are correct."

Henry said, "He's a bookbinder. My new assistant."

"Haynes?" Mr. Shirley's brows lifted. "A relation of Gideon Haynes?"

It was Ruth's turn to be startled. The man's manners and speech suggested that he was newly come from England. "You know my father?"

"I have a package for him, from Longman and Sons." His manner was exquisitely polite. "Extremely heavy for its size."

"My Caslon!"

"Come." Henry gestured. "Let's pick up the type at my shop and we'll escort you home. I'm sure Mr. Shirley would like a tour of town."

Ruth nodded, glad for something cheerful to distract her. "Thank you, Mr. Knox, Mr. Shirley. I'd love to."

5

May our land be a land of liberty, the seat of virtue, the asylum of the oppressed, a name and a praise in the whole Earth...
—Dr. Joseph Warren

*P*apa beamed to see the new Caslon type when they finally arrived at the print shop. Henry and his new assistant left, and Ruth shrugged off her cloak. Her fingers were freezing, and she fetched charcoal for the brazier, lit it, and warmed her hands. Then she went next door to the dispensary to help her aunt.

She'd just tugged on her kidskin gloves when the back door rattled. Her cousin Joshua elbowed his way in, carrying a small crate. "Packet boat from Virginia." He set the box down and went back out to the cart.

Ruth examined the wooden crate. Soap from Hannah? And knives from Jonathan, most likely. She hadn't seen the Russells in two years; they rarely traveled even as far as Philadelphia. But the occasional crate of goods or letter from the Shenandoah branch of the family found its way to the shop via one of the ships bringing passengers and cargo up and down the coast. This packet boat was the first of the season.

Was there a letter this time? She hoped so. She'd begun a correspondence with Hannah, the sister who made the soap.

Joshua returned and set down another box, longer and narrower. "More."

Her cousin was regarded as a halfwit, but truly he was just different. He was a loyal help to his parents and never complained. He avoided crowds, which made him nervous, and he had no notion of small talk.

A clatter on the steps announced her aunt's return from their rooms above. "Ruth? Oh, there you are." Aunt Betsy didn't seem to notice the crates. "Dr. Ward is not having a good day."

Ruth heard the hacking then. Over the past year his cough had progressed from soft and dry to violent and wet. A horrible, tearing sound.

"I want you to find Dr. Warren."

"Not Dr. Lloyd?"

Aunt Betsy's eyes filled with tears. "Dr. Lloyd says there's no hope …"

Dr. Warren had trained at Dr. Lloyd's side, but still, who knew?

Mixed emotions followed her as Ruth grabbed her mother's red cloak and went to seek the rebel physician.

DR. WARREN'S booted feet disappeared up the stairs behind Aunt Betsy. It was over an hour before they reappeared.

"Ruth." Aunt Betsy's shoulders sagged as she watched Dr. Warren stride away.

"What did he say?"

"He asked how long Dr. Ward had been coughing up blood. I said three months. Has it been three months?"

More like six. "Perhaps a little longer."

"Dr. Warren said he'd sent Josiah Quincy away south, but warned that when a case was advanced, it rarely did any good."

Ruth waited silently. She'd accepted the truth about her consumptive uncle weeks ago and had no more tears left.

"He said to get our house in order. He probably won't last the year."

"I see." In her own opinion, that was generous. Dr. Ward was nearly bedridden and could not sleep without laudanum.

"Well, tell me about the meeting." Aunt Betsy said, her tone falsely bright. She busied herself opening the crate from the Russells.

"Dr. Warren spoke, and he was well received."

"A letter." Her aunt handed it to Ruth and began lifting out long rectangles of soap. "She didn't cut it into individual cakes this time. We can sell it by the pound if we wish." She glanced at Ruth, her eyes bright with tears. "What do you think?"

Ruth blinked back moisture. "I like the appearance of single bars."

"How many attended the meeting?" Her aunt's code for "who was there"?

"Mr. Knox was there," she began. "With—"

"With a certain young lady? I thought that certain young lady might be you at one point—"

"Aunt Betsy!" Once Ruth had mooned over Henry, but that was eons ago. "No, he came with a man, a new assistant. A bookbinder. But no one we know," she added quickly, forestalling her aunt's next question. "From England, I believe."

Hacking sounded from above.

"Shoo, go read your letter from Hannah." Aunt Betsy's voice broke. "I'll see to Dr. Ward."

Ruth returned to the print shop and climbed the stairs to her room, her steps heavy.

THE PAPER SMELLED of cinnamon and cloves. And a hint of lavender, too, after having traveled many miles packed away with soap. Ruth's spirits lifted. Their first letters had been short messages about soap, but last year a true correspondence had started.

Dear Ruth,

Boston sounds interesting. I went to Williamsburg once but doubt if they have so many print shops and booksellers. You make setting type sound tedious but it sounds exciting to me. Although, I do love animals, and as my father breeds horses I cannot complain of my lot here. My filly is now perfectly broke. In fact, I tried her against Jamie Gibson's gelding, a horse with the longest legs you ever saw. She was ahead the first quarter mile and lost by only half a length. Her name is Boadicea after the warrior queen of the Britons, but I call her Bodie for short. Her sire was a thoroughbred and her dam a freight horse, and I think she has the best qualities of both. My father says she's sure-footed and tractable, which to him are the most important things. I neglected to tell him of the race. Nathan found out and gave me a long look. I promised I wouldn't race her again.

Nathan hauls freight over the Gap to Richmond. From Richmond there are ships that go downriver to Williamsburg, and so you can ship things from there to most anywhere. He loads his wagon with tobacco, hemp, and furs. Beaver are now scarce but we still get some from mountain men or even Indian traders. I hope to accompany him one day but he says I'm a lass. I say, I can shoot as well as most men. Then he said it's up to Da. Jonathan is against it, but Jonathan can be a real idiot.

You wished more about myself. Well, I'm tall and skinny. My hair is bright red like my uncle Roy's—more like copper than a carrot, if you know what I mean. I wish I had beautiful hair like Mother's blond locks, but she says we must each be thankful for our gifts, and that I had plenty of my own. I'm not sure what she means.

The first batch of soap using the rose oil was ruined, but the second was a success. I colored it with madder. The fragrance is mild but at least it looks right.

I mentioned your uncle's condition to her. She uses ginseng in soups and dogwood and bloodroot in a tea for chest problems. We haven't had anyone die of consumption here in a long time, as Mother says the climate is healthy. Your aunt and uncle are welcome to come to the valley for as long as they like, my father says.

Jonathan sends his greetings. He now gets his steel from Richmond as we discovered it there. But he hopes your aunt will like the knives he sent. He made me a folding knife for my pocket.

Affectionately yours, Hannah

If only they could go, Ruth mused. Would her uncle even survive the journey?

She scanned the letter again. It was amusing. Hannah was about her own age of nineteen. But not married yet, clearly, and probably not desiring to settle down, if the horse race was any indication.

Jonathan can be a real idiot. Ruth smiled. She hadn't seen the man in two years, but she could imagine him standing square in some rustic cabin doorway, telling his little sister she couldn't do this or that. For her own good, of course.

Thinking of the far-off branch of the family, her heart warmed with affection. Even for Jonathan the idiot.

∾

SEVERAL COPIES of the *Boston Gazette* covered Robert's desk in his cramped space above the bookshop. On top of them lay a sermon by George Whitefield and a eulogy of the minister written by a most unlikely young woman, an African slave named Phillis Wheatley.

Even slaves were educated? They wouldn't stay slaves long, if that were the case. Robert stacked the materials and set them on his bed. He needed to write the earl; ten days had passed since he'd arrived. Today was the Sabbath, and since both work and recreation were forbidden, he had time to pull out a sheet of foolscap and sharpen a quill.

His knife snipped off the edge of the jagged quill, and his mind wandered back to Leicestershire. When his father died, Robert had discovered a mountain of gambling debts. His mother had passed away long before, and now it was up to him to settle the obligations, which ate up the bulk of the estate.

Now he was landless and living with an uncle. The rest of his belongings were stashed in a room not much bigger than this.

He had no home, and no prospects. Well, a career as an officer might attract a merchant's daughter with a dowry. But now?

Who would marry a spy?

He dipped the pen in the inkwell.

Robert wrestled. He had to make it sound innocent, a nephew writing to a beloved uncle. The first sentences were painful, but it became easier as he went along.

Boston, March 15 1772

Dear Uncle,

I arrived in Boston harbor the fifth inst. after a quick passage of five weeks. We experienced a brief squall near our destination and arrived to find the town under two feet of snow. However, despite the weather the townspeople were gathering that very day to hear a Doctor Warren speak about the event they call the Boston Massacre. It was the anniversary of the event.

Warren is a genteel man, and well spoken, if one forgets that his words are seditious. The people listened attentively and with approbation, tho' I later determined that Boston is not all of one mind. Some of the better sort are quite opposed. I am enclosing a copy of the paper which includes his speech, in the event it does not reach you.

Boston is an interesting place. The people are lively, hardworking, and as you mentioned to me, religious. They are particular about observing the Sabbath. Schools are plentiful. There is a poorhouse, but few beggars, and I have yet to be troubled by pickpockets. In the square where the unfortunate shooting took place stands a pillory, their main form of punishment aside from imprisonment. They reserve execution for murder, and that only if there is "malice aforethought."

They seem welcoming and friendly, but that may be because Mr. Knox, my employer, treats me as an esteemed colleague rather than a servant. Only occasionally do I receive the sort of look one gets when entering a village for the first time. Their manners are kindly but rough-hewn. They are plainspoken and plain dealing as a rule.

The people are swayed by the opinions of their ministers, and I have learned that the governor blames the mob action in protest of the Stamp Act to be a result of a certain Rev. Mayhew's preaching. Mayhew himself is no more, but his words live on, and I have read his sermon on Romans the thirteenth chapter, preached on the anniversary of the beheading of Charles I. It seems mild enough, concluding with, "It becomes us, therefore, to be contented and dutiful subjects." He warns against extremes. Yet, the theme of these ministers and writers is to point out that the Crown is limited in power, and that a King may "unKing himself" by tyrannical actions. One may imagine the implications.

Laboring here in the bookshop is truly a godsend, as I have met a number of fine people, residents and officers alike, and have access to various publications. And strangely enough, I enjoy my trade. I repair books for Mr. Knox's customers, and it gives me a sense of accomplishment to see a volume restored to its former glory.

Winter has finally loosened her grip, and I am told the farmers are plowing their fields. I hope to explore the countryside soon.

Yours ever, Robert S.

He sanded the paper and prepared it for posting. He was vaguely troubled. For one thing, he doubted if this information was new. This letter was not worthy of a peer with Lord North's ear. Plus, there was no military information here. Perhaps in the future he'd be able to include something of tactical value.

Because the truth was, he was here under false pretenses. He was a spy.

6

Arbitrary governing hath no alliance with God.
— Samuel Rutherford, *Lex, Rex*

The Shenandoah Valley, April 1773

*J*onathan led Brutus up the path, casting his eye over the barley field to his right. Tiny grassy shoots stretched skyward, a pleasant sight. Ahead of him, the house was built at the top of a hill. "Russell's Ridge" was an exaggeration, as the slope was gentle. But beyond the house and outbuildings the Blue Ridge rose steadily in all its glory.

Tired after a day of plowing, Jonathan paused and looked back. The sun touched the western mountains, casting spokes of orange and mauve behind golden clouds. The snow had melted even on the high slopes, and the ridges had resumed their mantle of bluish green. It was beautiful.

For once the glorious sight was empty. He was lonely.

Jonathan took his horse to the barn and made his way to the spring. He plunged his hands into the frigid water and scrubbed, but it was futile; he'd never get all the rich dark soil of Russell's Ridge out from under his fingernails. He might pass scrutiny if his mother didn't look too closely.

He filled a bucket of water for his horse and stood, inhaling the rich smells of April. The lower cornfield was finished, and Brutus had endured the plow with only a few complaints. He strode to the barn, gave his horse water, then spilled a bucketful of cracked corn into the trough. He went to see what his mother had for his supper.

And he would eat with the family until he established his own household. For some reason, he pictured Ruth's clear brown eyes as he navigated the familiar path. He snorted and reached for the oak door of the pine-sided house, rejecting the image. Savory smells wrapped their arms about him, the printer's daughter forgotten.

After supper, he leaned back in his chair, his belly full of his mother's good cooking. Hannah plunked the dishes in the soapy water of the kitchen tub to soak, and soon the walnut table was clean, only the breadbasket remaining on its broad surface.

Da opened the old family Bible and found the place in their reading. They prayed, sang a hymn, and his father rose. "We'll start a new book tonight."

Every night after family worship—well, except during harvest, when work swallowed all their time—they read a chapter from some worthy book. Last night they'd finished *Henry V.* Jonathan loved the custom and wanted to continue it...when he married.

If he ever married. Sometimes it seemed unlikely.

Da lifted a volume and Jonathan caught sight of the title.

"Please no, Da, not Rutherford!" his sister pleaded.

Jonathan cut a quelling glance at Hannah, but privately he sympathized, as *Lex, Rex* was a meaty read. Normally they read something more entertaining.

But his sister ignored him, her gaze fixed on their father, who had just proposed they read through Rutherford's treatise on government. Mother's fingers stilled on her sewing as they all awaited the verdict.

One corner of Da's mouth lifted. "I've a suggestion. I'll read excerpts. And we can make application."

That was more like it. Application meant—well, to the present. To the tyrannical acts of Parliament. "I like the notion," Jonathan said.

Hannah relaxed and reached for her carding tools and bag of wool. "Thank you, Da."

To Jonathan's left, a lanky arm snaked out toward the bread basket on the table. His brother William was sixteen, skinny as a beanpole, and his stomach was never full.

"We'll skip the introduction." Their father turned several pages "Some of this doesna apply. Rutherford was writing in the sixteen hundreds, about the tyranny of Charles the First. King Charles thought that since God was sovereign in appointing him king, anything he did was right."

Hannah placed a chunk of wool between the carders. "Anything?"

"Aye. No one could question him. Some term this idea the divine right of kings. Rutherford wrote *Lex, Rex* in response, saying that even the king was subject to the laws of God and man, and the minister was exiled as punishment."

On the floor, Nathan wrapped his arms around his knees. "How does the treatise apply to King George?"

The room became quiet, and even William stopped munching.

Jonathan thought over the relative calm of the last few years, broken only by the burning of the *Gaspee,* a naval vessel that had illegally harassed shipping in Rhode Island. The Crown wanted the perpetrators.

The malefactors would be tried elsewhere, not by a jury of their peers. The residents of Rhode Island had closed ranks. No witnesses could be found.

It seemed such a small incident, yet it was tyranny to take away such a basic right as trial by jury—a jury made up of one's peers. And it bothered him. What—and when—should their reaction be?

Granting your thesis, what would you propose to do about it?

Ruth's words echoed in his mind. Did Rutherford have the answer?

Da took a deep breath. "The question is, when may a man lawfully resist God's appointed authority? And what form can that resistance take? Rutherford answers both questions, and he does so biblically."

He began reading, and the room itself seemed to relax.

The quiet *scritch, scritch* of Hannah's carding tools lulled Jonathan into a peaceful haze, and he leaned back against the wall, his muscles warm and achy from plowing.

Ruth's face reappeared in his mind's eye. Hannah often shared her letters with him. What would she think of Rutherford's biblical arguments?

Why did he care?

~

THE BOSTON SUMMER was warm but not yet hot. Ruth wended her way to the London Bookshop, wondering if Henry would be in. Often of late he'd been out drilling with the new militia unit he'd organized. Certainly, the man knew everything there was to know of artillery and military tactics; books like *Sharpe's Military Guide* always lay scattered on the bookshop counter, slips of paper marking Knox's place in his reading. Now that the bookbinder could spell him in the shop, he had more time for such activities, and Ruth could imagine Henry barking orders out on the Common on such a beautiful day.

The bell tinkled above her as she entered. She spotted a tall form behind the counter. "Mr. Shirley."

The bookbinder nodded. His clothes were ordinary, but Ruth could easily imagine him in a fine waistcoat like Dr. Warren's. "Miss Haynes. I am sorry for your loss."

He'd been at her uncle's funeral two months ago, the last time she'd seen either him or Henry. She'd been busy, helping her aunt and her father. "Thank you."

"How may I help you?"

Under his gaze she felt conspicuous. Her bodice was threadbare, her skirt salvaged fabric from one of her mother's gowns. Her friends Sarah and Lucy still kept up with the latest fashions out of London and Paris, but Ruth rarely purchased anything new. And now the Haynes's apprentice had fulfilled his term and left for greener pastures. Papa was working harder but bringing in less. She had a small amount of money she could spend on fabric, but she no longer had the time to sew.

"I-I need a pamphlet. Or book, I'm not sure."

"The author?"

"Rutherford. I have read Locke, but my family in the Shenandoah Valley recommends Rutherford."

"A treatise on government? Yes, here we are." He stood before a shelf. "We have two volumes by Rutherford." He pulled them out and placed them on the counter.

The first one was gold embossed on fine leather. *Letters.* "His correspondence?"

Henry entered the shop from the back, dusty and smelling of the field. A flamboyant handkerchief was wrapped, as usual, around his left hand, concealing the loss of two fingers while hunting. "Did I hear Rutherford? Rutherford is marvelous." He joined them at the counter and lifted the book. "*Letters* is a collection of epistles written when he was exiled. As a minister he sought to encourage his friends in the faith even as he suffered for speaking against King Charles."

"A minister?" she asked. This was a surprise, but knowing the Russells, maybe it shouldn't be.

Henry nodded and picked up the other book, entitled *Lex, Rex*. "Writing this was what got him exiled. Translated, 'The Law and the King.'"

Mr. Shirley's brow lifted. "Interesting."

"Both Rutherford and Locke describe what men may lawfully do under tyranny." Knox's handkerchief fluttered as his hands accompanied his words. "They agree in the right of petition. And the right to flee oppression. But if the first two fail, or are not options, resistance is lawful, under certain conditions."

Ruth recalled that Parliament had accused Charles of tyranny—and eventually, he'd been executed. *Horrible.* Killing a king seemed barbarous. "So what is the difference between these writers?" She'd read Locke and thought his treatise dangerous.

"Here's my understanding," he continued. "Rutherford says that active resistance can only take place under the rule and direction of magistrates. Individuals doing the same are rebels and criminals. While Locke's view was that men are morally free to resist individually."

Mr. Shirley leaned on the counter, forearms crossed. "How can Rutherford's scenario be plausible, if the government itself is tyrannical?"

"Consider Massachusetts. There is a governor, the agent of the Crown. But there is also a legislature, the General Court. Every colony is the same. Virginia has a House of Burgesses that makes most local decisions and raises taxes."

The bookbinder frowned. "Doesn't the Crown's authority supersede that of local magistrates?"

A good question.

Henry's cheeks puffed in a smile. "Not according to Rutherford. Not if the king has overstepped his bounds. And not according to Parliament. Remember what happened to Charles the First."

"Interesting." Mr. Shirley straightened. "I would love to speak to Samuel Adams about these matters."

"I think I can arrange that. Miss Haynes, would you like this volume?"

Ruth nodded. How well did Henry know Adams? The bookshop owner was friends with all kinds of people, Loyalists and British officers included. Surely he wasn't a member of the Sons of Liberty, those dark men who used fine words to provoke the mobs.

She completed her purchase. No new clothes this year.

THE BELL ANNOUNCED a customer to the bookshop. Behind the counter, Robert looked up to see a familiar form.

"Mr. Shirley?" Dark eyes in a pleasant face—the pleasant face of a rebel.

"Dr. Warren. How may I help you?"

"An invitation, if you will. For ale at the Green Dragon. Mr. Knox mentioned you."

The Green Dragon was one of the meeting places of the Sons of Liberty. "I am honored." He called Knox's brother to take his place and followed the physician out the door.

As they spoke of pleasantries on the street, nervous sweat chilled Robert's back. His assignment was to insinuate himself into this group. Or at least to try.

They reached the establishment, a multi-story brick building. From an iron crane over the door dangled a copper dragon, weathered to a bluish green.

Inside, the dank smell of beer competed with the pungent odor of tobacco. A large upstairs room contained a number of tables. Half a dozen men lounged about, talking and sipping from tankards. Smoke from several pipes lent a faint gray sheen to the air.

Robert determined to listen. He'd be careful in his words. He couldn't pretend to be a rebel, not exactly. But he could imagine himself as an ordinary man open to their arguments.

Dr. Warren led him to a middle-aged man sitting alone at a table. "Mr. Adams, may I present Mr. Shirley."

Adams rose. "Pleased to meet you." He cut a glance at Warren. "We have something of importance to discuss."

They sat. Samuel Adams was an ordinary looking man, dressed in ordinary clothing—the clothing of a tradesman or minor merchant.

For a second, Robert wondered. Could the Crown of the largest empire on earth be concerned about this seemingly inconsequential man?

"Hutchinson's letters?" Dr. Warren asked.

"The public deserves to know, not just the Committee."

Robert shook off the air of unreality and fought to focus.

Adams pulled out papers from his coat and spread them out on the table. A woman arrived bringing tankards. She set ale before each man.

Robert pulled his tankard closer but did not drink.

"Mr. Shirley, we have letters from Hutchinson, sent to London, that are most incriminating." Adams tapped the papers before him, and Robert noticed that his hands trembled, like a much older man's. "They fell into Mr. Franklin's possession, who sent them to Speaker Cushing. You'll see why he took such an unusual step."

He pushed one of the letters across the table to Robert.

Franklin's name he remembered—that pamphlet he'd read. So the man had contacts here. It seemed ungentlemanly to read private correspondence, but the eyes of the others were upon him.

I never think of the measures necessary for the peace and good order of the colonies without pain. There must be an abridgement of what are called English liberties ...

He scanned the rest of the letter, which continued in the same vein. The governor wished for firm measures, measures that ignored civil liberties. How would Adams and the others react to this? How should he react?

"Abridgment of liberties?"

"Precisely," Adams said. "Behind our backs our good governor has been conspiring to shackle us."

Robert schooled his features to look alarmed. Governor Hutchinson meant well. But it was a foolish thing to set on paper. Made public—why, there was no predicting the reaction. The present calm in Boston was illusory, he knew that much from the anniversary speech. The governor's words would serve as kerosene on a smoldering fire. The mobs could react without warning.

"Liberties by their nature should not be restricted because of the exigencies of the moment," Warren said, his gaze fixed on Robert's face.

Was this a test?

"What if the law is broken?" Robert ventured.

Adams raised his tankard. "Even a criminal deserves due process." He drank. "The people need to know the machinations of their rulers."

"What do you propose?" Warren asked.

"We publish the letters in the *Boston Gazette.*"

Robert's hands tightened around his tankard. No one in London had the slightest clue.

7

But O stupendous love! Whilst we were his enemies, God sent forth his Son, made of a woman, made under the law, that he might become a curse for us.
—George Whitefield

October 1773

Jonathan opened his eyes and struggled to remember where he was. Oh, yes. The minister's house. Their trip over the Gap—it came back to him.

The smell of coffee and bacon alerted him to the late hour. He glanced about the now-empty loft. Everyone must be around the breakfast table, and he was lying abed still.

He shoveled himself into his breeches, tucked in his shirt, and slid down the ladder. "Good morning, Mrs. Jarratt, Mr. Jarratt."

Everyone was crowded around the board table, all except his father, who was missing. Probably watering the animals.

The minister's wife brought him a thick piece of bacon on a slab of wheat bread. Saliva filled his mouth. "Thank ye kindly."

Jonathan was hungry, and ready for a day of rest. They'd been on the road for days. Nathan had loaded up his wagon with freight, mainly tobacco, and Da rode a three-year-old colt alongside, destined for a purchaser in Hanover County. Hannah had asked to come, claiming that someone needed to see that they eat.

They'd turned south, to spend the Sabbath in this out-of-the-way place. But Da said the man was a good preacher, and he said that about few.

With half an ear, Jonathan listened to Nathan as he talked to the minister. Hannah helped to gather crocks and put them in a washtub.

Da's face appeared in the doorway. "Ah, there ye are. Had your coffee?"

"I'll get it." The minister rose and poured black brew into a stoneware cup.

"Thank you." The drink was scalding hot. "Ye're a very kind host."

Jonathan sipped the coffee as the conversation resumed. Did the Jarratts always drink it? Sometimes they did on the Ridge, but often it was mixed with chicory. Tea was becoming unpopular.

News of the Tea Act had reached the colonies just this summer. Crazy things had come out in the newspapers, saying that tea itself was unhealthful, or that the East India Company, which now had a monopoly on the substance, abused and oppressed those who produced the tea.

All he knew was that Parliament didn't ask anyone here permission to create a monopoly. Its arbitrary economic decisions affected a lot of people. Da said the smugglers were outraged this time, because it was now impossible to undercut the price of legal tea. And warehouses full of tea were about to flood American markets.

The colonies had no say at all. Well, they didn't have to drink it, Jonathan mused. He handed his empty cup to Hannah, who placed it with the rest of the dishes to soak.

She frowned at him. "Fix your hair."

He wriggled his eyebrows at her. "Yes, ma'am."

Before she could punch him, Jonathan dashed out to see to Brutus. The blood bay colt was his pride and joy, a half-sibling to Hannah's mare, and even faster, if he were any judge. Best of all, the animal had tremendous wind. He saddled the horse, snaking the extra-long girth strap around the well-spring barrel. Once satisfied, he dunked his face and hair in the stream.

When everyone was ready, they left for the meetinghouse, a simple affair near a stream. Other vehicles stood out front, but Jonathan observed that most came on foot, children trailing behind parents. Most wore worn, plain clothing; this was not a wealthy district.

The inside was ordinary, the benches unfinished planks. Jonathan glanced up as the minister approached the large sermon desk at the front. He was wearing clerical garb and a piece of frippery around his neck. The colorful satin proclaimed him as Church of England.

Anglicans were "half-papist," according to his father. They were singing now, and it wasn't strange or what he imagined to be "papist." A rusty bellow emerged from the congregation, and a throaty counterpoint joined in from outside. Jonathan caught a glimpse of dark skin through the windows. There must be a fair-sized plantation nearby.

The singing ceased, and the minister opened to his text in Isaiah. "Chapter fifty-five opens with a pathetic call and affectionate invitation to all sorts of men, without limitation, to come and receive the blessings of the new covenant. 'Ho, every one that thirsteth,' that pants for happiness and the benefits of the gospel."

It was quiet, but Jonathan sensed an eagerness to receive, a careful attention.

"And lest any, through a sense of their guilt, unworthiness, and want of merit, should be discouraged and fear there would be no admittance for them unless they can bring some good in hand to make them welcome, it is added, 'And he that hath no money, come ye.'"

Jonathan sat up straighter. His own sense of guilt opened up before him like a dark pool. He flexed his hands, soiled with his sin.

"Oh, that you, my dear hearers, were but deeply conscious how wretched and miserable you are by nature and practice and how impossible it is for you to establish a justifying righteousness of your own by anything you can do or suffer."

He knew this already, didn't he?

"None but Christ can save you. His righteousness is sufficient for your justification, exclusive of anything else."

He soaked in the words, clasping them to his heart. *Help, Lord.* A dark face from the past accused him—could even this sin be forgiven? He thought all sins alike, but his heart couldn't seem to grasp forgiveness for *that.*

Sobbing came from behind him. But the preacher wasn't perturbed, his speaking did not falter.

"'Seek ye the Lord while He may be found, call ye upon Him while He is near; let the wicked forsake his way, and the unrighteous man his thoughts;

and let him return unto the Lord, and He will have mercy upon him; and to our God, for He will abundantly pardon.'"

Suddenly Jonathan became aware of sniffing nearby.

It was Hannah. Her face was covered with tears.

AFTER THE SERVICE, Jonathan lost track of his sister. He found her by the stream, with Boadicea's great chestnut head against her chest as she stroked the horse's glossy neck.

He decided to leave her be.

He found Brutus and led him through the reeds to the water. Nostrils flaring, the colt's black muzzle tasted the water, then lapped at it noisily. Jonathan stared at the ripples, his heart aching. His mind was split between hope and doubt.

Help thou mine unbelief.

Hannah looked up at Jonathan over the cattails. "Now I know what they mean." Her countenance held the glow of new discovery.

He maneuvered the colt nearer. His own heart was flooded with a bittersweet joy, seeing her face.

"I saw my sin for the first time." She paused as if speech itself were a new thing. "I knew I was a sinner, of course, but I didn't really *know.* Does that make sense?"

Jonathan nodded. "Aye, I ken the feeling." He'd experienced both the dread of wrath and the rush of enveloping forgiveness just the same—years before. And he'd almost forgotten. His heart had become like cornfields in winter, dry as kindling.

"I've heard the gospel so many times before. Why this preacher? Why now?"

He smiled. "Ye know that too."

A tear coursed down her cheek. "Amazing grace—nothing of me. It's all of Christ. I would have continued on my course unless God had intervened."

Brutus nudged him, and Jonathan reached up to scratch behind the colt's ears. Overhead, dark-bellied clouds threatened rain. A wisp of breeze toyed with Hannah's hair, sliding a tendril of coppery gold onto her cheek.

He wanted her joy, that fresh feeling of forgiveness. But it eluded him.

Jonathan's throat swelled and he couldn't speak. Whitefield was dead, but God was still working in the land, working even in his own family. He could rejoice for Hannah.

She smiled, and the shower poured in earnest, water seeking every crevice in his clothing. He needed water for his dry heart, cleansing for his soul.

～

RUTH LEFT a jug of cider in the print shop's work room for Mr. Shirley and Joshua. The bookbinder's presence still startled her sometimes; it had been just her and Papa for so long. He didn't notice her standing there, occupied as he was with the press.

Mr. Shirley's proposal had both surprised and cheered her. He'd approached her father with a business proposition, offering to supply much of the capital for publishing several books. Large print shops printed books, and now with a bookbinder, they could too. When Henry could spare him from the bookshop, Mr. Shirley was here, learning the press and laboring at their project.

Returning to the front room, she picked up a copy of the latest edition of their newspaper and scanned it for errors.

"Papa, what is this?" Ruth pointed to a column. "Who is 'Cicero'?"

Afternoon sunlight through the front window reflected from her father's spectacles. "I am."

Of course. She and her father were the only essay writers left.

"I decided to retire 'Silvanus.' Agricultural advice is not going to sell right now."

And Honorius was only attracting negative attention, she knew.

But still. "Papa, you write here that the King is wrong."

"He is." Gently, he indicated the essay. "Certainly, we may petition the King for redress. We have that right."

She studied his face. His eyes were shadowed. There was something troubling him—and he'd been so encouraged when Mr. Shirley had decided to help with a new printing project.

He placed the newspaper on the counter, concealing a sheet covered with scrawling handwriting. She reached for it.

This is a warning …

She scanned the rest of the threatening letter. Her heart thudded. "Papa."

He sighed and looked suddenly old. The familiar creak and squeal of the press in the workroom was the only sound for a long moment.

"Papa, this is probably from that rascal John Winthrop, who dresses up in that crazy costume of Joyce, King Charles' enemy, it's so insulting—"

"You're certain 'tis Winthrop?"

"You go to the taverns to hear things. I go shopping, and Winthrop owns a shop on the wharf. And he's head of that odious 'committee for tar and feathering.'"

"I had not thought it real. The committee, I mean."

Ruth crumpled the paper and threw it into the fire. "Either way, I need to give up Honorius." She couldn't subject her father to danger. They would not come after her. They didn't know she wrote the essays.

"Choose another pen name. We shall say that Honorius is retired. But I cannot bear to silence your voice of reason, even if it differs from my own view in some respects."

"I'll be careful, Papa." And she would.

Silence intervened. The press had stilled.

"Where'd you put that cider?" he asked.

They went into the back, where her father poured cider. Mr. Shirley peered at the sheets hanging to dry. Joshua still held the ink balls.

Ruth grabbed a rag and dipped it in spirits, wondering if the whole project was Henry's idea to begin with. She managed to get her cousin's hands partially clean before he wriggled away and headed out the back door, probably to see to the animals. Aunt Betsy had purchased a nanny goat, and Joshua loved the creature.

Mr. Shirley picked up a cup. He drank heartily, his Adam's apple bobbing, then drew out a handkerchief to dab at his mouth. Ruth held back a smile. Their apprentice would have used his sleeve.

She ran a finger along the edge of the nearest sheet hanging from the ceiling. Fine Edinburgh paper, much smoother than the local product they used for the *Observer*. Her chest swelled in gratitude. Their first project was an edition of Rutherford's *Lex, Rex*.

Henry had suggested the title. "I know it might not be your first choice," he'd said. "But it will sell."

And as she prodded the lead type into order with the composing stick, she absorbed the words of Rutherford. *The servant may resist the master if he attempts to unjustly kill him* …Not so bad. In fact, the Scottish divine seemed a reasonable man. And he drew most of his arguments from scripture.

The bell over the front door tinkled, and Papa left to man the counter. She hoped it was someone wanting to run an advertisement. They needed the funds.

"Mr. Shirley, how much will these sell for?" Ruth asked. The Hayneses would never recover their old prosperity. The horses and carriage, the dinners at the governor's home, all that was forever gone. Her mother's family had perished of smallpox just before her mother had contracted the dread disease, and the estate had gone to a churlish cousin. Every penny had to be earned.

The bookbinder's brows drew together, the last glow of the late afternoon sun highlighting his caramel hair. "The paper was expensive, but the calfskin we will be able to obtain for a better price than I expected." His face brightened. "We should inquire of Mr. Knox what he would accept as a good price. Yes, I will do that tomorrow."

Now that the weather was turning, Henry was less busy with his militia duties, and could spare the bookbinder more often.

"Can you fold octavo?" Mr. Shirley picked up a sheet from a pile and laid it on the broad workbench.

"I've never done it," she admitted. "But I set the type that way."

"A bookbinder normally doesn't do this step, the printer does."

"And now you are both." She helped with the first fold, long dimension together. She snatched a glance at him. He was handsome, with angular features, and his hands were fine and uncallused. "Mr. Shirley, why did you come to Boston?"

His eyes jerked up to meet her gaze, then he flipped the edge of the paper for the next fold. "What next?"

He examined the print, but Ruth knew the layout without looking. "This way."

Carefully Mr. Shirley made the crease. "My father passed. My mother had died in childbed years before."

"I'm sorry."

"I sold our property to pay my father's debts and lived with an uncle."

"And joined the Army?"

"The infantry, yes. I still receive half pay, so do not trouble yourself over the amount I am investing here." He placed the folded sheet on a table and picked up another.

That was a relief. Despite the handkerchiefs—fine linen, and embroidered with his initials—he was not a wealthy man, that much was obvious. They worked to fold the sheet.

"I wanted to seek my fortune. Not in the sense of becoming wealthy, but to …establish my name."

She waited, not wanting his expression to close up again. Mr. Shirley was a private man.

"One of my uncles was executed for murder."

What?

"He shot and killed his steward for refusing to do something illegal. Very famous case." He looked up. "Perhaps it was before your time. He was hanged over ten years ago."

"I am sorry."

"'Tis a stain on the family name."

She smiled, hoping to encourage him. "Here in Boston, the only thing you need to worry about is Governor Shirley's reputation."

His lips parted. "You had a governor by that name? I hope he was better esteemed than Hutchinson."

"A bit. He recently passed away. His beautiful home is in Roxbury."

"He hasn't been burned in effigy?"

"No, any controversies died with him." Ruth chuckled. "Now they just admire his house."

Sympathy tugged at her heart. She hoped Robert Shirley could find a place here. A home.

8

In short the Ministry may rely upon it that Americans will never be tax'd without their own consent ...
    —George Washington, *Letter,* 29th January 1774

*R*obert was glad for the Sabbath. All week he'd labored at the press, assisted by Gideon Haynes or his nephew Joshua, who despite his childish way of speaking was quite dexterous when it came to inking the type with the leather balls. Robert wriggled his shoulders. They'd hurt the third day of printing but had loosened up since.

Sitting on his narrow bed, he turned over the letter in his hands, recognizing the distinctive script of the earl, neat and restrained.

After a few days Mr. Haynes had offered him his old apprentice's room off the workshop, and Robert had instantly seen the wisdom of it. After a long afternoon at the press, all he wanted to do was eat and fall asleep, and the convenient nook spared him the walk to the bookshop.

Today he had time to read—and write.

A clatter from the print shop alerted him, and he slid the letter into his hymnbook, perched on the chest at the head of the bed. His palms grew cold as he heard footsteps.

"Mr. Shirley?" Ruth Haynes's voice.

He stood to intercept her, but she appeared in the doorway before he could move more than a step. He nodded a greeting. "How may I help you?"

"Mrs. Ward and I are going visiting—my, what a pretty book."

"A hymnbook. My godmother is a Methodist. A parting gift." The printer's daughter made him nervous. For some reason he'd revealed personal matters to her a few days ago. She was attractive and intelligent—too intelligent. He had to be more careful. If anyone could discern his true mission, it was her.

She studied his face. "Need anything before we leave?"

"Might I trouble you for a writing desk?"

"Oh, surely—I apologize for the room."

"I became used to much worse in the Army. It saves me walking back to the bookshop in the cold, a blessing."

She returned in five minutes with a traveling desk stocked with paper, quills, and inkwell.

"Thank you."

She smiled in response and left.

It wasn't until the door of the shop clicked shut that Robert took a deep breath.

That was close. He'd never be able to explain away this correspondence.

He slid the letter out and broke open the wax, stamped with the initials *W L*. The Earl of Dartmouth's family name, William Legge. At least the man hadn't used his signet.

Dear Nephew,

Your Mare is in fine Fettle, and her Colt is lively. His Conformation is promising. I am thinking of Names. Statecraft x Seabreeze suggests many Possibilities. Following Sea? Warcraft? I await your Pleasure.

I received your Description of Affairs in Boston after the Governor's Letters were published. The Man has no Tact. Of course, Incompetence may necessitate Replacement, but let us hope that Tempers cool. He has done good Service to the Crown and we hesitate to act prematurely.

The Tea Act is seen by many as a political Victory. A Decrease in the much-maligned Tax on Tea and Salvation for a crucial Company. I have not heard much from the Colonies, as I have retired to my Estate. But in any case, I have good Hope that if there are Complaints they will be restricted to Massachusetts.

Who knows? Perhaps all will soon settle and you may see to the Colt's training yourself.

Regards, your Uncle William

Robert scowled. The earl was being less than discreet. *We hesitate to act prematurely?* We, as in the Ministry—the small number of men who gave counsel to the King and presided over the functions of government. The earl had served as Secretary of State for the Colonies for the past year. He was the one man who might intervene, might help to resolve matters.

But Dartmouth had no conception as to what was happening. It took only a moment's deliberation to decide. Robert thrust aside his hesitation at the thought of correcting such an important man. He was going to have to destroy the earl's preconceived ideas, if it weren't already too late.

Dear Uncle,

I thank you for your letter. Since I wrote last my situation has changed. There is a small print shop here that has suffered because of the loyalty of the owners. They were looking for new sources of revenue, and the bookshop owner, Mr. Knox, has less need of me in the winter. I entered into a partnership with Mr. Haynes, the printer, in which I supplied a small amount of capital. We shall print and bind several titles. The first you may be familiar with, the treatise by the Scottish divine Samuel Rutherford. It is not quite as radical as Locke but I already have a buyer in Philadelphia for a portion of the print run. We may print a primer next.

The situation expands my contacts. Next door a relation runs a dispensary. I am not sure of the owner's sentiments yet. Most in Boston are sympathetic to the rebels. Some remain silent, probably afraid to express sentiments loyal to the Crown. The atmosphere has become especially fraught since Hutchinson's letters were published. Unfortunately, news of the Tea Act arrived immediately afterward, and the tension increased further. I have been to the taverns, where it is described as an insult. You might think a decrease in the tax would calm matters, but they think it arbitrary. In other words, the Mother country can act with no regard to the wishes or the consent of its citizens. The smugglers can no longer undercut the price of legal tea, and a large portion of the economy depends on smuggling. A broader range of people now have a stake in the outcome. I hear that ships full of tea are on their way here. I cannot foresee what will happen, but I fear violence.

Do you take the Philadelphia and Williamsburg papers? I am enclosing a copy of the Virginia Gazette, which I now make a point of reading. The Boston Committee of Correspondence now has children. That is to say, most of the colonies have organized in a similar fashion and communicate one with another. I conclude that a dangerous senti-

ment has sprung up—*the other colonies now take Massachusetts' injuries as their own. And some in Virginia are quite radical. The worst of the lot, a certain Mr. Henry, is reported to have said the following in their assembly: "Caesar had his Brutus, Charles I his Cromwell, and George III may profit from their example." Granted, his comment was expunged as treasonous, but it is revealing nevertheless. Sedition is not restricted to Boston.*

In gratitude I wish to gift you with the colt, if you think him likely. As for a name, I am flummoxed. Olive Branch, or Man of War? I fear the second will be chosen, and some nights I sleep poorly.

With affection, Your Nephew Robert

He sanded the paper and stared at it. Then he pulled out another sheet. He'd write his godmother, include a couple of those sweet-smelling soaps, and send everything to her. She'd get the letter to the earl.

He listened carefully for footsteps as he packed. He couldn't be too careful.

RUTH CLEANED her hands and straightened. Hours at the galleys caused her back to ache.

A thud and clatter intruded. Noises emanated from the dispensary next door, and she wondered at it until she recalled her aunt's mention of a ship at the docks. Another order?

She slipped out the back door into the November chill. Joshua was lifting a crate from the cart, which seemed overloaded with parcels and boxes. Molly, the free woman, emerged and grabbed a sack. Ruth scurried over to help. She chose the smallest container but could barely lift it. What did it contain? Printer's type? But no, they'd not ordered any. Was pewter that heavy?

"Let me help you." A masculine voice intruded—Mr. Shirley had come up behind her. He lifted the parcel as if it were weightless.

"Thank you."

She realized it was the time he normally arrived to operate the press. He must have followed her out the door.

"Come, come," Aunt Betsy fussed. She braced the door open with one meaty arm.

In twenty minutes the cart was unloaded, and Mr. Shirley and Joshua left. Arms akimbo, Molly frowned at the clutter before scurrying back upstairs. Boxes, kegs, and smaller parcels cluttered the back of the shop.

"What is all this?" Ruth sat on a keg and examined a box marked *candles*. Several boxes had no labels, only the Ward name.

Her aunt gave her a sober look. "There's trouble brewing. I survived a boycott but it was hard." She nodded at the containers. "I'll not be caught short again."

Some of the items were ordinary, like toothpowder and hair pomade. Others were not things the dispensary normally stocked. A large lumpy sack slumped against the counter.

She sniffed at the bag. "Coffee?"

"'Tis already growing in popularity. Folks only drink tea in secret, even if it's smuggled. What if trade shuts down?"

Ruth considered her aunt's words. Her uncle had been ailing a long time before his death, and even before that his practice had been limited. Aunt Betsy was the motive force behind the business. She knew what sold and managed money well.

Ruth stared at the counter, now fully stocked with scents, including some of Dr. Hunter's from Newport. "Many of these are luxury items."

"During the boycott I learned that there are always people with money. In times of trouble, prices increase. We will survive."

"But the cost—"

Her aunt harrumphed. "A few of these things are for friends in Cambridge. They helped finance the purchase."

Friends? Ruth wondered who these friends might be. She suspected her aunt of rebel sympathies. But then, most in Boston inclined that way.

She felt so alone. The scriptures said to honor the King, obey magistrates, render unto Caesar ... *Why, Lord? Why didn't they see? Don't they read the scriptures?*

Her heart smote her, knowing she'd been neglecting her Bible herself. She purposed to read it.

Right now, she felt like Job, the man who'd lost everything. She'd start her reading there.

Ruth rose and turned to leave but spotted the small heavy box lying on the floor. "What is this? 'Tis as heavy as type."

"Musket balls. And somewhere there's a keg of powder."

Had she been sitting on it?

9

There is a fountain filled with blood
Drawn from Immanuel's veins
And sinners plunged beneath that flood
Lose all their guilty stains
—*William Cowper,* Olney Hymns, *1779*

December 1773

*R*obert was ready. He shrugged on his greatcoat and tucked his hat under his arm, resolved to inform the earl as well as watch out for intelligence useful to General Gage.

One thing puzzled him. Tonight's meeting had been called by Samuel Adams quite openly.

Why hadn't the Crown arrested him and the others? The Sons of Liberty weren't hiding. Perhaps it was the earl's influence. He did not seem like a hasty man.

The meeting tonight was rumored to be huge, with men pouring in from the countryside to attend. Robert needed to be there.

He put on his hat and entered the front room of the print shop.

Stiff-backed, Ruth was facing her father, who was thrusting his arms through the sleeves of his greatcoat.

"But Papa—"

"I'll relay every detail of the meeting." He grasped her hands. "There's only one hope left—that Governor Hutchinson will grant the owner of the ships a special permit to leave without unloading the tea." His gaze met Robert's. "I'll have Mr. Shirley with me. Stay home."

"Take this, Papa." She handed him a pin-hole lantern. "'Tis already mid-afternoon. You'll need it."

Robert followed him out of the print shop into a cold drizzle. The glistening cobblestones echoed with their footsteps. Thousands had poured into Boston, but they had already gathered at the meetinghouse, and the street was empty.

Mr. Haynes did not speak on the way, and Robert held his peace. The memory of the sight of the huge frigates in the harbor, cannon trained on Griffin's Wharf, chilled him.

As a boy he'd exulted at the sight of a ship of the line coming into Portsmouth harbor after some great battle in the war with the French. Canvas bright in the sun, flags flying, multiple rows of guns bristling, the great frigates inspired awe.

Now they inspired dread. He knew the mood of Boston. They would not receive the tea. Hundreds of chests sat in the bellies of three ships moored at the wharf.

Would the Navy fire upon civilians if there were some kind of resistance? Even if they were armed, it counted for nothing. Cannon would obliterate the wharf itself. Surely not.

He hoped not.

As Robert had expected, the meetinghouse was packed, filled with the aroma of sweat, damp wool, and quiet tension. Robert spotted both Mr. Adams and Dr. Warren seated at the front as Mr. Haynes found them a seat near the back.

An hour passed as they waited for a reply from the governor—the final appeal for a special permit for the ships to exit the harbor without unlading. Boston was filled with attorneys, and perhaps it was not surprising that even the Sons of Liberty sought recourse in legal means above all. It elevated them in Robert's mind.

Dusk gave way to darkness, and candles were lit near the front. A quiet snore sounded behind Robert, and he was reminded of a tired congregation sitting bored under the drone of an uninspired preacher.

The mirage of fatigue vanished as a diminutive man walked to the front and spoke to Adams. Every man sat straighter. What had Governor Hutchinson decided?

Adams stood wearily to his feet and addressed the crowd. "There is nothing more that can be done."

A sigh seemed to settle over the gathering like the ebb of a disturbed ocean, preparing for a destructive break on the shore.

So the answer was no. Robert swallowed. The leaders were out of options, and if violence was planned, there was no way to stop it.

In the candlelight Adams's face looked serious. "This meeting can do nothing more to save the country."

Cries came from the doorway behind Robert. "Boston Harbor a teapot tonight!"

The murmurs around him grew louder. A few left hurriedly; some stayed and conversed.

Mr. Haynes frowned. "Let's leave."

Others had the same idea, crowding the aisles, but they finally made it outside.

The drizzle had stopped. Robert took the lantern, senses vigilant as he led the older man to safety. The harbor a "teapot"? Men darted past, some singly, some in groups. Who knew what mischief they were planning.

Once at the print shop, Robert scanned the street while the printer entered. A figure stood nearby, too close for comfort.

"Hail! Declare yourself," Robert challenged.

"'Tis only me, Mr. Shirley." The voice was Joshua's. "Speak softly. 'Tis a secret. 'Tis a secret."

Robert stepped closer and lifted the lantern. Joshua's face was covered in soot. He looked like a chimney sweep.

Joshua thrust a tin at him. "Use this."

He stared at the container. *Lampblack?* It was the basis for their ink. Surely Joshua didn't think Robert was connected to the Sons of Liberty.

"Hurry." Joshua grabbed the lantern to free his hands.

Robert took the tin. It was his chance. Feeling very strange, he smeared the black pigment on his face. The disguise would cloak him from both sides of the dispute, rebel and Loyalist alike. He followed the young man, and soon discovered their destination: Griffin's Wharf.

Dozens of men milled about, some with strange costumes or feathers in their hair. Axes and hatchets were plentiful, but he saw no firearms. All had blackened faces. Low in the sky, a crescent moon illumined the rigging of the ships. Robert sensed, rather than saw, the presence of the naval frigates beyond.

He thought of the earl then. The Earl of Dartmouth, Secretary of the Colonies, had not been able to prevent any of this. Events had seemed to take over, like a gale blowing a ship onto rocks.

In that moment Robert realized that he could do nothing to prevent this either.

One of the men returned from the nearest ship. "Here's the keys. The mate was helpful."

As if by prior instruction, the crowd divided. Some headed to the boats on either side. Robert followed the group boarding the ship just ahead.

"Harm not the boat, or any property, but the tea alone." A voice murmured an instruction which must have been agreed on long before.

So that was the solution. They wouldn't unload the tea. They'd destroy it.

It was brilliant and cheeky. And dangerous.

He clambered up the gangplank, and someone laid a hand on his sleeve. "See yon tackle? You look likely."

Robert nodded. He had no tool like the others, and someone had sized him up as strong. He studied the block and tackle and grasped the rope attached to the system of pulleys. He'd seen them used to unload cargo. It was simple enough. He stole a glance at the harbor. The warships sat silently, seemingly unaware of what was happening.

He hauled on the rope, hand over hand, and pulled the first pallet onto the deck. Others unloaded the chests, and he let the rope play out for the next load. He'd ache tomorrow.

The sound of axes biting into wood floated through the air. *Thud. Creak. Thud. Creak.* It was the loudest sound on deck. Silently, the tea was tossed overboard. The ruined chests followed; the sound of gentle splashes surrounded the boat. The pleasantly acrid smell of Bohea and the softer smell of green hyson filled the air.

Robert snatched another glance at the frigates. The moon was setting, but ship's lanterns spilled ripples of light as the vessels brooded over the dark water.

Surely such a large crowd of active men had been detected by someone aboard the frigates.

Perhaps not.

Behind him he heard the familiar sound of sweeping.

It was Joshua. "All tea must be gone. All gone. All clean."

"Empty," someone said in the cargo hold. Robert secured the block and tackle, rope and pulleys creaking loud in the silence.

Grumbling surrounded him. "Tide's out. Get the lads to clean up the muck."

Robert peered over the side. Below him, bits of wood bobbed in a murky sludge. Forward of the ship, a wet layer of tea coated the mud. It was a spring tide, and the water had retreated so far that the keel barely cleared the bottom.

What a waste. He should be outraged.

The men poured out of the ship as silently as they'd come. Still no activity on the warships. Robert let loose a quiet sigh as he gained the wharf and surveyed the mudflats below.

He was already soot blackened. A little more filth wouldn't matter. He grabbed the broom offered him and followed Joshua. He'd stay near the young man and make sure the fellow came home safely.

He stepped into the mud and joined in the seemingly hopeless task of pushing the cold mounds of wet tea into the oily harbor water, a mockery of the brew so beloved in English parlors. Brooms and sticks flailed. A few lads even removed their shoes and thrust and kicked the offending substance away with their bare feet.

Thank you. It was a prayer of sorts, a prayer to the distant God. There had been no bloodshed tonight.

10

The question, then, is whether these laws are to be submitted to. If the people of America say 'no,' they say in effect that they will no longer be a part of the British Empire …

—William Legge, Earl of Dartmouth

The Shenandoah Valley, May 1774

The news of a new act broke like the first fierce drops of a storm. Sheriff George Mathews called a meeting in Staunton, and Jonathan knew all the principal men of the area were planning to be there. He mounted Brutus and waited for Hannah as she led out her mare, wondering if the latest troubles with the Shawnee would eclipse Boston's new woes.

They set off for town, Da, Nathan, and Mr. MacLeod, the hired man, following in the clattering wagon.

Horses and wagons filled Staunton's main thoroughfare. Mathews's Tavern would be packed.

Jonathan dismounted and stepped inside. The aroma of tobacco and sweaty men assailed his nose. Once his vision adjusted to the dimness, he made out a number of familiar faces. Some, like the Mathews brothers and the Lewises, were also members of the Tinkling Springs congregation. Others, like Houston and Preston, lived to the south. Some were strangers.

One bear-like man approached them and addressed Da. "Name's Daniel Morgan. I hear you're a man to know in these parts."

His father returned the greeting, then added, "I hear you're a teamster. My son Nathan is of that trade."

Morgan laughed and shook his brother's hand. "Got a Conestoga for sale, iron rims on the wheels. I'm more in the farming line now."

Nathan brightened. Jonathan knew his brother had his eye on the huge wagons. And if anyone could get a heavily laden Conestoga over Rockfish Gap, it was Nathan, with his team of well-muscled horses.

They found seats, which was a surprise, but apparently the sheriff had anticipated the crowd and brought in chairs and stools from the courthouse across the street. Sheriff Mathews called them to order. "We've several grave matters to discuss."

"Boston!" someone shouted.

"We'll get to the Port Act presently." Mathews shuffled several papers in his hands. "First, Lord Dunmore is bringing men to fight the Shawnee."

Murmurs rose. "In person?" someone asked.

"If you can believe it, yes. The governor plans to help Pennsylvania with the latest imbroglio."

Colonel Andrew Lewis stood. "My men will be ready."

Murmurs of approval rose.

A chair scooted back and clattered to the floor. "Winchester will fight!" Daniel Morgan boomed.

Applause greeted this pronouncement.

When the noise died down, Mathews continued the meeting. Jonathan sat in a daze, thinking. Most of the men of Russell's Ridge were members of the local militia and would be expected to support the colonel. At least the corn was in the ground. But if Lewis was smart, he'd wait to muster the group until harvest was over.

And still … he wondered what his brother-in-law James Paxton would say, out beyond the western mountains, minister to a village of praying Indians. Jonathan would defend his home, but he had no special animus against the Shawnee.

Even after a Shawnee had killed and scalped Arch May, a day still vivid in his mind after all these years.

The truth was, Jonathan was reluctant to cross the western ridges, to go in search of dark-skinned men to kill. His mind shied away from the thought.

"We will now take up the matter of the Port Act." The sheriff's voice penetrated Jonathan's musings. "The port of Boston is closed."

The room stilled as the man picked up a newspaper and began to read.

Jonathan had read the article already. No ships could unload goods in Boston, except as necessary for the King's men, or for "fuel and victuals" for the townspeople. He worried for Ruth, but would the men of the valley care?

The sheriff finished and recognized young Houston.

"Boston is a port town. Shutting down the harbor is death to them."

Old Mr. Gibson banged his tankard on his table. "Can we trust the royal goons to allow enough necessities to get in?"

Murmurs rose.

"Order," the sheriff commanded, and when the hubbub had settled, he pointed to Colonel Preston.

"The King thinks the whole country will take fright and settle down and behave ourselves."

"Not likely!"

"Not while they take away our liberties!"

Sheriff Mathews simply waited until the comments subsided. "The law takes effect June first. The House of Burgesses of the Commonwealth of Virginia has declared June first a day of prayer and fasting."

The crowd absorbed this.

"However," Mathews continued, "Governor Dunmore disliked this action and dissolved the House."

A few colorful comments about Dunmore spiced the atmosphere.

The sheriff's mouth twitched. "Ladies are present."

Jonathan's father raised his hand and was recognized. "There is one problem we havena addressed. I agree that we canna trust the tender mercies of the King when it comes to Boston. They will need food and supplies."

Nathan stood. "I'll go. I'll pack a wagon and go to Boston."

Murmurs of approval swelled.

In that moment Jonathan made a decision.

What would he do about it? Ruth had asked. He could do this. He could go.

Not with Colonel Lewis. Not against the Shawnee.

He would go to Boston.

Bumps and clatters from the dispensary distracted Robert as he folded a sheet of the primer into octavo. He finished and laid it with its fellows. Only a few of the primer's sheets still hung from the drying racks, but he wouldn't be able to start binding the books until the leather for the covers arrived.

He sighed. If it arrived at all. Several boats were being unloaded in the harbor by men with taut faces, but they were the last before the Port Act took effect. Next week the harbor would close. All supplies would have to come by wagon.

The noise continued, and he looked out the window. A shipment must have arrived for the dispensary, for there were barrels and boxes in the cart. Perhaps he could help.

Robert opened the door, only to spot Joshua approaching carrying a crate. "What—?"

"Yours." Without further explanation, the young man entered the shop and deposited the large box on the floor with a flourish. Then he left.

Robert followed him outside, feeling a sudden urgency. The crate might be from his godmother, but it could wait. He was almost certain Mrs. Ward imported ammunition for the rebels. But what would be truly useful would be the names and locations of her recipients, and so far, he'd been unable to determine them. On the Sabbath, Ruth and her aunt visited shut-ins and widows, and Robert suspected, but could not prove, that Mrs. Ward carried more than foodstuffs in her baskets.

In any case, a woman's basket could only hold so much. A cart or wagon was another matter. And now that Parliament had essentially disbanded the local government, replacing Governor Hutchinson with a military general, Boston was strung tighter than ever. Robert had to know where these barrels and crates were going.

If General Gage could confiscate the ammunition from these caches, he might be able to keep the peace, such as it was. Without arms, there could be no widespread fighting. Robert had no desire to see bloodshed.

Joshua squatted, scooped up his nanny goat, and deposited her in the crowded cart. Her hooves clicked against the wood of crates and boxes. Unlabeled, the cargo could be anything. Robert eyed a cask, wondering if it was gunpowder.

"Care for company? I could help you unload. I'm finished for today."

Joshua squinted at him. "You can't tell."

"Who would I tell?"

"The redcoats. Bloody backs. But no, you helped with the tea. Come."

Robert jumped up to the narrow seat and Joshua clucked at the horse, a sturdy creature of about fourteen hands. The cart resisted the first efforts of the animal, creaking slowly out of the yard, and Robert jumped down.

"I'll walk." He laid an encouraging hand on the mare's bridle. "Where to?"

In this manner they left Boston and made their way to Roxbury. Robert wondered where the goat came into it.

"See the trees?" Joshua pointed. "Roxbury Green is beyond."

So that was it. The goat needed fodder, and Boston Common was all but useless for animals, being given over to both regulars and militia.

The trees ahead were decorated with tiny red objects. As the cart passed between them, the objects resolved into figures. Dolls. Red-coated toy soldiers, hanging by their necks.

Chilled fingers crept up Robert's spine.

They entered Roxbury Green, as the common was known, and Joshua tethered the goat to a full water bucket in the midst of knee-deep grass. They continued the journey. Sometimes Robert walked, and sometimes Joshua did. The afternoon sun shown in their faces by the time they slowed.

"Lexington," Joshua said. "Not all the way to Concord."

Journey's end?

The reins tautened and the pony halted.

"Colonel Parker knows you not." Worry lines appeared on Joshua's face.

Robert felt guilty to betray the lad, but it couldn't be helped. "I see. What shall we do?"

Joshua pointed to the tree line. "Wait there."

Robert headed obediently to the trees, but once concealed, he followed the cart from cover. Branches poked and pulled at his clothing, but he managed to find a place where he could see a building, probably a meeting-house—and the cart. A man was helping Joshua unload the cargo.

So, this was where the ammunition was going—or some of it, anyway.

General Gage was newly come from England, and Robert doubted the man would have had time to gather intelligence. He would get this information to him. But first, Joshua had mentioned Concord.

Robert needed to know more about munitions stashed there.

Perhaps a trip on foot? Catch a ride part way with a farmer?

On the way home shadowy plans began to form in his mind.

It was dark when Robert entered the back of the print shop. He stumbled against something on the floor.

It was the crate Joshua had delivered earlier. Robert lit a lantern and pried it open. A sturdy packet tied with ribbon nestled on top of other items carefully packed in straw and paper. He picked open the ribbon.

A rustle and flash warned him, and he stilled.

"You're back." Ruth stood blinking in the yellow light. "I heard a noise."

He took a steadying breath. She sounded nervous too, and he remembered the warning. A recent essay in the *Boston Observer* was thoughtfully critical of the dumping of the tea. One day, a warning from the committee of tarring and feathering had been plastered to the door.

No wonder Ruth was jumpy.

"'Tis only me." Robert opened the thick packet. "I received a crate from Leicestershire. From my godmother."

Several letters lay atop a number of thin booklets made of doubled crown-size paper nested together. He scanned the print. "Sermons. You may be interested."

He handed her the stack.

She angled the paper to catch the lantern light. "George Whitefield?" She pored over the booklets one by one. "I've never heard of most of these."

"I mentioned to my godmother that you wanted to print his sermons," he said.

Her eyes glistened. "Oh! We could print these individually, and then—"

"A collection." He smiled.

"Tell me more about your godmother."

"She knew Mr. Whitefield."

Her eyes grew round.

"She helped him and the Wesleys both. She lends her support to the training of ministers."

He peered into the box, wondering what else she'd sent. He opened a package wrapped in paper.

"Such fine linen," Ruth exclaimed. "Handkerchiefs?"

"Uh, no." He swallowed. The countess had sent him silk drawers. He rummaged quickly. "She sent stockings, and"—he opened a tin—"biscuits."

He raised the container in silent offering. He didn't mention what he'd glimpsed below the tin. A spyglass.

"How kind. Thank you again for the sermons. Oh, and Molly saved a meat pie for you and Joshua."

Her skirts swished as she left the circle of light and climbed the stairs.

Robert took a deep breath and removed the spyglass from the box. Made of rich mahogany, it was a marvelous gift.

And it would be useful.

His stomach rumbled, but the food could wait. Robert took the lantern and the letters into his tiny room. There was one from his godmother, and one with the tell-tale *W L* on the wax seal. He opened the one from the countess first.

Dear Robert,

I hope this Letter finds you well and in good Health. Thank you for the lovely Soap. It pleases me to know that it was produced in the Wilds of the Mountains. You know my great Affection for the Colonies and so I am grieved at the continued Trouble. I hope your Printer can make use of the Sermons. I am gladdened to hear that the name Methodist is not such a Term of Disapprobation as it is here. The College for Ministers prospers but I am concerned about the Orphanage. I hope Letters may at least travel to Georgia freely despite the recent Ruckus. In family News, your Cousin Lord Rawdon joined the 5th Regiment which I hear is being sent to Boston.

Lady Huntingdon

His cousin? Robert ran his palm over his face, roughened by the day's beard. He didn't like the man, but perhaps the military would be good for him. He slid his thumb under the red wax of the other missive.

Dear Nephew,

Your Mare is healthy and I plan to breed her again this Summer. Olive Branch is a fine Colt, quite lively and active. But alas, my yearly Sojourn to my Estate will be very brief, as the Pressures of the Office wear upon me.

I was not meant for this. To say so sounds froward, as I know my Creator is sovereign over all, but I have failed. To see these Acts pass through Parliament strikes me with such Dread I find my Sleep deserting me.

And yet, I cannot offer an Alternative. If Boston does not submit to the Crown, what options do we have? Your Letters convince me that the People of New England will not take kindly to Military Rule. Lord North is troubled too. He shepherds Parliament in the direction the King wills, which he knows to be his Duty. He feels helpless to avoid greater Conflict, which is clearly on the Horizon.

Destroy this Letter. If you discover Military Intelligence, report it directly to Gage.

Your Uncle William

Robert lit the brazier in his room. He ripped the letter into tiny pieces and fed them to the coals.

11

An attack made on one of our sister colonies to compel submission to arbitrary taxes is an attack made on all British America and threatens ruin to the rights of all …

—Virginia House of Burgesses, May 1774

July 1774

*R*uth tidied the print shop's front room, where they took classifieds and other orders. She bent to find a rag. Noise filtered in from the street.

She straightened and wiped down the counter. The noise grew. A sudden shout startled her and made her think of the bloody snow before the customhouse.

Heart hammering, she rounded the counter and looked through the window. Men were gathering in the street.

Her father's footsteps clattered down the stairs.

"Papa? What is happening?" Dread filled her. Was about her writing—but no, she'd been careful not to include inflammatory statements. Hadn't she?

The words became louder—and clearer. "Show your face, Honorius! Or is Marius your name?"

"Boot licker! Scoundrel!"

"Show your face, Marius!"

Ruth's stomach soured in fear. Marius was her new pen name, but they didn't know that. They'd think her father wrote the essays. They would tar and feather him. One man had nearly died, being stripped of his clothes and doused in hot tar in the dead of winter.

Her father peered outside.

Mr. Shirley rushed into the room, his apron speckled in ink. He joined her father at the window. "Sir, stand aside."

Papa hesitated, and Mr. Shirley tackled him. Both of them hit the floor just as a brick sailed through the window, shattering it.

Mr. Shirley rolled and scrambled to his feet.

Ruth screamed, then fell to her knees. "Papa, are you hurt?" She helped him to sit up.

"Ruth … get back." He fumbled to adjust his crooked spectacles, which had managed to stay on.

Joshua appeared at her side, rocking back and forth on his heels, inking brushes still in his hands. He stared at the brick on the floor.

"Joshua, get a broom," she said. "There's glass everywhere."

"Miss Haynes," Mr. Shirley said. "Stay back, away from the windows. I think I recognize one of those fellows."

He went outside, and she held her breath.

THE JULY SUN beat on his face as Robert scanned the crowd. The tradesmen and dock workers standing in the street were attired in ordinary shirts and caps, no fancy jabots. One or two looked familiar, but he couldn't be sure. That night on the wharf had been dark, and the men disguised.

Robert raised a conciliatory hand. "Good fellows—"

"Give us Marius!" The speaker was a dark, shambling sort of fellow.

"Mr. Haynes writes about agriculture."

"Not as Marius he don't!" someone else shouted.

A restlessness seized the group, and a lad to the left grabbed a loose cobblestone. His godmother's parlor, Lord Dartmouth's commands, seemed as far away as the moon.

"The printer is not the author." He watched arms and hands, wondering when a stone would sail his way.

A tall man removed his hat. "Are you the writer?"

Robert shook his head. Then the random shifting of the crowd revealed a pot full of pine tar. If the worst happened, the heat of the day might suffice to keep the viscous substance liquid. They wouldn't have to heat it to a dangerous temperature. Still, he couldn't bear the thought of such a humiliating fate for the gentle printer. If necessary, he'd take the blame himself—even if it destroyed his credibility with the Sons of Liberty. The earl could look elsewhere for a spy.

A fellow in a tradesman's coat made a gesture. "I recognize this man. He's one of the Sons."

A muttering arose as this was discussed. Tea was mentioned. Would his participation be sufficient to dissuade them?

A trickle of sweat rolled down the back of his neck. "I plead with you to overlook the opinions of an inconsequential essay writer. Mr. Haynes and Mrs. Ward are both upstanding people."

His arguments sounded stilted to his own ears. And they had little effect on the mob. Most of the men wore hard, flinty faces, and the younger ones looked savagely gleeful.

The tradesman's comment had not convinced them. He drew a breath. He'd need to confess to writing the hated essays himself. "I am—"

Several on the fringe of the crowd turned, and Robert looked in that direction.

Two riders approached, backlit by the sun. One was clearly armed, the muzzle of a rifle outlined above his shoulder. Robert couldn't make out the other. He raised his hand to shade his eyes. Friend or foe?

The dispensary door opened and Mrs. Ward emerged. "What on earth! Glass everywhere!" She wheeled on a young man and grabbed him by the ear. "What would Mrs. Cotton say to this?"

The crowd shifted and swayed like a boat caught in cross currents. Several men tipped their hats to her, but others scowled.

"Ho, Aunt Betsy! What's the trouble?" Clad in buckskin, the rider looked more like a hunter than a farmer, but clearly he knew Mrs. Ward. And his horse was a fine blood bay.

The second animal was a chestnut twin of the first. The rider was—a woman? Sunlight glinted on a pistol in her lap.

She raised it, and the closest men backed away. The buckskin-clad stranger reached for his rifle, and in one smooth motion he aimed it at the crowd.

"Who is responsible for this?" Buckskin asked.

As the firearm's muzzle swept over the crowd, they backed away, grumbling. Finally the last miscreant was gone.

Robert was relieved beyond measure. He watched the newcomers with interest. He didn't recognize the breed of their horses, but they were fine animals.

The fellow dismounted, gave Robert an assessing glance, and approached Mrs. Ward. "Aunt Betsy?"

"Jonathan? And is that—"

"Hannah, my sister."

The woman was tall like her brother. Clearly, this was some sort of family reunion.

"We had a bit of a problem, a brick thrown through a window—" Mrs. Ward said.

"A *brick?* Auntie, we came just in time."

She smiled, obviously relieved. "Meet Mr. Shirley, Gideon's bookbinder."

"Jonathan Russell, at your service." He stuck out a hand and Robert tested the grip, the callused palm. Russell was at least an inch taller than he was, and Robert was taller than most. Blue eyes in an honest face. "Robert Shirley, at yours."

Russell stepped to the side and introduced his sister.

Robert stared. She had the height and the blue eyes of her brother, but there was nothing masculine about her. She removed a straw hat, and the sun glinted gold in her copper-red hair.

She took several bold steps forward. He couldn't move. Her kerchief was carelessly tucked, and her skirts dusty from the road, but her easy grace and simple beauty would turn heads even in a London ballroom.

"Hannah Russell." She held out a hand.

He opened his mouth and choked out something. Then he kissed her hand.

❧

WHEN JONATHAN SAW the crowd in front of the print shop, the fatigue of the journey fell away. Most were bullies, easy to rouse, but just as easily dispersed. Still, Jonathan kept his eye on them until the last man was gone.

"Auntie? Is anyone hurt?" Was Ruth unharmed? He didn't see her.

"Only frightened. But that's what these scamps intended."

He nodded and led Hannah around the building to the small stable behind it, his pulse still thumping.

Jonathan kept a careful eye on the bookbinder, a Mr. Shirley. The man kept following Hannah with his gaze, and though he'd done nothing wrong, Jonathan's hackles rose.

The man assisted them in caring for the horses.

"May I ask their pedigree?" Mr. Shirley stroked Bodie's neck.

His posture, manners, careful phrasing of his words shouted *English*. Where did he come from?

"They seem to like you," Hannah said. "Half thoroughbred."

"And half freight horse." Jonathan ran a finger under the kerchief he'd tied as a stock. It was hot. "My father breeds Conestogas. They are sturdy animals that pull the largest wagons. We used them to bring a load of supplies. Corn, cider, barley, some other necessities. The rest of the family is out at Roxbury Green with the wagon."

"What's this I hear?" Gideon Haynes came through the back door of the print shop. "Supplies?"

Ruth came out behind her father, her face pinched and drawn. No wonder. Hoodlums had just smashed their front window. Jonathan's innards clenched. Was it in response to something published in the paper? If Ruth was still loyal, still a Tory, she was in danger. And would continue to be.

Aunt Betsy began organizing. "Joshua, we'll need the cart. Molly, we'll need a large spread for dinner—"

Ruth's gaze latched onto his sister. "Hannah?"

"Ruth? Is that you?" Hannah rushed forward and embraced her cousin. "Are you safe? We have been praying for your protection."

RUTH'S HEART CONTRACTED. Hannah's words, combined with the arrival of the supplies, swamped her with emotion. Several great, rolling sobs burst out of her throat.

"Come inside." Hannah steered her to a chair in the dim print shop.

Ruth forced a smile. "I'm sorry—" They'd only just met, but their correspondence made it feel more like a reunion.

"No, no, you've had a shock."

Jonathan came in, smelling of sweat and horse, and glanced about, taking in the press and hanging paper. "Who were those men?"

Ruth took a deep breath. Jonathan was bigger, taller than she remembered. "My fault. 'Twas my fault—"

"The committee for tar and feathering." Mr. Shirley curled his hands into fists.

Jonathan faced the bookbinder. "But why?" His blue gaze returned to her.

"Marius. Honorius. I wrote them, I wrote it all."

Puzzlement followed by a dawning comprehension traveled over Jonathan's rugged features. He must not have known she wrote for her father's paper.

"I believe they wanted your father," Mr. Shirley said. "No one knew who Marius was."

"But you did?" Jonathan stiffened.

"I suspected. And truly, she wrote nothing radical." Mr. Shirley rubbed his jaw. "In fact, it seems that the only acceptable opinions in Boston are either seditious or without sense entirely."

"Seditious." Jonathan seemed to spit out the word as bitter.

Ruth remembered the argument over sauced cod long ago. Seemingly, Jonathan had retained his opinions. For a brief instant she feared the men would come to blows, but the thread of tension broke as Hannah stepped between them.

"Ruth, I brought something for you." Hannah left the shop, only to return a few moments later with heavy leather saddlebags. She knelt before Ruth's chair, lifted a leather flap, and withdrew a gleaming object.

A pistol, with a polished wood stock and a shiny steel mechanism.

Jonathan crouched at Hannah's side, and his warm leather smell returned. "Not terribly old. Likely saw action in the war."

Hannah pulled out a pouch from the saddlebag. "Here's shot. Do you have powder?"

Ruth rubbed her fingers together. "I've never fired a pistol."

"Only rifles?" Hannah asked.

"No, nothing." Reluctantly she took the pistol in her hands. It was heavy.

A wide grin spread across Hannah's face. "I'll teach you how."

"I-I do not think I could." Images of glass flying into the room swirled in Ruth's mind. "And there is no need. I will no longer write—I cannot endanger Papa."

Jonathan's expression softened, and he asked for a copy of the *Observer*. Mr. Shirley went to a stack in the corner and handed him a copy. Brow wrinkling, Jonathan perused it.

"Miss Ruth, I've cleaned up the glass." At the door to the front room, Molly's gaze latched onto the pistol in Ruth's lap. "Your father has gone on an errand. I'll start supper now."

He might have gone to order a new window. Or get news. Or both. "Thank you, Molly."

Jonathan took the newspaper nearer to the window. "'Let us behave like children who have received unjust blows from a loving parent.' Why, this sounds like Dickinson."

Hannah squinted at him. "Dickinson?"

"Several years back—the 'Letters' that were published against the Townshend Acts. They were strongly worded but did not advise disloyalty." Jonathan cut a glance at Mr. Shirley. "Or sedition, if you will."

"I meant not to plagiarize the man." Ruth remembered reading the articles, thinking them bold and harsh at the time.

Jonathan closed the newspaper with a crisp rustle. "You could write elsewhere. Philadelphia is a peaceable town."

It warmed her that he cared. "Papa would never move."

"New York," Mr. Shirley ventured. "'Tis closer and—"

"Not now," Ruth said. "Not yet, anyway."

"Jonathan." Hannah's voice was firm. "She needs to rest."

"Would ye stay with her, Hannah? I need to get back to the wagon. They'll be wondering why we're not back."

The sunlight coming through the window picked up the coppery glow of her hair as she nodded her response. Yes, this tall, lithe, warm-hearted young woman was definitely a Russell.

"Miss Haynes?" Mr. Shirley asked. "I shall take my things to the bookshop to make room for your guests. But I will help with the supplies afterward."

"Thank you, Mr. Shirley, you are all kindness."

Jonathan nodded stiffly in acknowledgement as the bookbinder took his leave. He didn't like Mr. Shirley for some reason. That was clear.

Jonathan placed his hat on his head and fixed his gaze on Ruth. "I'll be back," he said softly.

She watched him as he left for the stable. The room seemed empty without him.

ROBERT STRODE down the cobblestone street, sea chest on his shoulder, feeling like a fool.

He'd never been affected by a woman in that way before. And she was— was—untidy!

A glorious, untidy Amazon of a woman. And that hair!

She'd ignored him. Oh, she was polite, friendly even—but what did he expect? She didn't know he was the nephew of an earl. A poor relation, granted, but no tradesman.

He clenched his jaw. But even if she knew, would she care?

He thought not. If fact, in this upside-down place, she'd probably disdain any pretension of rank or family. He smiled grimly. *Pretension* was right.

And maybe he liked her because she was so unpretentious, so easy in her own person.

Handling a pistol, yet fully feminine. And she spoke of *praying* for her relations. Devout, too? A good woman, then.

And utterly unavailable. His godmother would laugh.

Worst of all, he'd opened his mouth and exposed himself as loyal. The persona he sought to project was one of sympathetic moderation. Sympathetic to the rebels.

He stumbled over a loose stone. Seditious, indeed! Why had he used that word?

He quickened his steps, and in another minute he arrived at the shop, empty of both customers and owner.

William fairly bounced behind the counter. "Here to take my place?"

Robert was sorry to disappoint him. He'd seen several wagons along the way; the town hummed like a market day. "Nay, just bringing my things."

Five minutes saw him out the door again. He'd heard Miss Haynes mention the Shenandoah Valley—where was that? He'd find a geography book—

"Is that you? Cousin Robert?"

Robert nearly slammed into a red-coated figure that stepped into his path. It took him a moment to focus on the familiar face, the dark bushy brows over a rascal's gaze. "Francis!" Robert took in the gorget, the insignia of his uniform. "That is, Lieutenant …Lord Rawdon."

"Rawdon will do." His cousin surveyed Robert's attire. "And your commission?"

Robert became acutely aware of his surroundings. Fortunately, no one seemed to be within earshot on the street. Of course, the townspeople tended to avoid soldiers. "Inactive."

Rawdon's black eyebrows lifted as he studied Robert's face. "Inactive. At such a time." His mouth formed a doubtful moue.

Robert felt pinned like a specimen on a collector's board. He had to explain his presence, but how? He swallowed. He was under orders not to reveal his purpose.

"Let me guess. The countess … you were always her favorite. No, don't dispute it. But to dress you in rags here in this treasonous cesspool is not her work. Nay, I would put money on her friend the Psalm Singer."

Robert's lips parted.

"Don't look so surprised. Dartmouth has spies everywhere. But that commission can be reactivated at any time. We might serve together."

Robert's stomach roiled at the suggestion. Then he had a sudden thought. He lowered his voice. "You could help me. I need a contact. To get intelligence to Gage."

Dark beady eyes traveled over his face again. "I see. And if anyone asks, we are cousins." He jerked his chin in lieu of a salute, then spun on his heel and departed.

Robert stood in the street, the sweat under his shirt turning clammy.

"Mister, can I help you?"

He turned to see John Winthrop, the head of the tar and feathering society.

"You look pale," Winthrop said. "Did the bloody back trouble you?"

"Worse," he replied. "The man's my cousin."

12

The Act for blockading the Town has been executed with the utmost Rigor
and even beyond the Rigor of this cruel Act.
    —Rev. Samuel Cooper to Benjamin Franklin, Aug. 15, 1774

*J*onathan wormed his way on his belly to the front of the
Conestoga, the long, roomy wagon Nathan had purchased from
Daniel Morgan. Resting on the thick sacks of Connecticut wool
that covered the rest of the cargo, he propped up his chin and gazed out at
the August morning. The familiar clink of the doubletree and the rhythmic
clop of the team of four soothed him as he watched Nathan drive, riding
pillion on Lady Jane, the near wheel horse. They were taking another load of
miscellaneous supplies to Boston, but a Conestoga wagon had no seat in
front, and so Jonathan sat or lay on the cargo. He'd tethered Brutus to the
back of the vehicle for the day to give the creature a rest.

"Nathan, did you hear what Mr. Knox said about the horses?"

Images from their first trip to Boston remained impressed in his mind. In
Roxbury Green, children played and women gossiped as wagons from
various places, near and far, unloaded supplies for the townspeople. But the
dark tension of siege showed in the faces of the men.

Ruth had introduced them to a bookshop owner named Henry Knox, a local militia leader and a very interesting man.

Nathan turned his head. "Aye. He needs horses for artillery."

"Sounds serious. Sounds like war."

"No one wants war."

War. Following the passage of the Port Bill, four regiments of redcoats had been dispatched to Boston, and General Gage had replaced Hutchinson as governor. Boston was now under martial law, and the closing of the port had caused an uproar. The Quebec Act served as the last straw. With the stroke of a pen, much of the frontier now belonged to Quebec, and the Popish church was empowered to collect tithes from settlers.

Remote frontiersmen who cared little for Boston suddenly cared a lot about the actions of Parliament. Ironically, Jonathan mused, the actions of the British government had served to bring together all thirteen colonies—townspeople, planters, and backcountry settlers—as nothing else could have.

And in the belly of the wagon, underneath wool, cords of seasoned pine, and other assorted supplies, powder and shot served as ballast.

"Nathan, what will Ruth do?" He meant to say, the Haynes, or even, their relations, but *Ruth* just slipped out. "I suggested Philadelphia."

"And I take it they will stay."

"Hmm." Jonathan's mind was filled with Ruth's face, tendrils of dark hair escaping her cap to brush her cheeks. She was stubborn, yet vulnerable. Why he cared he wasn't sure. He couldn't marry, even if all *this* were not happening. He'd want to confess his dark secret, open his heart, but what good woman would marry him then?

Nathan pivoted easily to face him on the broad back of the horse. Knowing their business, the animals continued onward, keeping to the road.

"Things will get worse." Nathan's blue eyes were clear but full of concern.

"You never speak up at Mathews's—or even at home."

The breeze tugged at the brim of Nathan's hat. "In order for bloodshed to be avoided, the principal figure in this drama must desire a peaceful outcome."

Jonathan stared at his brother. "Principal figure?"

"The King, of course."

It was true. Folks tended to blame Parliament for everything. But it was whispered that the King controlled the House of Commons. They only whispered, because no one wanted to be accused of treason.

"By closing the port of Boston," Nathan continued, "they reveal a supposition that the trouble is local. A few rabble-rousers who will be brought to heel or hanged."

"And when it doesna work ..."

"Remember Culloden?"

They'd heard the stories of the rape of Scotland firsthand from Ian MacLeod, who'd been there, and it no longer seemed like a faraway tale. The lesson was clear. The King would show treason no mercy.

Jonathan rearranged some of the wool to create a seat. His head brushed the canvas top, secured by hickory bows arching overhead. The wagon was solidly built, and a good thing, too, with the distance they'd had to travel. "Scotland still hasna recovered from what Cumberland did. Crofts burnt, families killed or separated—"

"It didn't end with the battle. The Crown decided to crush Scotland so it would never rise again," Nathan said.

"So if we fight we must win."

"Live free or die."

Jonathan couldn't believe his brother's words, so calmly spoken. "But you—"

"Our life is but a vapor anyway. It's why I sell Whitefield's sermons."

"For almost nothing. I don't know how you are going to survive this." Someone had to be practical.

"Mrs. Lee gave me two shillings for the sermons, more than I asked." Nathan grinned.

Jonathan sighed. Perhaps it was better not to worry about money.

Nathan wriggled back to face forward again. "Ye ken well what the scripture says. 'Take no thought—'"

"Pah! Very well then, we shall trust in the Lord, ye scamp."

He lay back on the wool, thinking of the gunpowder underneath him. Would he end up fighting—killing? Not everyone understood the horror of it.... His mind shied away from that dark day. But he knew his duty—protecting his family, protecting his country was right. He couldn't wait to get to Boston, to get the gunpowder into the right hands.

∾

ROBERT PLACED the burning taper to the cotton wick. It caught, and he tossed the taper into the brazier. He stared at the burgeoning flame, knowing it would take several minutes before the scent would fill his cramped bedroom.

Bayberry candles were ridiculous in price, or so he'd thought at first. Until he bought one and realized that they were expensive the way a carefully aged wine was expensive. The scent was pleasant, but not cloyingly so. The smell was hearty, with a sharpness that hinted of forest and mountains. The strength of New England itself hid in the humble bayberry.

Robert gathered the rest of the candles together and wrapped them in paper. He couldn't imagine what his godmother would think of the gift; Old England smelled of lilac and roses, damp and smoke. But bayberry's strength was appropriate for a woman like the countess, who defied all English tradition by simple good works.

And the candles made him think of Hannah Russell. He placed a copy of the newly bound book of Whitefield's sermons and the candles in a straw-filled box and sat on the narrow bed. She was all that was good and grand about the colonies.

He loved this new world. And hated it, too. He hated what he had been sent to do. His loyalty to the King was absolute, but now it chafed at him. Ordinary soldiering was one thing; intelligence work, no matter how one excused it, was dirty.

The candle's aroma reached him, and he leaned back against the wall. He imagined riding his mare along a Massachusetts beach, then alongside a certain chestnut, whose rider wore red gold on her head.

He closed his eyes. Hannah smiled at him, a fey smile, inviting but full of warning. She raised a gleaming pistol.

Robert drew a forearm over his eyes and sat up. He'd fallen asleep. He wriggled his shoulders and took a deep breath, trying to dispel the image of the pistol. He needed to write a letter to the earl, though he had little to report, and a note to the countess.

He prepared a piece of foolscap and sharpened a quill.

Dear Uncle William,

Boston has been warm this summer, full of sunshine. Four regiments have barracked on the Common and I wonder how they will fare once the weather turns, as it will soon do. The officers sometimes patronize the bookshop, which is a help as the townsfolk have less to spend.

My employer has married. I would not mention it but for the circumstance. Mr. Knox is decidedly Whiggish in his politics, but never offensively so. He is welcoming to all, and courted a young woman from a respectable, loyal family. Recently Gage appointed her father secretary of the Colony. Mr. Knox married Lucy in June but her parents did not attend. Some say that the bookseller's antecedents counted against him —his father abandoned the family—but here in the Colonies, such things are not insurmountable. No, it was political, a sad commentary on the rift that now divides families.

An attorney named John Adams has joined his cousin Samuel on a trip to Philadelphia, where they will discuss the Intolerable Acts, as the Coercive Acts are here known. In particular, the Act to close the port of Boston is extremely unpopular. Supplies pour into Boston from as far as the Shenandoah Valley, five hundred miles away. The men of this town remind me of well-fed dogs, smarting beneath the whip, and all the more dangerous for that.

Hopefully, wiser heads will prevail in Philadelphia.

Thank you for the news of the mare.

Your nephew, Robert

He decided not to mention Rawdon. He could not include particulars like that in an uncoded missive.

He wrote to his godmother and folded the letter to the earl inside. He dropped the sealed letter inside the box with the candles.

Hannah Russell. He couldn't give her a gift, it was improper. But something for the family? He had several candles left.

Robert grabbed his coin purse and dumped it out on his bed. A few gold coins glinted amidst the silver and copper. With Boston closed, shipping to Leicestershire would cost a significant amount once he added the cost of freight to an open port. He separated out a gold ducat and a pile of shillings, leaving a lone gold sovereign and a few tuppence.

The Russells. They were coming any day from Newport with supplies. He'd speak with Mrs. Ward.

THE BRICK of the Brattle Street Church fairly glowed in the Sabbath sunshine. Ruth admired the tall, arched windows and the bell tower above the door. Construction of the new building had just been completed, and there were rumors that Franklin stoves would be installed in time for winter.

She spotted Mr. Shirley next to her father and her aunt, who'd come in the cart with Joshua. Ruth, accompanied by Molly, had elected to walk with Jonathan and Nathan, who'd delivered supplies just yesterday.

They entered the church and the scents of newly sawn wood and fresh paint met Ruth's nose. Molly slipped away to the gallery, where the slaves and freemen sat.

Ruth sat next to her father, and her cousins squeezed in on the other side. Suitably dressed in a well-fitting green waistcoat, Jonathan seemed especially gangly on the narrow seat, his knees reaching nearly to the back of the next pew. "Who's that fellow in the ruffles and braid?" he whispered. He smelled of Hannah's soap.

She followed his gaze. "John Hancock, he's a merchant. Now, shush."

The service was starting. She felt acutely conscious of Jonathan's presence. He stumbled through the psalter selections with a fine deep voice.

Finally the minister began the sermon. "Our text is Matthew twenty-two …"

Ruth settled back in the pew as Rev. Cooper preached on "giving unto Caesar." Next to her Jonathan leaned forward, broad hands on his thighs. The sermon seemed ordinary enough, although more political than usual. Perhaps it was necessary during this crisis to remind the inhabitants of Boston that they owed allegiance and duty to the King.

The congregation sat silent, attentive while the high ceiling reflected the minister's words. Ruth was acutely aware of Jonathan's warmth next to her. She closed her eyes.

"…a hundredweight of fish …"

Fish? Her eyes flew open.

"They were forced to haul their gift of fish over land, despite all assurances that the port was open for food and fuel."

Rev. Cooper had departed from the text. Or had he? "It is one more evidence of the cruelty of a government in which we have no voice, a far country which styles herself as our 'mother'. A mother may justly beat her child, but her motive is love, infused with the tenderness every woman knows by nature. Cruelty undermines the discipline of a parent. And so, when our mother country smites us, without mercy, without tenderness, how are we to respond?"

A murmur rose in the building. Rev. Cooper, as many suspected, was a rebel after all. Ruth sighed. Congregationalist ministers, almost without exception, felt this way. She shouldn't be surprised.

"Here in Massachusetts a man may not abuse his wife. She is subject to him by the authority of scripture and custom, yet she enjoys legal protection. Why should the colonies enjoy less?"

"Hear, hear!" someone shouted.

Jonathan sat bolt upright. On her right, Papa extracted a handkerchief and wiped his forehead.

The minister concluded his sermon, and conversation buzzed noisily, like a hive of disturbed bees. Slowly, in twos and threes, the congregation left the building.

She found herself standing near Jonathan, who was rolling his shoulders and blinking up at the sunshine.

"How d'ye bear it, all the redcoats about?" he asked.

Ruth glanced about the yard and surrounding streets. Three red uniforms dotted the small crowd that milled about, conversing.

"They are the King's servants." She didn't want to argue.

His gaze seemed to drill into her. "Precisely."

"We ought to give honor where honor is due."

Jonathan adjusted his waistcoat, which fit him well, but he seemed uncomfortable in it even so. "I agree with that. I ken the scriptures."

Somehow, his agreement needled her. "You can't mean that every law and decision should be subject to *your* approval before you obey it?" Her voice emerged loud to her ears.

Aunt Betsy looked her way, lifting a brow.

"Not every decision is legitimate. Not every law is lawful," he said.

This was the one point where Ruth stumbled. In theory, she knew he was right. But how—

"The King is subject to the law," he said. "We see that in the Magna Carta."

Mr. Shirley side-stepped closer.

"I know my history!" she hissed. Now she was angry. He was treating her like a child.

"Sir—" Mr. Shirley objected in an undertone.

They were creating a scene, but she didn't care.

Jonathan stepped closer. "The Parliament is out of bounds—"

"Who are *you*—"

He kissed her. Soundly.

Someone clapped.

"Dinna act shocked," he growled into her cap. He drew back and locked his gaze on hers. "Too many overheard you."

The fog dispersed from her mind. Her lips tingling, she nodded.

He tucked her arm in his elbow. "A wee argument with your beau is all they'll remember."

Heat flooded her cheeks. "I'll get you back for this, Jonathan Russell."

13

It is not in the still calm of life, or the repose of a pacific station, that great characters are formed. The habits of a vigorous mind are formed in contending with difficulties. Great necessities call out great virtues.

—Abigail Adams

March 1775

Chills seized Robert as he approached Cambridge. He staggered to the side of the Boston Road and leaned against an oak. Why was he shivering? There was snow on the ground, but even so. He'd been tramping steadily all night, his blood flowing. Layers of wool protected him. He shouldn't feel this cold.

Robert looked over his shoulder at the moon, a great silver eye descending toward the tree line in the west. His neck ached from the motion. Indeed, his whole body ached. An unexplainable fatigue had settled into his bones around midnight, and like a good soldier, he'd ignored it.

He felt horribly exposed, as if the moon mocked him, pointed out his duplicity. He wore no uniform, but he carried information about rebel stores in Concord.

He was no longer simply an observer. He was truly a spy.

He clamped his jaws shut to stop his teeth from chattering and stepped back onto the road. He needed to get this information to General Gage. A few dozen troops could seize the munitions in Concord and a crisis would be averted.

He forced his limbs to move. *Crunch, crunch.* He steps sounded painfully loud on the snowy road, but so far he'd been fortunate. No one out and about. All tucked snug in warm houses ... No, he couldn't think about fireplaces and hot coffee.

Keep moving. Rawdon's face swam before him. He'd have to stop by the Common, find the man. But shouldn't he write down the names, locations? He'd already scratched out a map. Hadn't he?

Thinking was impossible. He must be ill.

The moon vanished, and the blackness confused him. He stumbled into the bushes. Then he found the slight shimmer of the snow on the road and found his way again.

He was so tired. He longed to find a nook behind a tree and go to sleep. Just for a while.

But no—that was dangerous. And he had his duty. Duty came first.

A distant cock crowed, and Robert realized suddenly that the blackness wasn't absolute. As he approached Roxbury the faintest tinge of pink emerged on the horizon. Then orange. Then gold. He aimed his steps toward the red-gold of Hannah's beautiful hair.

Almost there, almost there.

Robert staggered into Boston. He saw Rawdon's huge black eyebrows. Then Hannah's copper hair framing her smiling face. And Gage. Where was Gage?

There was something important he had to do.

"Mr. Shirley?"

Something very important.

"Mr. Shirley, are you well?" That wasn't Rawdon.

He subsided into blackness.

RUTH'S FINGERS flew around the edge of the crate from Virginia. She hadn't heard from Hannah all winter—indeed, not since her brothers had left late last summer. Then Ruth heard rumors of a battle with Indians. Was everyone safe? Was Jonathan safe? She hated to admit it, but she worried about him.

"Here, use this." Aunt Betsy handed her a chisel.

In moments the box was open.

"Look, Aunt Betsy. What beautiful wool." Ruth pulled out a blue shawl crisscrossed with white. "And soap." Only a dozen bars this time.

Finely tanned leather gleamed underneath. She removed the soap to reveal four stout knives in tooled sheaths. Not case knives. These were huge.

Aunt Betsy lifted one and unsheathed the blade with a metallic swish. It glittered deadly in the light of the shop. "I can sell this, certain." She frowned. "What do I owe them?"

"Here's a letter." Tears sprang to her eyes. "Hannah gives the news ... they're safe ... oh, here. The soap and shawl are gifts. The knives are for consignment.... Consignment?"

"That means I repay him later."

"That's a kindness."

"I'll leave you be." Her aunt smiled.

Ruth wiped her face and returned to the letter.

Dear Ruth,

I am sorry for the delay, but in winter travel slows to a stop. As I write, Rockfish Gap is still blocked with two feet of snow. I am packing this crate to send by wagon north through Winchester and Lancaster. Last fall, Jonathan and Nathan came home after Colonel Lewis and the rest went to fight the Shawnee. In the end Cornstalk made a peace treaty with Dunmore (our governor). Many men in the valley grumbled at this. I am not sure if they just don't like Dunmore (it's true, they don't) or if they just want to have another try and kill or drive away all the Shawnee (stupid if nothing else, in my opinion). Many think Indians mere vermin to be exterminated.

My father says this treaty is incredibly good news, because with the trouble in Boston we don't need another war at our back door. I got to thinking about what he said. No one calls it war, but it makes me wish you were somewhere safer. Come to think of it, we have no printer in Augusta County.

Jonathan says the knives are for consignment and they cost him 6 s each to make. The soap and shawl are gifts. Mother made the shawl for you on a table loom. She was blessed by the bayberry candles Mr. Shirley sent. The smell brought back memories for her. The bookbinder is good-looking. I said this out loud and Da asked if he were a godly man. I protested that I was not serious. He said, "Never toy with a man's heart." I thought it sweet and did not gainsay him.

My brothers will stay to help with the plowing. I do not know what their plans are —indeed, we wait on events. My father insists that our Heavenly Father rules the kingdoms of this world, and we can rest in Him. In practice, that can be difficult. But I pray toward that end for myself, and I will pray for you.

In Christ, Hannah

Ruth pressed the paper to her heart. *We can rest in Him.* Yes, it was hard.

The dispensary bell tinkled.

"Ruth?" A familiar voice.

"Lucy!" She rose. "Come in—I haven't seen you in—"

"In months, most likely." Lucy Knox's dark hair gleamed, and a fine muslin gown draped her large frame. Henry Knox's new wife was an old friend, but she had other responsibilities now. "Have you seen Mr. Shirley?"

"Nay, he has not been by in several days," Ruth said.

"Harry is looking for him. What a pretty shawl."

"My cousins in western Virginia sent it."

Lucy's eyes rounded. "Cousins? Then it was a cousin who kissed you? Do not deny it, all of Boston knows."

Ruth's face warmed. "They are not cousins by blood. They brought supplies. How is the bookshop faring?"

Lucy's shoulders slumped. "Harry told the publisher in London that he can't pay him. Entreated the owner to speak for us to the government. The siege and the boycott are hurting British businesses, too."

"I'm surprised you're still here in Boston," Ruth said.

"If we go to the country, our property will be vandalized—"

"Could you go to Philadelphia? New York?"

Lucy's gaze fixed on Ruth. "I might say the same for you and your family." She sighed. "It may come to that. The anniversary meeting is tomorrow, and Dr. Warren has received death threats."

Ruth set out the soap and tidied the counter, wanting to ask a personal question. "Lucy, how did you bear your family's reaction?" she blurted. "To your marriage, I mean."

"When Harry and I met, my political views were unformed, but I enjoyed the atmosphere of the bookshop. Harry always encouraged the give-and-take of collegial conversation. Slowly, I became convinced that the rights of

Americans were being trampled." Her eyes twinkled. "By the bye, I did enjoy Honorius."

"You knew?"

"There were two pen names at the *Observer*, and Sarah Hutchinson let slip that you wrote for the newspaper. I could tell. Your piece on the destruction of Hutchinson's home was appropriate and well written."

"Thank you. But your parents—"

"'Tis hard. I haven't seen them since our engagement. Their loyalty to the King leaves no room for differences." Lucy blinked several times. "But I have Harry. He's enough." She cleared her throat. "Tell me about this fellow."

Ruth grabbed the shawl and held it up to her chest, as if it could cover her confusion. "I ... I—"

"What's his name?"

"Jonathan. And he's stubborn. Intractable."

Her eyebrows arched. "Oh, so you're alike."

Ruth's mouth sagged open.

Lucy's face was kind. "You both try to obey your consciences under heaven." She took the shawl from Ruth's hands and arranged it about her shoulders. "Let's go shopping."

"There's nothing to buy." On top of which, she had no money.

"Did I say we would buy anything?"

ROBERT OPENED his eyes and studied a crack in the plastered ceiling. Where was he? The sheets on his bed were damp with sweat.

He lifted a heavy hand and managed to clear the stickiness out of his eyes. Everything hurt. His skin itched, but he was too tired to scratch.

The last thing he remembered was a dark road. An important mission. He needed to get a message to General Gage.

He pushed himself up to a sitting position, but lights swirled in his eyes.

"What are you doing? Lie down." The voice was gentle, yet firm. And vaguely familiar.

Robert obeyed. Slanting rays of sunlight fell on the man in the doorway. He was well-dressed and wore a white satin waistcoat. The cravat, however, was modest rather than foppish. Robert approved of the man's taste. "Where—?" he croaked.

"My home is now a hospital." The man waved a ruffled hand. "Do not leave." The voice was steel, the gaze direct.

The familiar features resolved. It was Dr. Warren. "Why am I here?"

"You collapsed in the road. You have smallpox."

Horror swept over him. "I-I won't give it to you?"

"I have been inoculated. But most in Boston have not." He paced a few steps into the room and back. "Thanks to the British, this town is ideal for the spread of disease," he spat. "Mrs. Jenkins will attend you. You are still contagious. Mind her." He swept out.

Robert must have slept, because when he came to himself again the shadows had shortened. A spare, birdlike woman sat in a chair in the corner.

"Ma'am, what is the date?" He'd gone for information on the second of the month.

"Why, 'tis the anniversary celebration, the sixth." She peered at him. "Yesterday was the Sabbath, so the celebration is being held today."

He'd lost too much time. But he couldn't leave and risk spreading the disease. Was a message even possible? "How long will this rash last?"

The woman sighed. "Sorry, lad. 'Twill get worse before it gets better."

IT WAS TIME TO LEAVE. Ruth grabbed the pretty new shawl. The thick wool only came to her waist, not enough for the brisk day, but the crowded meetinghouse would be too warm for a cloak. "Ready, Papa."

He grumbled something unintelligible and they left, Joshua trailing. Ruth checked her pocket for the notebook she customarily carried, useful both for notes and occasionally even sketches. Mr. Shirley was nowhere to be found, and Papa needed help recording what was said. Joshua had been pressed for extra protection.

Papa worried, and in truth she worried too. The mood in Boston was very tense. She hunched her shoulders against the chill breeze and lifted her skirts to avoid the slush.

Once inside, they found a half-empty pew near the front. A number of scarlet-coated officers took up places nearby, and one found a chair on the side of the platform. A daub-hued figure took a seat on the other side—Samuel Adams. Soon the hall was filled with the sounds and smells of wool-coated men.

Ruth took out her notebook as Mr. Adams made the first remarks. Her eye was caught by motion to his side. The slouching officer in the front—a remarkably ugly man, with fierce black brows—dropped objects from his fingers into his opposite palm, one by one. At first, she thought they were coins. Then with shock she recognized them.

They were musket balls. *Clink ... clink ... clink.*

Next to her, Joshua wrung his handkerchief, tense as a startled deer.

"Here." She whispered, handing him the notebook. "Sketch that ugly redcoat."

The activity would keep him from bolting in panic.

The crowd cheered as Mr. Adams stepped down. The officers hooted and jeered.

A man robed in a Roman toga, like an orator out of a history book, stepped to the pulpit. Shouts of approbation, mixed with hostile comments from the officers, filled the room. Several redcoats struck their muskets butt first on the floor, tapping a protest at the visual insult.

It was Dr. Joseph Warren, and it was a brilliant piece of theater. The rebels idolized the Romans of the Republic. Cato and Brutus, who challenged the tyrant Julius Caesar, were their heroes. The officers were not ignorant of the message.

The cacophony ebbed away as the physician stared down the officers clustered at the front.

Ruth's heart caught in her throat. No matter any disagreement she might have with the man, she admired his courage.

He spoke of the obligation to defend personal freedom with clear ringing tones. "Our fathers having nobly resolved never to wear the yoke of despotism ... bravely threw themselves upon the bosom of the ocean, determined to find a place in which they might enjoy their freedom, or perish in the glorious attempt."

His voice sharpened as he traced the history of their present trouble. "... the property in this country has been acquired by our own labor; it is the duty of the people of Great Britain to produce some compact in which we have explicitly given up to them a right to dispose of our persons or property. Until this is done, every attempt ... to give or grant any part of our property, is directly repugnant to every principle of reason and natural justice."

Taxation without representation violated both law and sense. Ruth acknowledged Warren's argument. She simply couldn't countenance rebellion. Violence.

His remarks turned to the occasion, and he described the Massacre in moving, graphic language.

She remembered. Blood on the snow.

"Our streets are again filled with armed men. Our harbor is crowded with ships of war." His voice strengthened. The atmosphere was tight with tension.

Ruth swallowed. It was very warm. Next to her, Joshua dropped the notebook onto the floor.

"Our liberty must be preserved; it is far dearer than life …"

The charcoal pencil rolled away, lost beneath the pews.

"We cannot suffer even *Britons* to ravish it from us."

The ugly officer on the platform scowled in rage.

"Our country is in danger, but not to be despaired of…. Act worthy of yourselves. The faltering tongue of hoary age calls on you to support your country."

Joshua stood. Was he about to bolt? Ruth didn't know how he'd escape through the press of people.

Dr. Warren concluded his speech with a flourish of uplifted arms. The throng joined Joshua in standing, clapping, and cheering.

Joshua waved his ragged handkerchief in the air, his face glowing with enthusiasm.

Ruth felt alone, like an island in the midst of the sea.

14

Sovereign Ruler of the skies!
Ever gracious, ever wise!
All my times are in Thy hand,
All events at Thy command.
—*John Ryland, 1777*

April 1775

*R*obert made his way toward the Common. Well before he arrived, he heard the screams, a soldier being punished for some offense.

His body still felt strange, like a borrowed garment. After the illness had passed, and he'd passed from fevered dreams to full consciousness, the full weight of his duty had fallen on him. He wanted to believe that Gage's scouts and spies knew of all the caches of munitions tucked away in barns and meetinghouses. But the people of the countryside hated the regulars and could spot soldiers masquerading as civilians from a mile away. They even helped deserters to escape. Gage's intelligence was undoubtedly spotty, and Robert's contribution could be crucial.

His legs supported him as he strode over the cobblestones, but he was tiring. He'd paced the little room for a week as his pustules dried up: first slowly, step by step, then more quickly, hoping to build his strength.

He was closer, could hear the screams more clearly. And the lash.

Early on in his recovery he'd asked Mrs. Jenkins about his ramblings. His greatest fear was that he'd spilled who he truly was in the heat of a fevered dream. All he could recall was Dr. Warren's face and a bitter brew he'd been forced to choke down.

"Have you a sweetheart?" The little woman asked in response.

His face must have revealed something, for she chuckled, a surprisingly deep sound.

"A beautiful redhead, I take it? I wish you well." She handed him a mirror. "Your looks ain't totally spoiled."

Several pustules marred the lower half of his face. Frown lines sprouted in his reflection.

"Never you mind, they'll fade."

Was he truly vain enough to care? At any rate, he hadn't given himself away.

And he was alive.

Thank you, God.

Smelling the odor of the camp—smoke from cook fires, manure, and a sharper stench from the numerous latrines—Robert turned the last corner and entered the Common. Bound by his wrists, a soldier slouched against a pole. His screams had modulated to grunts and whimpers.

Looking fine in brushed coat and polished boots, Lord Rawdon stood near the poor sod under the lash. A sergeant gave the count while a dark-skinned drummer handled the cat.

"Ninety-four ... ninety-five."

The man's back was covered in crisscrossing welts. A number of them dripped blood.

Rawdon caught sight of Robert. "What happened to you?"

"Smallpox."

His cousin stepped back, brass gorget glittering in the sun.

"No, I'm not infectious. Couldn't leave quarantine until every scab fell off." The message for Gage burned in his pocket.

Rawdon glanced over his shoulder and, satisfied, turned back. "This man traded a musket for hooch."

Robert straightened. "Idiot. That's well-nigh treason to give these rebels arms."

"I gave him two hundred lashes. Can't lose them all. Just shot a deserter the other day."

Men survived two hundred easily. "'*Pour encourager les autres?*'" Voltaire's classic sarcasm certainly applied.

"I do mean to encourage them." He chuckled. "But the best discipline is to get them fighting." He lowered his voice. "Dartmouth needs to be replaced as secretary. We should have hung the ringleaders already."

It wasn't surprising the son of an earl had political opinions. "Most have left town," he murmured.

"I suppose you would know." Rawdon glanced back. "No slacking, Dobson! Make them count!" He turned. "Why are you here?"

Robert thrust the piece of paper, folded small, into his cousin's palm as he shook the other man's hand. "For Gage."

Lexington and Concord's secrets were now in Lord Rawdon's hands.

Black eyebrows lifted. "I see."

Robert spun on his heel and strode away.

He'd done his duty. But the whole transaction left him feeling dirty.

RUTH'S EYES blurred as she tried to focus on the galley in front of her. She needed an *f*. Her hand found the correct letter in the lower case. Then more of the small Caslon type followed the first to complete the word.

F-o-r-t-y. She glanced at her hastily written copy, but it was unnecessary. The sentence was vivid in her mind. The next word started with *d*.

Her fingers shook, but she forced herself to continue. Papa needed her to help print the paper, especially with such horrible news. Unspeakable news.

D-e-a-. One more *d*.

Her elbow hit the lower case, and type fountained onto the floor. Small lead letters lay scattered everywhere.

She knelt to gather them, and a single sob escaped her.

"Ruth, sweetheart, let me do that." Her father's spectacles were slightly askew, his eyes bleary.

"I'll get the type." She threw jerky handfuls into the box.

Papa squinted at the galley. "Only forty?"

"At least forty."

He took the last of the type from her hands and replaced it. "Let's say so then." He wielded the composing stick with the ease of long practice. "How many regulars dead?"

Ruth passed him the scrawled composition, then wrapped her arms around her waist. "They aren't saying. Some claim several hundred along the Lexington Road."

Her father turned and embraced her. "I will finish this. Go upstairs." He drew back and squinted at the hurried article in his hands, his face blanking into a familiar stare, his composing look. "Wait. Who fired first?"

"No one knows." She fled upstairs and threw herself onto her bed to weep.

A few minutes later, she quieted and wiped her eyes. She turned on her back, fingered her locket, and stared at the ceiling. No one knew who had fired the first shot on Lexington Green. She tried to visualize the scene. The militiamen—a ragged group of men of various ages, led by Captain Parker— did not resist at first, being greatly outnumbered.

But the British demanded they relinquish their arms. What a stupid request. Now, Captain Parker, hero of the French war, lay grievously wounded after a brief skirmish.

Other details were still arriving, but some things were clear. At Concord the soldiers boldly searched for munitions. One structure caught fire, and the countryside rose in response. Fearing for their own homes and families, militia of various townships swarmed against the redcoats.

Outnumbered now, the regulars headed back to Boston, with angry men taking shots at them from behind trees.

Over forty farmers had died. Her aunt was helping the wounded, and she had no notion of British losses.

Anger rose in her heart, not against Sam Adams, but against the King. Rebellion was wrong, but why ... ?

O Lord ...

What had Hannah written? That God was sovereign over all?

Behold, the nations are as a drop in a bucket ... To whom then will ye liken God?

She slid over the side of the bed and onto her knees. Boston was under siege. Her country was torn and bleeding. Their King was cruel.

"Lord, do You care?"

Are not two sparrows sold for a farthing? and one of them shall not fall on the ground without your Father.

Sparrows. She wiped her face. Yes, she felt like a sparrow. Strangely comforted, she rose and sat on the bed.

"Ruth?" Her aunt's voice echoed from downstairs.

With a brief glance at the mirror, Ruth left the room. Her aunt probably needed help with the wounded.

Aunt Betsy stood in the print shop. "Gideon told me he could spare you." Her hair was out of order, wisps poking out from underneath her cap, and there were streaks of blood and dirt on her apron. Her sleeves were grimy.

"Of course."

Together they searched the dispensary for supplies. Ruth grabbed the last of the willow bark. "What about nettle?"

Her aunt frowned. "Yes, take it. Take it all."

They loaded the cart with the last of the dispensary's supplies and a bolt of linen for bandages.

"Joshua is still at Cambridge. He's dedicated to helping Dr. Warren."

The cartwheels clicked over the cobblestones. "How many wounded?"

Aunt Betsy sighed and suddenly Ruth realized her aunt had lost weight. Her skin seemed to sag.

"I know not. Some militiamen fell in Concord, some at Lexington, only about half made it closer to Boston. There are about a dozen injured men at Cambridge."

Before them on the street Ruth spotted a familiar figure.

"Mr. Shirley!"

He looked up, his face pale.

ROBERT FELT ambivalent about seeing Miss Haynes and her aunt. Guilt darkened his heart as he greeted them. The bloodshed was his fault.

"You still do not look well," the older woman said. "We worried about you, once we heard you were ill."

"I am quite recovered, thank you." He answered their unspoken question. "I finished packing up Mr. Knox's inventory and wanted to help."

"Come with us," Mrs. Ward gestured to the cart.

Robert clambered into the back and found a place to sit. "I appreciate it."

"Henry is leaving?" Miss Haynes asked.

What to say? "He is known as a prominent rebel."

Miss Haynes turned, brows raised. Red rimmed her eyes. She'd been weeping.

"Is he in danger?"

"He and Mrs. Knox made it out of the city safely. I offered to stay behind, secure the inventory, and do what I could to prevent damage to the premises."

"I'm glad they're safe."

He found a comfortable position and closed his eyes, listening to the creaks and clatter of the cart's motion over the streets.

His thoughts wandered to the day before.

Yesterday all Boston had been electrified with the news of the skirmishes at Lexington and Concord. Rumors flew, none of them good. He'd waited until nightfall, then made his way through side streets and alleyways to the Common.

Rawdon's batman had ushered him into his cousin's tent, crowded with crates, a chest, and a cot. The light of a single candle threw sinister shadows on Rawdon's face as he sat on the cot, uncorking a wine bottle. A thick-stemmed cordial glass gleamed gray in the light.

"Care for some Madeira?" He indicated a camp stool. "Uncle Francis sends me a crate of supplies now and then. Even the cod-eating provincials eat better than we do."

Francis—The current Earl of Huntingdon, his godmother's son. "I would, thank you."

Rawdon used his left hand to pour the drinks, something Robert had not noticed before. Left-handed or not, all he knew was that his cousin had a reputation as a good shot.

Robert sipped at the Madeira. "What happened?" The intelligence he'd given his cousin had resulted in slaughter. Colonists at Lexington mown down, then the retreating troops under Pitcairn had been shot at from behind trees, houses, and walls, all the way back to the tiny hamlet of Menotamy, where scattered resistance had coalesced into full-out fighting. Injured regulars lay dying along the route; only the officers had been rescued in the desperate retreat.

Rawdon gave a scornful smile and gestured with his drink. "They fought back."

"Did they truly capture our wagons of ammunition?" An irony. Major Pitcairn's forces had managed to find very little of the rebels' supplies in Concord, but it was there—Robert had seen it. Did they move the powder to the woods? Bury the shot in the ground? They were farmers, practical. Nothing would surprise him.

Rawdon waved a dismissive hand. "There were mistakes. No matter. Your map was invaluable, I hear."

Robert took a sip. "The casualties—" So many soldiers had died.

Black brows jerked. "The rebels fought like savages." Rawdon seemed pleased at the thought. "Did you expect otherwise? They are insurgents, rabble." He smirked. "And that's how we shall treat them."

Robert sat up straighter. "I am not sure what you mean."

"This is not France, not a war between sovereign nations. We will crush the rebels and all their supporters. Like Scotland. Too bad we don't have Cumberland—only Old Woman Gage. Did you know his wife is American?" He refilled his glass. "Ban Tarleton's coming."

Robert's stomach soured. "I didn't know." Tarleton had protected Rawdon from bullying at Harrow; together they'd bossed a whole cadre of students. Robert tossed back half of his drink and choked.

"Look. Dartmouth can get you a position. Aide-de-camp. Mark me, Gage will be replaced, and so will Dartmouth. But he'll still be able to pull strings. Get you a situation … appropriate for you."

There was a touch of mockery in his voice, but Robert decided to ignore it. It was only the truth. His commission would be activated, it was only a matter of time. But he had no stomach for total war.

He merely sighed and finished the drink, the alcohol burning his throat.

Returning to the dark shop, he'd encountered Mr. Knox and his wife, two shadows leaving the building. He'd helped them down to the water and pushed off their boat, feeling very strange, as if there were two Robert Shirleys, one a British officer, the other …

He opened his eyes as the Wards' cart shuddered over a gap in the cobblestones, jerking him from his musings. He sat up as they neared the guardhouse and slowed to a halt. Every wagon was being searched. He closed his eyes again, wishing that the specter of war would all fade away.

But it didn't work.

15

Men of New Jersey, the Redcoats are murdering our brethren of New England! Who follows me to Boston?
—Joab Houghton, 1775

The Shenandoah Valley, May 1775

*J*onathan took a seat on the bench, and Nathan slid next to him. Across the room, William leaned against the wall. A thick ray of afternoon sunshine illumined the *Virginia Gazette* on the walnut table.

They'd arrived home last year in plenty of time for the harvest. The winter had come and gone, and events were cascading like spilled ninepins back in Boston. Jonathan longed to go back.

"Ho, I'm here," bellowed Uncle Roy from the doorway. He removed his hat, revealing his thick hair, copper fading to silvery gold at the temples.

Mother took a seat with her knitting in the bow-backed Windsor chair. Restless, Hannah finally settled onto a stool next to Da. Ian MacLeod crossed to the hearth.

Once the men of Russell's Ridge were all assembled, their father took up the paper. Most of those present had read it, but they wanted to discuss it.

"Dated April nineteenth. 'I have taken up my pen to inform you …'"

Listening, Jonathan closed his eyes and tried to imagine what it must have been like. Alarmed by a rider, the men of Lexington had assembled. Eight were shot dead there. The courthouse at Concord had been set on fire. But the rest of the tale sounded encouraging. Men from miles around had taken up arms and harassed the fleeing regulars for twenty miles.

"'It has been a most distressing day with us, and I pray God we may never have reason to be called to such another.'"

"But we won, didn't we?" William blurted, when Da finished reading.

Ian MacLeod growled. "That victory's like an arrow in a painter cat's paw. She'll turn and tear ye."

Silence fell.

"Why were the redcoats marching to Concord?" Uncle Roy asked.

"Same as Governor Dunmore. Tried to take their powder and shot," Da said.

"We didna let Dunmore do that here." Uncle Roy leaned on the table. "Dunmore's run like a dog with its tail between its legs."

Grunts of approbation filled the room, but Da looked thoughtful.

"MacLeod's right. This is our home, and we have the right to defend it. Even so, we face the greatest army and navy in the world."

Nathan took a deep breath. "Are we at war, then?"

"They willna call it that, aye?" MacLeod's gaze was far away. "We are rebels, traitors in their minds."

"Mr. Henry has gone to Philadelphia with the other delegates. Let us pray for wisdom," Da said. "There is still hope."

Jonathan wasn't convinced of that. "Da, the Haynes and Aunt Betsy—"

"I ken it," Da said. "We'll need to go. Help them get to safety."

Murmurs rose in the room, and Hannah's face tightened. She would want to accompany them, and it wasn't possible.

"There are men mustered at Winchester," Nathan said. "Gathered when Dunmore seized the powder. I heard at the tavern that Daniel Morgan may take them to Boston."

Da crossed his arms. "We canna wait for Morgan."

They spent the next hour discussing practical matters. Uncle Roy and Ian MacLeod left at dusk, and his father left to care for the animals.

Out of habit, Jonathan picked up a piece of elk antler destined for the heft of a belt knife and continued shaping it for some nameless man's hand. It would be a fighting knife this time, a knife for battle.

Hannah rummaged noisily among the kitchen utensils. She measured cornmeal with a tin cup and dumped it into a bowl with unnecessary force. She added other ingredients and stirred vigorously, frowning, while Mother tended a pot on the hearth.

"I suppose I'll never get to go," William groused.

Hannah hesitated in the middle of pouring batter into an iron skillet, and thick, gooey drops scattered. "I have it figured out. If Jonathan and Nathan take the wagon, we can go together, Willie. I'll need an escort home, in case—"

"In case we end up fighting?" Jonathan asked. "Or dead?"

"Say not so!"

"If Da says yea, then you'll obey me."

Hannah snorted. "If I must."

After the evening meal, Da still looked thoughtful. It was no good pushing him for a final decision. Jonathan returned to his work on the piece of antler, wondering if they should bring winter clothes.

A knock sounded on the door.

Jonathan jumped to his feet, and the antler clattered on the floor. No one came to the door without calling out first, especially after dark. His father reached the door and took down the rifle. Was it an emergency? A need for a midwife?

"Who is it?" his father asked.

Jonathan couldn't make out the voice on the other side of the closed door. But his father must have. He opened it, and a man swept in.

He looked vaguely familiar.

Mother stood. "Red Hawk? David?"

"Is everyone well?" his father croaked.

"Yes, all are well. We have moved farther west to the land called Kentucke."

David Sloan/Red Hawk, the Shawnee with blue eyes. A chill crept up Jonathan's spine. Such a strange man.

Silas Sloan's young son had been captured. While searching for him, Sloan had killed several Shawnee and in turn had been killed himself. Years later, Jonathan's sister Susanna had been captured by Sloan's son, who'd been raised as an Indian with the name Red Hawk.

James Paxton had gone to preach the gospel to the Indians and ended up marrying Susanna, who helped in the translation process. They were still out there somewhere, Jamie preaching to a group of praying Indians. Letters came occasionally, carried by Indian traders, but their neighbors conveniently forgot Susanna and Jamie, like family members who'd caused shame.

Why was Red Hawk here?

"Your family?" Mother asked.

"All are well. I have a letter from Susanna." He extracted a folded paper from a small satchel and handed it to her.

Jonathan scrutinized the man's outfit—he was dressed as a white man, like one of them, except—

His hair.

He caught sight of a bulge under Red Hawk's collar. It wasn't just a tail. The man had disguised his long dark queue by stuffing it down his shirt.

"Sit." His father gestured to his own seat. The very room seemed to exhale. "What news?"

Red Hawk pulled out the long tail from his shirt and seemed to relax. "I went north to visit my red brethren there. The Mohawk sachem you know as Joseph Brant sides with the King. I believe the Mohawk will help the red coats."

Not good news, but not unexpected.

"I also spoke to the sachem of the Oneida. They listen to Kirkland, who teaches the words of truth. Many have believed on the Christ. They also think that Kirkland is right about the wrongs done by the King. Of all the Six Nations, they are the only ones to side with us."

With *us?* "So, you agree with Kirkland?"

Red Hawk's blue gaze met Jonathan's. "Paxton refuses to tell us what to think, but he is not shy about his own conclusions, and I agree with him. All the same, I understand why many of my red brethren would choose another path. The King's words of 1763 mean that white men must keep to their side of the boundary."

"Unfortunately," Da said, "the King isn't here to enforce that edict, and men ignore that boundary. Supporting the King won't change that."

"But supporting the Patriots might make things worse. The Oneida take a risk."

Da's shoulders sagged. "What will ye do, Mr. Sloan?"

"You are the kinsmen of my heart. All I have I owe to you. Your daughter, Susanna, I stole from you. But through her and Paxton we heard the words of life." He looked to Mother. "I have a request. Would you cut my hair?"

Da blinked rapidly, and when he spoke his words wavered. "Ye do honor me. God is to be thanked. Abigail, your huswif?"

Jonathan swallowed. Didn't an Indian's hair mean something special? Have some sort of power?

What was Red Hawk planning to do?

Red Hawk sat on a stool in the center of the room. "Now that my trust is in my Creator, my Heavenly Father, I know my soul is bound up safe in Him. I can be all things to all men, as Paul said. I can help you."

It all became clear. Red Hawk was going with them, and he didn't want to look like an Indian, for practical reasons.

Jonathan felt awed. He didn't fully understand the sacrifice of the hair, what it meant to an Indian. But he knew the strength he'd gain from such a man at his side.

Mother snipped through his queue, and when it fell, they all heard the tiny swish of its impact on the floor.

THE ROAD to Boston was crowded with all sorts coming and going, even twenty miles away. Jonathan brought up his horse alongside Hannah's as a column of local militia crowded the road, going the opposite way. Hannah had convinced their father to come, but her presence put Jonathan on edge. Blood had been spilled.

William had to stay behind, and it was just as well. Someone had to help at home. Red Hawk rode on the other side of the Conestoga, eyes and ears alert. Everything considered, Jonathan mused, they'd made good time. Twenty-five days on the road, and that included stops on the Sabbath.

"You stink," Hannah said.

"Ye think I should stop at an ordinary and spend the night? Bathe in hot water and anoint myself with scent?" He pretended to consider it. "Nah. I dinna have a shirt with ruffles on the cuffs."

Besides, he didn't know if he could get into Boston if the Haynes were still there.

"I'm worried about Ruth." Hannah's words echoed his own concerns.

The afternoon shadows were still short when they pulled into Roxbury. The place was filled with armed men, animals, and wagons. Tents, brush arbors, and other structures lined the west side of town. An acrid stench perfumed the air.

On the east side a long dirt embankment snaked across the ground. Men swarmed over it, carrying rocks, wood, and shovels. Jonathan couldn't believe it. Or maybe he could. According to the letters they'd received from Boston, Mr. Henry Knox knew everything there was to know about both artillery and military engineering. The sight of the breastworks cheered him.

"Mr. Knox!" The large man was easy to spot.

Knox turned and squinted, his forehead gleaming with sweat. Amazingly, the events of the last few years had not stopped Henry Knox from gaining weight. A second chin now rested on his stock.

"Mr. Russell! Well met! May we expect militia from Virginia?"

"Probably, but I'm here for my cousins."

Knox wiped his face with a lace-edged handkerchief. "There's Molly." He waved the scrap of fabric.

A familiar woman with skin the color of a hickory nut grabbed at her skirts and picked her way over the ground. "Mr. Knox, sir?" Furrows of worry lined her face.

"Have Miss Haynes and her father got out yet?" Knox asked.

"No, sir. I just left this morning with Mrs. Ward and Joshua," the servant said. "The Haynes can't move the press. Can you help?"

Knox looked Jonathan up and down, then scanned the Conestoga. "Wagon's too big for Boston streets. And ye'll look like the devil himself to the British."

Jonathan became conscious of the weight of his long rifle, strapped to his back. He wore a belt knife and a tomahawk, and those were just the obvious weapons.

"One of the regulars was bashed in the head with an axe at Concord. Brains everywhere. Can't see you strolling into Boston like that." Knox stroked his chin. "Wait—wait here."

Knox wasn't gone long. He returned with a stack of clothing and a small bottle and gestured to a tiny hut.

Jonathan followed him, and changed into Knox's clothes, but he felt foolish when he stepped out of the structure to see Hannah staring at him. "Dinna laugh."

Her mouth worked. "You—you—"

"I really stink now." Jonathan had dressed in Henry Knox's finest outfit —all except the waistcoat, which hung on him—and then dabbed scent on his neck. "Did I use too much?"

The perfume enveloped him like a cloud. He didn't mind the fresh, woodsy scent of Hannah's birch soap. Now he smelled like a rutting stag knee-deep in lavender. His stomach roiled.

"Perhaps—"

"Nay," Knox broke in, having joined them. "'The regulars will be sure to smell you—and they'll think you're a gentleman. Only an officer might notice that the waistcoat doesn't quite match the coat."

"Or the shoes," Hannah said.

His shoes were sturdy but clashed with the silk coat.

"Here." Knox handed him a pair of gaiters. "These'll help."

Jonathan squatted and buttoned them on. "Now I need a wagon."

A wagon could not be found, but a roomy carriage was, and soon he was on the road to Boston.

The sight of artillery pieces on the Neck chilled Jonathan as he approached the guardhouse, but the red-coated soldiers waved him through. Knox had said something about permissions and papers, but apparently those were to get out of Boston, not to get in. How they would leave, he didn't know. As a sweet-smelling gentleman, perhaps some story would stick.

To his left, the sounds and smells of occupation drifted from the Common. He spotted one busy tavern with plenty of redcoats inside. But the town was eerily quiet. As he approached the print shop, a newspaper slid across the cobbles, startling one of the horses.

A frisson of dread snaked down his neck.

"PAPA, WE NEED TO LEAVE." Ruth wanted to say they could get another press, but one look at his pale face stopped her.

Mr. Shirley shook his head. "All we need is a wagon."

But the wagons were gone. The few residents who remained had sent their belongings to safety, and the British had commandeered the rest. Her aunt had managed to transport the bulk of their belongings to Roxbury via the little cart. Only the press remained, too big for the cart, and too heavy for Papa to lift, even with the bookbinder's help.

A knock sounded at the door. Ruth tensed. Soldiers? They'd come once before, confiscating weapons, and Papa had given them a rusty fowling piece.

Silently, Mr. Shirley raised a hand and went to the front room. The door creaked.

In less than a minute the bookbinder returned. "Mr. Russell is here. He'll be pulling in around back."

A grin spread across her father's tired face.

Ruth bounded out the back door and was met by a cloud of scent. "Jonathan?"

Perched high on the box of a bright yellow open carriage, he wore gleaming green silk, white linen spilling at his throat. "At your service." He gave a comical flourish with his hat.

She wanted to burst out laughing, but in her state she'd lose control and cry. "Lavender. Lavender and cedarwood." The smell seemed to fill the yard.

"I stink, but it's my costume."

Papa came into the yard and looked over the carriage, humming. "I think it will do. If we can hoist it in."

RUTH LOOKED TROUBLED, thinner. Jonathan wished he could cheer her. At least his get-up made her smile.

"Going to Philadelphia?" he asked her father. "New York is closer."

"I've a colleague in Philadelphia." Mr. Haynes brightened. "Plenty of news being made there."

He must be speaking of the Continental Congress. Ruth's face remained neutral. It couldn't be easy leaving her home.

Jonathan shrugged out of his coat and helped Mr. Shirley maneuver the heavy press out of the shop and into the carriage. The printing press was a magnificent contraption; the wood was aging, but the iron mechanism was well oiled and pristine.

The bookbinder brought out a parcel. "Your pistols," he murmured to Ruth. "I replaced the boards where they were hidden."

Jonathan's opinion of the bookbinder rose.

Ruth eyed Jonathan as she tucked several boxes in nooks and crannies around the press. "Guard these with your life."

The type, apparently. "Anything else?"

A single, plaintive bleat came from one of the outbuildings. "The goat! I almost forgot!"

They tied the animal on behind, and Ruth and her father squeezed into the crowded carriage, perching next to the press. The bookbinder sat next to him on the coachman's box.

Jonathan directed the horses toward the Neck. They just needed to get past the guard. How could they explain themselves? What if the guard objected? He felt naked, his only weapon a tiny knife in his boot.

A clump of soldiers, red as blood, thronged the gatehouse ahead.

The last few yards took forever, but it was not long enough. He still had no story.

"Wot's that?" A man wearing a sash over his uniform squinted at the press.

Jonathan's mind went blank. He forced his hands to stay relaxed. "It's … It's—"

"'Tis his grandmother's quilt rack," Mr. Shirley intoned, in precise language. He sounded like a blue-blooded gentleman. "Quite inconvenient, but we mustn't offend the woman. She's quite wealthy, you see."

"Of course, sir. Your papers?"

Jonathan let his companion continue the charade, feeling like a useless lump.

Mr. Shirley made a show of reaching for them inside his coat. He muttered a curse. "Silly me. I've left them behind. 'Tis late already." An expression crossed his face, as if he'd had an idea. "Say, my good man, I will not ever mention it if you'd be so kind …"

Gold flashed in his fingers, and just as quickly the soldier palmed the money.

"All in order here," the guard bellowed.

Jonathan signaled the horses, relief flooding his mind. Who was this bookbinder, really?

16

I wish this cursed place were burned.
—General Thomas Gage

By the time the Haynes's press was safely in the belly of the Conestoga, the gray mantle of dusk had fallen over the camp. Jonathan's belly rumbled.

Mrs. Ward bustled up to the wagon. "Mr. Russell!"

Jonathan turned. "Aye?"

"I can't find my Joshua. Have you seen him?"

Ruth came from behind the wagon and drew near to her aunt. "He might be with Dr. Warren." Her voice sounded tight, thin.

Jonathan scanned the area. "Where's Mr. Shirley?" He might know.

"He's gone," Hannah said. "Back to Boston, I think. Maybe Joshua is with him."

Jonathan followed her gaze to the dark city, where distant cook fires and lanterns glowed like fireflies. He had no time for missing persons. He needed to join a company. The British were rumored to attack any day, and every man would be needed. "Ruth, Hannah, Nathan. We need to find a better place. Away from the breastworks."

Ruth cleared her throat. "Governor Shirley's house—the grounds are extensive."

Once they'd made camp and the horses tended, Jonathan found his way to Knox.

"Prescott is digging fortifications near Charlestown tonight," the bookseller said. He looked tired in the firelight, but there was a keen edge to his voice. "Colonel Stark of the New Hampshire First is near Charlestown Neck —I daresay you'll like him. No-nonsense sort."

Weary, Jonathan agreed and made his way to the others, where a savory smell emerged from a pot. Nathan handed him a bowl, and Jonathan tore into the warm food.

"I'm going to join one of the companies for the time being," he said between bites. "Looks like there will be fighting."

There was no question about going. They were being invaded, and he did not need Rutherford or any fancy arguments to convince him of the rightness of it.

"What about ye, Nathan?" he asked when his bowl was clean.

"Not yet. I'll guard the women. But I'll pray for ye."

Jonathan's heart swelled with gratitude. He didn't deserve such a brother.

AT FIRST, Robert didn't know what woke him. It was still dark inside the windowless room at the back of the print shop.

Boom! The sound was distant but definitely a cannon. So it had started.

He felt his way out of the door into the front room. Through the windows a gray haze announced the new day.

He wished he could carry around a notebook, as Miss Haynes did, but as usual, he'd need to use his memory. He was feeling more and more useless in his communication to Lord Dartmouth; the man wouldn't see his message for six weeks.

And if Robert was correct, they were now at war, and the Crown needed spies, not "observers."

He went back to his room, dressed, and rummaged in his chest for his spyglass. He'd used it only once before, not wanting to be conspicuous. But there were mostly Loyalists in Boston now.

He'd do his duty, even if he thought it useless.

PALE PINK STREAKED the sky in the east as Jonathan sought the source of the ominous sound. A ship in the harbor was firing at militiamen digging entrenchments on a hill above the harbor, far off above Charlestown. From here, Jonathan couldn't see if the shot was hindering the effort.

Nathan was already hitching the horses to the wagon. "We'll follow you at least to Cambridge Common. There may be injuries—I'll help the women."

True. They'd packed herbs and bandages in the wagon, and Mrs. Ward still had a few items from her shop. He could trust Nathan and Red Hawk to keep the women safe.

Jonathan shoved biscuit and jerky in his satchel and mounted Brutus. Hannah laid a hand on the horse's neck and looked up at him, a line between her brows.

He took the reins. "Look out for Ruth."

His sister nodded. "I will. Dinna get killed, ye clot-heid."

He winked and pressed his heels to the animal's ribs.

As the stallion's hooves swallowed the miles to Charlestown Neck, Jonathan soaked in the sight of gathering men, camped everywhere. His pulse quickened at the sight.

The whole countryside had risen. They'd chase out the invaders.

Jonathan arrived and dismounted, but all was confusion. Men were everywhere, walking to and fro, and no one seemed to be in charge. Finally, he found Colonel Stark.

"Can ye use a rifleman?" Jonathan asked.

The strong-featured man looked him over. "How much powder and shot have ye?"

The familiar cadence of his speech marked him as a Scot born in Ireland. Knox was right; Jonathan felt easy in this man's presence.

"I've at least two dozen shot, and I know how to make each one count." Jonathan could take down a deer at over two hundred yards.

"Ye're better armed than some, then. Aye, I can use ye."

ROBERT FOUND a place to observe on the roof of Christ's Church. He wasn't the only one to have this idea; half the remaining population of Boston—rebels and Loyalists both—perched on rooftops or even ship's rigging, mesmerized by the spectacle of the cannon fire. He was reminded of a carriage accident in London. Everyone crowded forward to see the spectacle of death and injury. Bets were laid as to the fate of an injured horse, which was put down within the hour.

He drew out his spyglass and studied the fortifications on the hill across the water, just above the hamlet of Charlestown. The rebels were barely within reach of the cannon, and during the early morning hours the men seemed to have redoubled their efforts to entrench themselves, rendering the warship's efforts fruitless. But there were holes in their line—places infantrymen could easily flank them.

What were the generals planning? Howe, Burgoyne, and Clinton had joined Gage, and somewhere they were arguing over a course of action. Commanding by committee. Not the most effective way to do things, but Robert guessed they'd come to the most obvious conclusion and land men on the narrow beach at the end of the peninsula. Or perhaps on the far side, along the Mystic River.

Fighting uphill had its drawbacks, but all they needed to do was distract the main force. They'd flank them, and—

Robert slumped and lowered his glass. He didn't want to watch the slaughter of these misguided people.

A clatter sounded on the street below. Marching. Robert twisted, trying to see the soldiers' destination. He crossed the tiles, stepping around men, lads, and even one woman.

"Careful there!"

"My apologies."

Robert spotted a line of red-coated men disappearing in the direction of the Long Wharf. Time to get off this roof and see what the generals had decided.

ONCE ROBERT SAW THE WATER, he knew why it had taken so long to begin the attack. The tide, of course. Everything in Boston Harbor was dictated by the tide. The hidden shallows made it a dangerous place for deep-draft frigates; the shoals had claimed one ship already. But the water lapped high against the pilings now.

The Long Wharf was hot, noisy, and packed with men. Officers barked orders and regulars jostled for space aboard shallow red barges. There were dozens of boats; a few were already launched into the harbor, oars flashing, bayonets glittering above the red mass of men. They were being shipped out to the peninsula.

"Shirley!" Lord Rawdon's face was dotted with sweat. "Come with me. My man is sick. Can you reload pistols? Of course you can."

Horrified, Robert followed the man to the side of the wharf where Rawdon's batman kneeled at the edge, vomiting.

"Here." Rawdon thrust ammunition at Robert, followed by a satchel and pistols. "We need water, brandy, some foodstuffs. Enough for both of us."

While filling a canteen with water, Robert mused at the irony of being pressed into service. Despite the irregularity, there was no way to protest or resist; technically, with his commission inactive, he was available to be recruited at any time.

And by his cousin, no less! It chafed him.

IT WAS unclear to Jonathan who exactly was in charge. General Putnam had led a group out to the crest of a hill belonging to a local farmer named Bunker. Jonathan joined Colonel Stark's New Hampshire regiment in marching over the Neck to an empty pasture, the early summer grass up to his knees or higher.

He couldn't see them, but somewhere beyond Putnam's position, Prescott's men were building fortifications above Charlestown. Putnam, Ward, Stark, Prescott—Jonathan could barely keep the names straight, never mind figure out who was in charge. Colonel Stark himself hadn't bothered with the niceties.

"Putnam can do what he likes, but we've got to stop the redcoats from flanking Prescott," Stark had said, his voice clipped.

And with that, they'd headed out.

A boom was followed by the whistling roar of a passing cannon ball—too close—a lucky shot from the ship in the Charles River, hunting them from below like a coon dog.

"Steady, men!" Stark's raspy voice eased the impulse to bolt.

They crossed to the Mystic River side of the hill and were now out of range of the guns. Below, the beach glistened wet, lapped by the marshy water of the river. Ahead, a rail fence snaked along the slope. Instantly, Jonathan understood. The British could march down the beach and circle behind Prescott's men at the top of the hill. It was a wide-open back door.

"Bailey, take your men and reinforce that fence," the militia colonel shouted.

Half their number split off.

The distant sound of musket fire popped, at first in ragged bursts, then steadily. Jonathan's belly tightened. He could not see the fighting, but he could guess its location. At the fortifications above Charlestown, the battle had joined.

Stark led the rest of them to the beach and sent them to gather stones. Jonathan didn't have to look far. The ground of New England seemed to produce dark fieldstone like weeds, and the reedy banks of the Mystic were no exception. Within an hour the militiamen had constructed a crude wall using mud from the beach as mortar.

Colonel Stark walked in front of the stony barricade approvingly. "Line up in three rows. Only one row fires at a time." His square jaw and steely gaze inspired obedience.

It made perfect sense. It took time to reload; one group would be able to fire while the others reloaded.

But the colonel's next order was strange: pound stakes into the ground a certain distance away down the beach. When this was done, the shadows were beginning to lengthen, and Jonathan could smell smoke.

"They're burning Charlestown!" someone shouted.

ROBERT FOUND a place in the barge near Lord Rawdon. Only the oarsmen had seats, so the rest of them simply knelt, crouched, or sat in the bottom of the flat-bottomed boat. The red-coated, sweaty members of the Fifth Foot were packed like cod in a barrel. A few Robert recognized, but he doubted if they'd know him, dressed as he was. They pushed off from the wharf.

Most of Howe's men had already departed, and many had already disembarked on the beach at the end of the peninsula. Robert was weighed down with Rawdon's supplies, but he managed to extract his spyglass from his satchel. He found the redoubt on the hill, then sought the slope—had the attack begun?

He couldn't tell. The boat was rocking with the gentle swell of Boston Harbor, and it spoiled his view.

A gun spoke, followed by a full cannonade from one of the frigates. From their vantage point on the water, the bombardment of Charlestown seemed alarmingly close, with shudders of sound rolling over them.

Crunching and snapping rose from the target—the town of Charlestown. Then a tongue of flame licked up the side of a building. Then another. And another.

"Gor!"

The men in the barge were mesmerized.

Robert swallowed. It was a well-known tactic. The cannonballs had been specially heated in order to ignite the wooden structures, dried to kindling by lack of rain. He knew why the decision had been made—devastated once by snipers on the road from Concord, the generals weren't going to make that mistake again. And the rooftops of Charlestown would make perfect perches for deadly riflemen.

Surely the inhabitants had left by now—surely they had.

The soldiers around him hooted and cheered.

"Burn, rascals, burn!"

The sound of destruction crescendoed, a horrible whoosh and roar. Flame enveloped a church steeple and the structure became an awful fiery torch.

Robert noticed the faces then. Across the harbor, people perched on Boston rooftops or clung to ships' rigging, countenances glowing with the light from the scene—who could turn their eyes away from this?

Dark smoke billowed to the sky as the flames raged. The water of the harbor glowed orange.

"Beautiful, isn't it?" Lord Rawdon said.

BEHIND THE WALL, they waited. Jonathan leaned against the cool stone and listened to the others murmur jokes and tell stories about the officers. But tension showed on their tanned, hardscrabble faces.

Next to him, a young freckle-faced ginger spoke up. "Putnam was roasted alive by the Injuns. Or at least he was supposed to be. It rained and put the fire out."

"Stark was captured in the French War. Six weeks with the savages," came a voice from Jonathan's other side. The others seemed to find this a badge of courage as well.

"What's that?" The red-haired lad's low voice was urgent, and the discussion stopped.

He'd heard something.

"Steady on, men," Stark's voice rose above the rest. "Load. Third row goes first, but not until they reach the stakes."

Jonathan peered over the top of the wall. The stakes were close—so close. He opened and closed his fingers into fists several times before priming his rifle and closing the frizzen. He wished he could fire from farther away, but most of the militiamen owned muskets, not long rifles. He stroked the maple stock under his fingers. He could kill at a much greater distance. But a musket was worthless past one hundred yards.

Now he heard it too—the sound of men gathered on the beach.

His breathing quickened. He wished he could fire from two hundred yards. He didn't want to see their faces.

He wiped his hand on his breeches. These were intruders. The enemy.

"Here they come, lads."

Jonathan peeked again and saw a swath of red down the beach. Soldiers in bright uniforms, red trimmed with blue, and the glitter of deadly steel on their muskets.

Bayonets. The regulars, four abreast, marched quickly down the wet shore. The redcoats were planning to rush them and disembowel them with the dagger-like weapons.

But they were still too far away. Two hundred yards. Next to him, Red wriggled, the barrel of his long rifle resting uneasily on the top of the wall.

Jonathan glanced behind him. The third line crouched in readiness, narrow-eyed men dressed in rough farmer's garb.

Jonathan's heartbeat sounded in his ears. He could hear the soldiers now, their marching feet, the rustle and clank of their equipment.

He looked over the wall. They still weren't aiming their weapons, just holding them lance-like, a massive bristling phalanx rushing them.

They were close. Just a few yards now …

"Fire!"

Behind him the pops of musket fire merged to a roar.

Jonathan re-checked his own weapon. The frizzen was seated.

"Fire!"

The row right behind him fired.

He and Red exchanged a single glance.

Their line stood. Writhing bodies filled the beach. But more regulars stepped over and around them, like ants. Jonathan selected a target and aimed at the blue fabric crossing the man's chest. He tried not to look at his face.

"Fire!"

The man dropped, his body falling on top of another red-coated soldier.

Red yanked his arm. "Get down."

Hands shaking, Jonathan poured a new charge of gunpowder down the barrel. Patch, ball, ram it home. Prime the pan.

Their rank took another turn. Bodies piled up on the beach, red on red.

Another turn. And another. The sharp stench of smoke blanketed the sharp tang of blood.

Jonathan's hands reloaded automatically, knowing their duty.

Once, between the shots, a plaintive moan sounded from beyond the wall.

17

_____

The dead lay as thick as sheep in a fold.
　　—Colonel John Stark

*A*sh danced on the ripples as the water lapped the shore. Robert stepped out of the boat into the gentle waves along the rocky beach. He shouldered his supplies and followed the rest of the Fifth Regiment onto the land below the rebels' fortifications, hid from view behind the curve of the hill. Smoke rose from Charlestown on the left. Soldiers crowded the narrow beach, and it was clear that the Fifth would be the last to go into battle. Robert exhaled in relief. He didn't want to fight.

Rawdon led the company into formation behind the others. Ahead, the June sun flickered off soldier's buckles, tin canteens, and the brass and bayonets of their muskets. Beads of sweat were visible on flushed necks above red wool coats. The men were quiet, but the energy on the beach was palpable.

Once, Robert glimpsed General Howe, resplendent in gleaming buttons and braid, dark eyes firm and steady. His staff officers clustered around him while another man stood to the side, holding a tray with a wine glass.

Wine? Robert wondered whether Howe thought the action would be quick and easy, like a picnic, or if the man were simply so inured to war that bringing the niceties along was a matter of course.

A captain called the Fifth to attention. Without his uniform, Robert felt awkward. He was no longer a member of the regiment, not officially; he stood alone and apart, several feet from Lord Rawdon.

His cousin was clearly in his element. "About time," he murmured. "About time we punished these pretenders."

Surely one charge would be sufficient to dislodge the defenders and take the redoubt up on the hill. Then his old regiment could all paddle back to Boston. They'd be disappointed, perhaps, but Robert had no desire to fight the provincials.

The black pall of smoke over Charlestown shifted and spread, cloaking the sun in orange gauze and obscuring the hill.

Motion ahead caught his attention. Drummers tapped a cadence; one group moved right; another marched directly ahead into the haze. So, the attack had been ordered. The men of the Fifth remained behind, tense like greyhounds at the start of a race.

Lord Rawdon's gaze was fixed on the hill. "Pistols ready?"

"Yes." Robert had checked them twice. He handed one to his cousin, who slid it into his belt on his left side—the sword was positioned normally, on the left, for a right-hand draw. Despite being left-handed, Rawdon would charge into battle like a right-handed man and Robert would need to guard his left.

Artillery thumped above them on the hill. Were Howe's men marching into cannon fire? But the sounds diminished and finally stopped altogether. The way was clear.

They waited an hour, hot under the sun. General William Gage reappeared, disheveled but unharmed, his stockings soaked in blood. Few of his men returned with him.

And the man with the wineglass was nowhere to be seen.

HIS BACK against the stone wall, Jonathan slid his ramrod down the barrel. Muskets roared over his head.

The redcoats were still coming.

It was his turn. He rose and found a target. His mind went elsewhere, to a hunting trip he'd taken with his brother William, when the lad was just thirteen and still awkward with a firearm.

They'd found tracks, and Willie gasped.

"Quiet, now. Listen. Watch for the direction of the wind. Ye want it in your face if ye can."

"Why?" His brother remembered to whisper.

"Ye dinna want them to smell ye."

They spotted the animal, a yearling doe.

"I was afraid of that."

William cut him a questioning glance.

"Ye dinna want to take a young doe like that if ye dinna need to. But line her up in your sight just for practice."

The next day William bagged a handsome buck and bounced with pride all the way home. "Isn't he just grand?"

William had managed a lung shot. Jonathan pulled the trigger half a second later and took down the animal before it could suffer.

"Aim low, lads!" someone said.

No, he couldn't do that. A gut shot or a leg shot would stop them, but not kill ... not right away. Once, he missed. The man stumbled while climbing over bodies, and the ball only creased his shoulder. A flesh wound.

On the narrow beach, mere yards from the stone wall, men lay atop one another in red drifts, some writhing, some still. The uniforms had changed; the facings over their chest—his target—weren't blue anymore. Jonathan aimed, squeezed the trigger, and ducked behind the wall. Next to him, a rivulet of sweat ran down Red's face as his motions mirrored Jonathan's.

The scent of human excrement intruded into the smell of dank stone and marshy water. Jonathan seated another ball and waited his turn. Each time the horror of the killing threatened his mind, he remembered. The redcoats were invaders. He would protect his home, his family, to his last drop of blood.

Finally, the carnage ceased. Their guns fell silent, but up on the hill Jonathan could still hear the *pop-pop-pop* of musket fire. Once, a cannon spoke, an echoing boom from the other side of the hill.

"Who has rifles?" Stark examined all the men at the wall. "You!" He pointed at Red. The colonel's gaze landed on Jonathan. "You! I need sharpshooters to cover our retreat."

"Aye." Jonathan forced his legs into motion and followed Red up the hill and toward the narrowest point of the peninsula, or neck, where the men would have to pass in retreat.

Why should they think of retreat? But then he remembered Stark's first question—he'd wanted to know how much ammunition Jonathan had.

Holding the hill was a matter of enough men and enough ammunition. They might have enough men, but—

He broke into a jog and scanned the Neck for a likely tree.

REMARKABLY, the second wave of soldiers faltered and retreated, bringing wounded men back with them. The Fifth would fight after all.

Robert came to attention with the others as Captain Harris barked orders, feeling out of place. Typically, a batman was a soldier detailed to see to an officer's personal needs. Sometimes wealthy men brought their valets to serve in that capacity. But Robert was an officer.

The straps of the canteens and other supplies dug into his shoulders as he listened to the captain's instructions. They were to march in long, strung out columns.

The haze had grown thick, hindering visibility. Robert followed Rawdon up the long, sloping hill, grass to his knees or higher. To either side dark shapes appeared in the grass, then slid away. The bodies of the slain and wounded were spread across the terrain.

Were they marching to their deaths?

In front of Rawdon, Captain Harris marched briskly ahead. The steady pop of musket fire grew louder.

Robert planted his boot beside a limp white hand, vivid in the grass. He strode on, brushing the horror aside. Murmurs rose from the men as they reacted to the carnage.

Rawdon unsheathed his sword with a sharp metallic ring. He brandished it, calling out encouragement.

Cheers sounded from behind. The blood rushed in Robert's ears, and he laid his hand on Rawdon's second pistol. The pace quickened, and he found himself strangely eager for the battle.

Beyond Captain Harris the redoubt became fully visible, a dark lumpy wall of earth. A hat popped over the top, and the end of a musket flashed metallic in the unearthly light.

Pop!

A soldier in the column to his right collapsed.

Another rebel appeared and took aim, then another. Their fire was deadly, but it had become sporadic; were they running out of powder?

Rawdon turned and shouted to his men, sweat streaking his flushed face. They bellowed and rushed the fortifications.

Captain Harris clambered up the wall first, but his body jerked, then sagged. Hatless, he collapsed into Rawdon's arms. Four or five privates converged on the captain and pulled him off to safety as he cried, half-sensibly, "Let me die!"

The rest of the men roared, and breaking from their columns, swarmed over the earthen wall. Robert scrambled over the top behind his cousin. Inside the smoke-filled redoubt, chaos reigned. Rawdon thrust and parried with the sword, beating back half-visible rebels. He extended his left hand and Robert passed him a loaded pistol.

Robert stumbled over a body. Dimly he sensed rather than saw the confusion of the provincials as they fled the small stronghold before the rush of the infantrymen.

Having seen the bodies on the hill, the Fifth was out for revenge. "Conquer or die!" filled the air as they charged, stabbing and beating the few rebels who remained inside. The enclosure filled with red coats as the members of the Fifth continued to pour over the barricade.

Robert reloaded Rawdon's pistol and followed his cousin out of the redoubt. Once outside the smoke thinned, but Robert's throat was raw with smoke and shouting—yes, he'd been shouting too.

A thick knot of rebels stood a dozen yards away, covering the retreat. Rawdon cut several laggards down with his sword, then closed the distance to the others. The men of his company spilled through the grass, jabbing their bayonets at anything that moved, their throats filled with shouts. In turn, the colonials wielded their muskets as clubs. One even picked up a rock. Robert ducked as the butt of a musket sailed at his head; an infantryman pierced the man through in the next instant. The rebels weren't the King's men, but they certainly weren't cowards.

One man, clearly an officer, thrust and parried with a sword. He met Rawdon's steel with a sharp hiss and a clang, then side-stepped and went for Robert. The tip of the weapon reached his side, and a line of fire bit him, ribs to waist. Jumping back, he calculated that the wound wasn't fatal and ignored it.

Infantrymen dashed into the group of rebels, thrusting and stabbing, but the officer managed to parry the deadly steel bayonets as he backed, step by step, flanked by a number of others.

A glimmer of white caught Robert's eye. A white waistcoat. One of the other men several paces from the officer also used a sword, but he was dressed for a dinner party, a light-colored coat and ruffled jabot completing the ensemble.

Dr. Joseph Warren.

Robert's gut seized up. Mechanically, he reloaded his cousin's pistol.

Looking up, he saw a young lad at Warren's side, a familiar face, holding a musket.

Joshua. *No! Run, Joshua, run!* Why was he there?

The rebel defenders should have broken and run by now. Finally, their commander half turned and loped away, still parrying the attacks of a lone infantryman. But Warren stayed with a final handful of men, including Joshua.

Sweat ran down the physician's face as he faced Rawdon.

Robert passed his cousin a fresh pistol, who grasped the gleaming mahogany firearm and took a step forward.

Breathing heavily, Warren stepped back, his sword tip quivering and dipping. The man was exhausted.

The muzzle of Rawdon's pistol traced a deliberate arc from the sky to the physician's face.

Then the world exploded.

HE WAS IN HELL. Above him, the sky was orange. A hot poker stabbed his side, and a smith pounded on his head. Maybe he was alive after all.

A bird sailed overhead, incongruous in the deathly light.

Robert levered himself up, but pain swamped his head, and he lay down again in the trampled grass.

It was eerily quiet. He could hear a few pops of musket fire, but they were far away. Once, a ship in the Charles fired her guns.

Faintly, men's voices met his ears. And the soft wooden clink of oars in oarlocks from the beach far below.

The troops were leaving. Rawdon had left him for dead.

He had to get up. He pushed himself up, more slowly this time, but the pain made him grit his teeth. Then a sudden wave of nausea took him, and he vomited.

He fumbled for a canteen. He emptied it into his mouth and looked for the other, but it was nowhere to be found. Blood saturated the left side of his shirt. He removed his shirt and folded it into a rough bandage, securing it against the wound with a canteen strap.

The sun was low in the sky when he stood and took stock of his surroundings. A flutter of white attracted his attention.

Dr. Warren—or what was left of him. Robert stared down at the corpse, pierced many times with the bayonet, an unnecessary violence. The man had probably died instantly from the shot to his face. Robert curled his fingers. His own hands had loaded the pistol that had claimed this man's life. Bile threatened, but his stomach was empty. He staggered, turned, and spotted a figure in humble brown lying on the bloody, trampled grass.

Joshua. Could he—did he—live?

Kneeling, Robert laid several fingers on the lad's neck. Blood soaked one shoulder. More ominously, a bayonet had pierced his gut.

Yes, there was a flutter. He was alive. How long he would remain that way was unclear. But Robert had to get this lad back to his mother.

That meant walking up the Neck to the rebel side.

Robert didn't pause to ask if he could bear the weight, but squatted, braced himself against the agony of exertion, and lifted.

JONATHAN SQUINTED at the crest of the hill. From his vantage point in the gnarled oak, he could see all of Bunker's pasture and even a slice of the Charles River, where the white of canvas betrayed the location of a frigate. To his immediate right was—but no, he wouldn't look that way.

Ahead, someone was coming through the grass. He blinked, trying to clear his vision, but his eyes felt like they'd been sanded. The enemy? Bracing his legs around the thick branch where he sat, he lifted his rifle, which seemed strangely heavy, and sighted down the long barrel. He caught a glimpse of red and stiffened.

A redcoat?

He fought with the rifle. It wouldn't aim properly, the end of the barrel trembling and circling the target.

Jonathan lowered it and looked again. The man was perhaps two hundred yards away. But he wasn't alone—he was carrying someone.

Sounds from below interrupted his focus.

"Ho! Rifleman!" A white face looked up at him. "Colonel Stark is calling roll."

"Who are you?"

"Name's Corporal Bailey—what happened here?"

Below, Bailey's brown head bobbed as the man circled to the other tree —or what was left of it.

Jonathan managed to unlock his legs from around the branch and made his way down from the perch. His feet hit the ground and he wobbled, then spaced his limbs farther apart.

"Was there another rifleman here?"

"Aye."

He couldn't bear to look, to think about what had happened. A boom, a shriek, and then a sudden thud and snap had signaled the destruction of both Red's perch and Red.

"I'll send someone … for his remains."

Then Jonathan remembered the intruder in the field, and raised his rifle once again, but it was nearly dashed out of his hands.

"What are you doing? Those are two of ours." Bailey studied him and handed him a canteen.

The water tasted like liquid silver, fresh and sweet, and brought to his mind the stream near Russell's Ridge, cheerful and gurgling as it splashed into the South River.

"This is the best water ever."

"Ye're daft, man."

His vision cleared, and he followed Bailey into the pasture to meet the man, who had slowly closed the distance by limping steadily forward, deathly silent, blood on the side of his face and covering his side. In his arms, a young man lay senseless, limbs dangling.

The man's face looked familiar.

Bailey relieved the man of his burden. "He looks bad."

The bloodied man gave no response, only stared straight ahead, his eyes glassy.

It was Mr. Shirley, the bookbinder, and the lad was Ruth's young cousin.

O Lord, have mercy …

"Russell." Shirley spoke for the first time, but he wasn't looking in Jonathan's direction; his vacant stare was directed somewhere beyond. Then he fell, first with a sudden shudder, like a tree bitten by an axe. The rest of his body followed, his limbs flopping on the grass.

18

The sun's o'ercast with blood; fair day, adieu!
  Which is the side that I must go withal?
  —Margaret Gage, quoting Shakespeare's *King John*

*W*aking, Ruth opened her eyes to darkness, unable to see the wagon bed above her. But metallic clinks and grunts coming from the militiamen camped in the Common signaled the coming of dawn. Cambridge hadn't truly slept this midsummer's night; carts or horsemen had slipped through at odd moments, and the moans of injured men had become part of the background noise, a horrible counterpoint to the songs of crickets and tree frogs.

Yesterday, her aunt had been frantically busy. As the battle—if that's what it was—had ebbed to a close, men came back. Many were injured.

While helping her aunt, Ruth had kept one eye on the road, watching for Jonathan. As men trickled back, the news was patchy. Some said Dr. Warren had been in the fray—some even said he'd been killed.

"Ruth, I need you." Her aunt had waved a hand. "I need you to stitch this closed."

In the gloaming of the evening, she'd stitched a man's stumps where two fingers had been sheared off by a musket ball. Her stomach turned again thinking of it. But Ruth had forced her face into pleasant lines. "You'll be fine. And what a badge of honor to show the ladies."

Exhausted, sweaty, she'd spread a blanket beneath the Conestoga wagon at midnight. She kept seeing Jonathan lying dead on that hill. Restless, she'd tossed and turned. But she must have fallen asleep, for now she was waking up.

She lay there, listening, until the first birds began to chirp, then she rose and filled the kettle.

Hannah's head popped up from the wagon's interior, her hair tousled. "Howdy." She clambered out of the huge vehicle and wriggled her shoulders. "What's for breakfast?"

Ruth smiled. "We still have bacon."

Molly joined them, groaning that they had no bread—and no oven. Hannah went to the Conestoga and returned with a cast iron flat-bottomed pot and lid. "Here, try this. It's a Dutch oven. You can bake almost anything in this."

The goat bleated a complaint. She needed to be milked.

In the gray half-light, they fixed breakfast and tended to the goat. Papa, Aunt Betsy, and Nathan joined them, but only Nathan seemed to have an appetite. Her aunt picked at her food.

"Smallpox is spreading," she muttered restlessly, to no one in particular.

Hannah stared toward the ocean, where the sky glowed an ominous orange. "Come, Ruth."

Skirting several elm trees, they walked to the edge of the Common. The sun edged over the horizon, and soon an angry red orb hung suspended in the sky like a portent.

"'The fire-eyed maid of smoky war.'"

"Hmm?" Ruth shivered.

"Shakespeare. But I doubt it's a sign from heaven. I rather think it's the smoke. Where's your shawl? You're cold."

On their way back, Ruth spotted a tall, dirty man leading a horse.

"Jonathan!" Her voice joined Hannah's.

His sister bounded to him and wrapped her arms around his neck.

Behind him, his horse drew a tiny cart. Inside were two pale bodies.

One was Joshua, the other Mr. Shirley. Ruth signaled her father.

"Papa, they need a physician." Her words trembled. She had to focus; her aunt would need her now.

Her father strode off, and Ruth took command, spreading blankets and making pallets. Both were unconscious, but her cousin seemed the worse of the two. He lay pale and limp, unmoving. She pushed away her despair.

Mr. Shirley struggled and groaned, as if deep in some bad dream. Hannah bathed their injuries in chamomile tea and watered vinegar. Aunt Betsy fingered Joshua's hair and wept silently. Molly brought water, clucking her disapproval of men in general.

Jonathan gathered sticks to keep the fire going. "Ho, is that the man yonder?"

Papa was returning, accompanied by a man carrying a leather case.

"Dr. Hall Jackson." Drops of blood splattered the sleeves of his thread-bare coat. He glanced at Mr. Shirley, then squatted next to Joshua and laid his fingers on her cousin's neck. "This one's humors are low. But I can remove the ball in his shoulder quickly." He opened his case and displayed a blood-stained steel device. "I invented this myself. Have you spirits?"

"To clean your instruments?" Hannah asked.

"For the patient." He jerked his chin at Mr. Shirley. "That one will need to be dosed and tied down."

Jonathan and Nathan managed to get a few swallows of whiskey down the bookbinder's throat while Dr. Jackson laid out his instruments on a cloth.

He treated Joshua first. "He looks insensible, but you'll need to hold him firmly."

Aunt Betsy withdrew, and the men grasped Joshua's limbs gently. The physician leaned over her cousin's shoulder. When the steel dived for the ball, Joshua's body jerked once.

At least it was quick, as the doctor had promised. Aunt Betsy wrapped the wound with tender hands.

Dr. Jackson examined Mr. Shirley's head carefully. "Has he waked, or spoken?"

"He carried Joshua over Bunker's hill before fainting," Jonathan said.

The doctor pried open the man's eyes. "Indeed. That is hopeful. He's had a concussion, but the cranium is intact. The ball only creased his scalp."

He shifted his attention to the man's side. "He's lost some blood. Feed him beef tea and red wine."

Ruth noted he didn't give any such instructions regarding Joshua. But she forced herself to focus on the matter at hand, standing ready with linen for a bandage.

Jonathan laid his hands on the bookbinder's shoulders while the physician stitched the man's side. Mr. Shirley moaned and grunted, and Jonathan labored to keep him still. Steel flashed once and again, and finally the long rip was closed. It was over.

Hannah poured vinegar over the wound, and Ruth bound it up. Papa slipped a few shillings to the physician and murmured his thanks.

Ruth hoped the fever wouldn't be bad when it came.

JONATHAN WATCHED THE DOCTOR LEAVE. He was tired and filthy, but he fought the urge to collapse under the shade of a nearby elm. He didn't want to sleep, even though he knew he couldn't do any more than he had done for Shirley and poor Joshua. They were in the Lord's hands now.

Last night, after the battle, he'd slept little. When he finally drifted off, he'd entered an uneasy realm of red and black. Soldiers advancing, their bayonets like steel fangs, getting closer, closer, then pouring over the wall. He'd awakened then, thrashing and sweating.

No, he couldn't sleep. He sought his horse. "Hey, Brutus, want to stretch your legs?"

The stallion swiveled his ears forward, and Jonathan hefted the saddle onto the animal's back.

He left the Common and trotted east. Slowly the trees thinned, and Jonathan could see the harbor. He wanted to see for himself what the British were up to.

Soon the militias' entrenchments came into view. He could get a good view from there.

He slowed his horse as they made their way through a company of militia, homegrown tents and even lean-tos constructed of branches scattered over the pasture randomly. The scent of an indifferently dug latrine filled the air. Several men shoveled sandy dirt onto the top of the waist-high fortification of stone and topsoil. But most of the militiamen idled—smoking, talking, or playing cards.

A cannon boomed, and Brutus shifted his weight under him. Jonathan spotted the gun responsible. A faint trace of smoke rose above one of the ships in the harbor, a sleek warship with a single line of dark iron snouts visible above the waterline.

He dismounted. Could the breastworks stop a cannonball? Perhaps the smaller shot. From the chatter of the militia officers, he'd gleaned that there were different sizes of artillery and artillery shells.

A militiaman stood motionless at the breastworks, peering at Boston with a spyglass.

"Say, mind if I take a gander?"

The militiaman looked him up and down and must have decided he passed muster, for he handed Jonathan the glass.

Boston was busy, with red dots moving ant-like over the Common and other open areas. Jonathan lifted the glass.

"What am I looking at?"

"They're burying the dead." The man's voice was tinged with approval. "I know they say we lost, for we lost the hill, but what of that? I hear we slaughtered them."

It was true. Tiny soldiers wielding tiny shovels dug graves everywhere there was an open spot. Were there yet bodies on the beach—his mind shied away from the thought.

Jonathan's hand clenched convulsively on the spyglass.

"Aye ... we slaughtered them."

JOSHUA DIED AT DAWN. Ruth buried her grief in the need to take care of her aunt—and the dead.

"We'll go to Roxbury," she told her aunt. "Eliot's burying ground."

Aunt Betsy spoke little. Her tears had dried, and she seemed far away. Stiffly, she walked to the cart that held the last of the shop's merchandise. She returned with a long length of linen.

Ruth didn't need to be told what to do. But she'd need strong thread to bind a shroud. She went to the cart and rummaged for the embroidery supplies.

What was Joshua's favorite color?

Yellow. Yellow, that was it. He said that yellow made him feel happy.

She grabbed a yellow skein, and suddenly her vision blurred.

"Need help sewing that?" Hannah's voice was gentle.

Ruth cut a long length of linen, each snip of the scissors cutting her own heart. Her aunt washed the body, and the men silently helped move it onto the fabric.

As Ruth began to stitch, she raged against the British.

Why? How could you?

Broad yellow stitches slowly laced up the shroud.

Joshua ... Joshua. Why did you join the militia?

Then the yellow stitches covered his face, and they took Joshua's body to Roxbury. A good place. Joshua took his goat here sometimes.

But it wasn't the same. Earthworks ran across the eastern boundary of the burying ground.

"Seems wrong, to my way of thinking," said Molly. "This"—she gestured with a brown arm at the breastworks—"in a place of the dead!"

"'Tis war." Aunt Betsy's voice was hollow. "War and evil rulers."

No one said anything to that.

To lose a child ... it didn't matter if he was brave, even if the cause was just. There was no compensation.

The men took turns with a single shovel to dig a grave, and Ruth fought back tears, sitting near her aunt, offering no words of consolation, for she had none to give.

The patriarch Job had lost everything. He lost ten children and all his possessions. What had he said?

The Lord gave, and the Lord hath taken away; blessed be the name of the Lord.

Job had more faith than she did.

Jonathan climbed out of the grave. "It's done."

Help, Lord. Help us to bear this, because it's unbearable.

ROBERT OPENED his eyes to a bustle of activity. Where was he? He spotted one of the Russell brothers with a horse. Then Molly with a kettle. He was with friends, then, not captured as an enemy combatant. He closed his eyes again.

His head hurt, but it was bearable. His side was, if anything, worse, but it was neatly bandaged. He must have been shot or stabbed. He couldn't remember anything except the smoky confusion of battle.

He opened his eyes again to find Jonathan Russell crouched nearby.

"Can ye stand?"

With the help of Russell and a man he didn't recognize, Robert managed to mount a horse.

"We're going to Roxbury. Red Hawk'll help ye ride."

Red Hawk? A strange name, perhaps a nickname. The man was about his own size, with black hair and blue eyes, maybe of Welsh extraction. Red Hawk helped him onto a horse with strong, wiry arms, surely able to help him if he passed out again. Robert didn't think he would. He still felt as weak as a newly foaled colt, but the memory of the awful day was coming back. Dr. Warren ...

"What is the date?" His tongue felt thick in his mouth.

"Monday the nineteenth." Red Hawk mounted and took the reins from behind him.

He'd lost a whole day. "My injury ..." With the effort of mounting the horse, his side had begun a persistent throbbing. Thankfully the animal was moving slowly.

"The medicine man came and sewed it closed. He took a ball from Joshua, but ..."

Joshua. It was all coming back. "Joshua. Is he alive?"

The man cleared his throat. "No."

For a long moment Robert could not trust himself to speak. "Tell them he was brave. He was with Dr. Warren at the very end."

He could not face Mrs. Ward himself.

For the rest of the painful ride, he distracted himself by focusing on his surroundings, taking mental notes of the military encampments they passed, if "military" was the correct word. It reminded him of a militia training day holiday, so popular in Boston, complete with food and entertainments. But he'd seen them fight—no, they couldn't be discounted. Not that he could get the information to anyone in a timely manner, but estimating their numbers took his mind off the searing pain, freshened with each stride of the horse.

They reached Roxbury. The humble burial ground was littered with headstones of various sizes, some ancient and mottled with lichen. The men half-lifted, half-supported him to a large, sturdy headstone. Leaning back, he breathed deeply, slowly, studying a nearby weed to steady himself against the pain.

A shadow fell across the grass. Hannah Russell squatted under her voluminous skirts and placed one hand on his forehead.

He focused on her instead of the weed. "Fever?"

"Not yet. But it's early. Head hurt?"

"Some." He looked past her to where the men were bustling about, digging a grave, most likely. "How is Mrs. Ward?"

"Not good. But she has Ruth. Better than seven sons, she is."

"Ruth will make some young man very happy one day."

Hannah chuckled. "Aye, but he'll have to adopt her family or she'll no' marry him."

Robert smiled despite the pain. He didn't know why her faint Scotch brogue charmed him.

"Ye look peaked. I'll get you some laudanum."

"Later." He didn't want the mind-numbing drug.

She stood. "As ye will."

He closed his eyes. When he opened them, the bustle had ceased. Everyone stood about the grave, all but Mrs. Ward, who sat on a campstool, deflated like a doll with its stuffing removed. A single voice floated on the delicate breeze.

"We thank Thee, Father, for the gift of Thy Son. In this gift we find adoption and love. In this gift Thy son Joshua found hope and peace. And he was Your creature and Your child. We commend him to Thee."

Nathan Russell was leading the others in prayer about the grave. As Robert watched, the man opened his eyes and looked heavenward. "Please help those who have remained behind. You know we are frail. You know we are dust."

The formal thees and thous had slipped out of the prayer, and Nathan looked like a child at his father's knee, confident of his love. "You wept at the grave of Lazarus. We know You feel our pain."

A sob. It was Mrs. Ward.

As the prayer continued, Robert closed his eyes to stop the tears.

19

When we in darkness walk,
Nor feel the heavenly flame,
Then is the time to trust our God,
And rest upon His Name.

—Augustus Toplady (1740-1778)

*J*onathan joined Ruth and studied the man she tended. Sweat beaded on the bookbinder's flushed face, and his eyes were glassy. "We can put him in the Conestoga. But we need to leave —it's unhealthy here."

Some of the militiamen were coming down with the flux, and looking about him at those under his care, he felt a pressing urgency. Philadelphia would be healthier for Aunt Betsy and the Haynes. On top of which, he could not guess what the British were planning. Roxbury sat at the end of the Boston Neck, and the best way for the enemy to attack, in his opinion, was first to bombard them—he'd seen what a single shot could do—and then send infantrymen through the gate and up the hill, eight abreast.

Sharpshooters wouldn't be able to take them down fast enough, and simple breastworks wouldn't stop the infantry.

They were exposed, vulnerable. And periodically the British fired their artillery, breaking windows or scattering campfires with their shot. It was a miracle the cannonballs hadn't done more damage, but then, the British generals only seemed to be toying with them, as if the presence of fifteen thousand militiamen round about Boston was a mere irritation, like fleas on a dog's neck.

Was their resistance a fool's errand? From their campsite he could see the warships in the harbor, masts bristling like some dark, menacing forest. The colonies had no navy and very little artillery. The few pieces they'd had fouled early on in the battle. Useless. The odds were incredibly long.

He squared his shoulders and blinked to clear away sudden moisture. This was his home. He'd defend it.

Ruth squinted at him. "Hannah wants to look at Mr. Shirley's wound. She thinks it's festering."

Jonathan ran a hand over his stubbly jaw. "Aye, well. Let's see to it."

As the women heated water and vinegar, he spotted a familiar figure approaching. Henry Knox.

"Your plans?" Knox's sweaty face beamed encouragement.

Jonathan's smile was brief. "We leave at first light. The Haynes and Mrs. Ward need to go south."

Knox's face fell. "Heard about the lad. Sorry to hear."

"He stayed at Warren's side until the end."

The man blinked several times quickly. "'Twas a sore loss, to lose the good doctor. What about your servant—is she going south?"

"Miss Haynes tells me Mrs. Knox has need of help. They have asked Molly what she wants to do, and she's loath to leave the family, but she doesna want to go south."

Knox nodded and looked over the Conestoga. "Hear about Ethan Allen and Fort Ticonderoga?"

It was vaguely familiar. "Some place on the frontier?"

"Allen took the fort and all its artillery." Knox grinned. "Cannon of every description."

"Where is this exactly?"

Nathan joined them, listening.

"Up the Hudson River. About three hundred miles," Knox said.

"Three hundred ..." Jonathan grappled with the distance. "Roads any good?"

"We'll know more later. But we need to prepare." He gestured, silk hand-kerchief fluttering. "Wagons, harness, tents—"

"Feed," Nathan said.

Knox nodded, clearly in his element. "Know where to get rope? The thick naval kind."

Jonathan's gaze met Nathan's and a tacit agreement passed between them. Smugglers were flocking to Newport, bringing supplies of all kinds. Including stout rope.

But Jonathan couldn't even think past that. He'd been drawn into a war against his will.

~

THE STEADY RUMBLE of wagon wheels told Robert where he was. He opened his eyes and shut them again. The light inside the wagon was dim but still hurt his eyes. His mouth was dry, and an acrid smell of old sweat filled his nose.

He knew that smell—the smell of the sickroom. A sense of deja vu touched him, and he wondered how long he'd been fevered.

The last thing he remembered was Hannah Russell giving him laudanum. He opened his eyes again and studied his surroundings. Above him arched a canvas tarp, secured to wooden hoops. His foot rested on the oak frame of the printing press, and absurdly, that pleased him.

A shape to one side resolved into a woman. Hannah Russell was kneeling with her head against the wagon's sideboard, sleeping.

Robert raised a heavy hand to feel his face. The stubble was thick, almost a week's growth.

Hannah woke and gazed at him with sleepy eyes, her face framed with auburn wisps. "How do you feel?"

"My side aches, but not like before."

She smiled, then stretched and rearranged her limbs in what had to be a more comfortable position, sitting with her arms around her knees. "We were worried. I lanced the wound, cleaned it, then re-bandaged it."

"How long was I fevered?" Had he revealed his true purpose?

"Several days. We are close to New York. Can you take some cherry cordial?"

He nodded. Anything to clear the awful dryness out of his mouth.

She took out a tin cup and poured. "I've been giving you cherry bounce and beef tea, as much as you could take in your state. We didn't have wine, as the doctor prescribed."

He struggled to sit up, and she placed a sheepskin behind him against the wagon's sloping front. He closed his eyes as the fresh, tart juice struck his throat. "Thank you. This is good." He wondered what cherry bounce was.

"It's cherry season in Connecticut, and I made my brother stop and buy several bushels. And some kegs to put the juice in. But the cherry bounce we purchased from a tavern."

He felt pampered. Hannah was a lively young woman, yet so pleasant to be around. And forever beyond his reach. Beyond the reach of a British spy.

"Who is Raw-don?" she asked.

He jerked, and the cherry cordial splashed. "Rawdon?"

"Aye, ye said his name. Sounded like ye were angry."

He relaxed. What should he say? The truth, or as near as he could get to it. "Francis, Lord Rawdon is my cousin, and a lieutenant in the Fifth Regiment."

Her mouth formed an O. "A redcoat?"

He nodded. "He … he was the one who killed Warren."

"You saw it?"

"I was there."

"No wonder ye thrashed and cried out." Her shoulders sagged. "Jonathan says little about Bunker's hill. I want to help him, but I dinna ken what to do."

"Be patient. Death is a hard thing to witness, and killing a man is even harder, even though you feel it justified." He closed his eyes, seeing Rawdon's face above the fatal pistol. "We should be glad it is difficult. Some men come to enjoy it, and that is a truly fearsome thing."

"HE'S BEEN UNCONSCIOUS UNTIL TODAY," Ruth said. She was getting used to riding Hannah's big chestnut mare after days of travel, but her thighs were still aching. It was approaching midday, and she hoped for a good long rest after the main meal of the day to recuperate. The midsummer evening was better for travel than the afternoon.

"I dinna care for Hannah alone with that man. And I dinna know much about him."

"He used to be in the Army." Ruth appreciated Jonathan's doubts. In part, they were her own.

"Hmm. That explains some things. D'ye think he was an officer?"

"He must have been. From the little he's told me, I think his family is well connected."

"A gentleman. But why stoop to a trade?"

Ruth shrugged. Bookbinding was a good trade, not to be looked down upon, but perhaps Englishmen thought differently. Most of the leaders of Boston were tradesmen of some sort.

"Another thing. Officers can either sell their commissions or go on half-pay."

"He's on half-pay. He told me that."

Jonathan's horse sidled and pranced as he looked her full in the face. "Ye ken what that means. He's no' retired. He's still in the Army."

She frowned. "But—"

"He's not in uniform, but they can recall him to active duty at any moment."

"So he's still loyal to the Crown."

Jonathan lifted his chin. "No matter what he says, he's a redcoat. Dinna forget it."

It was hard to think of Mr. Shirley in the same category as the soldiers in Boston. But then, several times she'd seen officers in Henry's bookshop, browsing or conversing. She remembered one in particular, a lively blond man who cheerfully discussed natural philosophy with Mr. Knox.

Now they were at war, and the cheerful man could be lying dead. She sighed. "Tell me about Philadelphia. I've never been there."

"Has your father a position? Has anyone promised him?"

She shook her head. "He wrote a man named Mr. Sellers, but there was no time to expect a reply. How many printers are there in Philadelphia?"

Jonathan's eyebrows rose. "I've only passed through, never stayed long. But I happened to see several, and there are probably many more." He smiled. "It's a fair jewel of a city, with all kinds of shops laid out on broad streets. I suspect he'll find work, even if he canna set up on his own. Ye'll like Philadelphia. It's different from Boston. Plenty of Patriots, but on the other hand, I think it's safer for ye."

"For me?"

"Aye. For your writing. The folks of Boston were overwrought, like men under the lash. Not so Philadelphia."

Ruth was strangely moved and couldn't speak for a moment. "Thank you. I had not thought of writing—"

"Is it your calling? Your vocation?"

"I should help Papa." Her writing was secondary, wasn't it?

"The Continental Congress meets in Philadelphia. Ye can at least report on that."

In the rush of events in Boston, she'd forgotten all about the meetings.

"Oh. Yes, you're right." Ruth wished—oh, what did the strange swelling of her heart mean? That Jonathan could be part of her life somehow. But it didn't seem possible. She laid her hand on her bodice, her mother's locket just below. They were too different.

And this horrid war was in the way.

IT WAS three days before they found a place to bathe. Millstone River barely deserved the name—it was closer to a mere stream, in Robert's opinion— but in places it slowed and swelled into a pool, and the foliage screened bathers.

Robert felt filthy and knew he smelled rank. He needed to remove the bandage and take a look. The wound still hurt, but the pain no longer disturbed his sleep.

Horses came first. They were watered and tethered to a grassy spot while the women stirred up cornmeal batter. His stomach growled. But he was getting tired of hoecake and cherries. Sometimes they had beef pies or cheese, or whatever else farmers sold by the side of the road.

Mrs. Ward settled an iron pot on the fire with a clank. Then the women disappeared behind the foliage, carrying soap and clean clothing, smiling for the first time in days.

It had been a long road.

He found a place to sit and wait, his eyes on the road. A soldier's habit, he supposed. Or maybe just a man's habit—protecting the vulnerable.

A woodpecker's rat-tat-tat-tat sounded nearby. The sun felt good on his shoulders, and he felt grateful just to be alive. The landscape seemed only half-tamed, farms and hamlets alternating with large swathes of woods. Once, startled turkeys had whirred above the brush.

He slid a finger under the bandage. A pale ring surrounded a large central rusty spot. His shirt was slit to accommodate it, and he felt exposed.

No, he'd enter Philadelphia fully clothed. But what then?

The earl. He needed to write as soon as he could, tell him what he'd seen. But Robert had no faith that it would be useful.

"What's taking ye so long?" Nathan's tenor carried on the still air.

"My hair, ye twit," his sister answered from beyond the trees.

Robert smiled at the banter. Motion caught his eye. Jonathan Russell strode across the camp, cutting him a hard glance.

Robert sighed. Then he had a thought. Guarding his tender side, he rose to his feet. He fetched his godmother's gift and a clean shirt from his trunk. He found Nathan sitting on a stone by the river.

"I'd like you to have this."

"But why?" Nathan opened the book tenderly.

Robert had finally finished reading the volume of hymns compiled by the countess. "I can get another. I thought you would appreciate them."

Nathan turned a page. "Och, listen to this: 'Amazing grace, how sweet the sound, that saved a wretch like me.' Speaks to the heart. Who is John Newton?"

Robert slapped at a cloud of mayflies. "This I remember, because it surprised me. The converted captain of a slaver."

Nathan's eyes were bright with tears. "I will treasure this."

Robert blinked to clear away sudden moisture. "I need to get this bandage off."

"I'll leave ye to it." Nathan went back to the wagon, clutching the book to his chest.

Robert hung his clean shirt on a branch and carefully removed his clothes. He eased into the water gratefully. So far so good. He submerged his shoulders, then his head. Surfacing, he grabbed the bar of Hannah's soap —it smelled of oranges and cloves—and covered himself in the scented lather. Then he worked it into his greasy hair, careful to avoid the tender streak on his scalp.

He rinsed, then stood in a shallow spot to examine the bandage, which he'd left alone when he disrobed. It was loosening. He sat in the shallows and laved it.

A jingle and snort announced the presence of horses. Robert jerked the bandage off, wincing a little. No blood or festering, just an angry pink weal. He toweled himself with a cloth and drew on the shirt carefully before donning the rest of his clothes.

Through gaps in the foliage, he could see several on horseback. Friend or foe? Robert picked up his shoes and approached barefoot.

The Russells were speaking with a tall man atop a fine blue roan; just behind, a dark servant sat another horse. Jonathan's shoulders were thrown back, hands relaxed. He was alert but not afraid.

Robert stepped closer, the mud of the bank giving way to leaf litter beneath his feet. The glint of a scabbard caught his eye. The tall man was dressed in a fine blue coat with buff facings, gleaming boots, and a tricorne with a black cockade. The short sword marked him as military, and the fine boots marked him as an officer. Shiny epaulets on his shoulders marked him as ... a general?

His stomach contracted. This was genuine military information. Hannah's face appeared in his mind.

Could he betray them? Could he betray her?

The general dismounted with fluid grace and walked several paces forward with a peculiar gait Robert had seen in only a few—Jonathan and Mr. Sloan. The quiet step of a backwoods hunter. What an interesting man.

Jonathan gestured with his hat. "...and Mr. Knox asked us to find rope for his artillery."

Artillery ...

The ghost of a smile played over the general's features. He said something in return Robert didn't catch. But there was no mistaking the man's commanding posture, and when he remounted and moved off—north, toward Boston—Robert saw something else. The general sat a horse like he'd been born in the saddle.

He waited for the entourage to pass before emerging behind the trees. "What did I miss?"

"General Washington, is what," Nathan blurted. "Our commander-in-chief."

Robert saw Jonathan cut his brother a narrow glance.

Artillery and generals. His writing desk was packed somewhere in Mrs. Ward's cart.

He needed to get to it. Unobserved. But his duty choked him like never before.

Part Two

Philadelphia

ררר‎ז-‎ר‎ר‎5

20

My only hope of salvation is in the infinite transcendent love of God manifested to the world by the death of His Son upon the Cross. Nothing but His blood will wash away my sins.

    —Dr. Benjamin Rush (1745-1813)

*P*hiladelphia was astonishing. From her perch on the wagon seat, Ruth watched the vehicles and riders traversing Third Street. Like Boston, most streets were paved—but on these wide, airy streets, a Conestoga wagon could move freely. Two such wagons could pass each other without a problem.

The city smells—the scents of manure, chamber pots, and the distant whiff of the docks—reminded her of Boston, but the odors were lighter. Philadelphia was an open, clean town.

"Look there." Aunt Betsy rode on the cart's seat beside her. "An apothecary."

"And a print shop across the way."

Nathan Russell drove the Conestoga behind them, Hannah peering out at the sights. Jonathan and Papa rode, while Mr. Sloan walked, looking uncomfortable.

Savory smells flowed out of taverns and coffeehouses. Finely dressed men in satin waistcoats brushed against Quakers in dull clothing, and dark-skinned servants wearing colorful bandanas threaded the streets. The sight of sailors and journeymen was familiar, but the beaded, feathered Indian on one street corner was a surprise.

They passed Cherry Street, and to Ruth's left rose an impressive bell tower—a church. The bustle increased at the Market Street crossing. Finally Papa gestured to a neat, two-story building. A sign with gold lettering, *Hall & Sellers,* dangled from a brass bracket. Lettering spelling out *The Pennsylvania Gazette* was plastered in a window. The publisher of the most widely read paper in the colony would surely have work for her father.

But she doubted there would be a place for her.

THE GOLDSMITH GESTURED to a well-worn chair. Nervous, Ruth sat and adjusted her skirts. Beside her, Papa fiddled with the brim of his wool tricorne. Everyone else waited outside on the street.

"I care not for some ancient family feud," Mr. William Young told her father from across a scratched desk, his thick hair pomaded and powdered. "You may be at ease on that account." His gaze shifted to Ruth. "She should not suffer because of some disagreement between her grandparents and my father."

Papa had sketched out her relationship with this estranged branch of her mother's family after the visit to the print shop had resulted in mixed results. Ruth's grandparents had been more generous with money than affection. But she knew nothing of family conflict—or even that she had family here. Papa and Mr. Shirley had been hired by the *Gazette,* but there was no living space available except for a room above the stable—good enough for a couple of men. Philadelphia's inns and boarding houses were packed with members of the Continental Congress and refugees like themselves.

The printing press had found a temporary home in Jonathan's uncle and aunt's barn across the river, but Ruth and her aunt needed a place to stay.

Ruth took a steadying breath. Mr. Young's shop seemed prosperous, his clothing well tailored. She'd been torn from her home and felt at sea, adrift. But perhaps this was the Lord's provision.

"I can house you and your widowed aunt, but"—his gaze focused on Ruth—"you will need to earn your keep."

He began by asking her about her skills. "My wife has four children and needs assistance with the home."

"I have little experience with children. But I am well read, able to teach, and I have helped my aunt in her dispensary shop. I know the uses of all the common simples."

Mr. Young leaned back in his chair. "Have you a ready hand with a needle?"

Ruth was on safe ground here. "I can take apart a gown and remake it to any given style or fit." She'd had to, in the lean years after her mother and grandparents died.

The goldsmith's brows rose approvingly. "I've a final question. Your political views."

Ruth's throat seemed to close. She gathered her thoughts quickly. "I thought the Sons of Liberty to blame for the Boston Massacre. I thought they were mere rabble-rousers."

"You think differently now?"

"I am not sure what to think. I cannot call myself a Patriot. I have always been loyal to the King. But now I wonder if I must obey an immoral or illegal law. I find myself agreeing to many things the Patriots say, even if I am unsure of the rightness of all their actions."

"You disagree with taking up arms?"

"I have heard men say that they are justified in defending their homes, and they give the matter no deeper thought. But this is tantamount to taking up arms against the King, so I am, of course, hesitant."

"Even after what happened on Bunker's hill?"

Tears sprang to her eyes. "My cousin is dead. My aunt comes to you bereft of her only son."

The goldsmith arose and offered her a handkerchief. "I am sorry. Forgive me. You are welcome here for the duration."

ROBERT PULLED out a sheet of foolscap and set it on his writing desk in his lap—it was Miss Haynes's traveling desk, he realized with a start. He'd pay her father for it or buy one of his own.

He set the inkwell on the desk and opened the cap. It was dusty and dim in the cramped space above the stables, and too warm, but the lodgings would do for now. If Mr. Haynes came in while he was writing and asked any questions, he'd explain that he was writing his family.

But the printer wouldn't ask questions. He just wasn't that sort.

Robert began by sketching out the details of the battle. It took half an hour to describe the actions of both sides, and there were still many things he was leaving out.

Howe's wineglass. The gleam in Rawdon's eye. The gurgle from the throat of a man his cousin had cut down with his sword. The orange sky.

And his strange dreams. He still had headaches.

A horse snorted below in the stable. Robert brushed away the bloody memories, still so fresh, and fought to steer his mind to an analysis—information the earl could actually use.

They fight like fiends. No, fiends would not do. He labored over the next few sentences and was startled by a sudden creak.

Jonathan Russell knocked his head against the low lintel of the door as he entered.

Robert's hands froze—one on the paper, the other clutching the quill. "Is the press safe?"

"Mr. Haynes took great care, wrapping it in oilcloth and asking more than once, 'does this barn leak?'" His gaze swept the space before landing on Robert's hands. "Who're you writing to?"

Robert took in the hard lines of the man's frame and the weapons brushing against his bloodstained breeches. Russell was tall, well over six feet, and his reach was undoubtedly greater than Robert's own. In a fight he would be disadvantaged.

His side ached, and he voted for diplomacy.

"My uncle William. He cares for my mare on his estate."

Russell paused and blinked. Then he took another step forward. "Then ye willna mind if I read it." He swiped it from the desk.

Sudden fear coursed through him. The conflict was irregular, not a formal war—would their general, this Washington, hang spies? Robert ran the letter over in his mind wondering how badly he'd exposed himself—and the earl.

"Ye're very specific about the battle—both sides. Howe's men—how'd ye ken that, I wonder?"

"My godmother gifted me with a spyglass."

Russell eyed him briefly. "Warren's death, again very specific."

"I was there. Up until his last moments, then I was hit."

"Did ye see who kilt him?"

The brogue had strengthened in his voice.

"My cousin killed him. Francis, Lord Rawdon."

Russell's brows shot up. "Indeed." He continued reading. "Strength of the militia, plenty of details. And how'd ye explain this? 'They in no wise lack courage, will, or marksmanship. All they need is training, and some good generals.'"

"Most Englishmen view Americans as ignorant rabble. I do not hold that view, obviously."

"I wonder who this 'uncle' is."

Robert began to sweat. "He is well-placed and friendly to the colonies. He funds a charitable school in Connecticut. He asks for my observations."

It was as close to the truth as he dared.

"Well-placed? That could mean anything. It could mean he's the King's best friend. What it does mean is you're a spy."

"I am no spy."

"Perhaps we should let others decide that."

Could he do that? Arrest him? "A spy is a soldier out of uniform."

"Ruth said you were on half pay. Essentially, ye're a soldier out of uniform."

Russell believed him a spy, and so would Washington, if his work around Boston were known. And spying wasn't his idea or his choice.

Robert cursed. "And what shall I do now? I have two choices. Sell my commission or ask that it be activated—which it will be soon whether I ask or not, if I don't sell out. But to sell out now would raise questions at home. Questions of courage and honor. The family name." He stood, and the stool behind him tipped and clattered. "Do what you think best. What you think most honorable. I can only do the same."

Russell stared at him for a long, hard moment. "For Joshua's sake I'll do nothing." He ripped the letter in half. "Leave town, and I'll forget I ever knew ye." At the door he turned. "And stay away from my sister."

~

A SWATHE of green peppered by soft lilac and pink marked a garden between two houses. Ruth soaked in the sight, a restful balm that seemed to loosen the hardness that had crept into her heart, like crust on a stew left sitting too long. The warm, fresh scent of the flowers brightened the spot on the walk.

"It's beautiful. Boston gardens rarely have space for flowers," Ruth told Mrs. Young, who strolled beside her.

Homesickness flooded Ruth. But the Boston of her childhood was gone, replaced by redcoats and war. And the Russells had returned home to the Shenandoah Valley.

She missed Hannah—and Jonathan, if she were honest.

She even missed the goat, which had remained with Molly and the Knoxes.

Mrs. Young paused in her stride. "Yes—are those geraniums? The common areas are a mess, but these private gardens are a tribute to our city." Her stride resumed its decided pace along Walnut Street. "I want to show you the State House. 'Tis not far."

Rebecca Young and her brood were the warm heart of the goldsmith's home. The stair-step children, three boys and a girl, were well past leading strings, and the oldest, twelve-year-old William, learned metal-smithing techniques after his daily studies.

Benjamin was the youngest at six. Aunt Betsy had taken the little charmer into her lap yesterday, and the sight warmed Ruth's heart. Her aunt needed to love and be loved again.

"The State House—isn't that where the Second Continental Congress is meeting?" Ruth would record her impressions for her father, though his new position did not involve opinion pieces, at least not yet.

Her own well of creativity was dry. She didn't know what to think anymore.

"Yes—'tis right here on Fifth."

The goldsmith's wife had insisted on an outing, for she needed to place some fabric orders with a shopkeeper. But the true purpose, Ruth suspected, was simply to stretch her legs in the Philadelphia sunshine, away from the responsibilities of home and hearth, and with Aunt Betsy to mind the children, she could.

It was a warm day, but the heat seemed less oppressive in the open air. They turned the corner, and a massive structure came into view. Rebecca led her to the front. A clock tower perched like a mast on a sturdy red brick building with regular, large windows. Covered arcades ran to either side, joining the main building to two smaller ones.

"Let's circle to the back. There's a lawn. Not a garden, but pleasing enough," Rebecca said.

They found a seat on a simple iron bench behind some overgrown boxwoods and relaxed, the delicate chirping of a wren piercing the warm air.

"My oldest daughter needs a new skirt," Rebecca began.

"Out of the new muslin?"

"No, that's for you and your aunt. I'm thinking the worsted wool."

"You're too kind," Ruth said, her throat swelling with emotion.

"No—"

A clatter and voices sounded behind them. Ruth turned in her seat and glimpsed two men striding from the back door of the State House, slowing as they neared the hedge. One was tall and thin, dapper in a fine suit. The other, Ruth realized with a shock, was Boston's own John Adams, short and slightly rotund.

She met Rebecca's gaze but said nothing. The men were arguing, and it would be rude to announce their presence by making any noise.

"What is the reason, Mr. Adams, that you New England men oppose our measures of reconciliation?"

The muttered reply was unintelligible but carried the bite of sarcasm.

"Look, ye! If you don't concur with us in our pacific system, I, and a number of us, will break off from you in New England and we will carry on the opposition by ourselves in our own way."

Ruth cringed at the tall man's tone of voice, both petulant and condescending.

"Many accommodations will I make in the cause of harmony," Adams said icily, "but I will not be threatened."

He turned and left. The tall man departed in another direction.

"Who was the tall man?" Ruth asked.

"John Dickinson."

Ruth's lips parted. "You mean the writer of *Letters from a Penn*—"

"*Pennsylvania Farmer*. Yes, that's the one."

Ruth marveled. She'd thought Dickinson radical at first. Now he seemed the moderate. "I wonder what they were discussing. He spoke of 'measures for reconciliation.'"

Rebecca looked at her and smiled. "You are a printer's daughter, aren't you? I think we shall get along well together. As to your question, I've no clue. One last petition, perhaps?"

But blood had been spilled, Charlestown destroyed, and George Washington appointed commander-in-chief of a united army. "It cannot hurt matters. In fact, one might make the argument that if such a petition is rebuffed or refused by the King, it would bring fence-sitters to the Patriot cause and harden the resolve to fight."

"I heard you wrote for your father." Rebecca's eyes twinkled. "I can see your argument in the *Gazette* now."

Ruth flushed. Her aunt must have said something. They stood and made their way back, more slowly this time. She replayed the overheard conversation in her mind. The Congress was not all of one mind, that was clear. They had their disputes, and clearly some, like Dickinson, were loath to break with the Crown.

Like her.

They turned the corner and nearly collided with a man bounding up Walnut Street in the opposite direction.

"Forgive me, ladies!" Gray-blue eyes in an expressive, youthful face surveyed them with concern.

"No harm done, Dr. Rush," Rebecca said. "On your way to the State House?"

Despite his bright linen and silky cravat, Dr. Rush managed to look disheveled. He juggled the satchel under his arm awkwardly. "Yes, ma'am." He replaced his hat as if eager to be on his way.

"I've several seamstresses, and you need flags," Rebecca said. "Am I right?"

Dr. Rush's gaze sharpened. "How did you know?"

"You mentioned a committee the last time you spoke to my husband."

"Oh yes." His expression shifting quickly, as if a pattern of thought was falling into place. "We will send you the design." He nodded a leave-taking, and he launched himself down the walk again.

Rebecca grinned. "A sweet Christian man. He's not only brilliant, he's busy. I took the opportunity to volunteer our services—he wouldn't know whom to ask."

"Seamstresses?" Ruth suspected the answer.

"You and your aunt can sew, and a flag has no gathers or ruffles. I suspect it will be something with red and white stripes—how simple is that?"

Many of the militias had flags of some sort. The Continental Army needed a unique flag, Ruth supposed. "My aunt would jump at the chance."

And what about herself? So far, she'd sewed up injuries and helped the Cause in other small ways, but nothing any reasonable person would not do.

To sew a *flag*—why, that was different. It was participating in the rebellion.

Could she do it? Should she do it?

Rebellion seemed wrong, but the King's men had shed blood on Lexington Green.

The King's men had killed her cousin.

She would fight back, whether it was right or not. She would sew the flags.

~

RUTH WAS glad to see a gleam in Aunt Betsy's eye when they returned.

"A fellow came by with a package while you were gone. From the cabinetmaker's. With your name on it."

Covered in oilcloth and bound by twine, it was large and rectangular, as wide as a long loaf of Molly's bread. Ruth hefted it. Not quite heavy enough for books—but no, it came from the cabinetmaker.

"We don't know anyone here, Aunt Betsy."

Her aunt snipped the twine with a pair of scissors, and Ruth unwrapped the coverings. The gleam of fine pale maple met her eye. A traveling desk!

She ran her fingers over the satiny surface. Her own was old and cracked on one side. Did Mr. Shirley still have it? But then, the bookbinder had departed soon after they'd arrived, with no explanation, not even a note.

Papa had been mystified.

Ruth slid open the drawer. Paper! And all the other accoutrements of a desk were here—several quills and a capped portable inkwell.

And a note. Ruth's heart seized. It was Mr. Shirley's handwriting.

I am sorry for the suddenness of my departure. I will remember you all with great fondness. I left half of the sermons and primers with your father and took half with me. It was an honor to partner with you.

Yr Ob't Servant, RS

P.S. Below is my godmother's direction, in case of need.

In case of need? She scanned the address. Selina Hastings, Countess of Huntingdon. The rest blurred. *A countess?*

Who was Robert Shirley? Why had he come to Boston, really? And why had he left?

He was on half pay. It only stood to reason that he had rejoined his regiment.

He was now the enemy.

"What's the matter?" Aunt Betsy asked.

"I think he's joined the army."

"We'll pray for him."

Ruth didn't correct her aunt's assumption. Let her think Mr. Shirley had joined Washington. Because anything else would be too difficult for her aunt to handle.

She took a deep breath. She wasn't sure she could handle it herself.

21

Jesus, where'er your people meet,
there they behold your mercy seat;
where'er they seek you, you are found,
and ev'ry place is hallowed ground.
—William Cowper, 1769

England, October 1775

A footman stood ready to assist him, but William Legge, Second Earl of Dartmouth, ignored the proffered hand and descended from his carriage unaided, eager to breathe fresh air after a full day of bouncing over ill-kept roads.

He rolled his aching shoulders and glanced up at his coachman. "See the horses get the best treatment." They were hired, as he'd changed horses in St. Albans. But hired horses were still needy of attention, and the stable of an inn or tavern didn't always give good care to his beasts.

William turned his attention to the church spire. "I'll walk back to the inn," he said, dismissing both servants.

The unpaved road to the Olney Church was bordered by a welcoming grassy verge shaded by beech trees. The earl followed it until the tower and nave rose before him. He found his way inside the edifice of simple masonry and tinted windows, the odor of damp stone and musty books meeting his nose.

No one was about. It was nearly dusk, and the nave was empty, though the One the earl looked for must be here. He knew God inhabited every corner of His Creation, and yet for a flesh-and-blood man, this building of stone and wood seemed the best place to approach a God who hid His face.

He knelt behind a pew, a knee creaking in complaint. "Oh, Lord," he whispered, not knowing how to begin. What to say. What to ask.

Nothing was right.

The petition from the colonies, ignored. His fault.

And Robert Shirley marooned amidst hostilities, in danger of the noose. That was his fault, too.

He blinked and a tear rolled down his cheek. "Abba, Father."

The sons of the nobility were on ships headed west. The countess's grandson, Lord Rawdon, was in the colonies, and the rebels targeted officers. General Howe had just lost every single one of his staff officers—in one battle. And it wasn't over yet.

He closed his eyes, burdened with a fracturing empire. And a guilty heart.

Surely there was more he could have done. He was the Secretary of the Colonies, after all. He thought over each decision he'd made since taking the post three years before.

What if he'd been in London when Dickinson's petition had arrived? The weight crushed him.

But even here, in this place, God was silent.

Impossibly, he dozed, then a tiny sound brought him to himself again. He rose, knee aching, and sat on the pew.

A man clad in a dark cassock crossed the chancel at the front of the nave. A smile brightened his face. "My lord?" He made his way to the earl's side.

The smile quickly faded, replaced by a look of concern. "May I pray for you?"

William relaxed. John Newton was one of the few men of the cloth he felt totally at ease with. It had been through his own influence that Newton had received the Olney curacy. So many of the Church of England's posts went to hirelings ...but he squashed that depressing thought.

"Yes, I do need prayer." His sigh was almost a groan. "I have failed at my tasks in London."

Newton said nothing. Everyone knew the Earl of Dartmouth's position.

"Do you know, even after blood was spilled at Boston—and Charlestown burned—they sent a petition? A petition for reconciliation came to my desk. But ..." His voice faltered. "I was at my estate. I didn't see it."

"Let me guess. It was rejected out of hand by the Ministry."

William's brows rose. Newton was not political. "I was not there."

"Would it have made any difference?"

"As a lone voice, no. Lord North has no stomach for conflict with the colonies, but as Prime Minister he can do naught but carry out his sovereign's wishes. And the rest of the Privy Council is bent on a course of using force."

Newton sighed, and together they sat in silence. Then the curate stirred. "I want to show you something." Black fabric swishing, he made his way to the front, where he picked up his Bible. "Something I've been working on."

A hymn? His friend had written several.

Returning, Newton pulled out a crumpled sheet and began to read. "I asked the Lord that I might grow, in faith and love and ev'ry grace; might more of his salvation know, and seek more earnestly his face."

He passed the wrinkled foolscap to William, but the earl couldn't make out the words easily in the dim light, so he passed it back.

"'Twas he who taught me thus to pray, and he, I trust, has answered pray'r, but it has been in such a way as almost drove me to despair."

Despair? William began to listen more attentively as Newton's words described various trials of heart and circumstance.

"Yea more, with his own hand he seemed intent to aggravate my woe, crossed all the fair designs I schemed, humbled my heart, and laid me low." Newton lowered the paper. "I'm working on the last stanzas now." His voice took on a husky tone. "Does it feel that God is against you?"

"I believe that God is sovereign and has placed me where I ought to be. My duties are clear, though I may not hold this post much longer."

He didn't need to explain. Even without the present turmoil in His Majesty's government, Ministry posts were not life appointments.

"And you have done your duty with a clear conscience?"

"Yes, I have, but it has not been enough. We are at war with the colonies." *Humbled my heart, and laid me low.* "How will this song end?"

"'Lord, why is this?' I, trembling, cried; 'Wilt thou pursue thy worm to death?' 'Tis in this way,' the Lord replied, 'I answer prayer for grace and faith.'"

Grace and faith. If only such commodities could be purchased less dearly.

"May I copy your hymn?"

Newton's face settled into a smile. "I'll find some paper."

The earl thought of the countess, her steady gaze, her implacable faith. She had assembled several hymn books and would want to include this one. He'd give her a copy.

He wondered what she would say to him now.

"Think you that God is ignorant of your trials? How can He be ignorant when He planned them?"

He could almost hear her voice. It was the sort of thing she said.

In the silence of the nave comfort crept into his heart.

"How much?" the farmer's wife asked Nathan as she squinted at the sermon in her hand.

Jonathan's stomach rumbled with hunger as he listened to the exchange. They'd stopped to water the horses and mules at the New Haven Green on their way to Boston. The Conestoga wagon tended to attract attention, and sometimes Nathan turned the resulting conversation to greater matters, like now. Of course, Whitefield was a household name, and that helped.

"Tuppence." Nathan said. "Or, perhaps"—he smiled—"for a bit of what ye've baked this morning?"

The woman's expression brightened. "How did you know it was my baking day? Come. Men are always hungry."

"I'll stay with the animals." Jonathan didn't mention the cargo. Powder and shot for the Continental Army lay hidden beneath massive coils of naval rope, purchased from a smuggler in Newport. The rope was destined for Henry Knox.

In the smaller mule-drawn wagon, sacks of feed and other supplies were piled high, covered with an oilcloth tarp arched over willow framing mimicking the Conestoga design. Under the tarp, Red Hawk lay dozing. He disliked towns.

A large elm, golden with the turn of the weather, threw its shade over both wagons. Jonathan sat and leaned against its trunk, enjoying the play of the light through the leaves. Several gold ovals, like coins, fell fluttering to the ground.

Was Robert Shirley truly a spy?

He wasn't sure. Had he been right to let the man go?

Nathan returned, rose-gold hair escaping its tail. "She even filled my canteen with cider." He thrust a loaf of bread at Jonathan and sat beside him. "Lord, bless this woman's hands and provide her every need—spirit, soul, and body."

Jonathan ripped the loaf into three parts and handed a piece to his brother. It was dense, dark, and full of bits he couldn't identify. He took a piece to Red Hawk and returned.

"Here." Nathan opened his wooden canteen and shoved it at him.

Jonathan drank thirstily. "Thanks." He wiped his face with his sleeve and rose to get the horses ready.

Buckling the harness, Shirley's face sprang to mind. *Honor.* The man had spoken of doing the honorable thing. And yet the man had seemed torn, much like he was himself.

It was a casualty of this conflict, a casualty of the machinations of the British government, that men must make impossible choices.

Jonathan exhaled. Let Shirley do as he must. He just hoped he would never meet him in battle.

AS THEY APPROACHED ROXBURY, the road became busier. Heavily laden farmers' wagons stirred up dust along the wide track. Jonathan had no idea how many men surrounded Boston, but it was in the thousands, and they needed to eat.

As they drew onto the crowded Green, he cast his eye over the irregular lines of tents and brush arbors. The men weren't sleeping or playing cards, like the last time he'd been here. They moved jerkily, hastily, as though a stick had been thrust into an ant hill. Something had happened.

He jumped down from the wagon and approached a cluster of militiamen, Nathan following. "What's new?"

"Falmouth—have you not heard?" asked a lean man of indeterminate age.

Falmouth—where was Falmouth? Jonathan finally remembered it as an important trading town on the coast up north. "No, what happened?"

"Warships opened fire, burnt the town to the ground."

What? Why? Jonathan fisted his hands. Suddenly the gunpowder in his wagon seemed too small a contribution. "How dare they!"

"First Charlestown, then Falmouth—the British are no better than savages," spat a short man, with Liberty or Death stitched across his woolen cap.

"When did this happen?" Nathan asked.

Other men gathered round, eager to voice their outrage. Most carried battered muskets, but there were one or two rifles. One was unarmed except for an axe.

"A week ago—no, ten days now. Blasted redcoats gave folks a few hours to leave town. Then their great guns opened up and destroyed everything!" the lean man said.

"Fiends! The whole town was destroyed, and winter coming on. It was Charlestown all over again, for absolutely no reason." said a man with a long rifle.

Was this the strategy of the Crown? Raze the homes of innocents?

"General Washington is livid," Liberty observed.

"Where's Henry Knox?" Jonathan was going to help this man. They'd brought him rope, but Knox needed horses—and men.

Pulse thumping in his ears, he turned to Nathan, whose expression was sober.

They didn't need to speak. They were agreed.

With the help of his brother, Jonathan was going to get those guns from Fort Ticonderoga and fight back, if it was the last thing he did.

22

The soul becomes dyed with the color of its thoughts.
—Marcus Aurelius, *Meditations*

New York City, November 1775

The gusting north wind stung his cheeks as Robert strode up the street, crate on his shoulder. Paper was heavy, and there must be twenty reams in this box, but he didn't mind carrying such a load on this blustery day. The effort of his muscles warmed him as cold air snaked up his coat, speaking of frigid days to come. As the lowliest employee of James Rivington's print shop, Robert fetched, carried, and scrubbed. He also served as a third man on the press, but Rivington had a bookbinder already.

The sudden turn in weather on this late November day reflected the changing mood of the city. When Robert had first come to New York City in the summer, it had been a good place to lie low until he heard from the earl. The prosperous, complacent merchants and shopkeepers were loyal to the King and unperturbed by the boisterous sentiments in the newspapers.

But now, after all that had happened, the very cobblestones seemed to murmur. A few families had silently departed, usually giving some excuse, but everyone knew the real reason. Even this loyal city now had a fault line running through it. Robert could classify the newspapers by their political leaning—Holt was a rebel; Rivington, his employer, was a Loyalist.

At Wall Street, he waited for a carriage to clatter past before crossing. The road uptown curved away from the docks and past fine Dutch-style homes with scrubbed steps. Here and there, a larger red brick building cast cold shadows. Churches dotted the map, of every possible persuasion, and their bells pealed a discordant harmony on the Sabbath.

As he neared the Dutch Church, a familiar man on horseback appeared in the road, leading a group of men.

Henry Knox—there was no mistaking him. Few were as tall, and he was —if anything—heavier than he'd been in Boston. The bookshop owner had to be twenty stone.

Robert ducked behind the next building and set down his crate. He sat on the box, pressed his face to the rough brick, and adjusted the brim of his hat. He could observe without being recognized. At least, he hoped.

Dread curled in his stomach. He'd glimpsed the Russells just behind Henry. Why were they here?

Knox passed by, face raised to the buildings, taking in the sights. The Welsh man named Sloan rode a rangy gelding just ahead of the Russells' wagon. Jonathan looked about curiously, riding his fine stallion. Others formed a procession behind them.

Robert ducked his head lower. Washington was at Boston. Why were they here? They were traveling—but to where? Were they gathering food for their men or munitions? Both were critical. Washington and Russell's conversation had mentioned artillery.

A book in Knox's shop came to mind. A textbook on military science. Artillery was Knox's favorite subject.

There were cannon at Fort Ticonderoga, but that was hundreds of miles away, and winter was coming on. Surely not.

The intelligence might be useful—but he had no contact here. And truthfully, he didn't mind. It prevented him from spying.

The rest of the men passed, some on horseback, others driving wagons. Robert rose, hefted the crate to his shoulder, and made his way to the print shop. After his duties were finished for the day, he climbed the narrow steps to his garret room.

During the summer, it was hot as blazes, and now it was frigid. He needed to buy a brazier with his next quarter's half pay, which was already overdue. How much smoke would that make? The Haynes's little room had been snug by comparison.

He missed the Haynes. He even missed the little hymnbook. He picked up Marcus Aurelius's *Meditations* from the top of his chest and flipped it open.

But the words were cold and dry.

"Shirley!" A voice called from below. "The post!"

Robert scrambled down the ladder-like steps to claim the letter, then retreated to read it in the dim evening light. A note from his godmother was folded about one from the earl.

Dear Robert,

My Situation has changed. You may have read that Germain now holds my Post. I know his Mind. He will act quickly to subdue the Colonies by any Means necessary, and he will have no need of the Observations you have given me. I have made Arrangements regarding your Situation. You will hear from your Cousin soon. Your Godmother has sent your Belongings to him as well.

Uncle William

It was short, dry, terse. Undoubtedly the next editions of the newspapers would be full of the news—there must have been a reshuffling of the entire ministry. King George and the other hawks were undoubtedly angry and impatient. The costly victory at Bunker's hill would have been seen as a defeat.

Lord Germain. Robert knew little of this man, only that there was some dishonor attached to his military record. Would he now seek to squash the rebellion quickly? The earl seemed to think so.

This was not good news for the rebels. It was not good news for anyone.

RUTH TUCKED her needle through the blue wool, enjoying the task of constructing the flag's canton. It was more challenging than whipstitching the cut edge of the long strips of red and white. Aunt Betsy sometimes assisted them and spent the balance of her days at Marshall's apothecary, helping them while the owners worked for the Cause. She was there today.

The design of the canton troubled Ruth. Strips of red and white lay on her lap, waiting to be sewn onto a blue ground—the flag of the British Union. She'd seen this symbol every day in Boston for years, and now, after the recent bloodshed, it gave her mixed feelings. But as part of the flag of the united colonies, it made sense. Britain was still the mother country, despite having lost all motherly disposition.

Across the room, Rebecca squinted at the sewing in her lap. "The light is failing. But this is the last one."

Rebecca's lap was shrinking. Another child was on its way. Babies didn't consult the newspaper in order to time their appearance. But at least Philadelphia was safe.

Safe for now.

Ruth's pocket seemed to burn with the letter Mr. Young had given her earlier. She finished off her last stitch in the dim light, stood, and stretched.

"Here, take this." Rebecca handed her a pale candle.

"Thank you," Ruth said. After leaving her friends in Boston, she treasured Rebecca's companionship. She went upstairs and lit a taper in the coals behind the grate.

She touched the flame to the wick of the costly spermaceti candle, grateful for the pure, odorless light. She retrieved the letter from her pocket. It was spotted and stained, but the bold strokes and loops of the pen were perfectly legible.

Dear Ruth,

Some folks write journals, and I never have, as most days I have nothing to record but the weather, and who would want to read that? As a farmer, I know the signs of wind and sky, and know when the soil is parched, without any record of my own. Nathan keeps record of his thoughts or answers to prayer, and I decided to write letters.

I would begin by asking for your prayers for this expedition. I do not know whether Knox is a hero or a fool, but our cause is just. Perhaps you would not care for that sentiment, but I think I know your mind well enough to know that you are thoughtful. And fair.

I also need to ask your forgiveness. I am responsible for Mr. Shirley's departure. I know not whether he gave you the particulars, but let us say that my own feelings as a brother were part of it, which was foolish, as Hannah was leaving Philadelphia in any case.

Knox discovered a foundry just outside of New York City. Seems capable of casting small pieces of artillery. You can imagine his smiles. But for large cannon, we still need to look elsewhere. I suppose you can guess where we are going, though I am loath to reveal all in case this letter goes amiss.

Dec 1— Red Hawk (Mr. Sloan) left us. He scouts for us and does some hunting, but

I believe he wants to meet with some of the leaders of the Six Nations (Iroquois). The Mohawk are an important member of that confederacy and are thought to be Loyal to the King. It is very cold. Had to warm the inkwell under my shirt before I could write.

Dec 2 — Albany. I was surprised at the neat homes and streets. I was expecting to see a rough town like Staunton, but they tell me this place is very old. Brick and stone predominate, with a type of roof I also saw in New York City. Snow covers the ground, and the horses' breaths are white puffs in the still air. Nathan wrapped their legs.

General Schuyler was supposed to be with the army but he was taken ill. We spent an evening dripping on his fine carpet. He is a gentleman, with wide cheekbones in a spare face, and dark, shrewd eyes. His wife is gracious and doesn't seem to mind a herd of dirty men in her parlor.

Despite his finery, the general speaks Mohawk and smoked the pipe with nearby Indians to secure the peaceful travel of his men earlier this year. I will feel better when I hear what Red Hawk has to say.

There was a problem with the oxen. Schuyler tried to arrange for them but the prices for hiring teams are outrageous. Knox has resolved on horses instead, and Nathan has encouraged him, saying that horses are nimbler, and that is important on rough roads or when loads can shift. A teamster and his son have joined us, and they are lending their expertise as well.

I must close this letter, as Albany seems the last place on the trail I can post any type of mail.

Your Servant, Jonathan Russell

Ruth scanned the letter again. *I am responsible for Mr. Shirley's departure.* Yes, she ought to forgive him—in fact, it was probably all for the best—but her pulse throbbed in her ears. Jonathan Russell was a cheeky fellow, to ask for prayer and then forgiveness as an afterthought.

Frowning, she blew out the candle and climbed into bed, gathering up the cold blankets around her, waiting for the warmth to come.

Albany. There were on their way north, in the winter. Ruth put her anger aside and began to pray.

JONATHAN PULLED his cap over his ears and peered across the gray expanse of water. "I dinna see them."

"Two days to get there and back," Nathan said. "And it's only been two days. No telling how long to get the things in the boats."

Lake George was thirty miles long, but narrow, with multiple islands crowding the channel. Ice fringed the shore and a gray mist hung over the water. Knox had taken several dozen boats, of every size and shape, to fetch the artillery from the fort at the other end.

Jonathan and Nathan trudged back to the palisade. The tumbledown fortification had been erected during the French War and was now manned by a handful of ill-fed soldiers. A single large cabin served as an inn. Supposedly there was a British prisoner here, waiting to be exchanged.

Knox's men slept in six-man tents in front of the fort. The Russells' own tiny tent was sheltered nearby under a tree. As they drew near, the horses nickered a greeting.

Jonathan scratched behind Brutus's ear and noticed a man approaching them.

It was the head teamster, Mr. Becker. "Sleds will do us no good without snow."

They'd exchanged the wagons for sleds in Albany.

Two inches covered the ground, but Jonathan knew what he meant. They'd need a foot of snow just to cover the ruts in the road. The air was moist, and a cold snap might bring snow. Without it they were marooned here. "Let's ask the innkeeper what he thinks about the weather."

They ducked into the closest thing Fort George had to a tavern. The best part about the place was the hearth, which allowed the men to warm up, for the price of a cup of ale. A very overpriced cup.

A man in a red coat occupied a seat in one corner. A British uniform. Jonathan stiffened. This must be the prisoner. The sight of the blue facings running down the front of the man's red coat brought him back to Boston and the horrible stone wall. Red uniforms advancing, swarming, bayonets flashing—only to fall in heaps like gory snowdrifts. Jonathan had taken aim at blue facings before.

But this man was peaceful, unarmed, waiting calmly for his exchange.

Jonathan took a ragged breath and forced himself to be polite. "Jonathan Russell, at your service."

The stranger looked up, dark eyes in a handsome face. Surprisingly, he stood and executed a modest leg. "Lieutenant John André, at your service."

Jonathan presented his brother. Becker had ignored the soldier and was now speaking to the innkeeper, a rough-looking man with a pipe jammed in the corner of his mouth.

"Are you acquainted with Mr. Henry Knox?" André asked. His boots were shiny and well-maintained, interesting considering the fact that he was a prisoner in a crude tavern, in a crude part of the world.

Jonathan couldn't help but respond. "We are traveling with him."

"Such an interesting fellow! A bookshop owner—how marvelous to meet someone like him. We spent a wonderful hour discussing literature."

"You find time to read?" Nathan could put anyone at ease, and Jonathan was glad he'd joined the conversation. Hostility crept up Jonathan's spine. Which made him feel guilty, because André seemed the likable sort, if a bit dandified.

"I do now," André replied with a smile. "Any favorite writers?"

"William Cowper and John Bunyan." Nathan proceeded to explain why, and soon they were deep in conversation.

Jonathan requested ale from the innkeeper and found a stool. He sagged against the rough, untrimmed log wall, wondering if the officer guessed what they were doing. Knox wouldn't have volunteered their mission.

He sipped his drink. It was preposterous to believe that the polished lieutenant sitting across from him was any threat, but Jonathan's hand knew the exact position of his knife and the tomahawk strapped to his waist.

He gulped down the watery ale, wishing for something stronger.

23

Hail, sovereign love, which first began
This scheme to rescue fallen man!
Hail, matchless, free, eternal grace,
Which gave my soul a hiding place!

—Jehoida Brewer, 1776, found in Major John André's possession at his death

*J*onathan left the tavern and made his way to the tree line and their tent. Several minutes later, Nathan joined him. His brother rummaged in his satchel and pulled out a sermon.

Then he dashed back to the cabin. Jonathan guessed the pamphlet was for the prisoner. He clenched his jaw, wrestling with his anger. Even redcoats had souls.

"He loves to share the Creator's words."

Jonathan jumped, his hand at his hip. "You startled me."

Red Hawk found a place to sit near their fire. "I have news."

"Are we in danger?"

"I will let you decide."

Nathan returned. "Sloan! Welcome!" Without another word, he stirred the dormant fire and ladled out a bowlful of stew for the man.

Red Hawk accepted it. "Joseph Brant has gone to London. It is clear the King desires the help of the red man, and the Mohawks are listening."

Jonathan scooped out a generous portion for himself. Cold weather kept him hungry.

Red Hawk ate several bites and laid his half-empty bowl in his lap, his face pensive. "The Six Nations are divided."

Jonathan's spoon slowed its motion. Didn't they already know this about the Iroquois?

"The Mohawk chief Steyawa was the one who attended the council in Albany and met with the white men. He told Schuyler that this conflict is 'a family affair' between the white man and his father across the great sea. But I have discovered that the other Mohawk chiefs disagreed."

This was important news. Henry Knox was relying on General Schuyler's information about the Indians. Jonathan set his bowl aside. "A division among the Mohawks?"

"Something terrible has happened in the Iroquois League. Along with the Oneidas and Tuscaroras, this chief and his men came to the Council Fire of the Harvest Moon, where all the Nations meet once a year. Here Steyawa was castigated for his crime. He had no right to make promises to Schuyler as he did in Albany without the sanction of the entire League."

Red Hawk gazed into space, as if contemplating the enormity of the crisis. "Steyawa is an old and esteemed chief. He did not accept the scathing denunciations of younger men. When they were finished speaking, he came to the fire and stared into it for a long time."

Red Hawk looked at Jonathan. "You must remember that a council fire is a sacred thing, like the peace pipe. And the council fire of the Six Nations has endured for hundreds of years.

"Steyawa shouted, 'There is no more Iroquois League!' He marched into the fire, kicking and thrashing until the wood and coals were scattered and the fire died down. Then rain poured from the heavens and every trace of the fire was extinguished. It is a terrible omen, and word has spread."

"What does this mean for us?" Jonathan asked.

"It would be worse if every red man's hand were against you. As it is, Brant's men will obey the King, I am sure. But he's in London. Even those

Mohawk who would be hostile to us would not attack now. They will wait for Brant to return."

Jonathan's sinews relaxed. That was good news for the expedition. Providence had smiled on them.

Red Hawk handed his bowl back to Nathan. "My thanks. I will tell you one more thing. Returning, I came upon a man who invited me to join the Tyron County militia. I told him I scouted for Washington. He said to tell him the folks of the backcountry no longer wanted a redress of wrongs. They want independency. 'This is our country,' he said. 'Tell him that. We want a new nation.'

"I do not pretend to understand omens and providences. But one thing I can see without calling myself a prophet—the red man's sun is setting, but the white man's is rising."

Nathan studied Red Hawk's face. "And you do not know what to think, because you walk in the place between."

∾

THE LETTER WAS POSTMARKED New York, but Ruth wondered. Boston's postal service had been suspended, and yet messengers came and went. It was impossible to know exactly where this letter had come from. She slid her nail under the wax and broke the seal.

Dear Ruth,

I am alive. At one point I had my doubts as to my survival, but first, let me explain. We are hauling artillery, I suppose you guessed. You remember my brother's horses. They were chosen to haul the heaviest cannon, a bronze monster, but Nathan says it's about the same weight as a loaded Conestoga. But on a sled—well, I think even he had concerns. One morning, we woke to a cold so dreadful I feared for the animals—we hired over one hundred horses plus a few oxen, all told. Nathan harnessed the horses, but the sled wouldn't budge because the runners had frozen into the icy snow. "Gee!" His voice carried in the frigid air like music, and the horses leaped to the right as one. "Haw!" And they lunged left, and a great crack echoed from the trees. The sled was free. We made good time that day.

As we approached Albany we came upon a new problem. The terrible cold had frozen the river, so that when we needed to cross even a heavy cannon could traverse the ice safely. But it warmed, and the ice thinned, and it was hard to tell how much. At this point I was walking alongside the sled, a pole in my hand, and a rope wrapped around it. We thought to steady the sled in case of a slip by slamming the pole into the ground. We were also ready with knives and tomahawks to cut the horses loose should the worst happen when crossing the river.

Well, it did. The ice splintered beneath us, and the cannon, which we had named Big Martha, began to sink. I dove for the traces and sliced through the harness with my hatchet, but as a result I ended up underwater, in a dark and freezing place. I must have kicked myself to the surface, for the next thing I knew, Nathan had me by the hand. It was several hours before I recovered and the harness was mended. Amazingly, the people of Albany poured out to assist us, and we managed to save the cannon too. It now has the more stately name of "Albany."

But that wasn't the last of our troubles. Poor Lady Jane strained a tendon as we went through hilly country. She is an amazing wheel horse and became quite upset when we replaced her with Brutus, who'd been kept in reserve for such an event. She nipped him and crowded him and finally Nathan simply rode her close alongside, taking up the reins from her back. Foolish animal. We saved her life but she showed no gratitude.

I close this letter for now, grateful myself that our trek is almost over. We lost no men or cannon, and I still marvel at Knox's achievement. I hope it will do some good in the end.

Your Cousin, Jonathan

Ruth traced the loops of his handwriting with her finger, her pulse thudding. So close it had been! Moisture sprang to her eyes. Did she care for him so much?

Her feelings surprised her. She folded the letter and clasped it to her chest.

Thank you, Lord.

THE FULL MOON cast eerie shadows over the trampled ground, slushy with old snow and cold mud. Behind them in Roxbury, several cannon spoke in unison, startling Brutus, and Jonathan murmured nonsense as he stroked the creature's head. Ahead, a man whispered commands to his oxen, and the cargo dipped and slid along on its journey to Dorchester Heights.

It was a preposterous end to a preposterous effort. Every cannon had survived the trip—even the largest, the Albany—and now the ultimate goal was so close.

The British warships bottling up Boston harbor would wake in the morning to artillery trained on them from above. As long as Knox's plans remained secret, unobserved.

Every tool was tied in rags, lanterns were shuttered, and only the snorts of animals and creaks of axles marked the movement of hundreds of men. The cannons were here, ready to be placed on fortifications, but the March ground was frozen. Unsurprisingly, Knox had a plan.

Jonathan's horse was hauling barrels filled with sand. They would be placed behind the wooden fortifications they were making, ready to roll down the hill and stop any attack by British regulars. Behind him, Nathan's team hauled timber frames which, once filled with bundles of sticks and baskets of gravel, could stop small arms' fire as well as earthen breastworks.

Artillery fire barked behind them—a few of the Ticonderoga guns had been placed at Roxbury and other locations. They now bombarded Boston, a noisy diversion to keep the sharp British lookouts from noticing what they were doing.

It seemed impossible that they wouldn't.

A clatter of dropped tools sounded preternaturally loud, and Jonathan cringed. Guns roared behind him, hopefully serving to distract from the sound. He darted a glance toward the harbor and saw twin flashes over the water, illuminating a warship. Twin shells traced fiery arcs across the dark expanse.

Boom! Roxbury answered. And so it would go.

The moon brooded almost directly above. Half the night was gone. A frisson of urgency snaked down his spine.

Another five minutes and they reached the place where General Thomas was directing construction. Then back for another load. Then up the slope again. Brutus began to grumble, and Jonathan paused to water the beast.

Then he saw Knox. The man now wore a uniform and the rank of colonel.

"We are ready."

That needed no interpretation. The fantastic fortifications—their design spotted in a military book and created in a few hours under strange conditions, were now ready to receive several dozen artillery, including the Albany.

Jonathan harnessed Brutus to one of the smaller guns, and Nathan backed his team before the Albany.

"Just one more trip, fella, and we'll get their goose." Jonathan stroked his stallion's nose, then led him forward.

The moon was hanging over the trees in the west when a new swarm of men silently took the places of those who had worked all night. The exhausted teamsters and carpenters melted away.

Jonathan's hands were stiff, his body damp and clammy from sweat despite the cold, and he wished for a place to collapse into sleep.

But not just yet. He sat on the end of the now-empty cart, watching the activity, as Brutus dozed in his traces. Ammunition was hauled to each gun, and the groups of men resolved into artillery teams, their long rammers and botefois catching the last light of the moon.

A silhouetted man on horseback inspected the line. It was Washington, whose quiet encouragements had animated the tired men all night.

Jonathan nodded off, and when he opened his eyes the moon was gone, and the quiet hush of pre-dawn settled over the knoll. An easy clop of hooves made him turn.

Washington was still there. "Remember the fifth of March!" he bellowed.

A murmur rose in response. Jonathan had forgotten the date. Today was the anniversary of the Massacre.

Washington's mount trotted along the line. "Avenge the death of your brethren."

Huzzahs greeted the dawn.

24

I went to bed after 12 but got no rest. The cannon continued firing, and my heart kept pace with them all night.

    —Abigail Adams, letter to her husband John

Boston, March 1776

*S*pyglass in hand, Robert climbed the steps of Faneuil Hall in the gray dawn, his regimentals as stiff and unfamiliar as his new rank of captain. He'd done nothing to deserve the promotion, but he suspected the earl had been practical as well as generous in purchasing the commission: an aide-de-camp with the lowly rank of lieutenant was ludicrous.

When his cousin had given him his trunk packed with his uniform, along with a captain's insignia, he'd mistaken Robert's smile for gladness at the promotion. Robert hadn't corrected his impression. He was no longer spying, and that was a huge relief.

The hush from the hills around Boston was almost deafening after the long night. Irregular artillery fire from Roxbury had turned the town into a madhouse, with the remaining residents running out into the streets, sometimes coalescing into fire brigades, sometimes simply screaming. Others ran up to officers with impossible demands.

Robert was tired, and his eyes felt grainy, but there was no doubting what he'd seen.

He passed through the inner door and spotted General Howe, bent over a map. Red-rimmed eyes looked up as he barked a command to an aide. Then he spotted Robert.

He lifted his hand in a salute. "General, I spotted a chandelier-style fortification on Dorchester Heights, the peninsula to the south. There are ... cannon."

Thirty-six cannon, Robert had counted them, but who would believe it?

Howe straightened. "Show me."

They went outside and strode quickly down the street to gain a better vantage. Robert handed the general his spyglass, but the man had already spotted the long dark smudge on the ridge. Orange light from the rising sun glinted off a string of round muzzles pointed their way.

Howe lifted the glass and was silent for half a minute.

"Where did these come from?"

"Ticonderoga?" Robert ventured.

"I fail to see how." He stared at the fortifications and shook his head. "The rebels have done more in one night than my whole army would have done in a month."

Admiral Shuldham joined them, and Howe handed him the spyglass.

After a brief survey, the admiral spoke. "We have an untenable situation."

"You have guns," Howe barked. "Blast them off the hill."

RUTH BREATHED DEEPLY of the April air and settled on the stoop in front of the shop, spreading her skirts. Linen-colored clouds lazed against the clean blue of the sky. In Rebecca's small garden to her left, the glad yellow heads of daffodils nodded above the tender green of phlox and geraniums, whose flowers would emerge later in the summer.

She tugged her shawl closer. In Boston, she would have needed a cloak at this time of year. Here in Philadelphia spring came earlier, and every day after the noon meal Ruth slipped out to breathe the fresh air. Twice she'd walked to the library, and once to the State House, but Rebecca had stayed indoors, where a red-faced newborn dominated the household. Christened

Mary, the baby girl brought a smile to her mother but a furrow of concern to her father, whose mind was already troubled by the conflict.

An open two-horse carriage jingled past, its narrow wheels dipping through a muddy spot on the cobblestones. Two weeks ago, a nor-easter had blown through, rain pummeling sideways and sending loose shutters into the streets. Deposits of mud were the only signs left of the gale.

A horse and rider turned from Fourth Street onto Walnut.

That horse—that tall form—it was Jonathan Russell. She swallowed, her heart hammering.

He was safe.

Jonathan approached slowly and reined in before her. "Hello."

His face was dusty and lined. Fine crow's feet bracketed his eyes—that was new. Or was it? How long had it been since she'd seen him? "Come, let me water your horse."

He dismounted and followed her down the lane to the Youngs' stable. "Thank ye kindly."

She spoke to the stableboy and soon Brutus faced a bucket of grain and an armful of hay. "He looks thin."

Her words sounded weak to her ears, inconsequential, when she really wanted to know so much more.

"They all are," Jonathan said. "The horses, I mean. Nathan took the Conestogas to my uncle's farm across the Schuylkill. We … we plan to stay for a few days, at least. They need to graze."

They walked back out to the street.

"You wrote that Lady Jane was hurt."

His head bobbed eagerly—too eagerly. "It's dangerous for a horse to strain a tendon like that. Nathan may retire her."

"Oh?"

"On top of which—" He stopped altogether, his expression comical.

"Lady Jane will be well, won't she?"

"Lady Jane will have a foal in a few months."

She smiled. "That should be good news."

"Oh no, Nathan near smacked me." He looked at the street, his boots. "Brutus is the sire."

"I see," she said, then thought quickly. There was one way they could continue a private conversation. "Would you escort me to the State House? After such a long winter, a walk sounds fine."

Awkwardly, he extended his arm and she took it. It was a few minutes before they spoke again, though Ruth was bursting with curiosity about Boston. She knew the siege was broken, but the news was sparse.

"I need to ask your forgiveness," he said. "About Mr. Shirley."

"I forgive you."

He slowed. "I mean—you do?"

"Yes."

"I was going to explain that I had to tell him to leave, but, well—"

"It was a difficult decision."

"Precisely." His gaze traveled over her face. "You understand hard choices, don't you?"

She hooked his elbow and jerked him along. "Tell me what happened. The *Gazette* said the British left Boston. I want the details."

Jonathan slowed again. "Henry Knox and General Putnam had a military book."

Of course Henry had a book. She smiled. "That does not surprise me."

"The ground was frozen, and we couldn't dig ordinary fortifications. The book described special breastworks made out of wood and gravel. We built those in one night, secretly, and mounted the cannon right above the harbor —right above all those warships."

The ships would be vulnerable. "I see."

"The frigates bombarded us in the morning, but most of the shot fell short—Dorchester Heights is too high, you see. We knew Howe would have to attack, there was no way he could let the guns threaten his ships. So, we prepared for another battle like the one at Bunker's hill."

They arrived at the State House, and for a few moments Jonathan's gaze traveled over the archways and clocktower.

"The Congress meets here," Ruth said.

Jonathan's lips parted. Then he seemed to collect himself. "The truth of it was, we hadn't the powder to do much. A few cannonades, a day's battle —that was it."

Ruth's heart quickened, imagining the tension. "And then?"

His eyes glistened. "The most amazing thing. A storm hit, and not an ordinary storm. Powerful, like something ye'd read about in the Bible. General Howe took his men and left."

Ruth recalled their own storm. Philadelphia had been affected too. "The whole army? All the ships?"

"Well, some ships were abandoned and scuttled. But many of those had stores in them. The British sailed so fast, they left horses, hay, goods—many of the houses and shops were damaged, but General Washington was pleased overall. Most of the Tories left with Howe, but some stayed and pled for mercy, which of course our commander-in-chief granted."

A familiar man came through the State House door and approached Ruth with a smile.

"Dr. Rush, my cousin, Jonathan Russell." She made the introductions. "Dr. Benjamin Rush."

Without preamble, Dr. Rush opened his satchel and pulled out a sheet.

"A new design." He handed it to Ruth. "What do you think?"

Thirteen stars were sketched on the canton in place of the Union Jack. "I like the stars in lieu of the British flag," she said. "What is the color scheme?"

The sketch was black and white. Jonathan stepped closer and peered at it.

"Blue ground. White stars," Dr. Rush said.

"Thirteen stars for thirteen colonies," Jonathan said approvingly.

"Thirteen is a difficult number to arrange," Ruth pointed out. The sketch was indifferently done, five-pointed stars tossed haphazardly over a square. The stripes were the same as before.

"I'm sure you ladies will find a way." The physician smiled. "I'll leave this with you." He excused himself and left.

"Ye make flags?" A teasing smile played on Jonathan's lips. "*Patriot* flags?"

"'Tis the King's fault I have no position. I must earn my keep somehow."

He thrust out his elbow for her to take. "And so ye must."

RUTH SLID her needle into the blue wool. According to the *Gazette,* General Howe and all the men and ships had retreated to Halifax, but no one imagined they were gone for good. She was almost finished with the last star of this flag—three across, then two, then three, then two, and then a final row of three. It was the best arrangement they'd thought of so far and possessed a pleasing symmetry.

The Youngs' parlor was filled with wool bunting of various colors. Sitting across from her, Rebecca joined a long strip of red to white. "Have you reached a conclusion about Thomas Paine's *Common Sense?*"

While sewing, their conversation flitted from recipes to politics and back again.

"It shocked me at first, but I told you that already. Paine rejects the very idea of kingship, of monarchy, and that seems to go against the New Testament."

Rebecca laughed. "The man classes kings with ruffians! But he does make a good case."

"His case is partly based on Israel's mistake in asking for a king. That kings are heathenish. But if you take Romans chapter thirteen in the balance, I think his argument is more descriptive than directive."

"What?"

Ruth chuckled. "In other words, kings may be heathenish, but that does not justify rebellion." She tied off the last stitch.

"What does? The king's tyrannical actions?" Rebecca raised a brow.

"Hmm. Perhaps. You know I still wrestle with that."

"I hear they are debating independency even now."

Ruth swallowed and held her peace as she finished the last stitches. She held up the canton for inspection. "Care to sew the next one?"

"Nay, I know you enjoy that task. As long as you do the cutting."

"Certainly." The flags were large and the material cumbersome. They had to cut the wool for the stripes on the floor. "Although the next one is silk—and smaller."

The next flag was meant to carry into battle as a standard, and silk was lighter than the wool bunting they were using. Ruth pictured the banner snapping above a clearing while muskets fired and cannon boomed. Smoke cloaked the landscape, then thinned to reveal dead bodies—bloody bodies, scores of them.

Men—husbands and fathers and sons, lifeless on the grass. Would Jonathan be one of them?

Ruth blinked the nightmare away. Thomas Paine and so many in Congress were set in their convictions, firm in their course, yet the end of that way was death.

Was it worth it?

~

"PAPA?"

Ruth's father stood on the Youngs' doorstep, smiling. "Come with me to the State House." He extended his arm.

Ruth tied her hat under her chin. Spring had melted into summer, and the gardens of Philadelphia celebrated with pink and purple. Even Rebecca ventured outdoors with baby Mary for short distances. But gauging from Papa's face, something had happened.

The peal of a church bell startled her as they crossed Third Street. Today was Monday, not Sunday.

Several more churches joined in, a cacophony in brass, a joyously random rhythm.

People poured out onto the walks and overflowed into the street. The clatter of iron-shod hooves on the cobblestones announced approaching carriages. A clot of women dressed in Quaker brown emerged from Fourth Street and headed toward the State House. Men in coat and cravat mingled with dirty apprentices, all striding in one direction.

"Papa?" Ruth began to suspect the reason for the public meeting—for clearly, that's what it was. Rumor had it that Congress was debating independence from the mother country.

"Careful." Her father guided her around the corner. A crowd spilled around the State House, on the lawn and in the street. Carriages and wagons blocked traffic. They drew as near as they could and waited in the July sunshine.

Finally, a man walked through the main door, a document under his arm. He stood on a modest platform and unrolled a parchment.

The crowd settled and hushed as they all sought to hear.

"When in the course of human events it becomes necessary for one people to dissolve the political bands which have connected them with another and to assume among the powers of the earth, the separate and equal station to which the Laws of Nature and of Nature's God entitle them, a decent respect ..."

So, they had decided on independence. Ruth strove to take it in, to digest the words.

"We hold these truths to be self-evident, that all men are created equal, that they are endowed by their Creator with certain unalienable rights, that among these are life, liberty and the pursuit of happiness. That to secure these rights, governments are instituted among men, deriving their just powers from the consent of the governed ..."

The consent of the governed? But yes, even Rutherford would have agreed with the sense of this document.

Tears filled her eyes as she listened to a long litany of the King's abuses. No longer was blame laid on Parliament or the "Ministry." The veil of careful speaking was swept away.

This declaration was treason. But it was also the nucleus of a government.

A government.

The reading finished with a record of the signers. Ruth turned away before he finished, struggling with her thoughts. For a long time, her heart had been torn—rebellion was sinful. Rulers could be evil, but God was the one to raise them up and set them down.

Now Pennsylvania—Massachusetts—Virginia—all the colonies—had formed a new nation, with a government. Great shuddering sobs rose from her chest and spilled out her throat. Ruth thrust her hand into her pocket but found no handkerchief. She wiped her eyes with the back of her sleeve.

The cheerful crowd swirled around her, and an elbow jostled her. Her hat became dislodged, and she restored it clumsily. Where was Papa? Somehow she'd lost track of him. She began to stumble home, but before she reached Walnut Street a man in a dark coat appeared in her path.

"May I help you?" The face was kindly over a starched collar, like a minister's.

Her mind spun. "The document—the Declaration—"

"Lass, does it trouble ye?"

The Scottish cadence of his voice warmed her, reminding her of Jonathan. "Nay, the opposite." She wiped her eyes with her fingers. Why was she speaking to a stranger? But it was a strange day. Her world was upside down.

"Here." He handed her a handkerchief.

"*Lex, Rex.*" She was babbling. "Samuel Rutherford. I know I make no sense, but he would have approved."

"Ye make perfect sense to me."

"You have read him?" As soon as she asked the question, Ruth felt foolish. He looked like an educated man. And he was Scottish. Wasn't Rutherford Scottish?

"I have a copy of the treatise ye mention in my library." His mouth twitched into a half-smile. "I have a great regard for Rutherford."

Ruth wiped her eyes again. "Then you understand the implications."

"And what are those?" he asked as a tutor would drill a student.

"We now have a government and can resist tyranny lawfully. Of course, the colonies had governments before this, individually, but they were *colonies* of another country. Now they are nations—states—and we are a union of states."

"These United States. Of course, we must fight for the right to be such." The smile disappeared and the man looked off into the distance. "If we lose, we are colonies once again and every traitor hanged." He returned his gaze to her face. "Every man—and woman—must count the cost. Is your life and safety worth more than liberty from tyranny? Better to settle it ahead of time than put your hand to the plow and turn back."

"Will we win?" She asked softly, wondering if he heard her over the hubbub.

"Only by the help of heaven. I believe our cause is just. But God's ways are not our ways. One thing I have learned in my sojourn here is that the Almighty is faithful, and He will carry you through the dark times. Trust in Him."

Tears filled her eyes. "Thank you."

The stranger took his leave, and another man took his place.

"Dr. Rush!" She wiped her face, realizing she still had the stranger's handkerchief.

"I see you have made the acquaintance of Dr. Witherspoon. A dear friend."

"A physician?"

"Oh no. He's a former president of the Presbyterian college at Princeton, and he serves as chaplain to Congress." His eyes followed Witherspoon's form as it disappeared in the crowd. "He signed the Declaration." His gaze met hers. "Pray as you never have. The die is cast. We are all dead men if caught. Traitors to the Crown."

"Thank you. Thank you for this … Declaration." Ruth couldn't explain what this document meant to her. But her insides felt light as air.

25

These are the times that try men's souls. The summer soldier and the sunshine patriot will, in this crisis, shrink from the service of their country; but he that stands by it now, deserves the love and thanks of man and woman. Tyranny, like hell, is not easily conquered ...

—Thomas Paine, *Common Sense*

Staten Island, August 1776

The gibbet loomed large and ugly above the rows of grenadiers standing at attention. Lord Rawdon dismounted behind them, and Robert followed suit. Though the British camp on Staten Island was swollen with new arrivals, the usual smells were minimal as the latrines were still new.

As was the gibbet, crude gallows probably slapped together that morning. Sweating under the noon sun, Robert longed to run his finger under his stock to quell the itching but dared not, as he was an officer, and it mattered not that he wasn't in command of these men. He kept his face impassive, his manner and posture correct.

He spotted a man on the platform with his hands bound, presumably the wretch about to be hanged. A clergyman was speaking to him.

"Desertion?" Robert asked.

Rawdon kept his gaze forward and replied in an undertone. "Too much beef. The men are well fed."

Robert rubbed the leather of the reins between his fingers. Several new regiments had established camp here, and morale was high due to good food supplied by local farmers, mostly loyal to the Crown. Shipboard conditions were always abominable and the food execrable, and the infantrymen rejoiced in fresh air and rations. But how did beef—?

At the tree line stood a girl. Apron fluttering in the breeze, she stood next to a man dressed like a farmer, presumably a family member.

"Lasses here are not as generous as their fathers."

Robert's stomach curled. He was no prude, but Rawdon disgusted him. The man's lechery was not unusual; he boasted of amorous conquests just like his friend Tarleton. Even General Howe flaunted a mistress—a married woman.

Rawdon's chin jerked in the girl's direction. "She's pressed charges, you see."

The rope settled upon the grenadier's shoulders, and the hangman, a sweating corporal, awkwardly tightened the knot.

The girl's companion—probably her father—pressed her face to his chest.

Robert wished he could turn away.

He was no longer a spy, but his new role pinched him like ill-fitting shoes.

BRISTLING SHIPS' masts dominated the view of the harbor as they returned. Robert tried not to think of the hanging.

What would he do, where would he go, if he could sell his commission? Raise horses? The earl's generosity might make that possible. Seabreeze had foaled again.

Maybe one day.

The horses eased into a trot and ate up the distance to the shore, where a flatboat would take them to the Howe's flagship, the *Eagle*. The harbor was filled with ships of every description. Last week mercenaries from the German state of Hesse had augmented the number of regulars now thronging the island. And yesterday more thousands of regulars had arrived under Sir Parker.

Sir George Germain, the new Secretary of the Colonies, had wasted no time in mobilizing a fleet of warships packed with men. Ironically, General Howe had sent out a peace overture to Washington just yesterday. Howe was authorized to grant pardons for treason, but no more than that.

He meant well, Robert decided. Knowing the colonists, they'd think such an offer an insult.

Once on board, he accompanied Rawdon amidships, where a canvas awning created a shelter for a table and chairs. Howe relaxed next to Mrs. Loring, his mistress. Eyelids drooping, Lord Percy slouched on the other side of the table.

A dragoon scurried up the plank. "Sir, General, sir." The lieutenant was pop-eyed and nervous, a missive clutched in his hand.

Howe waved him closer. "What is it?"

Mrs. Loring ignored the commotion, fanning her pink cheeks, but Lord Percy opened a sleepy eye.

"Mr. Washington refused the letter. Said 'twas incorrectly directed—"

"What?" Howe straightened. Percy looked interested.

"The form of address, the title. Said it should be *General* Washington, not Mister."

Howe blinked, and even Mrs. Loring's fan slowed.

"Sounds like vanity to me." Rawdon gave a correct bow.

Howe's face remained impassive. The man rarely lost his temper. Robert decided to take a chance. "I respectfully disagree. There is a practical reason to acquiesce, in my view."

Percy roused. "Which is?"

"I have seen the man. He is no bumpkin, and I doubt if vanity is his sole motive."

Howe toyed with his cup. "You gave Dartmouth intelligence, did you not?"

"Yes, sir. After this Declaration of theirs, they wish to style themselves independent. Subject to the ordinary usages of war. Military titles are part of the whole."

Howe's gaze remained fixed on him, and Robert found himself sweating anew, but not from the heat.

"I suggest 'twill benefit both parties if you humor him. If we maintain them to be mere criminals, and treat prisoners accordingly, our own will suffer. This way, we can set up exchanges when necessary. We would desire our own men returned."

Eyebrows raised, Percy addressed Howe. "I agree. If Germain fusses, you have a practical explanation."

Howe harrumphed. "Give me that."

In three minutes, the missive bore the correct form of address, the dragoon was dismissed, and Robert found himself at the stern with Rawdon.

Robert's heart was still pounding.

Rawdon's lip curled. "Took a chance. But he bit. There's hope for you yet."

"Hmm." His cousin judged others by his own ambitions. Robert looked past the forest of masts to the hills beyond. "'Tis a big country."

"We have the navy, the manpower, the munitions. How can you doubt?"

"They will be crushed. But I believe it will be more difficult than some think."

Rawdon leaned on the rail. "I hear the leader of the Mohawks was fêted in London. They will fight for the Crown."

Robert winced. Savages wielding tomahawks didn't seem like honorable allies. And Hessian mercenaries? How could the "mother country" hire foreign soldiers to fight her supposed children and expect any affection at all?

No, affection was dead. Dead and buried.

Hannah's face came to mind. He feared for her and her family. His own prayers went no higher than the canvas of his tent, but perhaps another—

Yes. He'd write his godmother tonight.

JONATHAN CROSSED two faded dry corn husks and grabbed another ear to start the plait. Women usually braided the corn at harvest time, but he enjoyed seeing a long string emerge from his hands.

Mother carried a steaming covered dish to the long plank table set up under the walnut tree. The savory aroma made his mouth water. He had also heard talk of apple pie, but they wouldn't eat just yet. It was only mid-afternoon.

Nearby, Hannah and Nathan stripped corn of their husks and added to the pile at Jonathan's elbow. Beyond them, the Robinsons tackled another pile of harvested corn. At the end of the harvest season, the laborious shucking was turned into a frolic of sorts for the families around Russell's Ridge, with food and even games for the children.

He folded more papery husks together, then added another. The pattern was soothing. Glancing up, he spotted one of the Robinson lads talking to Jane MacLeod near the barn. In Jonathan's opinion, Jane could do better.

Rip, rip, rip. Hannah's quick rhythm broke into the haze of his thoughts. Her hands grabbed each ear as if at war with it. *Rip, rip, rip.*

"Hannah?"

Her brows lifted. *Rip, rip, rip.*

"Troubled by something?" He reached for another ear.

She snorted. *Rip, rip, rip.* She flung each stripped ear into the pile at his feet. "Washington. He's retreated."

Jonathan blinked several times. In his opinion, New York was a lost cause. But Washington had taken his men south after Howe pulled out of Boston. "Ye're upset because the man retreated?"

Hannah swallowed. "I suppose he had to. And—and—they say Providence smiled on him, sending a fog to cover the retreat, but—"

Nathan tossed an ear to Jonathan. "A fog?"

The *Gazette* had made no mention of an unusual fog. "Who says?"

"Ruth. I had a letter from her yesterday."

Jonathan's hands stilled. "Ye didna read it to us."

Hannah made a face at him. "The harvest."

For the past several weeks family devotions had been minimal. Everyone worked, ate, listened to a brief passage, prayed, and fell into bed. There'd been no time for other reading or discussion.

Nathan picked up an ear and slowly pulled off the withered husk. "What did she say?"

"Ruth has changed her mind. Or rather, she's banished her doubts."

Jonathan paused in his work. "What do you mean?"

"The Declaration settled it for her. We can lawfully resist tyranny because we now have a government. We have magistrates."

Could it be? "We had magistrates before now."

Nathan stripped another ear. "It's an answer to prayer. I'd hoped she'd settle it one way or another."

"Surely ye canna mean the Tories are right."

Nathan cut him a glance. "Every man must be convinced in his own mind. A clear conscience is a great treasure. What a good woman she is, to have such a tender heart, and yet by long wrestlings she has settled it."

Jonathan toyed with a husked ear. By whatever means, Ruth was now a Patriot. He tried to take it in. It was hard to imagine not arguing over this. Perhaps they'd fight over something else. Affection swelled in his breast. Perhaps they wouldn't fight at all. "Hannah, that's good news. What's eating you?"

Hannah got to her feet and brushed corn silk from her skirts more vigorously than necessary. "He's losing. We're losing. And Ruth says the enlistments are up at the end of the year. There will be no more army. No more country." She looked to be on the verge of tears.

The image of Ruth's face filled Jonathan's mind. "How far is it from New York City to Philadelphia?" A rhetorical question. They'd made the trip several times.

"Just one hundred miles." Nathan's gaze locked with his with comprehension. "I suspect Washington's men need supplies."

"I reckon they do."

Hannah's face lit.

Jonathan felt for his sister. "No, ye canna come. But we'll need help. It's a good time of year to ask folks for donations—we'll go after the hogs are slaughtered."

Yes, they would help with supplies, but more was needed—so much more. The British Army was mere days from Philadelphia—and Ruth. He pushed away the image of Red's broken remains on Bunker's hill.

Duty called him, nightmares or no. "And I'll lend Washington my rifle."

26

The time is near at hand which must probably determine whether Americans are to be freemen or slaves ... the fate of untold millions will now depend, under God, on the courage and conduct of this army.
—General George Washington

December 1776

The fence was completely obliterated. In the field beyond, Jonathan could see where the rails had gone, as there were circular dark splotches in the snow.

Old campfires.

"We've found the army," he said unnecessarily. He urged Brutus forward, and Nathan followed in the wagon, the wheels scrunching on the snowy ground as they left the road. The smell of shallow latrines threaded through the air, not nearly as bad, Jonathan suspected, as what it would be in summer.

A blind man could follow this trail. Past the fields, they made their way through a copse of trees, denuded of all low-hanging branches.

Jonathan didn't know what Nathan thought of his decision to head straight to the camp without stopping to see the Hayneses and Aunt Betsy in Philadelphia. His brother had merely grunted assent to the suggestion. But the truth was, Jonathan's feelings were ambivalent regarding Ruth. The way was clear to court her—they were of one mind about the Cause—but the other thing, the dark secret, well … He couldn't marry a woman without laying bare his heart.

And he wasn't ready to confess *that*.

In the next field Nathan pulled the horses to a halt, slipped off the wagon seat, and grabbed something on the ground. "Shoes." He lifted what used to be a stout pair of boots, the soles detached from the uppers, clinging by mere threads.

"Ye're collecting rubbish, are ye?"

"I've harness leather, and a buckskin in here somewhere. I can repair them."

"One pair of shoes?" Jonathan was cynical. Even their wagonload of supplies would barely make a dent in the needs of just one regiment.

"Only one pair, but it would make a world of difference to one man."

After an hour they spotted gray threads of smoke rising above the trees. A man with a musket over his shoulder squinted at them dubiously.

"Password?"

Jonathan shrugged. "Come to join, me and my brother Nathan. And our rifles."

The sentry caught sight of the supplies in the wagon and his suspicion faded. "You got rum? It's mighty cold out here."

Nathan tossed him an apple. "Who's quartermaster?"

Once past another stand of trees they came upon tents pitched in a haphazard fashion over a field. Men huddled before fires. Few of them seemed dressed for the weather.

Beyond stood a house guarded by a scattershot array of men, like a lad's clumsy attempt to line up his lead soldiers. The door opened, and a man came down the steps dressed like an officer. He was tall and broad.

And warmly familiar.

Colonel Henry Knox's cheeks glowed red in the cold air. "We've several Virginia regiments here." His gaze fastened on the horses and he grinned. "Surely the quartermaster has no need of these lovely animals."

Jonathan returned his smile, though the sight of the ragged army had blackened his spirits. "Nathan?"

"My horses remember artillery, sir."

"I've sixteen guns." Knox scrubbed his jaw with a paw-like hand. "And some of my animals are overburdened." His expression turned mischievous. "And, of course, if I capture more cannon, I may need more animals."

The large man explained that they were going against the Hessian stronghold at Trenton, just across the river.

"I'll lend you my horse too." Jonathan decided to march with the others. He was no officer nor cavalryman and had no need of a horse during a battle.

Knox's face lit. Nathan agreed to mind Brutus—anyone could guide the Conestoga geldings, which knew their business better than most men.

Jonathan removed his gear and bedroll from his horse and carried it to a group of men he'd noticed on arrival. They seemed to belong to no particular regiment and looked half-dead with fatigue.

He neared their fire and threw a few sticks into the flames. "Howdy."

Their beaten appearance depressed him. Like Ezekiel's vision of dead bones one had to ask—*can these bones live?* Can this army win a single battle? They were all dead men—or worse, crushed men—if they didn't win this struggle.

A man looked up, his young face weary, but his eyes showed life. "Welcome to our fire. Regiment?"

"Thought I'd join Daniel Morgan, but he isna here."

"John Greenwood, twenty-sixth Massachusetts." He reached into his haversack and pulled out a fife. "My usual task—but they say the musicians are to fight tomorrow."

The musket at the man's elbow was battered and scratched. His clothing was thin, and his shoes had loose soles, flapping and nearly useless.

"Eaten yet?" The men here looked too exhausted to cook, and Jonathan saw no women attending to them as the other regiments had.

"Not much—we arrived yesterday. From Montreal."

Jonathan was speechless. No wonder their shoes were destroyed. He scanned the group and found one or two who still looked hearty. "Come, we'll fix supper."

As he worked he grappled with the stark sacrifice these men were making. He'd made his own decision to act, yet never imagined such suffering as part of the fighting. He'd seen bullet wounds outside of Boston, seemingly a lifetime ago, but this was different.

Two pounds of parched corn were soon cooking in a large kettle finagled from a camp follower. It would make a good gruel for these men. Jonathan used his knife to shave bits of jerky into the pot. Men began to stir. Some rose and added roots and scraps from their rations.

His heart squeezed at the sight. Hannah said Washington was losing, but she couldn't see this—the broken shoes, the skimpy rations. It all seemed pointless—and yet, he knew the cause was just. He had to do what he could.

Nathan arrived and repaired the shoes of several men.

Waiting for the stew to finish, Jonathan looked skyward, wondering if the weather would hold. Mare's tails covered the east, an ominous sign. He turned west, and his heart sank. The sky was red.

These men would die. Maybe they would all die.

He swallowed. He wanted to live, to make a life with Ruth, if he could ever come to that place. But maybe it was not meant to be.

THE NEXT DAY'S march was confusing, with starts and stops. Once Jonathan caught a glimpse of General Washington as he rode up and down the lines on his stallion. Nathan was out of sight, with the artillery near the front of the strung-out procession.

Jonathan kept an eye on the Massachusetts men. Some left bloody tracks in the snow. With an army like this, what could they hope to achieve?

The weather held until they reached the Delaware River at sunset. The sight of the ice-choked water sent a shudder down his spine. Then darkness fell, the clouds occluding the moon. He could see nothing. Rain lashed their faces, then sleet, then snow as the temperature plummeted.

Ahead, boats creaked and watermen shouted. Jonathan gave no thought to the coming battle and focused on the next few minutes, the next few steps, and the men who clustered around him as if for courage.

The lading took forever. While waiting their turn, one man fell out to the side, half frozen, and lay prostrate in the snow. Jonathan took out a blanket from his bedroll, roused and covered the militiaman, and forced him to walk in circles until he no longer felt sleepy.

His comrades clustered around in support, though most of them were nearly as bad off.

Finally it was their turn to be transported. The evacuation of Long Island might be a miracle, but if anything, the Lord's hand seemed to be against them here.

Then Jonathan heard Henry Knox's bellow above the sound of the wind. The huge bookshop owner was in charge of the crossing. Hope rose in Jonathan's heart.

"Ye go in first, Mr. Greenwood, and I'll help this fellow."

By dint of encouraging words and helping hands, the Massachusetts militiamen clambered onto several broad-beamed river boats, and they were poled away from the invisible shore.

The crossing was eerie. Time and again the boatmen would fend off an ice floe with their poles. Once, a resounding thunk shuddered through the craft. The men crouched uncomfortably, unable to sit in the watery bottom, and ducking their heads to avoid the sharp bite of the icy wind.

Halfway across, light pierced the darkness. Fires had been lit on the opposite side. The men took courage. The boat bumped against the shore, and they half-crawled up the frozen bank.

The militiamen joined the others in demolishing a fence and throwing the rails into the building flames. They turned before it like rabbits on a spit, warming first their fronts, then their backs. No matter how great the fire roared, the heat wasn't enough to fully warm them, and yet Jonathan's heart swelled with thankfulness. They'd survived the crossing.

Greenwood's countenance glowed in the firelight, relief on his face.

After less than an hour's respite, barked commands penetrated the thick air, and the mass of men found their officers and coalesced into formation.

The road was so rutted beneath the snow that the men walked on the shoulder. Light from dark lanterns and the artillery men's torches shone intermittently through the swirling flakes. Jonathan felt his way along, listening to the breathing and soft curses of the men, grunts of the horses, and creaking of the artillery carts. They made their way by starts and stops, occasionally colliding with each other in the dark.

Suddenly, Greenwood was no longer at Jonathan's elbow. Fear rippled through Jonathan as he slowed and searched for the man.

"Anyone seen Greenwood, the fifer?"

The men of the Massachusetts regiment shrugged and sighed. No one knew.

Jonathan retraced their path. Hope was dimming when he almost fell over a dark shape.

It was Greenwood, sitting motionless on a tree stump.

"Hey, get up—ye'll freeze."

Jonathan chafed the man's arms and hands, then replaced the musket that had tumbled off into the snow. But there was little response. Desperate, Jonathan unwound his own thick scarf and wrapped Greenwood's neck and lower face.

"Get ye up, man!"

Greenwood stood and began to shake violently. Jonathan forced him to walk in a slow circle around the stump, but the man's legs were stiff. Then Jonathan caught a glimpse of his shoes.

The man's toes were visible through the broken leather.

"Sit down."

Greenwood obeyed.

Jonathan sat in the snowy verge and pulled off his boots. He exchanged his footwear with the fifer, knowing that fit was not an issue: his own feet were large.

He rose. Hopefully it wouldn't be far now. "Come, lad."

By the time they caught up with the rest of the regiment the front of the formation had halted.

Whispers and murmurs brought the news down the ranks. "Stirling's men are taking the river road. The rest follow Washington and Knox."

They were dividing up. They had to be close to the town.

As the men stumbled into sluggish movement, Jonathan realized that the darkness was not absolute. The outlines of hats and wrappers were visible in the eerie gloom.

Dawn was almost here. It was Christmas. Did Hessians celebrate Christmas? Were the Jägers ready for them? Total surprise was inconceivable.

A quarter hour later, the roadside became visible, but the sun was cloaked behind a wall of whiteness as the storm renewed its fury. The swirling snow changed into driving pellets. Jonathan could no longer feel his feet. It was all a cruel joke. They were marching to an icy doom.

Or perhaps the Hessians would find them and put them out of their misery.

A gray shape rode by—Washington, erect in the saddle. "On, boys! Onward!"

Then, horribly, the horse's hind legs slipped on the ice-covered verge. The commander-in-chief would be thrown.

Jonathan watched, stupefied, as Washington laid broad hands on the stallion's mane and jerked the great head back. The animal's center of weight shifted, and it regained its footing.

Gasps of astonishment rose from the regiment. But it wasn't just brute strength, Jonathan knew. He had just seen a demonstration of unusual horsemanship. The man was one with his beast.

The feat seemed to enliven the half-frozen, exhausted men. They straightened their shoulders and picked up the pace.

The next few minutes stretched long as Jonathan fought the wind and the brutal cold. It helped that they were strung out in several long columns, each man partially blocking the weather from the next.

He flexed his fingers, unwilling to trust them. How could he fight in a blizzard? How could he aim, shoot, and reload, not to mention, would his rifle even fire?

He wrapped his hands around the matchlock and blew on the priming pan. He scrubbed away the frozen chunk of powder, and forced his stiff fingers to pour a small stream from his powder horn. It was the best he could do.

A cannon boomed. Then again. It seemed so close in the whiteness. Jonathan couldn't tell whose artillery he was hearing.

Ahead, Henry Knox shouted something unintelligible, and then Jonathan knew.

The cannon fire was their own. His pulse thrummed in his ears.

Shapes loomed in the whiteness. The shapes resolved into buildings.

A cheer rose from the throats of the men ahead. Sporadic musket fire peppered the air.

Jonathan clutched his rifle tightly and rushed into Trenton.

27

Here succeeded a scene of war, which I had often conceived, but never seen before. The hurry, fright, and confusion of the enemy was [not] unlike that which shall be when the last trump shall sound.

—Colonel Henry Knox, December 28, 1776

Thank you, miss," the soldier said, his dark eyes hollows in a pale face. "Did you hear about Trenton?"

Ruth nodded. "Corporal Sprague told us. Marvelous. Rest now."

The soldier closed his eyes, exhausted from the effort of eating, and Ruth tucked his blanket around him carefully. His injury—a long, slashing saber wound—was less angry today, and she had hopes for his recovery. At least the man had good shoes. Not all of them did. She brought the spoon and bowl to the servant who did the washing.

Bits and pieces of news about the battles at Trenton and Princeton had filtered back. But the rumors were confusing, and outlandish claims were being made of hundreds of Hessian prisoners. All she knew with a certainty was that Dr. Rush's hospital was not busy. Only a few wounded men had crossed the river and stumbled into town. In the months since Ruth and her aunt had volunteered their time to nurse the wounded, the numbers had swelled and ebbed with the tide of war. The hardest cases were civilians. Silent girls with empty eyes.

But now, there were empty beds.

Fear crept down her spine even so. Hannah had written that Jonathan and Nathan had joined the army. Corporal Sprague had lost two toes to frostbite. Jonathan might not be here, but the weather had been frightful. He could be frozen to death, lying in a ditch.

Ruth checked the shelf of medicinals. A hodgepodge of containers marched along the unpainted wooden ledge: tin, stoneware, glass. A large container of this latter sort was obviously empty. A single bottle of laudanum stood at attention, its contents doled out carefully to the worst cases.

"No more yarrow." Her aunt wiped her brow and turned her attention to a crock of balm she was making. "And Mr. Marshall sent all of his stock to the army."

Ruth rolled her shoulders to loosen them, then began to straighten the vessels. "What about Bartram's?" Old John Bartram was one of the premier botanists in the world—certainly the best in the colonies, and he had acres of plants just across the Schuylkill.

"Hmm. If we borrow the carriage we can be back by sunset." Her aunt finished and covered her crock. "Come now, Dr. Shippen and his assistant are here. I need something hot to drink."

With only six men needing attention, the doctor wouldn't need help this afternoon. Reluctantly, Ruth grabbed her cloak. Dr. Shippen was well regarded, but she missed Dr. Rush, who insisted on cleanliness and good diet as essential to recovery, which she appreciated. He was also cheerful, with a good word or verse of scripture frequently in his mouth. But he was away with Washington's army.

They stepped outside, where fingers of clouds veiled the thin sunlight.

"Have you faith in the words of the corporal?" Ruth flipped the hood of her cloak over her head to block the cold early March wind. Their patients brought news as fast or faster than the newspapers.

Aunt Betsy looked both ways before they crossed the street, treacherous with refrozen slush. "Almost a thousand prisoners taken at Trenton? Sounds like a fever dream. But they say both Trenton and Princeton are in Washington's hands. And based on the small number of wounded—"

"I hope there are no more this winter." Ruth wanted to ask, *Where is Jonathan?* But she didn't want to voice her fears.

They reached the other side and passed a tavern. Ahead, a dark figure stumbled on the icy pavement.

The tall form was familiar, but the shoulders were hunched against the cold. It was Dr. Witherspoon, looking strangely frail.

Aunt Betsy swept up to his side. "Headed for the coffeehouse?"

A single nod was all she needed to guide the man indoors. Ruth thrust away her worries and followed them, the warm air thick with the aroma of coffee. The Youngs brewed theirs with scant spoonfuls of grounds, and some used chicory or acorns, but in a place like this the smell alone woke her.

Once he had coffee in hand, Dr. Witherspoon became fully alert. "Am I keeping you?"

Ruth had seen him in the hospital several times, praying with soldiers. He was about Papa's age, but today he looked like an old man. Bertram's gardens could wait.

Ruth led them to sit away from the knots of men discussing business in the corners. "Has Congress returned from Baltimore?" The proximity of fighting had sent Congress fleeing.

He nodded. "They are back. The victories in Trenton and Princeton have encouraged us all."

He did not sound encouraged.

Ruth warmed her hands around a cup of fragrant coffee. "What troubles you?"

He picked up his cup and set it down again without tasting. "Princeton." He took a gasping breath. "The College ..."

"Has not Washington taken Princeton?"

He nodded, a tiny smile touching his lips. "I should be thankful. But ..."

Again he lifted his cup and set it down. "The library—" The words caught in his throat.

Tears started in Ruth's eyes. Washington's men were not the first to hold Princeton. "The British?"

His voice was a whisper. "Completely destroyed. The College library ... all my books ... completely destroyed ... why?"

～

THE MOON HAD SET, but golden light from the windows of the house banded the snow. Robert stood in front of the house commandeered as Howe's headquarters and peered into the darkness of the trees, wishing he'd worn his woolen muffler, but he'd only thought to be waiting a few minutes. The reality was, he'd wanted to escape the fog of tobacco smoke and oppressive, brandy-laced conversation. He didn't need to watch out here like a sentry.

They were expecting a message from a Hessian commander, and it was overdue.

New Jersey was proving more difficult to subdue than New York. Supposedly, men loyal to the Crown abounded here, but the reality had proved different.

He cringed at the rumors. Hessian soldiers breaking into houses, abusing civilians—and now traveling parties of Jägers and British dragoons were attacked and even killed. It seemed the whole countryside was rising up against them.

And Washington had taken both Trenton and Princeton in a sudden turn of events. Rawdon still mocked the man, but Robert wasn't sure what to think. True, the rag-tag colonials had melted away before their fire on Long Island, but Washington's men had retreated in some order. The escape across the East River still made Robert smile. And now gutsy moves in the dead of winter had reset the chessboard. Washington had taken Trenton in a blizzard—a blizzard! Brilliant? Or desperate?

He thought of a badger he'd seen once. While chasing a fox, his uncle's hounds had stumbled upon a boar badger. One mutt clamped his jaws on its dark pelt, but the loose hide of the creature enabled it to twist and claw its assailant. In no time the animal was safe in its burrow—a vast maze inhabited by dozens more. Exterminating badgers was no easy task.

Washington the wily badger still survived, and the farmers of New Jersey were angry. Not a good situation.

A welcome gust of warm air and the click of the door signaled a presence. Lord Rawdon.

"Still no word?" his cousin asked.

"No. Think they've been ambushed?"

"'Tis cold out here. I wouldn't trouble yourself. If we lose a few more Hessians, what is that in the scheme of things?" Rawdon mused. "I hear Washington's men do not even have shoes."

"True." Robert turned, but as he did his eyes caught the glint of tack and saber. The feather-soft sound of horses making their way through snow ghosted through the night. "Wait."

In moments, a cavalcade emerged from the trees. Dozens of riders glowed like specters in the light from the house.

"Message for General Howe." The speaker dismounted and Robert escorted him inside.

Dozens of men to guarantee a single routine message. No, it wasn't good at all.

He turned, but Rawdon caught his elbow.

"I need you to go with me tomorrow. Reconnaissance."

There was no help for it. He could only hope that wearing his butternut greatcoat over his crimson regimentals he'd be less vulnerable to angry farmers.

After a handful of hours of sleep, Robert pulled on his uniform. This time he'd wrap warmly with a scarf under his outer garment. It was early March, but the last few days had been fiercely cold, one last gasp of winter.

"Here's where we're headed." Rawdon showed him a crude map after they packed their saddlebags with foodstuffs for the day. He laid a finger on a location. "We need to see if Washington's patrols are here"—he shifted his hand—"or here."

It was a long ride just to get to the general area, and Robert's horse seemed to resent the outing even more than he did. He brought up the last two battles in conversation to distract himself. A college at Princeton had been ravaged.

"Why the college?" Robert pressed his heels to his mount's ribs. Lord Rawdon had the better horse, a bay gelding with fine conformation, and it was difficult to stay abreast of the man. "Why'd they destroy a library?"

"'Tis difficult to restrain the men after such an order. Howe's order."

All "extra" supplies found in the homes of New Jersey civilians now belonged to the British Army, by Howe's command. What exactly was extra was a matter of opinion. British regulars and Hessians both were looting and pillaging.

"How is it honorable?"

They slowed their horses as the ground sloped to a creek. Once on the other side, Rawdon looked him in the eye.

"We have to make them suffer," he growled. "Realize the folly of rebellion."

Total war—it was Rawdon's philosophy. Robert was reluctant to believe that General Howe felt that way. But his orders had the same effect. It was a distinction without a difference.

"We will drive them into Washington's arms," Robert pointed out. He thought of Ruth Haynes then, loyal to the Crown. What would she do if her home were attacked by soldiers? Would she take up a pistol?

Rawdon nudged his horse into a trot, and Robert fought with his animal to match its pace.

"You're a thinker." His cousin's bushy brows lifted. "Just like Captain André. Can you imagine him at the head of a regiment of cavalry like Tarleton?"

Robert pictured the young man—handsome, well spoken, well educated. Ambitious, but a merchant's son. Charming rather than lecherous—and the women loved him. "I agree. He would do anything if asked, but he hasn't the bloodthirsty drive your friend has."

Rawdon guffawed. "And André *has* been asked. Secret service—he doesn't work just for Clinton."

They stopped briefly to rest and water the horses but built no fire. Robert stamped his feet and stretched to keep warm while the horses pawed at the snow, looking for forage.

"So, André is intelligence."

"Yes, and say nothing to anyone," Rawdon said. "Not to Tarleton, Simcoe, or any of the others."

Robert raised questioning brows.

"I do not have you pegged as a bold commander, either. And with loyalties confused or changing, we need information." His cousin made a sweeping gesture, indicating their current mission. "Anyone with a good mount, a good seat, and half a brain can do reconnaissance. What André does is quite different."

Spying. Robert's stomach curled as they remounted. He thought he'd finished that underhanded work.

"He'll show you the ropes. Don't look at me like that. 'Tis only a matter of making contacts. Finding Loyalists who will bring us information." He fended off a low-hanging branch. "Information that will bring this bloody war to an end."

"I do not want to soil the Shirley name." It was a feeble excuse. Nothing about this war was honorable.

They pulled up at a fork in the road.

"Who's to know? Once this is all over, we'll go home with rank and honor, and no one will ever know John André was a spy—or you." Rawdon scanned the area. "I'll go left, and you take that path. We'll rendezvous here" —he took out his watch— "at two."

That gave him about three hours. Robert nodded and urged his mount down the path at as brisk a walk as the beast could manage. His seat was already sore with the horse's jolting excuse for a trot.

Several miles down the road the trees thinned, and Robert spotted a split-rail fence. A nearby farm. He dismounted and led the horse along, scanning the terrain, looking for the highest point, a place he could use his spyglass. Even a tall tree would serve.

"Hands up!"

Just off the path an old man aimed a blunderbuss in his direction. Robert dropped the reins, took a step to the side of the horse, and raised his hands.

"Open your coat." The man spoke around a corncob pipe clenched in his teeth. "Hurry!"

Robert complied, wondering how old the weapon was. Seeing the red uniform, a rebel might shoot him on the spot, but a loyal man would not.

Part of him was terrified, but he ignored it. Fear would kill him.

The man guffawed but neither pipe nor firearm wobbled. "I'm loyal to the King. May he live long and stay many miles away." He seemed to be enjoying himself. "Give me your horse—and your greatcoat. It'll be some small recompense after what our dear sovereign has taken."

Robert didn't argue. He slung the coat over the saddle.

"And the scarf."

The scarf joined the coat.

"Now your shiny boots."

He studied the man's firearm. It might misfire, but who knew what the man had loaded it with. Nails could tear a man apart. "Nay, sir, this footwear is now my sole means of locomotion. I insist they remain."

To Robert's surprise, the farmer grinned. "As you say. Be off with you. And lively, now." He raised the blunderbuss. "Step lively!"

Robert trotted back the way he had come, cold sweat rolling down his back. After a hundred yards he slowed. The range of the weapon was limited. The terror and embarrassment of the ambush was quickly replaced with a wry thankfulness.

Thank you, God. He hadn't joined the few dozen who'd simply disappeared, dead in a ditch somewhere.

The man hadn't taken his satchel or pistol, hidden in a discreet sheath. Or his regimental coat, without which he'd freeze.

He certainly didn't miss the animal, though it would be a long, cold way back on foot. Even the distance back to the fork took him over an hour. Once there, he ducked into a stand of birch and took out his watch. Almost two.

It was a cold wait. The shadows began to lengthen, and still Rawdon had not returned. Robert stomped and marched in place to keep his blood moving. Thoroughly chilled, Robert pulled out his watch again. If his cousin had not returned by four, he would head back—as it was, there was no way they'd return by nightfall, even on horseback. And it was dangerous out here so close to Washington's army.

Distant movement flickered through the naked trees—then a soft tattoo of hooves breached the stillness. The sound quickly crescendoed, and two horses thundered into the crossroads.

Face red with cold, Rawdon sat astride his bay gelding while gripping the reins of another animal, a sleek black mountain of a horse, feathery mane and tail flying as the creature arched its neck and snorted.

Robert's mouth fell open. "What—?"

"Where is your hack? Never mind, take this animal. We need to go."

Robert reached for the reins. Once on the stallion's back, he waited for an explosive reaction—but it never came. Apparently, the animal was well trained despite its high-stepping nature.

This time he had no trouble keeping up with Rawdon's horse. They cantered briskly for several miles before slowing enough to talk.

"Anything useful?" Robert decided that Rawdon would explain the horse in good time. The stallion's motion was glorious, the trot smooth as silk.

"I found one of Washington's raiding parties—and they didn't see me, but when I passed through a farm on the way back, I saw this fine creature and remembered the general's order."

"Definitely surplus," Robert responded dryly.

"The owner saw me and gave chase."

Robert recounted his own adventures, and Rawdon laughed.

"You ride this animal well enough, and I have a problem. Some general will commandeer it. Don't you dare let Tarleton see it—he kills horses. Rides them to death."

"Sell it to me. I've ten guineas, though it's worth much more." He thought of Hannah Russell. A plan was coalescing in his mind. "And I'll need a pass."

THE COLD AFTERNOON shadows were long as the carriage left the ferry and headed back into town. Ruth sighed quietly, not wanting to disturb her aunt, who dozed at her side. Philadelphia was no longer bright and welcoming. There was a curfew, and members of the Committee of Safety patrolled even in the daytime, accosting folks thought to be Loyalists. They reminded her of the mobs in Boston.

Ruth was no longer a Loyalist, but she didn't know if anyone knew that. In any case, she put no trust in the discernment of ruffians who flocked to the Patriot banner. How would they know which side she was on? The carriage turned from Market Street onto Fourth, jolting on the icy ruts. A lamplighter darted from one pole to the next.

She slid her hand into her pocket and touched the cool steel mechanism of the pistol inside. Hannah had taught her to shoot in Roxbury before they left for Philadelphia.

"Dinna cock this weapon unless you mean to kill," Hannah had said, pinning an old newspaper to a tree. "Settle it in your mind. If a man sees ye dinna mean to use it, he'll take it from you."

Ten paces away seemed close, but Ruth couldn't hit the target.

"Let's try five paces," Hannah said. "If ye are defending yourself or your family, it will be up close."

At five paces Ruth hit the paper. The sight of the hole jarred her.

"Self-defense is honorable." Hannah took the pistol, fired, and a hole appeared a finger's breadth away from Ruth's. "Dinna fret."

"'Bertram's was a disappointment." Aunt Betsy said, interrupting Ruth's musings.

"But they did have some lavender and chamomile, and we haven't a need for yarrow just now anyway." Ruth hugged the package of herbs under her cloak, their presence a comfort.

"What think you?" Aunt Betsy asked. "Will the Youngs leave?"

Several Patriot families had left Philadelphia recently. Howe's army had withdrawn to New York for the winter, but that could easily change. The trickle of departures could turn to a flood with the spring.

"I heard Rebecca discussing it with her husband. The journeyman left last month, and business is slow." Ruth shrugged. "I know not."

The carriage slowed as they drew near to the house.

"Ruth." Her aunt's voice was low and quiet. "Who's that?"

A horse stood before the Youngs' home, and behind it a filthy man slumped on the front steps. Ruth set down the packet of herbs on the carriage seat and withdrew her pistol. Committee of Safety? But he looked tired, like a traveler.

The horse lifted its head, its winter-heavy coat a familiar red. Was that Brutus?

Ruth replaced the pistol and jumped out of the carriage.

"Ruth, wait!"

It was Brutus—was that Jonathan? Could it be?

Her aunt's steps quickened behind her. "Jonathan!"

Ruth's chest seized. Was he hurt?

28

God often takes a course for accomplishing His purposes directly contrary to what our narrow views would prescribe.

—John Newton (1725-1807)

*R*uth rushed to Jonathan's side while Aunt Betsy summoned the stable boy to come and collect the horse.

Jonathan seemed half-asleep. Her pulse pounded in fear. Was he injured? "Jonathan, wake up."

Glassy-eyed, he smiled at her. "I gave the message. Washington's message."

Ragged and sour smelling, he was clearly delirious.

Ruth felt his forehead. Burning hot. "Come inside."

Her aunt returned and they maneuvered him through the door. By the time he was situated in the kitchen, the entire Young family had gathered.

"A soldier!" Little Benjamin was entranced.

"Let's allow the women to feed him." Mr. Young steered him away.

Her face creased with concern, Rebecca went to and fro, gathering blankets and linens. Aunt Betsy laid an assessing hand on Jonathan's forehead.

"He's fevered, but not as dangerous as some." She turned to Ruth. "I need to check for injuries."

Ruth handed her a sheet. "I won't look."

"I'm no' so terrible to look at …"

"Jonathan, what are those on your feet?" Ruth squatted and gently disengaged the leather remains of what might have once been boots. "Aunt Betsy, can we make a foot soak?"

Her aunt waved a hand. "After I check the rest of him, which is not for you to see. Why don't you brew some willow bark for the fever and put together marigold and chamomile for his feet."

Ruth knew when she was being dismissed. Tears welled, tears of joy. Jonathan was safe.

SITTING ON A WELL-CUSHIONED CHAIR, Jonathan sipped the foul-tasting brew. He wouldn't complain about the medicine. Not after beef broth and corn pudding shiny with butter. For the first time in months, he was both clean and full.

And Ruth was here, a sight even more welcome than the food. He hoped she hadn't been part of the bath—he was unsure of that. The last thing he remembered was giving Washington's message to Mr. Thompson, secretary of the Congress.

Beneath a warm quilted blanket, he was wearing a shirt and stockings but no breeches. He couldn't remember if he had an extra pair in his saddle-bags. But no matter. The parlor was warm enough, thanks to the Franklin stove.

His brethren in arms had none of these things. The Morristown encampment was cold, the men devouring all the wood in the district like termites to keep warm.

Aunt Betsy bustled in and inspected his cup. "Good." She laid a hand on his head. "Better. Your fever is down. I bandaged a cut on your side. But you've got a nasty case of chilblains, and Dr. Shippen may need to look at your feet. I hope you don't lose any toes."

He coughed.

"Hot soup. Let's see if we can nip this in the bud." She turned and spoke to someone through the doorway. "Come on in."

Ruth looked thin, but she was still pretty. A lock of dark hair swirled against her temple. Why wasn't she married yet? Why, anyone who saw her would think her irresistible.

"Irresistible?" Ruth asked.

"Did I say that aloud?"

Ruth's cheeks were an interesting shade of pink. "Yes, it's the fever talking."

"I feel perfectly fine. Where are my weapons? My rifle and knives?" He felt naked without them.

Ruth brought a chair next to him and sat. "Your rifle is in the hall. Everything else is here with your saddlebags, and we're washing your clothes. Some may end up in the rag bag."

As soon as he felt better, he'd clean the rifle. For now, just looking at Ruth made him content.

"Tell me—tell me about Trenton."

Jonathan's mind went back to the snowstorm, to Greenwood and his fellows. "Henry Knox won the battle."

He told her about the river crossing, the falling temperatures. "But I heard Knox's voice, and I felt hope. Ye ken the man—and his bellow was better than a bugle. By the time we arrived at the town held by the enemy, the weather was a wall of ice. There were no sentries—no one could stand sentry in that. We set up the artillery and began to fire just as the Hessians poured out from the buildings like ants."

"Did they have cannon too?"

He coughed. "Yes, a few, but we got the jump on them. In fact, Knox captured theirs."

"I'm glad you weren't hurt."

Jonathan adjusted his blanket. "I got a wee scrape at Princeton. But the Lord was gracious. Those redcoats love the bayonet."

He couldn't say more. Seeing men wounded in the gut with the wicked steel weapon was too much to bear. He'd heard the English complain about the long rifle, that it was outside the pale of civilized warfare to kill men at four hundred yards. But at least they died quickly.

"It seems Providence has smiled on us for once," Ruth said.

"Aye, He has. Though I would prefer it if He'd simply make this whole thing go away."

Had he said that aloud too?

~

In the kitchen, Ruth heard rumbles of conversation, Mr. Young speaking to Jonathan about the war. The rest of the family had gone to bed. She turned to her aunt. "I don't like that cough."

"'Tis not as bad as some," her aunt said. "He's strong—he'll shake it off. Let's get some of this chamomile tea into him before he falls asleep."

Rebecca had made up a pallet in the parlor for their guest, but Jonathan was still awake in the chair when Ruth returned with the tea.

His expression twisted. "More?"

"There's a chamber pot right here." Ruth was embarrassed, and she didn't know why. They'd been caring for the soldiers at the hospital, and chamber pots were an ordinary fact of life.

"As long as ye close the door—"

A knock echoed in the hall.

Her aunt's face appeared at the doorway. "Who could that be at this hour?"

"Get my pistol, just in case." Ruth twisted her apron between her fingers.

Jonathan scooped the blanket around his hips and lunged for his saddlebags.

"'Tis probably a neighbor," Ruth said to calm him, but there was a curfew. It could be someone who needed her aunt's skills with herbs. At least, she hoped that was the case. The so-called Committee of Safety terrorized Loyalists.

Jonathan sat warily in the chair with a wicked-looking knife in his hand. "Call and I will come."

The knock repeated, softer this time. Ruth padded to the front door and lit the dark lantern on the hall table. "Coming."

Aunt Betsy passed her a pistol and kept the other for herself. Ruth cracked the door open.

The lantern light fell on Robert Shirley's face.

She scanned his form. He wore a long linen duster, but at the throat she caught the gleam of his officer's gorget. So, he was in uniform. His caramel eyes and familiar features slammed her with emotion.

"'Tis a neighbor, Aunt Betsy," she said, using a voice that carried. Then she whispered, "Do not let Jonathan outside."

Her aunt scowled but nodded. Ruth slipped her pistol in her pocket, then slipped outside and closed the door.

"What are you doing here?" she hissed.

Then she saw the horse, a shadow against the dark street, eyes gleaming in the light of the lantern. Rags swathed the animal's hooves.

"I have a gift of sorts. May we speak in the stables?"

This was a dream, and she was going to wake. But was it a good dream, or a nightmare? Robert Shirley was a British officer. She liked the man. Respected him—but everything he'd done for them had been under false pretenses. Could she trust him now?

She led him to the stable, and instead of waking the stable boy she guided the new animal to a stall herself—as far away from Brutus as she could. Thankfully, it was so dark it would be impossible for Shirley to recognize Jonathan's horse.

"Tell me about the horse." Even under the narrow beam of the dark lantern the animal looked impressive. Stomach tight and roiling, she grabbed an armful of hay while Shirley set a bucket of water before it.

"Stolen in New Jersey," he said, his voice barely above a whisper.

"So, you're not just a deceiver, you're a thief?"

Shirley blinked but remained poised. "I purchased it from the officer who'd stolen it. I think it's a Dutch horse, valuable. The Russells might be able to find its owner, and in the meantime ..." He shrugged. "They breed horses."

Ruth's anger subsided. "You're thinking of Hannah Russell."

The look on his face was comical.

"'Tis impossible, you know that."

His expression firmed. "I do. But would you assist me in this?"

"I will." She watched as the stallion raised its head, wisps of hay dangling from its mouth. "Seems tractable enough."

"One thing the army is good at is killing horses."

"Not to mention men." Anger resurged in her heart, but she checked herself. It wasn't his fault, not really.

He stroked the horse's neck. "I know you must hate me, I don't blame you."

"I think you are doing your duty."

But his face did not look like that of a man doing his duty with a clear conscience. It smote her heart.

"Do you? I have tried. But ..." He took a deep breath. "I was with my cousin at Bunker's hill. I loaded the weapon that killed Dr. Warren."

What! She was horrified, but so, it seemed, was he. His expression was empty, as though he looked into a dark, yawning pit. "He treated you when you were sick, didn't he?"

"Yes," he replied, his face a misery. "Dr. Warren saved my life."

"Stay here, I'll be right back."

ROBERT TENSED, unsure of what she went to fetch. Hopefully not a rebel. Philadelphia was full of them, and many times he'd silently blessed the black color of the horse as he'd made his way through side streets and alleys to this house.

Would she expose him? It was war—most would quibble and say they were simply putting down a rebellion—but semantics aside, they were engaged in real battles and real intelligence. And people did strange things in war.

The rustle of skirts marked her return. "Here." She thrust something into his hands.

It was a book—a New Testament, one of the small volumes printed here in the colonies. "Thank you."

"Read it."

"I will." He slipped it into his pocket. His godmother would be pleased. The Bible she'd given him lay gathering dust in Leicestershire. He would read the testament. Roman philosophy was all very well, but he couldn't imagine anyone thrusting *Meditations* into his uniform before a battle. He sighed. He still had to do his duty, as unpleasant as it was. "Are your loyalties still with the Crown?"

Her expression hardened. "My loyalties are first to the King of kings. Our dear King George has decided to throw natural law and English civil liberties to the wind."

"Please keep your voice down."

"He has reneged on his own duty to the people."

"But he is your sovereign." It was hopeless.

"We have our own government now." She bit off each word. "Don't you dare ask me to spy for you."

The rebuke pierced him. "I will not." His voice was hoarse. "Thank you for the gift."

He turned and fled, his steps heavy with regret.

"WHAT A SHAME." Jonathan stroked the stallion's black neck and turned to meet Ruth's gaze. "Such a bonnie fine creature, and now I must make him ugly."

Three weeks and a painful scraping by the surgeon had rendered Jonathan almost as good as new, although Aunt Betsy clucked over several toes that remained numb. Seeing Ruth again was worth any number of toes. He'd stuffed any questions of their future together into some mental saddlebag, not to be opened until later. He didn't want to deal with all it would entail, not just now, with the British at their doorstep.

Quite literally. "I canna believe Robert Shirley gave us this animal." His feelings toward the man were confused. He hoped not to meet him in battle. "And I canna believe—"

"Did you truly think I'd let you know he was here? Here, I have the scissors."

Jonathan subsided. They'd had that discussion already. They set to work trying to conceal the stallion's obvious lineage. Dutch horses were high-stepping, sturdy creatures blessed with long, showy manes and tails. Before long, the mane was mere stubble, and long black strands littered the straw.

"Might yon stable boy fetch us some mud?"

Ruth's mouth fell open.

"He'll be under harness, but even so," Jonathan explained. "Once I get the Youngs to the country, away from the armies, it won't be as dangerous." The goldsmith and his family were packed and ready to leave in the morning.

They both understood that the main danger was the British army, and no one knew General Howe's intentions now that spring had arrived. Armies needed horses, and they didn't ask permission.

"So after you see the Youngs safe, you're headed to the valley?"

He nodded. He had to get home for spring planting. After that, he'd be returning. "Nathan will stay with General Knox." Jonathan reached for a glob of mud and spread it along the withers and barrel of the horse. "Ruth, will ye come with me now?"

"Papa is now one of the principal composers at the *Gazette*. As long as the newspaper stays here, he will stay. We will both stay, and I can continue with the sewing."

Jonathan stood. His hands were dirty, but he didn't care. He reached for her and laid his hands on her arms. "Please. I canna help worrying."

"Worrying? Hah! You march off to war, straight into danger, and you worry about me?"

He let his arms fall.

"Ruth, Ruth!" Mrs. Young swept down the track to the stable. "Promise me you'll leave town if the British come anywhere near."

Jonathan picked up handfuls of straw and rubbed it over the sticky mud to dull the animal's hide as he listened to the conversation.

"We will pack tomorrow," Ruth said. "We'll be ready to go at any time."

Mrs. Young grasped Ruth's hands. "Be careful." She looked at the stallion. "What have you done?"

Jonathan squinted as he examined the stallion from both sides. "A disguise. Make him look like an ordinary hack. I'll keep it to a walk as long as we are in town, and it will fool most people."

"Thank you for your assistance." Mrs. Young drew out a handkerchief. "I-I cannot repay your kindness." She spun and left.

"'Tis difficult for her," Ruth said. "Uprooting family—she has little ones, besides." She stepped to the feed bin, scraped out a cupful, and poured it into Brutus's trough. "Maybe you should dress him the same, with mud."

"Aye, you're right." Thankfully the horses were now used to each other's smell. They might just make it home without any serious equine arguments. "Da's coming later this year with a wagon for you and your father's printing press, but dinna wait if the danger is near."

Her jaw worked. "Papa will not wish to leave."

"Ye ken General Howe is coming—"

"We *ken* no such thing. That other general—Burgoyne—is up north, and I do not see why Howe would want Philadelphia."

He snorted. "Ye may be right, except that capturing Congress would defeat us at one stroke."

"Hard to capture men with feet. They fled for Baltimore once."

"Exactly. They ken the danger, even if ye dinna." He was angry, but not at her. Not exactly. "Shirley is the enemy. For your own safety, dinna forget that."

Ruth was silent for a long moment. "Robert Shirley is a man with a troubled conscience."

The words smote him like an arrow, and he fumbled for a reply. "Even a man with a troubled conscience kens his duty. And Shirley's duty is to kill me and hang Washington."

29

There is not a single instance in history, in which civil liberty was lost, and religious liberty preserved entire.

—Dr. John Witherspoon (1723-1794)

Philadelphia, August 1777

*H*eat blanketed the city like heavy wool. Deciding she'd rather brave dust and insects than suffocate, Aunt Betsy had opened the door and propped the windows open, and Ruth was glad for the air.

Sewing woolen flags was hot work. Thankfully, the hospital was almost empty of patients, and Ruth found time for the needle. According to the paper, General Howe had packed his army onto ships and departed. But to where?

Long strips of bunting lay across Ruth's lap as she gazed out into the street. No battles, no injuries, and no deaths. Congress was still here, and many other Patriots, but a large portion of the population was Quaker, and The Society of Friends forbade taking up arms. Therefore, Quakers were considered Loyalists whether they truly were or not.

Ruth felt sorry for some of the Quakers she knew. Many saw the injustice of the Crown's actions but simply stayed silent. Patriots harassed them.

On the other hand, if General Howe expected Philadelphia to rejoice if he captured it—well, the residents might give that appearance. But she wasn't sure how many would actively help him. Perhaps the wealthier sort. And those who feared retribution.

At her side, her aunt's chin lifted. "What's the fuss?"

A man darted down Third Street. Then another strode down Fourth, a block farther down. On Walnut, a woman peered out a window.

Then another man—it was Papa! He approached the house in great bobbing strides, looking as if he wanting to break into a jog.

Ruth thrust the bunting away and stepped to the doorway. "Papa?"

He reached the steps, puffing. "News. Howe has landed. South of here. Washington coming."

"Come in, I've lemonade."

It was more like switchel—she'd had but the one lemon, and she added vinegar to make up the difference.

By the time cups were passed around, Papa had caught his breath. "No one knew for sure where Howe's ships would land."

"You said he'd gone down to the Chesapeake." At one point Ruth had opened a geography book in Logan's library to make sense of the bits of information in the *Gazette*.

Her father fished a handkerchief out of his pocket and wiped his forehead. "Yes. We didn't know where he was headed—would he turn north and head toward Baltimore or Philadelphia? Or would he continue south to Charleston."

Ruth nodded. "But we suspected Philadelphia." Feared was more like it. "It doesn't make sense. Why would he put all his men on ships when he could simply march through New Jersey?"

Papa shrugged. "It certainly took longer. And rumor has it they were caught by a storm. Lost some of their horses."

Aunt Betsy harrumphed. "Well, Gideon, I say that's the hand of Providence against the rascals."

Papa smiled, but it was a grim one. "Washington is marching through Philadelphia today. He's headed south to mount a defense."

Aunt Betsy stood abruptly, and her empty cup fell over and rattled on the table. "Why didn't you say so? Down what streets do you suppose? Ruth, do we have bunting we can use?"

Ruth scurried after her and picked up an incomplete flag. She had an idea of what her aunt wanted. "A running stitch on either side would work."

In twenty minutes, the red-and-white bunting was ready. Papa escorted them to a likely location on Fourth Street. Clusters of people had gathered on the street corners, and the lawn of the State House was crowded. Aunt Betsy clasped the bunting before her like an apron.

The faint tapping of a drum penetrated the low rumble of the crowd. Then Ruth heard the shrill of a fife.

"They're coming! Our boys are coming!"

The crowd cheered. Aunt Betsy pressed forward and flapped the bunting.

They came, marching to the cadence of the drum, some a little out of step, but each wore a sprig of green in their caps in remembrance of the Liberty Tree.

The Liberty Tree. Ruth remembered the Boston symbol of liberty and resistance to tyranny with mixed emotions. The mob had used it as a focal point in some of their most egregious actions. Tarring and feathering—what honor was there in that? How did that promote justice?

True liberty was about justice. Equal justice for all, according to the law, and not by the whim of man. She thought about Robert Shirley then, who was trying to do his duty while surrounded by the questionable actions of the British Army.

Mobs could not dispense justice. But neither did King George. Had they exchanged one evil for another?

But no—the Declaration of Independence specified each unlawful action of the King, and by implication, acknowledged and established the law.

As they marched by, the Continental Army became individual faces. Many were young—too young, she thought. Others were bronzed by the heat of decades of sun in the fields. A few—officers, she guessed—looked like tradesmen, merchants, or even scholars. A few rode, but most were on foot, their clothing ordinary, stained and frayed. Many were thin. But all carried their weapons proudly.

The cheering swelled. "General Washington!"

A man on horseback came into her field of view, the same man they'd encountered on the road to Philadelphia. Under his hat his natural hair was perfectly tied and powdered; his blue uniform was immaculate; only his boots were dulled from the dust. His erect form and poise commanded respect. And yet, there were lines on his face she hadn't seen that day on the road.

Instinctively Ruth straightened as he crossed in front of her, vaguely aware of Aunt Betsy's cheering, which was nearly lost in the roar of the crowd.

Then the general passed, and an empty space seemed to open behind him. The dust of the street parched Ruth's throat as the joyful sounds subsided. The people were hopeful, and Washington's appearance had bolstered that hope, but the reality was, their ragged soldiers were going up against the greatest army in the world.

THE NEXT DAY, Ruth did the laundry. In Boston, a servant had done all the heavy work, and before the Youngs left, Ruth and her aunt had helped with sewing, mending, and cleaning, but never this. Thankfully, the needs of two women were small.

Clouds scudding across the sky provided the only relief from the heat in the space behind the house where the fire pit was located. Ruth dumped the clothes into the wash kettle. As she stirred briskly with the paddle, steam redolent of lye stung her nose and eyes. She consoled herself that the task came only once a week.

And maybe this would be the last week, the last time she'd do the wash here. They'd packed the trunks and were prepared to leave at an hour's notice. Some families had already left—if Washington did not defeat Howe, the British would be here in mere days.

She tried to focus on the task at hand, not wanting to think about what the redcoats would do to civilians left behind.

Her shoulders began to ache. The yard around her looked large and lonely. It wasn't her home, and now she might leave it, too. Boston seemed far away. A settled home was a mere dream, an illusion.

"Ruth?" Aunt Betsy stood on the back steps. "Two packages have arrived!"

Ruth almost dropped the paddle. Mail of any kind was sporadic and highly valued. Her gaze flew from kettle to washtub where rinse water awaited.

"Here, I'll finish." Her aunt took the paddle. "Go and take a look."

Ruth wiped her hands on her apron, but it was useless—her apron was both dirty and wet. She begrudged every hindrance—a wet rag to clean herself, a fresh apron—but finally she was in the parlor where two packages greeted her.

One was wrapped in coarse paper and twine; this sat on a settle. On the floor nearby was a small crate, addressed in Hannah Russell's handwriting.

Ruth snipped the twine around the paper-wrapped parcel, which turned out to be well-protected. She found oilcloth beneath the layers of paper, and below that, more paper.

A letter lay atop colorful fabric. A gown?

She pried open the wax seal—it was from Lucy Knox.

Dear Ruth, thank you for your last letter. Molly is well, truly a godsend—

Ruth checked the letter's date. July. Her own letter had gone out in March and had included mostly commonplaces, with only a little about the soldiers in the hospital. It was unthinkable to burden Lucy with the realities of war, when her lonely imagination would inflate them, thinking of her "dear Harry."

But a gown was an extravagant gift. She scanned the letter till she found a mention.

General Arnold courted one of my friends, an insupportable situation as she had no interest. But he pressed on, supremely self-confident! After he left Boston, he requested of me that I give her a token of his regard—he sent a whole chest full of gowns! She turned down the gift, quite wisely in my humble opinion.

Ruth smiled, hearing Lucy's voice through her written words.

I wrote the general and asked what he wanted me to do, also requesting he give me a shawl that was in the chest. (The gowns do not fit me, and I have not your hand with the needle!) General Arnold has not responded, but then, I suppose he is busy with the war. So, I decided to give them all away. There is suffering in Boston and even I am counting my pennies. I saved the best for you.

Ruth lifted the heavy chintz gown from its nest of wrappings. Vibrant hues of blue, green, and red swirled across the fine fabric, delighting the eye without overwhelming the senses. She stood and lifted it against herself, feeling strange. Her hands—oh, the hands that were coarsened by all the sewing and chores—held the dress of a princess, or at least a merchant's wife.

It was something her mother might have worn. Tears sprang to her eyes.

"Ruth?" At the doorway, her aunt wiped wet hands on her apron. "How lovely! Who sent it?"

"Lucy Knox—'tis a long story."

Aunt Betsy quickly determined that the garment was two inches too long. "I will take in the bodice for you. 'Tis probably too large."

"But ... but—" It was extravagant.

"No, Ruth Haynes, listen to me. Your mother isn't here, but I am, and I will tell you what she would say. You will have occasion to wear this. Certainly for your wedding, if nothing else. And if you've worn your fingers to the bone helping your father, helping me, and now serving your country, that doesn't make you less of a woman. You need a woman's things. And this time will pass, and good times will come, a time of weddings and babies and making merry. And you'll find that husband, if you haven't already."

A tear ran down Ruth's cheek. "Thank you, Aunt Betsy," she finally managed. "I think that box might have something for you."

And sure enough, the crate from the valley, packed with yarrow and other wild herbs from the mountains, distracted her aunt enough for Ruth to recover her composure.

She tucked Hannah's letter in her pocket for later.

THE SETTING SUN cast its rays lengthwise down Walnut Street, casting long, jumping shadows from a passing horse and rider. Ruth sat on the front steps of the house and opened the letter. She skimmed the greeting, and in the next paragraph Jonathan's name made her heart jump.

Jonathan returned safely with the most amazing horse, but of course you have seen it. Da clucked and raised a brow and clucked some more. He will put out an advertisement at a safer time and will stand it at stud for now. Truly was it from Mr. Shirley? My brother won't tell me anything more.

Jonathan joined in the spring planting with all his might, though his manner was strange. You should have seen the way he wrestled with the plow, as if he fought with it. I am not sure if it has to do with the war. As a practical matter, he was torn between two regiments. A few lads around here have joined Morgan's rifles, though most of that regiment hail from the Winchester area (north of here). But George Mathews has organized the 9th Virginia, and many in the Staunton area have joined. Jonathan doesn't like Mathews, but he is esteemed as a leader and there is no doubt of his courage. And he and his brother helped put together the Augusta Resolves two years ago, when all this started. He understands the principles of natural law and what we are truly fighting for. I knew you would appreciate that.

Anyway, Jonathan decided to join Mathews. I do not know what Nathan will do, whether he will stay with Henry Knox or join Mathews. My younger brother William fussed because he could not go too. Finally, Jonathan said, "If we survive this year, I will stay home next year and you will go."

It sobered us all to hear those words. He did not need to say that all of my brothers could die if they all go, leaving Mother without a son. Willie stomped off to go turkey hunting, but when he returned, he was in better humor. He understands.

Jonathan is preparing to go, and he still seems vaguely out of sorts. I snapped at him once. Da asked me to help him with a mare, and he spoke to me in the barn. "A man needs to face his troubles alone. If he wants help, he will ask."

I couldn't bear to stay silent. "But Da, the Bible says the wife is a 'help'." Surely a sister could be that too.

He grinned. "And that she is. Do ye ken what your mother does for me? How she helps me?"

I could not think of a thing. Except maybe supper, but that seemed trivial.

"She does many small things. Everyday things, like keeping my shirts mended and my socks darned. After a hard day in the field, I am greeted with a kind word and fresh switchel for my parched throat. These are small things. But I wonder if they are truly small. One day we may see all things with their true valuation and know that we have esteemed some things large that were ultimately insignificant, and some things small that were truly of great worth."

I remembered a verse. "'She is more precious than rubies.'"

He smiled again. "Aye. And remember this for your own wedding day."

I knitted Jonathan several pair of socks and threw them at his head when he started packing. "I'm coming, too—with Da when he comes for Ruth."

He was not pleased, wanted to tie me down. But we're coming for you and the printing press. I'll find a way to make Da let me come!

Ruth smiled, imagining the socks. And she made a mental note to enlist a few neighbors to knit stockings. Not every soldier had a sister like Hannah.

She folded the letter, thinking of Jonathan marching with his regiment—he'd be well on his way by now. Maybe he was already with Washington's army.

Well on his way to meet General Howe's forces.

Worry clutched at her. *Lord, keep him safe.*

30

If there are any Shoes & Blankets to be had in Lancaster or in that part of the Country I earnestly entreat you to have them taken up for the use of the Army.
—George Washington to John Hancock, Sept 23, 1777

September 1777

The misty morning fog over the Brandywine River had burned off over the course of the morning, only to be replaced by drifting pale gray smoke of cannon and musketry. Fighting ebbed and flowed along the bank, sometimes approaching Jonathan's position along the Philadelphia Road with the rest of the Ninth Virginia as they waited for the order to fight.

At first, the Ninth had braced along with the rest of the regiments under General Greene to take the brutal shock of the British advance. When the redcoats appeared on the other side of the river, the lads from the valley primed their weapons.

Then, the British shifted their position south. Then back again. What were they planning? At least Washington's men now had plenty of ammunition, thanks to the French. Keeping an eye on Colonel Mathews, waiting for a signal to move, Jonathan smiled grimly. No one from the valley had any love for the French—not after that nation had incited Indians to attack them. But gunpowder was welcome, no matter the source.

The shadows were long when the order came.

"General Greene says follow him north," shouted Colonel Mathews to the regiment, his voice hoarse with the smoke and much shouting.

Out of habit, Jonathan patted his satchel, checking his ammunition, then scanned his companions to his right and left. Those like him with long rifles brought up the rear. Rifles had no place to attach a bayonet and were at a disadvantage in close combat.

Sweat-grimed, Abel Robinson was reloading. Rob Kerr perched on a rock, catching his breath.

"Ho, lads, let's go." Jonathan took a swallow, wetting his dry throat, then handed Kerr his canteen, and the young man drained the last of it. Kerr was perhaps eighteen, and Robinson sixteen. The Ninth was a hodgepodge of sturdy men like Mathews, lads like Kerr, and indentured servants sent by their masters. Most had gumption, but few had much training.

And Jonathan had a bad feeling about the order. It could mean only one thing: they'd been flanked, or soon would be. And this was the last defense of Philadelphia. If they lost, the British would come pouring into the city.

Ruth. He would do everything in his power to stop them.

AFTER AN HOUR'S march through orchards and cornfields, sounds of battle and white smoke became discernible through the trees. Jonathan wiped his face with his sleeve and checked his flint. It had all become clear. General Howe had divided his forces, and while they'd been busy fighting one division all day, the British general had moved infantrymen to the north —here—like pieces on a chess board.

Ahead, a man darted through the trees and tossed his haversack away, face twisted in fear.

Jonathan tensed at the signs of panic. Howe had succeeded in flanking them—was all lost? The men they were supposed to reinforce were dashing into the woods, leaping fences, escaping pursuit, real or imagined. How to stop cowards from shirking he had no idea.

He could only do his own duty. Greene's men—their own regiment and several others—were all that was left to prevent a rout.

"Look lively, lads," he cautioned those next to him. "Dinna fire till the order."

It was their worst problem. Green recruits fired as soon as they saw the enemy, not only wasting their ammunition but essentially disarming themselves until they could reload, which could take as long as thirty seconds, an eternity in battle.

Colonel Mathews led them through a stand of trees and into a buckwheat field, eighteen inches of nearly ripe grain. The cover would suffice almost as well as a wood for a sniper. They could reload on the ground.

Mathews strode up and down the line, exhorting them. "Hold your fire, lads! Hold your fire!"

It helped a little. When the grenadiers' pointed caps first emerged over the slope, no one fired. But the redcoats were still over one hundred yards away when a musket barked. Then another. And another. Worthless shots.

"Lads, pick your targets," Jonathan shouted to the other riflemen, knowing they could easily kill at this range. He sighted, pulled the trigger, and fell into the buckwheat. He rolled onto his back and reloaded, then got up to fire again.

After his third shot he had to pause. The grenadiers were closer; smoke obscured the field, and the multiple clicks of steel on steel signaled the slide of bayonets onto their sockets.

As the sun touched the horizon, Colonel Mathews screeched a yodeling charge, and all the regiment followed, raising such a din Jonathan jumped eagerly forward despite his fatigue.

JONATHAN WOUND the bandage around Mathews's midsection. "Should mend." None of the colonel's bayonet wounds would be fatal unless they festered. The man's coat was worse, ripped and punctured in multiple places. There was no questioning his bravery.

A small fire illumined scattered blanket-wrapped lumps, the exhausted men of the Ninth Virginia.

Mathews cursed the British. "Another defeat."

The British had slipped past them. Jonathan forced the gloom away. "We failed to defeat the mightiest army in the world, aye. But thanks to you, we covered the retreat. Stopped the grenadiers in their tracks. The best of the best."

Grenadiers were chosen for their size, that much he knew.

Mathews merely grunted. "At least we didn't lose any—except Robinson. What happened to him?"

"I've his rifle—misfired. Told him I'd check it out."

Jonathan had not told such a blatant lie since he'd been switched for one at twelve. In Washington's regular army, the penalty for desertion was execution. But the militia? He had no idea. In any case, Abel Robinson had been missing for mere hours. Perhaps he'd show.

"Should'a known ye'd doctor me well." Matthews slumped, his weariness plain. "With your ma like she is."

Jonathan's mother was a midwife and the closest thing to an apothecary in the area near Russell's Ridge, well known for her skill. He handed the colonel his blanket and left to find his own spot beneath a tree, away from the probing light of the single fire.

Miraculously, the British hadn't followed the retreating men. Jonathan leaned against the tree and wondered how long he could stay awake. Maybe he didn't need to. Maybe the lad would never show.

Above, the strange spectacle of the aurora borealis shone through the branches. Sleepily, he wondered at it, thinking it a phenomenon reserved for the far reaches of the north. The gossamer-thin band of green light danced above, a mesmerizing glow against the velvet-dark sky.

He closed his eyes.

"Russell?"

Jonathan jerked awake with a start, clueless as to how long he'd been asleep—a minute or an hour, he didn't know. "Abel?"

"Aye—was I missed? Had a stone in my shoe."

No one would admit to panicking. "Mathews asked for ye, and I explained your rifle misfired. Just needs cleaning, lad."

"Oh—thank you." Robinson's voice cracked. "Did we … win?"

"You decide. The British just won the Brandywine, and perhaps Philadelphia—but Greene's division kept the army from disaster. We covered the retreat and stopped the British advance on our flank."

The shuffling of leaves marked the place where the lad bedded down to sleep. "Washington still alive?"

"Oh, aye. I saw him today once, out in front of his men, riding that fine horse of his too close to the river, within range of any sniper. But God protected him."

Robinson's voice was sleepy. "All is well, then."

Yes, it was chess. Their king was still on the board, and hopefully they hadn't traded away a crucial piece.

Philadelphia might be lost, but Jonathan could only think of Ruth. Would she and her family get out in time?

"PAPA! WHAT HAPPENED?"

Ruth held the front door open, and her father slipped inside. The early dawn light revealed a disheveled street littered with a child's toy, a broken wheel, and a fluttering kerchief. The clatter of wagon wheels on cobblestones had kept her awake most of the night. She'd finally given up any pretense of sleeping, though Aunt Betsy managed to snore in a chair before the stove. Philadelphia had panicked last night—or at least, some people had.

"John Russell came. He's across the Schuylkill."

That didn't explain her father's sooty face or the torn sleeve of his coat. "You're filthy."

"We moved the press."

She led him into the kitchen. "Our press?" She set the kettle on and rummaged for rags.

He plopped into a chair. "No, the *Gazette's*." He dampened a rag and wiped ineffectually at his face. "We hid it, but we'll still print, as soon as we find a safe place."

Despite his fatigue, there was a crow of triumph in his words.

"Gideon?" Aunt Betsy stood in the doorway, blinking owlishly. "You look wretched."

"Give me your coat, Papa, and I'll mend it."

Ruth retrieved her sewing kit from the parlor, and her aunt set the table with day-old bread and thin coffee. At least it was real coffee.

He sipped at the beverage with obvious relish. "I'll escort you both over the ferry."

She pushed the needle through the tough fabric of his coat. "Papa, what about you?"

He stared into his cup. "I need to stay with the paper."

The news of the loss at the Brandywine River had penetrated Philadelphia and with it a conclusion that Washington had failed, and the city was now open to the redcoats. For her part, Ruth did not know where Washington's army was, or if there was another chance at stopping the British.

"Where are the British?" she asked.

"Does it matter? I doubt if they are more than two days' march away."

A chill ran up Ruth's spine. "But Papa, where's the paper going?"

"Head out toward Lancaster. I will meet you there."

Tears sprang to her eyes. They'd left Boston. Now the Youngs' home was no longer safe—and there seemed to be no hope left. Not for them, not for the Cause.

THE NIGHT SETTLED in over General Grey's men. A single bright rectangle shone from a lantern carried by Grey's principal aide-de-camp, and Robert kept his eyes steady on the beacon as they traveled north, seeking Anthony Wayne's militia.

Robert welcomed the darkness. It hid the long ears of the mule he rode —no cavalryman would take the creature, but if he was to accompany Captain André, he needed a mount. And many of the horses had died on the rough voyage down the coast and up the Chesapeake Bay. General Howe's own mount had survived, but its ribs still protruded. Even Tarleton was unhorsed, and the burden of the recent battles had fallen on the foot soldiers. This mule had undoubtedly served a local farmer until someone in a red coat had snatched it.

"How do you get it all done?" Robert nudged the mule closer to Captain André's mount. "The records, the meetings, all in addition to your other duties."

André now served as junior aide-de-camp to General Grey, and Robert had been assigned to help André in his secretarial duties and as a sort of intelligence protégé.

"Once we take Philadelphia and enter winter quarters, we will be able continue developing contacts without the pressure of daily maneuvers." He paused. "Do you dance well?"

"Dance? Tolerably enough."

"The Loyalist population of Philadelphia includes women and cultivating them may prove helpful."

Robert had no doubt that André would do well among the fairer sex, with his handsome features and charming manners.

They came to a crossroads where there was a brief halt. Commands were grunted down the ranks. "Remove flints."

Rustles and sharp clinks sounded as the men disarmed their muskets. No shots could be fired to give away their position. An attack in the deep of night seemed ... well, less than honorable, but everyone agreed they'd sustain the fewest casualties that way.

The darkness seemed to deepen. From the foliage at the side of the road, a bat flew suddenly overhead, a blur of motion, black against black. Then the foliage parted to reveal a veil of crimson velvet across the northern sky.

Robert's throat dried. Last night's friendly green aurora borealis had shifted to an ominous hue.

And then shall appear the sign of the son of man in heaven ...

He'd finally finished reading the book of Matthew. Jesus' words were at turns sweet, puzzling, alarming. Nothing like what he'd expected.

But no. The color of the heavens meant nothing. He wrapped his fingers around the comforting hilt of his sword and loosened it from the sheath. He could at least defend the general.

Before and behind, the thuds and clinks of marching men filled the cooling air. The infantrymen were eager to attack the rebel militia they were hoping to surprise. General Wayne had been harassing General Howe's army, nipping and biting at his sides. The militia would get a trouncing if these men had anything to do with it.

But didn't Wayne know they were coming? The nimble Pennsylvania militia would know the countryside.

Robert murmured the question to André, and in lieu of reply, the man rummaged through a pouch and lifted out a folded paper. "Intercepted."

So, General Wayne suspected. "They are awaiting reinforcements?"

"That will never come."

"Nice work," Robert whispered. One of André's informers had relayed the position of the rebel detachment, and now this.

Metallic swooshes and clicks rang deadly in the cool night air, the sound of bayonets being fixed. Robert understood the necessity of not giving away their position by firing, but now he understood the full plan: they were going in silently to skewer unwary men, or worse, to kill sleeping soldiers in their beds.

They had to be close. A halt. More marching. A rising moon struggled to shed light through the trees, but it had to be near midnight, and the rebel sentries might be sleepy.

Robert glimpsed the feeble flicker of a fire ahead. Moments later, shapes rushed from the tree line, firing upon the infantrymen, tiny flashes accompanying the tell-tale *pops* of gunfire.

The sentries hadn't been sleeping, after all. Robert unsheathed his sword.

"Dash on, light infantry!" General Grey's bellow was heard down the ranks, and Robert's mule danced about in confusion for several moments. Riding a farm animal into battle might not have been the best choice. He kicked its ribs, and the mule lurched forward.

Robert gained Captain André's side soon enough to see the attack. The sentries' fires gave enough illumination to glimpse the camp beyond, where rebels rolled out from crude lean-tos or tents in clear surprise. Some had even left arms behind.

Cheering filled the air as Grey's men rushed forward, bayoneting every man they saw. Shrieks of the wounded filled the air, competing with the gleeful shouts of the infantry.

Then bursts of light flared here, there, and in another place. The infantry were setting the huts of the militiamen on fire, the flames casting ghostly shadows among the trees. The soldiers laughed as they stabbed those who escaped their burning shelters.

Those who managed to fire their muskets were cut down, the flash of their musket pans marking their location in the darkness.

Robert sheathed his sword and raised his pistol, hunting for a target. Advancing through the melee, he saw a rebel emerge from a burning tent— the man a human torch, clothes and hair on fire.

Horrified, Robert shot him. The mule bucked, and for several minutes he fought the creature, finally bringing it under control.

With the scent of smoke, blood, and human waste filling his nostrils, he sought André, but the battle had swept south among the trees, and only pockets of men remained. He approached one such pocket—red-coated men circling a lone rebel, who danced to evade the silvery thrusts of flashing bayonets.

Blood trickled from multiple wounds on his arms and legs. He screamed as a corporal raised his musket high and thrust the bayonet into his shoulder. They were toying with the man.

"Is this man a prisoner?" Robert barked.

The infantrymen paused in their macabre game, and the rebel slipped from the circle and disappeared into the trees.

Robert fought rising nausea as he made a show of reproving them for losing the captive. Then he turned the mule.

He wished he could escape too. And maybe he would, if he could find an honorable way. But there was none.

31

The annals of the age cannot produce another such scene of butchery ...
—Major Samuel Hay, 7th Pennsylvania Regiment

*T*here's a dry spot." Jonathan jerked his chin in invitation. The intermittent rain had ceased for now, but the mud remained. "I'm sorry about your horse."

Nathan took his pack off and set it down. His face was streaked with grime and gunpowder. "Aye, Wilson was a faithful creature. I left Luther with Henry Knox. The horse knows his job better than some of the artillery crew."

"Aye, Luther is as canny as they come."

Wilson, one of his brother's prized horses, had perished at the battle along the Brandywine. On foot now, his brother had joined the Ninth Virginia, which was currently sprawled about a grove, snacking on filched apples or foraging along the stream. The quartermaster had given them nothing since noon yesterday, and Jonathan's belly gnawed with hunger.

Nathan leaned his long rifle on the broad tree trunk behind him and sat before the campfire. "Where'd ye get the birds?"

Yellow tongues of flame sputtered at the drips of grease from two roasting geese propped on makeshift spits. The savory smell attracted a few glances. The sure shots of the Ninth fretted over the order to conserve ammunition. Some used snares, but few caught anything.

"Lured them with a few kernels of corn." Then he'd grabbed their necks in one quick motion.

The birds were delicious, autumn-fat. The brothers shared with several who stopped by the fire, including Colonel Mathews.

"Finally. The quartermaster is doling out bread and rum," Mathews said. "I spotted Knox, Greene, and the others going in and out of headquarters." He looked them each in the eye. "We'll fight again soon."

"We won't get Philadelphia back," Jonathan said. Congress had fled; the government was safe. He had yet to hear from Ruth.

Mathews finished the goose leg they'd given him and licked the bone clean. "Think about Brandywine. What if we hadn't been flanked?"

Jonathan saw his point. They'd fought well, just been outmaneuvered. "We will sleep on our arms again tonight."

The massacre at Paoli's Tavern horrified him. The Ninth and all of Washington's army had been sleeping fully clothed on the muddy ground, firearms loaded and primed at their sides, ever since. The men were furious.

Matthews' eyes narrowed. "And we'll get our revenge. Russell, I want you on the left of the regiment. And you"—he glanced at Nathan—"on the right."

Jonathan grunted in acknowledgement. If Mathews charged at the redcoats again like a crazy man, at least they could cover him.

Mathews departed, and Jonathan dozed. The shadows were lengthening when another man approached. A familiar man.

"Red Hawk—howdy! Come sit at our fire." Jonathan gestured a welcome. It had been a long time since he'd seen the man, and he fought his impatience, silencing the questions coming to his lips.

Red Hawk eased himself down. "Are you well? And your father?"

"My father should be west of the Schuylkill River by now, escorting the Haynes and my aunt to the valley—or at least, out of danger." Jonathan didn't know if Ruth had actually agreed to go to the valley or not. And he had no clue as to her father's plans.

Eventually Red Hawk described his own activities up north, scouting for Washington and parleying with the Oneidas.

"A group of Oneida I left in New York, fighting against General

Burgoyne. They also serve as scouts. Some have come with me, and I suspect, more will follow."

More men were always welcome. "I have a favor to ask of you," Jonathan said.

"You are my brother."

"Brutus—take him. We will fight on foot with the Ninth, and you might have need of him." What Jonathan did not say was he feared his horse would be killed.

Red Hawk's blue gaze was fixed on his face. The setting sun highlighted the lines framing his eyes. "I can keep Brutus for you. And after my duties are completed here, I will ride west and see to your family's safety."

Jonathan's heart swelled in gratitude. "Thank ye kindly."

Brutus snuffed once before consenting to Red Hawk's gentle handling.

"I will lift your name before the throne of grace."

Jonathan nodded. *Grace.*

It sounded sweet. But it just seemed so far away. Jonathan watched Red Hawk trot away and ran his fingers over his jaw. The stubble no longer itched. He suspected some of the Ninth would simply let it grow into an early winter's beard, but his heart was restless, and the hair did not rest easily on his jaw.

He picked through his haversack, pulled out his shaving kit, and strolled to the nearby stream. Golden light reflected off the surface of the water, breaking up into tiny suns. He suspected that Washington would give the command to march well before daybreak.

Would he be ready?

He scraped off the beard slowly and methodically, wanting to somehow cleanse himself, prepare himself for the upcoming battle. According to Red Hawk, Indians purified themselves before marking their bodies for the warpath.

The throne of grace.

He stared at his reflection in the water, his features pulled apart by the dancing ripples.

His face was clean, but his heart was not. *Help, Lord.*

～

THE WAGON SLOWED AND STOPPED. Ruth glanced at Aunt Betsy, whose gentle snores had not stopped since they'd left before dawn. The turmoil of the last few days had tired them both. A folded blanket helped to cushion the hard wood of the sea chest Ruth sat upon in lieu of a seat—the Conestoga had none. Papa's printing press gleamed dully in the wagon bed behind her.

Ruth clambered out into the dim morning, thick with cottony mist. Why had they stopped?

Jonathan's father was examining one of the mule's legs, his rifle still strapped to his back. John Russell was a cautious man. His gaze checked the horizon, still invisible beneath the cloak of early fog. The only sounds were the final nighttime pips of a lone frog and the twittering of a few brave birds on the Lancaster Road. There was no sign of the British.

Hannah dismounted from her large mare. "Lame?"

John Russell lifted a foreleg and inspected the upturned hoof. "Bruised hoof, I think." He released the animal and straightened. "All this rain and mud make for treacherous footing."

Several September downpours had drenched Philadelphia and nearby towns. Clouds still threatened, but they'd seen no rain on their journey—all five miles of it. Mud still clogged the low places of the roads.

Ruth tried futilely to see through the mist and decided sound was more reliable. Certainly there were no hoofbeats or marching feet following them on the Lancaster road. But the British Army was somewhere near. Jonathan's father thought some of Howe's brigades were to the north of them.

He didn't need to mention that some were behind them to the east— right across the river in Philadelphia. The sound of their drums and music had followed Ruth and her aunt as they'd escaped the city and crossed on the ferry. Papa—where was Papa? And now this.

"Da? What are we going to do?" Hannah's question echoed Ruth's own.

John Russell took a deep breath. "Bodie's broke to harness."

"She hates it."

They harnessed Boudicea in the place of the mule, which was then tied to the back of the wagon.

"Slowly, now." He walked before the animals, one hand on each bridle. The mare tossed her head once but submitted.

Ruth joined Hannah who walked behind the wagon, keeping an eye on the limping mule. "How did you get permission to come?"

"Into danger, you mean?" Hannah looked her in the eye. "When we made preparations, we didna know where General Howe was, and the danger seemed small. In Winchester we got word that his ships had landed, and in Lancaster we read that he was approaching the Brandywine River." Her voice dropped. "Da started grinding his teeth after that."

They made it only a single mile before the metal rims of the wagon wheels began to suck and pop in a muddy stretch.

"Take the reins, lass," John Russell said to his daughter. "I'll push."

They made it out of the mud, but the going remained slow. After another couple of miles, John Russell checked the mule's hoof again.

"We need to stop and let Rufus rest," he said.

"Where?" Hannah spun about, indicating the landscape.

Trees flanked either side of the road. But even if they found a farm, would the owners be friendly?

He indicated one side. "We'll follow this road."

"Road?" Ruth asked Hannah.

"See? Near the stream."

Faint twin tracks of dirt ducked under the foliage, presumably flanking a stream. It looked rough. But at least they would be out of sight of any redcoats.

AFTER A QUARTER HOUR on the track, both the fog and the trees thinned. Aunt Betsy woke and peered out at the trees, her mouth a grim line. Ruth thrust her hands in her pockets, but her pistols were in the wagon, wrapped safe from the wet.

The trees parted.

A small stone farmhouse was nestled at the bottom of a misty hollow. Apple-laden trees guarded the far side; behind the house, fence rails rose over half-harvested fields. A neatly swept front yard lay empty.

Might they claim hospitality?

"Halloo, the house!" John Russell signaled the women to stay behind the wagon.

Ruth followed Hannah to the front wheel of the Conestoga and peeked from behind it.

The house looked so peaceful … maybe too peaceful. It was quiet, without the customary clucking and squawking of farmyard fowl. A modest outdoor brick oven sat to the side, its cover missing. As if someone had removed hot bread and galloped off.

"Halloo, the house!"

Hannah crouched, withdrew a pistol from her satchel, and laid the muzzle of the gun against the rim of the wheel.

Her father examined the door. "It's open!"

Hannah stood, but he waved her back.

After several minutes he returned. "No one's here."

Had they fled the army?

Jonathan's father helped Aunt Betsy from the wagon. She swept inside, and Ruth followed her in. The floors were old, scarred pine, and she lifted her skirts to keep their muddy hems from soiling the clean surface.

A quick glance revealed a simple layout—two rooms above, a narrow staircase, and two simple rooms below. A large, cracked bowl sat on a narrow kitchen worktable. The single hearth was large, and the box was still full of firewood.

John Russell returned from the other room, holding a brown broad-brimmed hat. "They left in a hurry."

Aunt Betsy claimed the kitchen, and Hannah's father went outside to see to the animals.

Hannah nudged Ruth. "Let's see if there's a kitchen garden."

Ruth turned to the open doorway and paused on the top step. On the other side of the yard, beech saplings dressed in yellow-tinged leaves rose between broad stumps along the line of the stream. Beyond the foliage, the eastern horizon was hazy. But not with fog.

She took several steps toward the stream, trying to see better.

"Hannah?"

"Aye?" Hannah was at her elbow.

The distant basso voice of a cannon shuddered through the morning. "Is that—"

Hannah's warm hand curled over Ruth's cold fingers. "It's started."

～

JONATHAN DIDN'T KNOW what had wakened him. The birds and crickets were silent, and only the katydids still filled the night with their chirping.

It was very late, but it wasn't morning.

"Russell," a voice said. "We're marching. Get the others."

Jonathan wiped the sleep out of his eyes and reached for his brother. "Nathan."

"Already?" But the muffled complaint was followed by the rustles of quick movement.

"Send Robinson to me and put Kerr on your left," Jonathan said.

Soon the riflemen were awake and took their positions behind those with muskets, bumping each other in the darkness. The moon wouldn't rise for hours—assuming they could see it through clouds or mist. The blackness was pierced only by a few dark lanterns, their small squares of light bobbing like fireflies.

For what seemed like forever they marched in columns, Robinson just behind him, sometimes treading on his heels in the darkness, grunts and low words marking the positions of the other men of the Ninth. Once, Jonathan heard General Greene's voice rise above the murmurs and rustles of the masses of men, shouting instructions to Mathews and the other militia commanders.

Then they stopped. A sudden shove sent Jonathan on his face on the wet ground. He got to his knees. "Watch yourself, Abel Robinson!" The man had run right into him.

"Sorry, sir. It's so dark, sir."

After Brandywine, Mathews had promoted Jonathan to the militia rank of lieutenant. It was probably a concession to the Russell name—rank in a militia had more to do with popularity than anything else. The "sir" irked him a bit but since he bossed folks around, he might as well have the authority to do so.

"Never mind."

They waited under the trees for a long time. Finally the birds began to chirp, but their song faltered at the tap-tap-tap of distant musketry.

Then a cannon boomed, and then another, and the sound seemed to surround them in the gray misty dawn. Where was it coming from?

Jonathan dropped to his knees and hunted a dry patch of ground. He didn't want to be flanked again.

"What are you doing?" Robinson asked.

It was an Indian trick. Jonathan laid his ear on the ground and listened for a long while until he was sure. Finally he rose. "The battle is before us." He pointed. "Right that way."

Mathews summoned them. "Attack formation. Forward march."

The members of the Ninth cheered as they formed rows. Jonathan primed his rifle and nodded to Robinson to do likewise. Then they advanced. Trees and fences loomed out of the wispy fog, obstructing their way. But the Ninth Virginia had its blood up, ready to avenge Paoli, where men had been bayoneted in their beds, and the men to either side of Jonathan poured over and around the obstructions like disturbed ants. Boots and moccasins slapped on the leaf litter to Jonathan's right, and to his left, the murmur of another regiment's advance filled the woods with ominous sound. They charged through and around every barrier.

Jonathan clutched his rifle tightly, his blood thumping in his ears. The tap-tap-tap of musket fire sounded louder now, closer than the cannon.

A sudden glimpse of red sent his pulse racing. The trees and fog slipped away to reveal the red of British uniforms. Instinctively, Jonathan leveled his long rifle and sought a target.

He paused, listening for a command. But there was none. Instead, the Ninth Virginia seemed to act as one body, all rushing against the enemy.

Then Mathews shouted, and a ragged *pop-pop-pop* sounded from the front of the regiment. Jonathan lifted his rifle and squeezed the trigger. He reloaded, glancing about. Robinson's face was a study in concentration—he too was reloading, hands flying.

Dark gray smoke mingled with the remaining fog. Colonel Mathews shouted again, and again they advanced, cheering and shrieking. Jonathan found his own throat raw, though whether it was from shouting or the acrid smoke he couldn't tell. He managed to get off two more shots and had the satisfaction of seeing a British officer spin and fall.

He couldn't see well because of the musket smoke. It seemed they were still advancing, but it was becoming difficult to find targets. Then, suddenly, all was confusion. Musket fire sounded to his right and to his left, and the haze blinded him. Someone screamed, and a horse whinnied in distress.

A blow slammed into his shoulder, turning him around and sending him to his knees. Red clouded his vision, but he fought to get to his feet. His left shoulder felt numb, and his left arm wouldn't obey his commands. Standing, he lifted the rifle with his sweaty right palm.

He tightened his jaw and willed the sight to come up. Through the gray smoke he saw the long ears of a mule.

A mule?

The breeze parted the smoke and he saw a cluster of red uniforms on either side of the mule. He chose one at random and fired.

His knees weakened, and his shoulder burned. He knelt to reload, but it proved impossible with one arm. Hooves appeared on the blood-spattered mud nearby. Strong hands lifted him, and pain enveloped him.

"Come."

It was Red Hawk on Brutus. He must be dreaming. Why would Red Hawk be here?

ROBERT NUDGED his mule forward to assist Lieutenant Foster, who was supervising the surrender. Before them, a white shirt impaled on a bayonet rose pleading above a large group of grubby men. Foster's men pointed their muskets at the enemy, some of whom were on the ground panting or clutching their wounds.

"Hundreds, sir, there are hundreds." Foster waved a gloved hand. "But we just lost our captain." To one of these riflemen, no doubt, and the expression on Foster's face was one of fury.

An entire rebel regiment had been captured. The men wore no uniform that Robert could see. Some wore ordinary coats, but most sported leather hunting jackets with fringes. Unshaven, gunpowder-blackened faces stared back, some furious, others mystified. They truly looked like rabble.

Even those not wounded were near collapse with exertion. They had fought with great courage and effort, charging up against the British position until—impossibly—they found themselves behind the lines.

Washington was withdrawing, and this island of men was completely surrounded.

A sorrel horse looking remarkably like Jonathan Russell's burst through the hazy mass of trees and men at a gallop, but he could not discern the rider's face in the haze. The animal's hindquarters nearly touched the ground as it came to a sudden stop next a single crouched man—one of the wounded, no doubt.

Foster raised his pistol as the rider deftly hauled the wounded soldier onto the horse and took his place behind him.

Was that Jonathan Russell?

The rider charged straight for them, seeking a way of escape, the broad-chested sorrel's gallop startling Robert's mule, sending it straight into the lieutenant's mount.

The lieutenant squinted and aimed at the escaping rebels.

Robert thrust his hand under the barrel of the pistol and sent the shot skyward.

"What—!"

"You idiot! Have you no sense? We are sitting in a circle, we cannot fire at a moving target, we'll hit one of our own!" Robert was becoming a very good actor. He could sound like a tightly strung martinet if he wished.

Robert wanted to survive in this army, and it was the only way.

He twisted. The horse and rider had disappeared.

32

I trust the same Divine Being who brought us together will support us ...
    —Henry Knox to his wife Lucy

*R*uth returned inside and joined Aunt Betsy at the kitchen worktable. "Might I help?"

Her aunt's strong fingers wrestled with a large lump of dough made with flour she'd scrounged from a nearly empty crock. "See what's upstairs. We'll need to sleep, and I can't imagine the sheets will be fresh." Ruth headed for the narrow oak staircase, but the ominous gray band of smoke on the horizon remained on her heart.

Cleaning would distract her. A broom made quick work of freshening the ceilings and floors of cobwebs and dust. Ruth stripped the beds. She shook out and folded a multi-colored quilt made of carefully pieced triangles, artfully arranged but faded with time. The owners had undoubtedly snatched away the best of the blankets, but they'd left this labor of love behind.

Why had they left? Were they Loyalists—or Tories, as some called them —afraid of Washington's army or the Philadelphia Committee of Safety? Or was the situation reversed, and they had fled the redcoats?

Ruth stared at the lumpy mattress and her eyes grew moist. She knew what it felt like to lose a home. Was someone living in their home in Boston?

Was someone sleeping in her bed?

Once, this conflict roiling over land and sea had been an argument of minds—which argument was sound, which argument was scriptural.

But it wasn't that way now, and it wasn't that way for the inhabitants of this house. They'd feared for their lives.

A clatter of hooves and a man's shout sounded from outside. She scurried to the small window. Unable to see much, she scrambled down the stairs and dashed to the front door. Hannah was already outside, her apron splotched from the garden. Her aunt, dusted with flour, joined Ruth.

Brutus! Ruth's pulse raced as she recognized the horse, carrying two men, his master and David Sloan. Blood covered Jonathan's left side as he slumped in the saddle. Sloan relinquished him to John Russell's arms.

"Ruth! Hot water! Bandages!" Her aunt helped the men with Jonathan.

Ruth dashed for a bucket.

"I'll make a pallet." Hannah's voice was low pitched, her face drawn.

John Russell helped Jonathan navigate the steps, though Ruth didn't think he was fully conscious. He seemed dazed.

She wondered where Nathan was. Sloan's presence was a mystery—how did he know they were here? But then, they weren't far from the main road. She could only feel gratitude for the man's ability to track them down.

The men eased Jonathan onto the pallet and examined the wound. Ruth unrolled her huswif to find scissors and thread. Aunt Betsy brought in steaming bowls of vinegar water and bandages. Hannah spooned laudanum into his mouth.

A wave of emotion washed over John Russell's face as he removed most of his son's shirt with a knife and pressed wads of linen into his shoulder, quickly turning crimson. "Miss Haynes, we'll need your needle." His expression had settled. "Can ye sew a wound?" She nodded, and he addressed Mr. Sloan. "Red Hawk, hold him."

The men braced Jonathan's limbs. Ruth saw the injury clearly for the first time. A musket ball had passed through his shoulder. Had it nicked a bone?

John Russell splashed a little vinegar water over the wound and Jonathan yelped. "It's gone through, a good thing."

The warm, metallic smell of blood met her nose, and the vivid memory of the Boston physician removing a musket ball from Joshua's shoulder curdled Ruth's stomach. She took a deep breath. With her largest needle she probed the wound for bone fragments. Jonathan groaned and shifted as she levered out a long chip. Once the blood-covered fragment was free, she stitched him steadily but quickly, forcing herself to treat him as she treated any soldier she'd nursed at Dr. Rush's hospital.

A strand of hair fell into her face, but she ignored it, fighting against the tears, fighting for focus. When one side was stitched, the men eased Jonathan over and she repeated the process, finishing with a final splash of vinegar.

Maybe he'd still have full use of his arm. Time would tell.

Aunt Betsy handed her sassafras and together they bound up the wound.

Jonathan began to stir. "Da? ... Da?"

"Son?"

"Nathan ... Where's Nathan?"

Ruth relinquished the bedside to the men. She began to tidy the common room, worried. His wound might fester. And Nathan ... Had he been fighting alongside his brother?

"I'll find out for ye," his father said. "Rest now, get your strength back."

Jonathan tossed his head once and then subsided into an exhausted sleep.

John Russell studied his son's form, then turned. "Red Hawk, I'll see ye on the stoop."

Hannah took her father's place and knelt next to her brother. The men went outside and sat on the front step. Ruth busied herself near the small front window, levered open to air the house. She thrust her broom into the corner and made cleaning motions while listening.

"The whole regiment was captured. There were redcoats on every side," Mr. Sloan was saying. "I did not see Nathan, but there were many men and much smoke. I will return and scout the area."

"The British will still be there. Be verra careful."

Ruth squeezed the broom's handle and a sliver of wood slid into her finger. Sloan, or Red Hawk as he was known, was going back.

Nathan ... captured?

A desperate idea began to form in her mind.

MR. SLOAN—RED Hawk—returned well after dark, clutching a man before him in the saddle. Another man was strapped to a crude travois harnessed to the horse.

Ruth's breath caught. Was either man Nathan?

No, they were strangers. Soon both men lay on the common room floor. Ruth lit several candles while Aunt Betsy and Hannah scurried about with water and bandages.

John Russell's face was grim as he examined their injuries. One of them had been stabbed several times by bayonets. The other had a musket ball through his leg and a bayonet wound in his shoulder.

"See to Zeke first, he's hurt bad," Musket Ball said. His leg was bloody but apparently no bones had been broken.

Ruth staunched and sewed until the flow of blood was stopped and the men were resting easier. Weary, she laid a hand on Jonathan's head. No fever yet. Jonathan had even taken a little broth, but she wasn't sure if these soldiers would survive. It was then she heard Red Hawk talking to Jonathan's father.

"I saw no trace of Nathan. Some of the wounded were left behind in a house guarded by a sentry, I could not check inside. I saw several dead lying in a field, and these two as you see."

"Any rumor as to where the able-bodied prisoners were taken?"

"The army was moving to Penn's town—Philadelphia," Red Hawk said.

"So presumably the prisoners would go there as well."

"Yes."

Ruth took a candle, went upstairs, and found her writing desk. Heart pounding, she washed her hands in the ewer's basin and wiped them on a clean corner of her apron. It was important she write this carefully.

She sat and inhaled deeply. Her hands were still trembling, but she willed them to form smooth strokes with the pen. Mr. Shirley—Captain Shirley—would be with Howe's army. Hopefully a sentry could get it to him.

To Captain Rbt. Shirley,

A scout has returned with information. Send the bearer with a time and place to meet.

Honorius

Cold sweat trickled down Ruth's neck. She studied her words. She had not given anything away, nor promised anything. Not exactly.

But he would help them, she was sure.

Almost sure.

She folded it and labeled it, then picked up the candle and tilted it to drip a crude seal on the letter. She stepped to the top of the stairs.

Red Hawk and Jonathan were talking below. She retreated and set the candlestick down so the light would not betray her.

"Here, drink this." Red Hawk's voice.

"I dinna need a nursemaid." Jonathan's voice was still weak, but Ruth was cheered by his words.

"In the morning I will find your aunt some cattail. She has no more yarrow but cattails will work just as well for bleeding."

"Must ye be so cheerful?" There was more to Jonathan's banter than his typical playfulness. His mood was dark. But then, he didn't know if his brother was dead or alive.

Red Hawk sighed. "Your heart is sick, my brother. It needs more than herbs."

Jonathan was silent for so long Ruth decided he'd fallen asleep. When he did speak his tone was different. More sad than angry. "Red Hawk, I do have a sick heart. A sick spirit. And I do not know who else to tell."

Ruth inhaled abruptly. Everyone else was upstairs, asleep or preparing for bed. She had promised her aunt to check on the men one last time, so no one else would think to come down.

Should she eavesdrop? But she didn't want to disturb the moment. If she moved from her place at the head of the stairs, she would most certainly be heard.

Her heart ached for Jonathan. She'd seen what Red Hawk had seen—the grayness that pinched his features at odd moments.

"I killed a man."

How was that strange? They were at war. But Red Hawk said nothing in reply. He simply waited until Jonathan spoke again.

"I was hunting out past Buffalo Gap. Hadn't seen anything in a day and a half, so I decided to cross the next ridge. Past Mathews's last trading post."

Ruth peered over the banister and saw Red Hawk nod. "I know the place."

"I was nervous. I knew Shawnee might come that far in their hunting. I

—" His voice choked. "I saw a rustle, a dark head rise from the brush, a hand ... and I fired."

Jonathan settled back on the pallet as if exhausted from the confession. "I killed an innocent man. I killed a man I knew. I killed George the Indian trader." He curled up on his good side and grasped his belly, groaning. "He ate at our table."

"That is too heavy a weight to carry alone," Red Hawk said. "I am honored that you chose to tell me."

Jonathan relaxed onto his back. Wetness glittered on his face. "But what do I do? I know God forgives ... but it plagues me. There must be something more I must do."

"You know I am named after David in the scriptures. Think on his sin. Did God forgive his sin of bloodguilt?"

"Aye, He did. But ... didn't King David suffer as a result?"

"David stole and killed. God did not require his life—the Son of God died for his sin—but He required restitution. The law says that you give back four sheep for a single stolen animal."

Jonathan's brow wrinkled. "How on earth do I give restitution?"

"The people have a custom for this." Red Hawk's voice tightened. "A life for a life." He paused. "George was Uchee, they are a peaceful people. They may accept you as a replacement for the one they lost. They may treat you well."

Ruth's knees weakened, and she lowered herself slowly to sit on the top step. *They may treat you well.* They might kill him as soon as he confessed. How could Jonathan even think about trusting himself to Indian justice?

"I will pray about it, but already my heart is light."

"Sleep well." Red Hawk remained until Jonathan's eyes fluttered closed. Then he stood.

Ruth picked up the candle and made her way down the steps. "Red Hawk."

He faced her and in his expression it was obvious he knew she'd been listening all this while.

"Would you grant me a favor?"

"If it is within my power." His gaze fell on the message in her hand.

She handed it to him, and he studied the direction. "You are sure?"

"If you can deliver it safely."

Red Hawk nodded and slipped out the front door without a sound.

Her heart numb, Ruth felt Jonathan's forehead, but he did not wake at her touch. Only slightly warm. She crossed to the common room and tended to the other men, changing their bandages.

Nathan was captured, and once he healed, Jonathan was leaving, she was sure of it. Hopefully Papa had escaped Philadelphia—traveling or hiding with the rest of the *Gazette's* printers.

She couldn't imagine sleeping. But she ascended the steps as silently as she could, Robert Shirley's face in her mind's eye.

On the landing, Hannah's half-dressed form startled her.

"What?" Ruth hissed, then pulled Hannah into the bedroom and closed the rickety door as quietly as possible.

"I'm coming." Hannah's pale face was blotchy from weeping.

"Coming where?" What had Hannah guessed?

"Nathan—he's been captured, and I see you have a plan. You sent Red Hawk with a message."

There was no denying it, but she had to keep Hannah in the dark about Robert. "I know not what will unfold precisely."

"You have friends in Philadelphia."

Ruth nodded. She'd let Hannah believe that. "Yes, I will try to find a way —but I will not know anything until tomorrow night."

Hannah sank down on the bed. "Da says in two days the soldiers will be able to travel—if they survive."

They had two days to find Nathan, two days before they had to leave for their own safety.

And Jonathan was wounded, which took him out of harm's way for now. But when would he leave on his hopeless journey to find peace?

33

We cannot hold mortality's strong hand.
    —Shakespeare, *King John*

*J*ohn Bertram's garden reposed on the West Bank of the Schuylkill River like a queen spreading her royal robes. Masses of herbs, trees, and rare botanical specimens from all over the world adorned her acres. Riding pillion behind Red Hawk, Ruth took a deep breath of the night air. They must be close to the garden and the rendezvous point.

She wouldn't be entering the garden itself. The note had been very plain. *Bridge before B's Garden, midnight.*

She'd pacified Hannah by promising to reveal what she discovered. The moon had set, and it was very dark on the road. The horse's hoofbeats sounded loud to her ears, and her pulse thrummed in her throat. Any moment now.

"We tether the horse here," murmured Red Hawk.

They continued the journey silently on foot, the better to escape detection. The British were just across the river and could have sentries along the road.

The British. Ruth's stomach roiled as she thought of Zeke, the soldier lying on the common room floor, dying. One of the bayonets had pierced his belly, and he wouldn't survive. Zeke was just a lad, really, a long-limbed youth who may have lied about his age to fight.

The wonderful words of the Declaration of Independence were fading just now. The King's fist had struck them again and again, and yes, maybe they'd fought courageously, but courage was no match for the brutal force of His Majesty's Army.

And now Nathan ...

What would she say to the King if she had the chance? What would she write? She wouldn't write as Honorius. No, she needed another name. And not Marius, either.

Portia.

The name leaped out at her like an epiphany. Shakespeare's Portia in *The Merchant of Venice.* The woman who took on a man's garb and argued for justice in a courtroom.

The quality of mercy is not strained ...

She'd always liked that play, the story of a bitter moneylender who insisted on "a pound of flesh" as collateral.

The bond doth give thee here no jot of blood ...

Walking in the dark, with Red Hawk beside her, she silently composed a letter.

My King, my liege lord, thou hast broken the bonds of common mercy by insisting on the slavery of thy subjects. When they resist, thou pursuest them to blood and death. Women are driven from hearth and home ...

Ruth's throat swelled and the words fled. It was too hard.

Red Hawk paused. "Just ahead. I'll keep you in sight."

Somehow she knew he could, despite the darkness. But he couldn't be part of this tête-à-tête.

Ruth shivered, her cloak no longer warm enough. The trees blocked out the faint light of the stars, and she felt her way forward, each step uncertain. Then the wooden planks of the bridge creaked under her feet. Underneath, the stream gurgled gently.

A light glimmered ahead. She turned the bend.

"Miss Haynes?"

The black awfulness fell away and there stood Mr. Shirley, familiar except for the red coat. He was the same—almost. A subtle shadow marked his handsome face. A new thought struck her—would he get in trouble for meeting her?

"Yes, 'tis I. Are you well?"

"As well as might be expected." He lifted the lantern higher. "But this is not a social visit."

"Nathan has been captured," she blurted. "We-we are looking for him."

"Is he an officer?"

Ruth frowned. "I doubt it. Just an ordinary militiaman."

He sighed. "If he were a regular officer, it might be possible to exchange him. Maybe. But mere militiamen—even militia officers—well, they have no standing."

The King, and General Howe, regarded them as criminals, not prisoners of war. She suspected that only necessity—the capture of their own top officers—would motivate them to release some of them in exchange.

"So, he is simply imprisoned for the duration?"

She wondered what Shirley's rank was. He was no longer "Mister" Shirley. Lieutenant? Captain?

"You said you had information."

She took a deep breath but had no words to speak. She would not give him what little she had. It was a ruse, and by the expression on his face, he knew it.

"You will never betray your friends." The lantern light glinted off his officer's gorget. "And I am not your enemy."

Tears welled in her eyes. "What can I do?"

"Most of the prisoners are in the Walnut Street jail. I can make arrangements for this time tomorrow night. You can visit, or at least communicate through a window. But do not come alone. The streets are not safe for a woman."

CAPTAIN ROBERT SHIRLEY found it painfully easy to bribe the provost, a man universally despised, and for good reason. He was abusive to prisoners and skimmed off a portion for himself from any donations that came their way.

For the wretches lived on charity—mostly from the Quakers, who may have abjured violence but neither could abide cruelty. And since the

Quakers were viewed as Loyal, they were mostly left alone. They quietly brought food and medicine to the rebels.

The provost was a lover of good food and drink, and it showed on his face. The sovereign Robert slipped him would be gone in a day. But the man asked no questions.

It was almost midnight, and the bulk of the Walnut Street jail loomed menacingly in the street lamps—a few of which were still lit, thankfully. There was no moon.

He heard singing. It was thin and weak, but it was singing.

Jesus, lover of my soul …

He knew this hymn—Charles Wesley.

Hide me, O my Saviour hide …

"Till the storm of life is past," he mouthed. "Safe into the haven guide."

O receive my soul at last.

Receive my soul—receive my soul at death. Wesley was speaking of death.

The singing stopped.

Robert scanned the streets again. It was foolhardy for a woman to come to Philadelphia. At this hour, the only soldiers about were foxed and looking for a good time.

Movement caught his eye. A man strode down Walnut, probably a Quaker by his dress, bearing a haversack. The broad-brimmed hat shadowed his features—

Wait. He watched as the man slowed and looked about. There was something strange about his gait. He was tall, but—no, this was no man.

His heart thudded in his chest. *Ruth?* Disguised as a man?

The woman passed near a streetlamp, and he caught a glint of red-gold hair, tied back like a man's.

Hannah.

He gasped and stiffened. She hadn't seen him, standing across the way in a puddle of shadow. He needed to stay close. He waited until she neared the jail, then crossed the street.

If he spoke, she'd recognize him—wouldn't she? His regimentals felt heavy on him, a malignant weight—malignant in her eyes. He tugged his hat down. He'd change his voice. Mimic Lord Dartmouth's cool vowels.

"May I help you?" The moment of truth. Would she recognize him?

Hannah Russell turned, and her gaze barely touched his form. "I need to see my brother."

The haversack was probably laden with supplies. "You may speak through the window."

It was the best he could do. He still had no clue as to Nathan Russell's location or condition. The men inside would probably know.

Hannah wavered, and he placed his hand under her elbow, something he wouldn't do to a man, but she didn't seem to notice he'd penetrated the disguise.

"Where?"

He guided her around the side of the building and retreated, staying in the shadows but within earshot.

"Nathan?" Her plaintive voice sailed through the bars of the window.

Robert caught the stench then. Human waste mingled with sweat and a faint coppery scent of blood. The jail was crowded, packed with the hundreds captured at Germantown.

"Ma'am? Miss?" A voice answered her. "Who are you looking for?"

"Ninth Virginia. Nathan Russell. I'm his sister." She laid her hand on the rough stone of the building.

Her voice had strengthened, but Robert felt her tension as if a cord bound them.

After several moments, the voice answered. "A fine man. The best."

Hannah's face barely reached the bottom of the window. She rose on her toes and leaned against the building, the hat tumbling from her head. "Is he there?"

"Not anymore."

Robert's heart sank.

Hannah curled her fingers around the bars. "What? Where?"

"Nathan taught us a song. And scripture verses. He kept saying them, you see, and his face would light up even though—"

"Was he injured?"

The voice inside stumbled and coughed. "Yes, miss, he was hurt but we helped him walk. We thought he would mend, he was so cheerful."

Hannah took several great breaths and dug her fingers into the stone.

The voice continued. "He was so cheerful," the man repeated. "We encouraged each other, speaking of home, and he said, 'Yes, I'm going home. To a better country, whose builder and maker is God.'"

Hannah crumbled, landing on her knees. Silent sobs wracked her. Robert waited.

"I'm that sorry, miss. They took him out this morning."

After a minute she seemed to come to herself and felt for her sack. She made her way awkwardly to her feet and began rummaging through the bag. "I have some things I brought for him." Mechanically, she slipped them through the bars.

Robert caught a whiff of fresh-baked bread.

"Thank you, miss."

The task complete, she seemed to remember Robert's presence and he shrank within himself, keeping his face in the shadows.

"Where—where—would they take him?"

Robert wasn't sure, but he could guess. The British Army wouldn't expend effort on the burial of dead prisoners. Somewhere behind the building was his best guess. He motioned her forward, and between the dark outbuildings, they found a stretch of ground.

Between an empty chicken coop and a long-unused pigpen were several fresh graves—one had been dug that very day, by the looks of it. The mound of dark soil bore no trace of autumn leaves or rubbish.

Hannah rushed forward and flung herself down on her knees. She thrust her hand into the damp soil and squeezed it. "How could you, Nathan!"

Robert scanned the area. She wasn't loud, but still … He saw no one, but his neck prickled. Someone was here.

Just like last night. Ruth's companion had been totally hidden by the foliage, and if it hadn't been for the chance glimmer of lantern light on an unsheathed blade, he would have stayed hidden.

So close, too. Not ten feet away.

The same man was probably near—a good thing, Robert supposed, but he decided to make no threatening moves. He didn't want a knife in his back.

Curling over, Hannah sobbed and heaved.

Robert yearned for her, yearned to wrap his arms around her, speak nonsense into her hair. There was nothing he could say that would help.

I am sorry for your loss. What a trite, unhelpful utterance, so common in English parlors. It would be absolutely despised by the vital, half-tamed woman before him.

He was six steps away, but he might as well be an ocean's distance. He would never court her, love her, provide for her—did women like that even need a man?

Maybe he could help in one tiny way. He searched the ground. It had possibly been tilled at one point but neglected since. Misshapen lumps dotted the yard. He found a large piece of fieldstone, roughly rectangular, and brought it to her.

He worked to keep his voice disguised. "A marker?" The words emerged half-strangled.

She accepted it and laid it on the grave. Then she stood. "I will not thank you. You killed him."

"I—"

"You are the King's man. You seek to crush us. You killed my brother." Her breathing deepened, hoarse and quick.

He reached out. If she became hysterical it would attract attention. "Miss, let me escort—"

"Dinna touch me!" The light of a street lamp fell on her flushed face. Then the flash of a blade.

He stepped back and raised his arm to block the blow, but he was too late. His cheekbone stung.

He retreated and pressed a handkerchief to his injury, acutely conscious of the guardian in the dark.

He took another step back.

A whisper of fabric, a muffled footfall, and she was gone.

The cold, empty night settled around him as he stood there holding the cloth to his face. Finally, he turned and walked back to the grave. He knelt and with his free hand reached out to the stone.

A better country. What did it mean?

Robert didn't know, but he hid the words in his heart, like foreign currency he would need later.

Someday, the pieces would come together. He hoped.

34

Tis a day of doubtfull expectation, Heaven only knows our destiny.
　　—Abigail Adams to her husband John, Oct. 6, 1777

*M*orning-damp tree limbs grasped at Jonathan as he thrust his way through the orchard. His sling-bound shoulder ached, but the pain seemed far away. He emerged from the trees and stumbled into the next field, gasping for breath. He wobbled to a stump and sat.

Yesterday he'd slept late, dreaming bloody dreams, only to be awakened to a living nightmare. Last night he'd barely slept, trying to absorb the news Hannah had brought back.

Nathan was dead.

Jonathan was numb. It didn't seem possible. But why should he doubt? This was war. Men died in war. Why not Nathan?

An ugly thought intruded. Could he have prevented it? Red Hawk had rescued him—but what if he'd stayed behind with the rest of the regiment? Stayed with Nathan? Was it his fault?

A fresh ache from his shoulder argued against the idea.

Back at the farmhouse, Zeke fought for his life on the pine floor. Another man who would likely die.

War had immersed them all in a miasma of blood and death. He'd seen it on the beach near Bunker's hill. He'd seen it at the Brandywine River and now Germantown.

But Nathan? It seemed impossible. It seemed that if he only turned around his brother would be there, joking or quoting Whitefield. How a man so devout, with such a fervent love for Christ, could be so full of joy seemed paradoxical.

Or maybe it wasn't. When Jonathan had decided to travel to the Uchee, a great burden had lifted. He felt like a heavily laden pack animal loosed from the weight of kegs and sacks after a long journey. Strangely light.

"Nathan," he whispered. "I wish you were here now." He wished him here to discuss the journey, to pray for him—to pray with him.

Had he suffered? To have succumbed after only a few days meant he'd been wounded—seriously wounded. He swallowed back a sob.

Hannah—poor Hannah—had relayed his final words. *A better country.*

So he was lucid, speaking of his own departure. Hopefully, his suffering had not been too grievous.

Jonathan wanted to feel angry, wanted to hate, to rush back into battle, but all he felt was an emptiness. Nathan was gone and would not come back.

His mother. He could not conceive what her grief would be like. He sat there for a long while, his mind empty, breathing in the smell of the field. The delicate call of a warbler hovered over him.

Lord, you know our needs before we even ask. I ask for my mother.

He wiped his eyes and rose. They might need him. Hannah would need him—and what about his father?

Jonathan returned through the orchard and ducked under the boughs of the sturdy old trees, their limbs dripping with red-tinged leaves. He resented his weakness. They needed to leave as soon as possible, and he could do little.

Wisps of smoke emerged from the outdoor oven, and he smelled bread. Then he smelled something else. The distinctive odor of turned earth, normally a pleasant, sweet smell he associated with spring plowing, but now—

He spotted Red Hawk's shoulders. He was digging.

Digging a grave.

Jonathan quickened his steps. "Zeke?"

Red Hawk stopped and straightened, beads of sweat on his temple despite the autumn cool. "Yes, early this morning."

Jonathan's shoulders slumped, and a dagger of pain tore through his shoulder. "Where's Da?"

His father never spared himself because of his age. Why wasn't he here, helping with the task?

"Went to Philadelphia at dawn, with the last of the apples from the orchard."

"What!"

Red Hawk sat on the edge of the shallow trench. "You were sleeping. He said he had to see his son's grave. I told him where to look. He went as a farmer, selling apples."

Jonathan clenched his fists and took a deep breath.

"He's dressed like a Quaker. Like your sister was."

"My eejit sister!" He clenched his jaw then sighed. She'd returned safely. But now Da ... Jonathan studied the dirt. "Wish I could spell you with the shovel."

"The horses need attention."

Jonathan went to the barn, his mind a tumult. It was easier to go into battle himself than to fret over his family. Hannah could have been—

He stopped himself them. No, Red Hawk had been with her, made sure she came to no harm.

But his father—

One careless word or action and he'd be captured. And from the tale Hannah had returned with, prisoners did not fare well.

He stroked Brutus's warm neck. "Hey, boy. We're leaving soon, ye'll be glad to stretch your legs."

Jonathan fed and watered the animals, then found a worn brush under a broken bridle. He curried his stallion one-handed, taking extra care in all the tender places. Brutus nickered softly.

"Nathan's ... gone." His voice cracked. "I dinna ken if ye understand. Maybe it's a blessing not to."

The animal laid his head against Jonathan's chest, and the warm horse smell soothed him.

"Ye're a good horse."

A noise stirred him. He poked his head outside.

It was his father, an empty basket dangling from his arm. Jonathan rushed to greet him, then slowed as he saw his gray, drawn face.

"Da."

His father dropped the basket and embraced him with one arm, careful of the sling. "Son."

Jonathan breathed in his father's sweaty scent, grateful he'd made it back safely. They'd harness the animals and leave—

And go home. "Mother."

His father's grip tightened, and his frame shuddered in a single, soundless sob.

There could be no words, no help for her grief. Only heaven's care would do. Jonathan released his father.

"Did ye find the grave?"

"Aye." Da's face was unreadable. "Let's go inside."

Several loaves of bread lay cooling on the kitchen table. Ruth scrubbed the common room floor, now bare of soldiers. The surviving man now sat on the kitchen floor, leaning against one wall. His face was pinched.

Jonathan wanted to know about Philadelphia, and he searched his father's face, willing himself to be patient. "We lost the other man."

"Let's see him proper into the ground first."

They went outside, and with his father's help, the grave digging was soon completed. Before the sun was high everyone gathered to pay their respects.

Jonathan ached as the shrouded body was slowly lowered into the earth. Instead of the unknown soldier, beneath the linen he saw his brother's face.

Nathan, smiling, joyful, his red-gold hair always threatening to come out of its tie. Nathan, running on the beach, laughing.

Goodbye.

He swallowed and fought back the tears. Perhaps it was best he hadn't been with him at the end. He could remember his brother as he'd lived.

He blinked and realized Ruth was next to him, her hands red from scrubbing. He'd buy her better soap or find some way to keep that from happening. She glanced at him, her dark eyes glistening with tears, and he longed to take her hand in his.

Da led the prayers. "Keep us, Lord, and give us the courage to walk in Your light and truth, even when we walk in darkness ..." His voice faltered.

Red Hawk spoke. "Grant Your people strength and joy and keep our steps. Have mercy on our enemies, as Your Son bids us to do. Amen."

There was silence as everyone laid stones on the grave to give it extra security against animals. Then they went inside.

"Da, did you find it?" Hannah asked in a small voice.

"Aye."

Jonathan found a stool. His legs were still weak.

His father's face was haggard with grief. "I found Nathan's grave. It had a stone to mark it."

"Aye." Hannah's voice could barely be heard.

"I dinna understand it. His name was engraved on the tombstone."

Ruth gave a small sound as she inhaled sharply.

Hannah shook her head. "Da, it was just a fieldstone."

"I am no' dreaming it. Simple, it was. 'Nathan Russell went to a better country.'" He sketched out the size with his hands, about the size of a loaf of bread. "Small but would have cost money for the carving."

"There was a man," Red Hawk said.

"A redcoat." A line appeared between Hannah's brows. "A guard or something."

Ruth's mouth dropped open. She must have a good notion of who it was.

Jonathan wasn't about to speculate. Not aloud. But he had a good notion too.

⁓

"JUST GET ME TO CHESTER." The surviving soldier, Sykes, moved stiffly. "I've kin there. Real sorry about ..." his voice trailed off in the pre-dawn darkness.

"Shush," said Aunt Betsy as the men helped Sykes into the wagon. He was healing, but it would be a long time before he could fight again.

Ruth rode behind Hannah to ease the burden on the mules. Every mile away from Philadelphia was a relief, but Ruth knew that scouts or raiding parties could accost them at any time. By the time they reached Chester, she was exhausted, and when the soldier thanked them again for saving his life, she barely acknowledged him.

She ate and climbed in the wagon, where sleep claimed her. Much later, long insistent rays of sunlight struck her face, and she reluctantly opened her eyes.

The wagon shook and rolled underneath her. Aunt Betsy was snoring, her chin on her bosom as she sat leaning against the side.

Ruth scooted closer to the open front of the Conestoga. Red and gold spangled the trees by the side of the road. How many days had it been since she and her aunt had left the house on Walnut Street? It seemed like forever, the hard days and worse nights blending together. The leaves announced the change of season, and the cold would come soon.

Jonathan's father rode pillion on the near wheel mule. The sound of clanking harness and muffled hoofbeats was soothing. No wonder she had slept so long. Just beyond the lead mules Hannah rode next to her brother.

The lines of Jonathan's back looked rigid as he rode Brutus. His shoulder must be painful. Even with the sling keeping his arm immobilized, riding would aggravate the wound. She would re-bandage it as soon as they stopped.

Nathan. The full nightmare came back to her then. A shoulder wound was the least of Jonathan's troubles. And then there was the journey he meant to take, if that late night overheard conversation meant anything.

Would he confide in her? She ached for him but knew she had no claim on his affections.

Jonathan must be exhausted. No sooner had the thought passed her mind when Jonathan's father called a halt.

"Mark the birch trees? I remember a goodly stream hereabouts."

Ruth relished stretching her legs. Once camp was made under the yellow foliage of the river birch, she sought out Jonathan.

"I'd like to check the bandage."

"Hmm." Every line of his body sagged.

They sat before the infant fire as Red Hawk fed it patiently.

Aunt Betsy thrust a canteen at Jonathan. "Switchel."

"Thank ye, Auntie." He upended it and drank the sour beverage thirstily.

"Maybe you should be in the wagon, not me." Ruth loosed the bandage. The place was pink and angry, the seepage mostly clear. Just a little blood, and no pus that she could see. Vinegar would do for cleansing the wound. Or even switchel.

He was quiet for a moment, watching her. "Da says we'll stay in Lancaster a few days."

"How far is that?" She grabbed his canteen and dampened a cloth with switchel.

"We'll—ouch! We'll be there tomorrow."

She laid a clean wad of linen over the injury, wrapped it snugly, then sat back on her heels. "I'm sorry," she said gently.

A wave of sorrow passed over his face. His Adam's apple bobbed. "And now I'm leaving them all behind, like a coward." He frowned. "I didna ask Hannah about Mathews."

"Who is he?"

"Our colonel."

Ruth thought of Robert Shirley's words. "They wouldn't exchange him, not a mere militiaman."

"Butchers." He sighed. "I know I ought to forgive, but it's beyond me just now." He caught her gaze. "You were involved in this, weren't you?"

He wasn't asking a question. He knew.

She nodded. "I found out where they were, but I couldn't go myself. Zeke was fevered—and in any case, Hannah insisted."

He took a deep breath. "Aye, I ken how she is." He studied her. "You met with Shirley."

She almost choked with surprise. "He told me where they were being held."

"When Da spoke about the stone, I guessed it."

"There was no one else to help ..." Her eyes welled with tears.

"Ruth Haynes, ye are the bonniest, most courageous woman I know."

Her throat swelled, and for a moment a rich silence lay between them. The fire popped.

"You're leaving ... you're a brave man, Jonathan Russell."

His jaw worked, and he squinted at her. "Ye make no sense."

"I heard you and Red Hawk."

He sighed, and his whole body seemed to sag. "Aye, I need to make something right. I dinna think folks will understand."

"I think you are obeying your conscience." Half of her wanted to beg him to stay. But she couldn't ask him to go against his conscience. Go against God.

She laid a hand on her bodice and felt the hard lump of her locket underneath. She had an idea.

35

I see grace groweth best in winter.
  —Samuel Rutherford

*L*ancaster was crowded. Every tavern and ordinary was packed with travelers and refugees. The shops did brisk business, but the prices were outrageous.

Ruth followed Aunt Betsy into a store. Some shelves were empty.

Her aunt snorted. "They want that much for beans?"

"That's the price in continentals." Ruth said. "I suspect you'll get more with hard money."

"Hmph. We have none."

It was true. Ruth had mere pennies in her coin purse and only a few continental dollars. Not enough to buy supplies for the rest of the journey. She had only a vague idea of the distance to the Shenandoah Valley, but they'd need beans and cornmeal at the very least.

They purchased a small sack of beans and returned to the campsite beside the river. The horses and mules grazed contentedly, and the men sat around the fire, talking.

Papa was not here. But someone in a tavern said Congress was in York, and the *Gazette* would surely follow. Surely Papa was safe, if he was this far from the British. Waiting chafed her, but it was good for Jonathan. He needed several more days for the wound to fully close.

As they drew closer to the fire, Ruth overheard Red Hawk's voice. "I wish to go hunting."

John Russell's gaze locked with Red Hawk's, a tacit understanding traveling between them. She didn't think it was just about hunting.

"I'll go with ye."

Less than an hour later, they were gone.

"Well, at least we'll have meat for the pot." Her aunt's expression was unreadable. "And if the Lord wills, extra for trading."

And perhaps the quiet of the woods would help a father's awful grief.

ROBERT ENTERED the room where Captain André sat at a desk, writing. The man was always writing, even in the evenings.

"Have a seat, Shirley. I must say, the scoundrel has good taste."

Robert had to agree. They shared Benjamin Franklin's Philadelphia home with Lord Rawdon, and while some in London would consider the man's taste to be rustic, Robert liked it. The Queen Anne chair he chose was spare and elegant, with just enough blue padding for comfort. He sat. "More correspondence to copy?"

"No. I wanted to show you my system."

Robert looked more closely at the book under André's hands. "A record?"

"Yes. When I make a contact, I record it, like so." He turned the book so Robert could see.

A spy book. It was impressive. "You have some abbreviations."

"You would make sense of them easily enough. We must keep tactical intelligence recorded to make any use of it at all."

Robert's mind was on the battlefield. "You are thinking of reports, of course."

"Naturally. The general needs a full report with adequate information, given him in a timely manner. Otherwise, it's all a game. A pointless game."

What André did not say was that they had no guarantee a commanding officer would use their intelligence. A familiar frustration.

"I spoke to Edward Shippen," Robert said. "You are right, he seems loyal to the Crown, even though his nephew is a rebel."

"His nephew the physician, you mean?" André took out a piece of paper and laid it on top of the book.

"Yes. But this loyal merchant has a daughter. I mentioned the general's dinner and our need of female guests to even the numbers."

"We also need to plan a dance. A ball." André dipped his pen.

Robert's chest tightened. He was glad Ruth was no longer here. Knowing her—and Hannah—they'd try to infiltrate the Loyalists and do their own spying. No, that was impossible. He knew their identities, and they knew he was here. Ironically, it would keep them from harm. "I fear I dance poorly."

The *scritch, scritch* on the foolscap was the only sound for a few moments. "No matter. You and I wear a fine uniform, and by using a little sense, we can chat up the ladies to good purpose."

"You mean flirt."

André chuckled. "Yes, I mean flirt. Nothing more, I assure you. No attachments. That is why you would make a better intelligence officer than Tarleton or Rawdon. They don't understand that women can be dangerous in this game."

"Yes, well—"

"Yes, absolutely. They think anyone who is not a rakehell is a monk or worse."

"What are you doing?" It was a drawing, he was sure. The man was a musician, wrote tolerable verse, and was rumored to draw and paint.

André lifted the sheet. "A good likeness? 'Tis only half finished."

Spare lines captured a thoughtful man on a graceful chair. Did he really look like that? "I am impressed."

"Here—for your sweetheart."

"I-I have no—"

"Hah. I know now that you do!"

A clatter rescued Robert from any interrogation. Not that André would, of course. The man was discretion personified. But still.

His cousin stood in the doorway. "Heard the news?" Rawdon's voice grated on Robert's ears.

"Enlighten us," André said, but Robert doubted his cousin heard the dry humor in the man's tone.

"Burgoyne. Surrendered. Surrendered to Gates."

The words opened a sudden well of silence in the room.

André dropped his pen. "I knew things were not going well up north, but—"

Robert was stunned. "How?"

"There were several engagements near the town of Saratoga. The second battle near Saratoga was fatal. Burgoyne was surrounded." Rawdon let loose a string of expletives. "General Simon Fraser killed. Many officers lost." A hard line appeared in his jaw. "Remember two names: Daniel Morgan and Benedict Arnold. Morgan's riflemen took down many of the officers. A bunch of scruffy backwoodsmen. I will get Morgan in my sights if it's the last thing I do."

Robert's chest tightened. He'd heard these names before. Suddenly he was back on that bloody hill above Boston, where he'd handed a loaded pistol to his cousin. That pistol aimed at a figure in white—

"And Arnold?" André asked.

Robert blinked and focused. Arnold. He wondered what André knew about the rebel general.

"Supposed to be brave. But"—Rawdon eyed the spymaster judiciously—"he is barely tolerated by the others."

"What do you know, precisely?"

"They say he is ambitious, but Washington won't promote him."

André nodded, looking thoughtful. "I would like to know anything else either of you hears about this man." He tapped the quill on the desk. "About the surrender—what are the terms?"

Robert tensed. A lot could hinge on the terms. Or lack of them.

His cousin slouched against the doorjamb. "Still being negotiated when the messenger left."

A good sign. Hopefully their officers would be paroled, at least.

"So," André said, "we may assume the general usages of war are being respected."

"They can't jail the whole army." Rawdon smirked. "Gentleman Johnny must be humiliated."

"No doubt." Robert crossed his arms. "But what are the implications? We know the rebels are courting the French."

It would be a month before the news crossed the Atlantic—to both London and Versailles. But what then?

"What are the implications?" André repeated. "The French already supply Washington with arms and ammunition."

Rawdon pursed his lips. "The French will always seek a chance to cut into our gains from the last war, or at least seek revenge."

"If they commit their navy there could be a problem," Robert said.

"Rawdon, tell me this. Did we lose these battles or did the rebels win?" André asked. "At any rate, what will the French think?"

His cousin sighed. "From the little I know, I would say the rebels certainly held their own on the field."

They had their answer then. Sooner or later, France would launch her navy.

Things had become a lot more complicated. This would not be a short war.

RUTH BUSIED herself as best she could while waiting for her father. The third day in Lancaster, Hannah approached Ruth and Aunt Betsy. "Let's go foraging. We might find late berries, and maybe chestnuts."

"And herbs." Aunt Betsy's manner was cheerful, if a bit forced.

Ruth readily assented. Anything to distract her thoughts was welcome.

The three armed themselves with sacks and baskets and set out along the river. Hannah carried a shotgun, and Ruth, a pistol, at Jonathan's insistence. By the time they returned, late in the day, laden with hickory nuts, watercress, cattails, wild onion, and several half-ripe persimmons, a stranger was sitting with Jonathan.

The man rose and approached them. No, not a stranger. He was dirty and dusty, but the familiar spectacles remained.

"Papa!" Ruth dropped her basket and threw her arms around his neck. Her father smelled sour, as if no one had washed his clothes recently.

He squinted at her through his spectacles. "You look thin."

"What about the *Gazette*?"

His brows lifted. "In York. Where Congress is. But I ..." He took a deep breath. "Mr. Sellers doesn't need me. He has two faithful journeymen, and only the one press now."

Ruth's heart accelerated. "So—"

"Would you mind terribly if we all went to the valley?"

"I think it's a marvelous idea." Jonathan would approve, he had desired it from the first.

"Your young man told me about Nathan."

His words fell heavily between them.

"He was captured, and …" She steeled herself, trying not to cry.

"You remind me of your mother." He placed his hands on her shoulders. "She was always so brave, but the truth was, I could read it in her face when she suffered. She simply couldn't hide it."

Ruth studied her father. She'd never thought of her mother that way. She remembered silk and satin, a pot of French rouge hidden in the dressing table drawer, a fine silver hairbrush. And trips to the governor's mansion for dinner. A life graced with fine things.

"Her parents opposed our marriage, you knew that. I was just a journeyman, but we attended the same meetinghouse, and saw each other frequently. I worked hard and saved. My hope was to buy a press, go into business, and become prosperous enough that I'd be accepted. I did manage to buy the press, but—"

"They never accepted you."

"No. Two horses and a carriage for a wedding gift. And as long as your mother lived, her father gave her significant sums from time to time as gifts. But her mother would not speak to me. Or worse, to her daughter."

Much of this Ruth knew or guessed. "But she married you despite their disapproval."

He shrugged. "In some respects, they were well meaning. Wanting the best for their daughter. But in truth, they themselves caused her greatest suffering."

"I remember her as cheerful."

"She was, most of the time. But I saw her tears. And her efforts to be brave." He took a deep breath. "And now … can you bear a new home? In the wilderness?"

Ruth felt rather than heard Jonathan's approach. He smelled of leather, sweat, and horse.

"It's not so bad as all that," he explained to her father. "We've killed almost all the wolves." A dry humor underlay his words. "And Staunton isna quite as large as Lancaster, but we've a courthouse and two taverns. And several stores. And since Maggie McClure retired to her rocking chair, we dinna have an apothecary. Aunt Betsy would be welcome."

Ruth's heart swelled with thankfulness at his words. But what about Papa? She could help him start a paper. She'd have a purpose too.

"My press?" Papa was asking. "You brought my press?"

Jonathan jerked his chin toward the wagon, then froze.

She followed his gaze. A rider was approaching. The horse trotted to a standstill nearby, blowing.

"Halloo! News!"

They all gathered around the man, whose face was sweating despite the chill of the day.

"Burgoyne surrendered! Gentleman Johnny is going home!"

Could it be true? Or just a wonderful dream?

~

JONATHAN WAS STUPEFIED. Then a thrill shot up his spine. "What do ye mean, surrendered?"

British General "Gentleman Johnny" Burgoyne was somewhere up north, fighting Gates's men—and Daniel Morgan's riflemen. That was all he knew.

The messenger wiped his brow, and Aunt Betsy motioned for him to dismount.

"Come settle and have something to drink." She handed him a canteen.

"Thank you, ma'am."

Ruth's father drew closer. "How did it happen?"

The messenger took a long swallow and wiped his mouth with his sleeve. "Morgan's men took down many of their officers, and I know they lost a general. They say General Arnold's bravery—or foolhardiness, depending on who you ask—made a big difference. Burgoyne was surrounded and sent word to Gates. He refused to use the word surrender, but that's what it was." He grinned.

Hannah whooped in delight.

Ruth handed the man a persimmon, and he nodded his thanks.

Jonathan remained where he was, seated on a log, trying to absorb the incredible news. "How big is Burgoyne's army? Five thousand?"

"More than that, but I don't know how many exactly," the man said.

"Mr. Haynes, what happens to those redcoats?" Jonathan asked.

"There are protocols for this sort of thing. Those regulars will not be fighting again."

At least five thousand out of commission. Out of the fight. The odds were better now.

He gazed at Ruth. The victory was a token for good. Looking at her, his heart felt torn—he'd miss her. But he knew the Lord's will; his path was marked. When he'd made the decision to go south, peace had flooded his heart.

He'd see her again. He just knew. And now the way was clear.

The messenger stood. "I must go to the courthouse and give them word. And then on to York. Thank you for your hospitality."

The rider departed, and they all watched him go silently. It was a long minute before anyone moved.

Ruth approached Jonathan. "What does this mean?"

"It means we have a chance. And who knows, the French may help us." He stepped closer and took her hands in his. "Would it be too forward of me to ask … to ask if ye'll wait for me?"

He held his breath. It could be a very long time.

She blinked rapidly several times. "Jonathan. I … I will wait for you." She released his hands and fumbled with a clasp behind her neck. "Here. I want you to have this. A lock of my hair."

"But …" Jonathan examined the locket in his palm. The top was glass, the dark coil of hair fully visible inside. "I thought you carried your mother's miniature in this."

"I plan to purchase a little frame for that. Wear this next to your heart."

He swallowed. "I will return as soon as I can."

O Lord, bring me back to her.

Part Three

The Backcountry

1780-1782

[in code] I expect soon to command W[est] P[oint] and most seriously wish an interview with an intelligent officer in whom a mutual confidence could be placed.

—Gen. Benedict Arnold to Major John André

The Shenandoah Valley, April 1780

*R*uth squatted and thrust her knife into the soil. Several broad-leafed ramps joined the others in her basket, their sharp oniony smell tart and refreshing. She stood and felt a twinge in her back.

Whenever she needed to be alone, she went foraging on the slopes of the Blue Ridge above the Russells' home. Wild leeks, or ramps, were among the earliest finds of spring and made for a good excuse.

She'd been in the valley with her father and Aunt Betsy for over two years, and she'd learned the secrets of the slopes and hidden bounty of the forest. The cobblestones of Boston were fading in her mind. Even the war seemed far away. The Shenandoah Valley was like a secluded enclave, hundreds of miles from the fighting.

She tried to forget the war. Papa scrounged for news, and so it faced her again and again, and since Burgoyne's surrender at Saratoga, the news had rarely been good. But under the friendly oak branches on the slopes, her mind could rest.

Ruth found a gray outcrop and sat on the cold stone, wishing her leather half-cape were longer. The day was cloudy, and the sun's warmth didn't reach the ground.

She smoothed the stems in her basket into parallel formation, loosening the clumps of dirt still clinging to the bulbs. Her fingers found one stalk that was snapped above the bulb, limp and broken.

Jonathan was dead. That's what they were saying in Staunton. She didn't believe it, not really, but sometimes at night the dark loneliness pressed in and he seemed truly gone.

At first, there had been whispers of "injun lover," but only whispers, as the Russells were respected in the valley. Then, the morbid rumors started. It was a dangerous life over the mountain. Even now, with no tribe on the warpath, individual Shawnee or Cherokee would not view a white man favorably, which was why folks thought he'd been killed.

She'd given him a lock of her hair, but she had no token from him, and now, two years later, she could barely remember his face.

Others had returned. Members of the Ninth Virginia who'd been kept in the Walnut Street jail had trickled their way west after the British had left Philadelphia the next May. A few, like Nathan, had perished from wounds or ill-treatment, and some had been sent to prison ships in New York, never to be heard from again.

Jonathan had been swallowed up by the wilderness. When folks assumed he was dead, or whispered that he was a coward to have left the army, even Papa did not argue, his face cloudy.

The peace she felt now and again in the meetinghouse was elusive. God seemed far away, and the war—well, ever since the grand victory at Saratoga, Washington's strategy seemed to be simply to stay alive. The French had formally declared war on Britain, but that seemed to be making little difference.

Ruth rose and made her way toward the Russells' house, basket over her arm. The oak trees were awakening, small bright leaves springing forth in merriment. All of Creation seemed joyful in spring, ignorant of human sorrow. Inhaling the spring air made her soul ache.

The barn appeared through the trees, and beyond that, the brood mare paddock, where several blood bay colts gamboled with their dams, sons of Jonathan's stallion, left behind to stand stud. Several animals turned their heads at her approach.

Motion caught her eye. A dark head of hair, a set of strong shoulders—Ruth dropped her basket.

Jonathan?

No, it was William, leading Windsong, his filly, out to pasture.

She scrambled for her spilled greens. William didn't truly look like Jonathan, but his tall form, and the color of his hair—

A shadow spilled over the ground.

"Ruth?" Hannah squatted and helped her rescue the ramps. "I'm going to town after dinner. Want to come?"

THE SHADOWS WERE STILL short when they pulled into Staunton. Ruth jumped down from the wagon seat, and Hannah tied the horses to the post in front of the print shop.

Ruth stepped inside. The smell of fresh pine and linseed oil ink never failed to lift her heart. Broadsheets hung drying on a rail—mainly classifieds, but still. Augusta County now had a newspaper, and her father an occupation.

John Russell had provided the lumber for the modest building and more recently had been making noises about a house. But Aunt Betsy had moved in with the McClures, who treasured her help in the store. Evenings, she could be found knitting next to old Maggie's rocker.

Papa rarely returned to the Russell homestead, finding the back room of the print shop adequate to his needs—and inclinations. Ruth herself had visions of a cozy home with embroidered curtains ... but there was no one to share it with.

For now, Ruth slept in a cozy room upstairs at Russell's Ridge, with Hannah in the adjoining space.

"Billy Bob." She addressed the apprentice, who at her entrance had grabbed a broom and pretended to work. Clearly William Robert Cunningham, otherwise known as "Billy Bob," had been lounging about while her father was gone. "Where's Papa?"

The lad's front teeth seemed too big for his face. "Over to the courthouse for the news."

Outside, Hannah was halfway across the curiously busy street. A number of men were conversing excitedly in front of the courthouse. Ruth grabbed her skirts and hurried to catch up.

"What's happening?" Ruth asked, but Hannah shrugged.

They went inside the crowded room where Ruth caught a glimpse of an old man with spindly arms and legs. Papa helped him to a chair and Colonel Lewis pressed a tankard into his hands.

Aunt Betsy came in and stood close behind them.

"Who's the old man?" Ruth whispered to Hannah.

"He's not old. That's George Mathews, colonel of the Ninth Virginia."

Aunt Betsy muttered something sharp under her breath about redcoats.

Papa extracted himself from the crowd and urged them outside, a bundle under his arm. "They kept Mathews in a prison ship." A rare bitterness edged his voice. "Took two years to exchange him. Most of the others died."

Aunt Betsy scowled and marched away. Ruth guessed she was plotting something. Starting with soup.

Papa handed Ruth several letters, but she barely glanced at them. Mathews was skin and bones. How had he managed to travel? There were wagons coming and going; folks must have pitied him, fed him.

O Lord, how long? How long must we suffer under the British?

"MAY I COME IN?"

Hannah's voice came through the bedroom door. Glancing at the letters on the bearskin coverlet, Ruth decided it was pointless to indulge in self-pity. Sharing them would cheer not only Hannah but also herself.

"Come in."

The second-floor bedroom at the Russells' was narrow, but comfortable. Ruth patted the bed.

"Sit. I've two letters."

"I've one as well."

"Rebecca Young wrote me." Ruth opened the smudged missive and scanned the page.

"Is she back in Philadelphia?"

"Oh yes. And back to sewing flags, apparently. Seems it has taken a long time to repair the damage from the British occupation." She decided to skip Rebecca's ruminations on that subject. Too depressing. "I want to see what Lucy says, I haven't had a letter from her all winter." She popped open the seal. "She's writing from Boston. Let's see. She wrote this in February. Hmm … She complains about her separation from her husband, then she describes the army's situation. 'My poor dear Harry. Conditions in the camp are wretched, as the weather has been atrocious. Six feet of snow, and the cannon had to be dug out lest they be ruined. I suppose it is well that we are apart, as I am in an interesting condition once again.'"

Ruth raised her hand to her mouth and smiled. "She's expecting. Now for the gossip. She knows everyone, you see. 'A friend in Philadelphia tells me Gen. Arnold is courting Peggy Shippen, and she is allowing his attentions! I cannot credit it. Peggy is not only intelligent—have you met her? She is so beautiful she could have any man in the City. To settle for a crude man like Arnold is beyond belief. His table manners alone would repel any woman.'"

Ruth raised a hand to her mouth to stifle a giggle.

Hannah raised her brows. "Is this the great general she is describing?"

Ruth recovered. "Yes. Although I suspect the man has little to his credit besides that one action at Saratoga. According to Lucy, he has two goals. A woman, and preferment. And maybe not in that order." She folded the letter. "You have one?"

"A friend in the Waxhaws."

The name was unfamiliar. "Where?"

"On the border of North and South Carolina. Some folks moved there from the valley—one of the McClures lives down there." Hannah opened her letter. "It's from my friend Eliza Jackson. She describes rumors about the British invasion."

"Savanna?" Ruth's knowledge of the geography of the south was muddled. "I know they've captured Savannah."

"That's Georgia, farther south. No, this is South Carolina. Oh! Eliza says here they've landed. Many ships, thousands of soldiers. Charles Town is under siege." A line appeared between Hannah's brows. "She says, 'My oldest son Hugh has joined Lincoln's men there. You may imagine my mind, only sixteen and gone for a soldier. The backcountry is divided, some loyal to the Crown, and others have taken up the Cause of Liberty. Every man's hand is set against his brother. I will trust in the Lord, both for myself and my sons. It is all I can do.'" Hannah looked up. "They won't be content with Charles Town, you know."

Was anywhere safe?

ROBERT ROUSED THE LOITERING MEN. "SIMMONS." He couldn't recall the other's name. "Aren't you two on latrine detail?"

As aide-de-camp, Robert served as Lord Rawdon's right-hand man in getting the Irish volunteers, his cousin's new regiment, into proper discipline. Just making camp, and all that went with it, was a challenge. The South Carolina soil, sandy and boggy by turn, seemed to fight against them. Latrines quickly became smelly swamps and had to be filled in.

Simmons grimaced. The other, a tall man with a bulbous nose, stood erect.

"We just dug a new latrine," Bulbous said.

"Nevertheless, a fresh one is required." Robert sincerely hoped the man wouldn't make any trouble. The new regiment was comprised of Loyalists, and his cousin understood the tendency of provincials to resist authority, but he also would not hesitate to use proper discipline.

Both men stepped forward, clearly aggrieved.

"Why not piss against a tree?" Simmons complained.

Bulbous scowled. "I just dug one."

"Pick up your shovels."

Simmons hesitated, but Bulbous took another step, hands curling.

"Attention," Robert commanded. The situation was deteriorating. If they didn't respond he'd have to arrange for discipline—the cat o' nine tails.

Bulbous narrowed his eyes and swung, landing a blow square on Robert's jaw. He fell back and hit the ground, but quickly regained his feet.

Robert felt his jaw. This was serious. But did they understand? "Striking an officer is punishable by death."

The faces of the men paled. They truly didn't know. Surely there was a way out of this.

"Look," Robert said. "I'm the only one who knows. I can overlook it on one condition."

"We'll dig the latrine." Simmons was obviously horrified.

Robert stepped toward Bulbous and swung his fist. The impact against the other man's jaw was satisfying. Bulbous staggered once, then fell on his rump. "That's my condition. Now get to work."

He pivoted and headed back toward his tent, rubbing his jaw and brushing off his coat as well as he could. He quartered with Rawdon, whose batman had been killed in New York. Robert saw to his commanding officer's clothing, sending their shirts out to a laundress, but there was one line he would not cross. He would not clean the man's boots.

Flexing his aching hand, Robert skirted the main part of the camp and stepped along the verge, where grasses and scrubby shrubs dominated. He stepped around a bush that resembled a New England bayberry, only to step in mire.

It was truly a foreign land. Almost a thousand miles from New York, South Carolina boasted an intimidating landscape. Cypress swamps circled Charles Town, making the location of campsites critical. Even after choosing a dry hillock for the Volunteers of Ireland, they still had problems with latrines.

And it was warm for May. Robert's shirt felt clammy with sweat, and it wasn't even noon. The moist, marshy air lay on the camp like an oppressive blanket. Summer would be nasty, and fevers thrived in the climate.

The noise of boisterous conversation ahead caught his attention.

Before the tent stood Lord Rawdon and Captain Banastre Tarleton, talking animatedly.

They were all smiles. Seeing them together, Robert was reminded of how ugly his cousin was—thick black brows, a weak chin. By comparison, Tarleton shone. He was not classically handsome, but his features were pleasant and his form graceful. His auburn hair glinted red in the sun, his green uniform neat and the hat under his arm custom made, a black plume arcing above the crown. He possessed a charisma attractive to some women, though others knew him for a rogue and avoided him.

Best of all, from the Army's point of view, he was superb at commanding both man and beast. And fearsomely aggressive in battle.

"Shirley!" Tarleton called. "Hear the news?"

Suddenly Robert became aware of the silence. Come to think of it, he hadn't heard any cannon fire all morning. Yesterday had been especially disturbing. Heated shot had started fires in Charles Town, and he'd been reminded of the Massachusetts town of the same name, surrendering to the flames. Haze still drifted over the area.

"Lincoln surrendered." Rawdon smirked. "Over three thousand men."

Tarleton gestured northwest. "One large mopping up operation. We've all but won."

Robert considered. "News of this will certainly weaken the hands of any rebels in the backcountry."

Rawdon led the way into the tent, where he broke out a celebratory bottle of Madeira. Robert shrugged out of his coat and tossed it aside.

Tarleton handed him a glass.

"A toast," Rawdon lifted his goblet. "To brethren in arms."

"Here, here," Robert joined in.

The Madeira was welcome. It had been a long war. He thought back. He had come to Boston in 1772. Eight years ago. Half of that time, he'd served under arms.

Well, much of that under the tutelage of Major André. He missed the man, though not the task. In some respects, Robert was suited for intelligence. He was educated, literate, and well spoken. But his heart was not in it, and he lacked André's driving ambition.

The major had some big fish on his line, whereas Robert had only been able to collect tactical information—strength of the enemy's troops and observations about the terrain that helped his commanders, when they chose to listen. But he refused to turn a man against his family or beliefs. Betrayal was betrayal.

André played a deeper game. He'd befriended Margaret Shippen, and never told Robert what his plan was, but when the woman married Benedict Arnold, the disgruntled rebel general, it was easy to see.

"I know," André told him one winter night over mulled cider. "I can see it in your eyes. You dislike much of what we do." He sighed. "So do I." He swirled the amber liquid in his glass. "I compare it to battle. What man enjoys killing men with whom he has no quarrel? In the same way, the secret service is honorable."

When General Clinton's forces moved south as part of a change in British strategy, Robert had been assigned to Lord Rawdon as aide-de-camp. No more intelligence missions. No more sneaking around—he'd be busy with the daily minutiae of the new regiment.

Robert was relieved, even though he disliked his cousin. And the strategy was clearly working. Now that Charles Town had fallen, he could imagine an end to this interminable war.

Rawdon's voice interrupted Robert's musings. "Shirley, give us a toast."

What should he say? To King and country?

He raised his glass. "To the end of this bloody war."

37

We are going away to another country; you are, as it were, only lodging here, for a night.

—Jeremiah Burroughs, 1648

*J*onathan squinted through the trees and wondered what day it was. In the village, time was reckoned by moons and not by weeks. At first, he'd fought to retain his knowledge of the date, and worship on the first day of the week, but as the weeks and months passed, those things had slipped away.

In the end, he'd decided to worship every day. Read a few verses from his New Testament, if he could. Pray in his heart, if not aloud. Sometimes, when alone in the woods, he'd sing a hymn. It helped him to remember English, to remember who he was.

His ear caught the tinkle of a creek. He followed it downstream and found the place where it fed into a stream, a welcome sight in the late summer heat. He filled his belly and his canteen gratefully, then splashed some down his neck. Ruth's locket dangled out of his shirt, and he tucked it back underneath. It was a miracle the thing had survived.

Thank you, Lord. Thank you for keeping me safe there and back again.

And his conscience was now clear, clear and sweet as the soft summer breeze. An inestimable treasure.

He looked for a place to camp. He found a place where the trees thinned, and the rocks formed a natural defense.

A stand of beech was familiar. It was here that Red Hawk had taken his leave and returned to his village. He'd escorted him this far, given him directions, and then left.

That meant the Shenandoah Valley was less than a week away.

Jonathan sat on a stone and soaked in the surroundings. He debated whether to stay here several days or not. Without a rifle it took longer to find food. He'd never completely mastered the bow, and in any case, he did not have one. He'd need to fish and trap. But his heart urged him to keep going. The memory of Ruth's face was elusive, and sometimes he'd look again at the small lock of hair, trying to remember exactly how her hair would slip out from the pins and curl on her cheek. Or fall onto her shoulder.

In the end, he decided to stay a single day. Jonathan pulled out his rusty traps from his haversack. A tiny sound made him freeze.

A rustle, followed by movement under the trees. An animal? He was close to Cherokee country. His fingers slid onto the hilt of his belt knife.

The foliage parted, revealing a man and a mule, laden with packs. Friend or foe?

"Ho, stranger!" The man bellowed.

The appearance of the buckskin-clad trader—or trapper—startled him. The abundant beard and blue eyes felt out of place. But of course, the fellow was not Tsoyaha. He was a white man.

A man like himself. And so, he must answer in the same language.

Jonathan raised his hand in greeting. "How—howdy."

"Hear about Charles Town?"

By the time the stranger went on his way, Jonathan felt like his feet had been shoved into boots a size too small. The war had come crashing down on him once again.

A war he wasn't sure he wanted to be a part of anymore.

"WHY, IT'S THURSDAY," Samuel Houston said. "Join us for supper."

Jonathan nodded. He'd navigated Goshen Pass and followed a game trail onto the Houstons' land. The sight of the buildings through the trees had cheered him. Slowly he'd approached the house, uncertain of his welcome, feeling very much the stranger, until Houston's broad grin had chased away the cloud.

Timber Ridge Plantation was twenty miles southwest of his own home, only a single day's travel away. He forced his shoulders to relax. His belly was hollow, and he needed to rest before the last leg of his journey.

"Thank ye kindly. Thank ye for your hospitality."

The large, solid timber house felt empty. Sam was his own age, but his parents had passed away. He had a passel of sisters, most of whom were married and lived elsewhere.

"Jonathan!" Maggie Houston's beaming face welcomed him. One remaining sister lived at home.

"I remember ye as a wee lass." He was suddenly conscious of his scruffy appearance, his ragged beard.

"Shush! Come and eat."

In the last two days he'd only eaten a single small trout and a few creamy-sweet paw paws. He obeyed willingly.

Buttered turnips and a large slice of pork pie were set before him. The smell was heavenly. Saliva flooded his mouth.

"Simple fare," Houston apologized.

"Oh no, it looks wonderful. Thank ye, Maggie."

They asked a blessing and began eating. Thankfully Houston skirted the obvious questions, merely asking about the weather and his health.

After supper, Houston pulled out his pipe. "Let's go out for a smoke." Once outside, he motioned toward a bench. "They say ye're dead."

Jonathan's chuckle died on his lips. "I almost was." He sat and thrust out his legs before him, debating what to tell the man. "I was adopted by the Uchee, or Tsoyaha as they call themselves, learned their tongue, lived as one until they released me." He omitted his motives for going. He wasn't sure if folks needed to hear all the details.

"Hear about Charles Town and the Waxhaws?"

"Heard we lost Charles Town. Wait—ye served under Morgan."

Houston removed the pipe and blew a puff of smoke. "I did. But Morgan is retired up Winchester way. There's thousands of British prisoners there, sent by Washington."

"Passed through there several years ago." Jonathan had glimpsed barracks full of ragged men.

"Even more there now. Morgan hired a bunch of Hessians to build a new house. I wonder if the news will bring him out of retirement."

Jonathan frowned. He didn't want to fight, but if the war was in the south, he might have to. He'd fight under Daniel Morgan willingly enough. "Tell me about the Waxhaws—that's the backcountry, isn't it?"

"Just got the news. Terrible thing. A massacre. Our man Buford surrendered, then the British cavalry slaughtered them anyway."

"What?" The British were harsh foes, but this was bad, even for them.

"Cavalry's led by a man named Banastre Tarleton. 'Bloody Ban,' they're calling him. Makes my blood boil."

Jonathan sat silently, absorbing this. "But what does this mean for Virginia?"

"They're coming—and they show no mercy. I haven't said anything to my sister yet—or to the woman I'm courting—but if Morgan calls a muster, I'm ready."

They show no mercy.

He was thankful he was back in time to defend his home.

THE NEXT MORNING, Jonathan stared at the man in the mirror. Familiar, yet strange. A new jagged white scar snaked over his left cheekbone, courtesy of the Uchee. Blue eyes—like the trapper's, his eyes looked strange, like a splash of winter cold after a long summer. One night on the trail, Red Hawk had confided how he'd felt discovering his heritage. He'd always known he was captured as a young child, he had vague memories of it, but never guessed he was a white man—and that his blue eyes proclaimed his race to all and sundry. He'd finally made peace with his origins, but it had been a shock at first.

Jonathan had no qualms about who he was. But immersed in the Tsoyaha language and village life, being cared for by a brown-skinned woman who'd accepted him regardless, adopting him over the protests of some—that life was hard to shrug off after so many moons. Maybe he never would.

He understood the stories now. The stories of captives who'd either refused to go home, or lived permanently in between the two worlds, red and white. Some of those lived as mountain men, alone, or with Indian wives.

He sharpened the razor on the strop, then brought it to his face. The blade scraped once, and a clump of hair fell away. The skin beneath was pale.

Houston had lent him a razor without comment. Jonathan appreciated the man's careful kindness, not asking too many questions. Back in Staunton not everyone would be so understanding.

How could he explain his decision? Did he need to?

He'd labored over two years for the family of the man he'd killed They received his vow as sacred, after the initial shock—and the beating that had ensued. Several cousins had decided pain was required as part of his recompense. He'd almost died.

Now, he was back, his heart fresh, with only one worry: would Ruth still receive him? Had she waited for him?

THE PRINT SHOP was pleasantly warm, and it was making Ruth sleepy.

"One more time," she said, forcing herself to sit straight.

Mouth puckered, Billy Bob copied the sentence again. The child was literate, but just barely, and Ruth wondered sometimes why her father had agreed to take on an apprentice with such a limited education. A printer needed to be able to compose.

The little academy named Liberty Hall taught Latin, history, and mathematics to a few, but for those whose fathers could not afford to send them, or whose sons never learned basic reading and writing, it was inaccessible. The children needed a school.

The shadows were lengthening. Time for them all to go. "That's better. Off you go."

The lad bolted for home.

Ruth looked for her father but the shop was empty. He'd probably gone to the courthouse or Mathews's Tavern for the latest news. She stepped outside and scanned the street.

"Ruth!" Hannah crossed from the courthouse. "I've a letter."

Ruth gestured to the bench in front of the print shop. "Who's it from?"

"Eliza, down in the Waxhaws." The folded and sealed paper was tattered. "Oh ... Oh, no." Hannah passed her the letter.

Dear Hannah,

It is late, and I finally have time to scratch out a few lines. I am sure others have brought word about Buford's defeat and the terrible massacre. Buford's men surrendered, but Tarleton's cavalry chopped them to pieces. Over one hundred dead, and the wounded filled the church. The boys and I spent long days and nights caring for them, but some perished despite all our efforts. Their cries haunt my dreams. I can only pray that the God Who Sees will have pity on us. E. Jackson

"Where is the Waxhaws?"

"South, through Maggoty Gap, past Charlotte. It's a ways—"

"But closer than Charles Town."

Hannah nodded.

There was a commotion in front of the courthouse. Several men surrounded a tall individual in the middle of the dusty street.

Hannah stood, and Ruth followed her lead. *Who was it?* Hannah strode forward, long legs eating up the distance. Ruth hitched her skirts and struggled to keep up.

The circle of men parted, and she saw a buckskin-clad mountain man. Blue eyes, dark hair, and a clean-shaven face that looked curiously two-toned, bronzed across the nose and cheekbones, pale beneath. He'd just shaved a heavy beard.

Hannah screamed her brother's name.

It was Jonathan.

Later, remembering, Ruth didn't know how she managed to close the distance before Hannah did. She threw her arms around his neck.

The sweet smell of sweat and leather filled her nose. Then she slid back, abashed, awkward. "Are you well?"

His shirt was ragged and hung on his collarbones. At the base of his throat hung her locket, strung on a dark, oily piece of leather. He still had it.

Tears filled her eyes.

Jonathan smiled and placed his hands on her upper arms, touching her tentatively, as if he wanted to embrace her but imagined she were made of glass. "I-I am well."

Hannah slugged his shoulder. "Ye clot-heid! What took ye so long!"

Jonathan released Ruth and embraced his sister. Then he wiped his eyes. "Is Da here? Or up to the Ridge?"

"He left ten days ago," Ruth said. "Took a wagon of supplies up north, for Washington. And a couple of horses."

The crowd thinned and dispersed, some with outsized grins, others wiping surreptitiously at their faces.

"Jonathan." Hannah's eyes glistened with tears. "Come home. Mother has sewed you four shirts."

"And I'll guess ye knitted socks—go on ahead, I'll follow."

He extended his elbow, and Ruth accompanied him, but he was silent until they'd left the busy street. When they reached the bridge over the creek, he stopped. Hannah had disappeared up the road, and they were alone.

She studied his face. So familiar, the furrow between his brows a little deeper. A new thin white scar—there must be a story behind that. But his expression was rested, peaceful.

He fumbled inside his shirt and drew out a ragged linen wallet. "I've something for ye." He pulled out a handful of purple and white beads that resolved into a strand. A necklace?

"The woman who spoke for me, she made me shoes." His words were slow, rusty, as if he hadn't spoken in years.

Ruth's gaze fell to his feet. Neatly crafted moccasins, plain except for a few porcupine quills.

"She wanted to use these on the moccasins, and I reminded her that I was spoken for."

There was a story, a long story behind his words. Ruth studied Jonathan's face. There was a story in the lines of his face, in the small scar that hadn't been there before.

"The purple is special."

These weren't beads, like the traders sold. No, these were wampum, the little shells that Indians painstakingly pierced and strung. Wampum belts were exchanged as part of treaties.

Jonathan's fingers brushed her neck as he tied the necklace on. She couldn't breathe.

"Ruth, I want to build ye a house."

Embroidered curtains. She would make curtains.

For a moment she couldn't speak. Then she found her tongue. "I would love that."

38

The truth of the matter is this: the doctrine of our regeneration, or new birth in Christ Jesus, is hard to be understood by the natural man.

—George Whitefield, sermon, *On Regeneration*

*H*e was going to have nightmares. Robert scraped off the mud from his boots—not just any mud, but swampy, South Carolina mud—and tried not to think about the wretched night just outside Camden.

Lord Rawdon had led his men around the swamps and engaged the rebels in a hellish darkness lit only by the intermittent fire of the enemy.

Afterward, they'd crept forward, groping, hesitating to create a single light lest they give themselves away, and looked for dead bodies.

Had to feel them, examine their uniforms, or lack of them, to determine which army they belonged to, for burial.

Once in a while, Robert's fingers discovered a dismembered arm or leg, the body shot to bits by their mobile three-pound mortars. Other times, he'd grasped a limb only to discover the man was still alive, moans for water his last words.

And *that* was a victory.

It made his stomach quiver to think about it. Tarleton was ecstatic, of course, and Robert's cousin wore a satisfied smile. Victory was the way to promotion, and Tarleton, in particular, needed it. He was the son of a man who'd made his money in the slave trade and had no social rank at all.

Robert found a heavy streak of blood on his coat. Perhaps he'd consult one of the laundry women. Normally he cleaned the garment himself, but blood was problematic. The rest was simple filth, garnered when his horse had slipped and he'd fallen in the mud while reconnoitering the terrain. He cleaned off as much of the gummy mud as he could, then examined his gorget. It wasn't very dirty, and he quickly restored it to a brilliant brassy sheen.

A victory *was* a good thing. Especially this kind of victory. General Gates had turned tail and fled. The only army Washington had in the south was shattered. The local militia were unreliable, and one of the most competent of the leaders, Colonel Pickens, had been captured, and the man had given his parole. The feisty rebel was out of the war.

And maybe they all would be soon.

Carefully, he eased off his grimy shirt, the cuffs stiff with blood. The washerwomen would be busy the next few days.

Robert put on a clean shirt and eased himself onto his camp bed, his bruises making themselves known. He didn't know where Rawdon was. Probably celebrating, and there was no reason to wait up for him. He leaned over and snuffed out the lantern. No telling when his cousin would be back.

The hard cot felt good beneath his aching muscles. He was exhausted, but sleep eluded him.

Flashes of gunfire erupted again behind his closed lids. He heard the howls of the enemy, the huzzahs of Rawdon's Volunteers.

He felt the slick stickiness of blood beneath his fingers, his hands on a corpse.

No. He had to think of something else. He sought a quote from *Meditations*, but he hadn't opened the book in a long time, and words of the Roman sage eluded him.

Instead, a fragment from the Gospel of John slipped into his mind.

Verily, verily, I say unto thee, unless a man be born again, he cannot see the kingdom of God.

He'd finished the New Testament and begun it again, feeling as though he was missing something. John's gospel was especially obscure. The words stabbed him, nagged at him, sometimes beautiful and attractive, other times bringing fear or a dreadful guilt. But always there was a veil.

Born again. What did it mean to be born again? The passage indicated that the man to whom Jesus spoke those words didn't know either.

So Robert wasn't the only one who didn't understand. It was a comfort. A small comfort, but he had nothing else.

RUTH WOKE HAPPY. Jonathan was here, Jonathan was safe.

She went downstairs, thinking about what needed to be done. September was a busy month.

After breakfast, Mrs. Russell gave Ruth a small but heavy cloth bag. Seed, she guessed.

"Would you take this to Jonathan?" Mrs. Russell's gaze slipped down to Ruth's neck.

Ruth nodded, conscious of the necklace that peeped out above the folds of her kerchief.

Mrs. Russell laid a hand on her own bodice and drew out a simple blue stone on a chain. "John gave me this." She paused. "You have my blessing." She blinked rapidly a few times and smiled.

Ruth gave her a shy smile in return and slipped out the door. She found the harvested bean patch, where Jonathan's shoulders flexed and rolled as he worked, his hoe chopping the clods left after plowing under the stubble. The loamy autumn soil lay open to the slanting golden sunshine, smelling fresh and hopeful.

He straightened and the hoe stilled. He looked at her with eyes that expressed so many things without words. He seemed peaceful, relaxed.

They hadn't spoken again about the house since he'd returned two weeks ago. She'd decided not to press him, not with so much on everyone's minds and hearts.

"Your mother sent seed." *And her blessing.*

He nodded, and together they labored easily in the cool morning. The small field was planted quickly, and Jonathan scanned the sky above the western hills.

"Will it rain?" she asked.

"Wrong kind of clouds. But maybe in another day or two." He gave her a gentle smile. "Turnip seeds are canny. They'll wait days for rain, then give them a good soak, and they dinna waste any time in springing up. And the frost willna kill them. We'll harvest them before the snows."

No wonder they were a staple, even when corn and potatoes flourished.

He turned and looked up at the rolling swell of the Blue Ridge. "Come with me to the birch grove."

Ruth insisted on stopping at the house for a basket of food, and they climbed the gentle slope behind the house, a jug of switchel swinging from Jonathan's hand. Rhododendron branches snatched at her skirts, and they ducked under the limbs of dogwood and white fir. Strong saplings surrounded the wide stumps of harvested oaks.

They paused at a chestnut tree, and Ruth caught her breath. The slope was becoming more difficult.

"Just a little farther," Jonathan said.

Soon a great grove of birch appeared, the familiar oval leaves edged with the first yellow of autumn. They sat on a fallen log under the shade.

She had so many questions, but she passed out the food first, meat-filled pasties, day-old cornbread, and a few wrinkled apples.

"What were the Uchee like?"

Jonathan made short work of an apple. "It was strange. Traveling south, I was filled with the greatest peace I'd ever known. Even before I'd come to the village, before I'd labored for them, I knew God was with me. Does that make sense to ye?"

She nodded. "I knew something of that peace after the Declaration of Independence was made and I ceased my wrestling."

He smiled. "Once they accepted me, the Uchee taught me a trade. Metal-working. They fashion copper they find in the hills. But they dinna smelt it, they pound it. That's what I did." He raised a hand to the locket. "They saw this, esteemed it. Hair means something to them."

Hair? The question must have shown on her face.

"Aye, they think hair has power of some sort. For you to send me forth with your hair meant ye'd given me something of yourself. Something with power. They respected that and named me 'He-Who-Is-Spoken-For'. But the name had a double meaning, for a relative of the man I killed claimed me, spoke for me. I worked for her."

Ruth's heart swelled with thankfulness once again. "God protected you."

He nodded, and his eyes grew gentle. "Where would ye like your house to be?"

"Who will live in it?"

Red crept up his collar to the tan line on his cheeks, which was still slightly visible. "I-I'm sorry, I didna ask ye proper." He turned to her and grasped her hands, lightly, as if he feared she'd reject his touch. "Will ye marry me?"

"Of course I will, ye clot-heid." Her lips twitched upward, but the darkness of the outside world intruded, and her smile fell away. "I need not live in town. Once I marry, I will go where you go, live where you live."

"But ye're troubled."

"Camden. All of it. Everything. Can we even plan?"

Jonathan released her hands and his shoulders sagged. "Camden. There are still some good men in South Carolina, but they are scattered. Colonel Pickens gave his parole, which means he can't fight anymore."

He reached up and broke off two twigs, then handed one to her. He studied the remaining twig as if for answers.

She picked at the outer bark of her twig. "What if … we lose?"

"I've been thinking about injustice. Ye ken the vestry tax? Virginians have never had the liberty to worship the way folks do in Pennsylvania. Everyone must attend the Church of England and pay the tax. It helps that there's no parish church within miles of here. We have a certain freedom west of the Blue Ridge." He smiled grimly. "But we pay the tax, always have, even though it's unjust. If they win this war, we will simply have to bear even greater burdens."

"Even here? Somehow this place seems far away from the reach of the British."

He sighed. "Maybe, maybe not." He looked toward the western hills, barely visible through the foliage. "Kentucke might stay free. Aye, I can imagine the coast being occupied by redcoats while the rest of us find homes elsewhere." He thrust the twig in his mouth and chewed it.

"I wonder what Nathan would say." Her chest ached even as she uttered the words. She hoped she hadn't spoken out of turn.

He was silent for a while, then he lifted his face toward her. His eyes were wet, his lashes clumping. "I had a lot of time to think while I worked in the village. I thought about Nathan, about his life, about his last words."

"A better country?"

"A better country—a heavenly, as Hebrews says. For so long I thought of Canaan as the land of promise—and it is. A physical place, promised to Abraham's descendants. But the patriarch wasn't focused on that, not entirely. He was seeing heavenly things all along."

Ruth's heart swelled with hope. "We have a better country too."

"Aye. And no matter what happens, we will have that. We will have the only country that matters. The only kingdom that matters."

"And the only King."

JONATHAN ENTERED the cornfield and inhaled the dusty scent of the ripening stalks. Soon they would turn dry and brown, ready for the shucking and braiding of the husking bee.

It was good to be home. His father was miles away, his last letter posted from Philadelphia on his way to the Continental Army encampment. But the rest of the inhabitants of Russell's Ridge, his uncle and his family, the MacLeods, the Kerrs, and the Robinsons, had surrounded him with love and sharp-edged teasing.

Best of all, every Sabbath he could sit on a worn pew and let the voice of the minister wash over him, the words of scripture working their way into his very joints, warming and easing his heart.

And Ruth. Best of all, she hadn't married in his absence. None of what he'd feared had come to pass. She had seemed to fit right in, helping his mother in the garden, foraging, and sewing or knitting in the candlelight.

"Read for us, Jonathan," his mother had asked, not long after he'd returned. With his father gone, family worship continued, though abbreviated as it always was during harvest.

"Isaiah. Let's turn to Isaiah." He didn't know why he'd chosen it, but they turned to Isaiah and started with the account of the Assyrians besieging Jerusalem. They read half a chapter every evening.

The prayer of Hezekiah still echoed in his mind from their reading the night before.

"Now therefore, O Lord our God, save us from his hand, that all the kingdoms of the earth may know that thou art the Lord, even thou only."

A king had oppressed them, too.

Deliver us, Lord, for Your name's sake.

He grasped an ear of corn on a half-dried stalk, testing it. Another week.

The sight of the corn brought him back to the Uchee village, the women bent over the green stalks, nurturing the coming harvest.

Indian men didn't work the soil. They insisted women were life-givers, so the women would bring life from the fields. Men hunted and fought. Jonathan's time was eaten up by the hard labor that any settlement needed —hauling water, preparing firewood.

He didn't miss that.

But he did enjoy pounding metal into useable shapes. His weak shoulder had been forced to full strength. And the bright copper cheered him in his exile.

He turned and made his way up to the house. A flash of red hair behind the trees betrayed his uncle Roy, dismounting from his favorite mare. Another man followed close by, an old man, moving slowly, painfully.

It was Daniel Morgan. Not so old then.

Morgan caught his eye and flashed a grin. "Ho, Mr. Russell, I hear you're back from over the mountain."

"Welcome to Russell's Ridge." Jonathan followed them inside.

Once they were seated around the kitchen table, ale and cider flowed. William joined them, then Ian MacLeod, and finally Hannah, who cut suspicious glances at the men while helping her mother serve the drinks.

Jonathan didn't see Ruth, who was probably still helping her father as she did several days a week.

"What brings ye?" Jonathan asked after all the greetings were made. The obvious answer tightened his gut.

Morgan took a long swallow of cider. "Gates is beaten, but we haven't lost yet." His gaze found Jonathan's. "The mountain men are rising. They've heard about Camden. And they've heard about the atrocities of the Loyalists, about Bloody Ban, and the church."

"Church?" MacLeod asked.

"One of the redcoat commanders burnt down a church. For no reason a'tall. And Tarleton burnt thirty plantations. Once, he locked folks inside their house, then set it on fire."

"What?" Hannah's knuckles turned white about the flask she carried.

"They managed to escape. But folks are boiling mad."

"So the mountain men will fight?" Jonathan said.

Morgan nodded. "There's a muster in the hills, the best marksmen I know of." He took another swallow. "And not only that, folks tell me Clinton has turned on those he paroled."

"What do ye mean?" Uncle Roy asked.

Jonathan understood that a paroled man was bound by his honor—his word—not to fight again. But the obligation cut both ways.

"Clinton established martial law in the Carolinas. Then, he proclaimed that everyone—including those on parole—must take an oath of loyalty and offer themselves to fight for the Crown."

"What!" several men said in unison. "He canna do that!"

Jonathan curled his hands into fists. The British had gone too far.

"Colonel Pickens refused to fight for the King, and they plundered his plantation. All these folks content to sit things out won't be any longer. We've a chance, and I'm raising my own regiment, bad back or not. If I have to be dragged over the hills, I'm going to the Carolinas. Who's coming with me?"

Jonathan's throat was dry. He'd promised Ruth a home. But this could be their only chance.

He hoped she would understand.

39

Nothing will serve these people but fire and sword.
—Lt. Col. Banastre Tarleton

*M*ixing dough in the kitchen, Ruth turned at a noise.

"Where've you been?" Hannah asked William, who had just come in the door. He was filthy and stubble marked his jaw. "Ye need to dunk yourself in the stream, I dinna care how cold it is."

Ruth felt a frisson of irritation. William's dark hair and broad shoulders reminded her painfully of Jonathan. She turned to the hearth and pretended to busy herself with the kettle.

"Militia duty. With Colonel Preston's men gone to fight the redcoats, Colonel Johnson's mounted militia is the only defense we have."

Ruth peeked at him. His stance was broad, his chest puffed out. He'd been disappointed in not being able to accompany Jonathan and the others who'd gone with Morgan, but not for long. Colonel Mathews, still thin and frail-looking, was busy, training and organizing the men who were left. Colonel Johnson now led a promising group of mounted men.

"And today the colonel promoted me. It's Captain Russell now."

"Ye'll be insufferable now. Captain Russell of the Shenandoah Cavalry."

Hearing their banter, Ruth's annoyance faded. As soon as she'd heard of Morgan's plans, she'd known Jonathan would go. And she'd refused to hinder him, knowing he'd stay if his conscience allowed it.

But it was still hard.

"Nay, I'm just poking fun at ye," Hannah said. "Ye heard what Mother said, that we needed men here."

Ruth turned. "William, have you a uniform or insignia of rank? Perhaps we can help."

He smirked. "At least someone is good with the needle around here."

Hannah growled and threw a skein of wool at his head.

"Oh, and here." He deposited a newspaper and several letters on the table, then left, presumably to wash up.

"The *Virginia Gazette!*" Hannah cried. "I rarely see it, and look, it's only a single page."

"Papa has been getting his news from the Philadelphia paper, and of course, from the birds of the air." Ruth set about to fix some chicory coffee. October had arrived, and coffee of any sort was welcome.

Hannah smiled. "He's good at that. According to the *Augusta Observer*, the over-mountain men are hot on the trail of a Tory regiment. He's even listed some of the names of the commanders—of both sides."

But not Morgan, Ruth mused. Morgan was not in the news. Maybe that was good. "Who are the letters from?" Anything to distract her.

No matter how busy she was, how exhausted, at night she thought of Jonathan, out on a cold battlefield, injured … even dying.

"Interesting." Hannah lifted a letter. "From England. I dinna ken anyone in England."

Ruth poured the coffee into two mugs and pushed one toward Hannah, who nodded her thanks. She popped the seal and scanned it, then read it aloud.

"Dear Miss Russell, I hope and pray you are well. My godson gave me your direction, and I hope this missive has not gone astray. He informs me you are a follower of Jesus Christ, and so I enclose a few hymns you may find encouraging."

Hannah unfolded the sheets underneath the top one. "Aye! Hymns—but who is this godson of hers?"

Ruth stared into her cup. "Who's it from?"

"Selina Hastings, Countess of Huntingdon. A countess! What is that?"

"I believe 'tis an earl's wife." How much should Ruth tell her?

"I dinna ken any earl."

"Robert Shirley is her godson."

Hannah's eyes widened. "Shirley—the man injured on Bunker's hill. He brought your cousin back." Her face grew thoughtful. "He was fair spoken."

Ruth nodded silently. She couldn't reveal everything. "Is there more to the letter?"

"'I pray every day for the end to the hostilities. The war has made it difficult to communicate with Bethesda orphanage, with which I was entrusted after the Rev. Whitefield's death. If you think upon it, will you pray for these little ones?'"

Hannah sat up straighter. "The orphanage? She's in charge of the orphanage?"

"She sent me a number of Whitefield's sermons while Mr. Shirley worked as our bookbinder."

Hannah's mouth formed an O.

"Drink your coffee. 'Tis cold, but—"

Hannah waved a hand. "But why is she writing me?" She sipped her coffee. "He must have told her about me, but why?"

"Who knows?" Ruth had seen the way Shirley had looked at Hannah, but nothing could be said about that. She poked at the second letter. "Who's this from?"

Hannah picked it up and squinted. "Da's writing." She opened it, grinning. "Let's see what he says."

This time, she did not read it aloud. Ruth watched her face. Hannah's expression changed from gladness to concern and back again.

"He's well—and coming back soon. But he has a story to tell." She pushed the piece of worn and dirty paper toward Ruth.

Tappan NY Oct 2

To all at Russell's Ridge, including my dearest Companion,

The supplies for the Army were welcome, including the horses. Please tell Miss Haynes that General Knox is in fine fettle despite the privations the Army has endured. I gave him one of Nathan's mares for a saddle horse, as his size requires a sturdy mount.

A British spy was captured and sentenced to death. He carried the plans to West Point in his boot, and I regret to say that Gen. Benedict Arnold gave him the intelligence. But the traitor fled and escaped. His wife, the former Peggy Shippen, claims she knew nothing of his perfidy, and she has been charged with no crime, but I suspect her tears are merely for show.

The spy is a Major John André, a fine-spoken gentleman. I had the opportunity to speak to him about his soul and made sure he had access to the Scriptures. I also gave him a newspaper clipping I had in my saddlebag, a moving hymn in long meter. He seemed quite taken with it.

Today they hanged him. I believe he requested the firing squad, but hanging is the prescribed punishment for a spy. The officers in particular seemed affected by his death. The Major was a likable man and went to the gallows with great bravery. His last words were that his death would be "only a momentary pang."

I heard one man say that he wished Arnold had been hanged instead. I write all these details partly for the relief of a grieved mind. But I do have hope for the man's soul.

I plan to return soon. I will spend another week with the foraging parties. Sometimes we bring down turkeys or even a deer, but game is scarce, and so my usefulness is limited.

My prayers for all, especially Jonathan.

Jn Russell

"'Especially Jonathan.' He knows not that Jonathan returned."

Hannah's smile was strained. "Aye, but he needs the prayers. And did you see when they left? Morgan's men didna take a single supply wagon, only a few pack mules."

Ruth suspected that Hannah had taken note of every animal, firearm, and sack of beans on their way south with Morgan. "What are you thinking?"

"Nothing. Let's start the cornbread. I want to make extra. William will be famished when he comes back."

Hannah was planning something.

"Let me know if you need help—with anything at all."

~

ROBERT FOUND the magnolia tree he'd noticed the previous day. The leaves were still shiny and green, despite the cooler weather, and he wondered if the plant ever lost its leaves. October had brought relief from the killing heat, and the mosquitoes had retreated, but Robert longed for a frost. A dry, bracing sort of cold. He doubted he'd get that here.

He leaned his back against the trunk and flexed his tired hands. Correspondence had occupied the entire day. Lord Rawdon sent frequent messages, and everything coming and going had to be copied. Records kept and filed. His cousin sometimes even dictated his journal entries, always slightly supercilious, as if he were some great personage.

It had been a long day. Robert thought about his evening chores and ablutions. Even the act of removing his boots loomed before him as troublesome. Ever since they'd received the news about Major André, Robert had become an automaton, every movement like swimming through molasses. Only the occasional walk enabled him to breathe freely.

By all accounts, John André had gone to his death bravely. But what was on the other side of that great divide? Marcus Aurelius had no clue, writing of mere possibilities. Robert's New Testament proclaimed eternal realities with great assurance. But what puzzled him was that Jesus spoke of the kingdom of heaven as if it existed both in this life and in the life to come.

The concept was just out of reach.

Robert walked back to his tent. His cousin had reacted to the news of André's execution with great anger. In fact, Robert had never seen him so disturbed. Rawdon kept his fury under wraps for the most part, but before Tarleton had departed to hunt down local militia, Robert had overheard a conversation.

"What did you expect?" Tarleton's voice.

"Some consideration," Rawdon said. "He's—he was—a gentleman, an officer. What an ignominious way to die!"

"Everyone liked him. He had the patience of a saint, put up with Clinton for years. But look around you—these backcountry traitors string up their neighbors on the nearest tree. We cannot expect much better from their so-called army."

Their voices moderated and Robert heard no more. Tarleton was right about the backcountry, but Robert wasn't sure the Army was much better. The debacle at the Waxhaws had given every redcoat a bad name, not just Tarleton.

Once inside his tent, he tugged off his boots. With Ferguson and his men on a foray to crush mountain militia, and most of the rest of the men away with Cornwallis, the camp here at Camden was quiet. Rawdon sometimes slept elsewhere, and Robert neglected to imagine where the man might be.

He was too tired, anyway.

Reveille woke him at the usual time, but before his stock was snug against his throat a loud tapping disturbed him.

Robert opened the tent flap and stepped outside. Several privates wielded hammers, the source of the sound, and another was lifting a long board, probably torn from the side of a nearby barn or shed. As Robert drew near, he could see a crude platform taking shape.

"Corporal Stubbins, what is the purpose of this structure?"

The corporal turned, hammer in hand. "Why, it's a gallows, sir."

Robert fought to keep his expression stoic. "Gallows?"

"For the prisoner, sir. He's to be hanged tomorrow morning."

"Carry on." Comprehension flooded him. A man had been brought in who'd refused to take the oath of loyalty to the King, a member of a local militia who'd been captured and released under parole.

How could he be hanged as a traitor or spy if he'd given his parole? Robert marched to the large sprawling tent that served as headquarters.

Rawdon was not alone. Several of his Volunteers stood about. Robert forced his breathing to remain steady. It would not do to dispute his cousin's orders in front of his men.

Instead, he picked up yesterday's paperwork and sagged into a camp chair. He'd wait. He sat and focused on his breathing, focused on what he'd say.

The men left and they were alone.

"I heard the hammers. We need gallows?"

"Payment," Rawdon said. "We can hang spies too."

"I was not aware we'd caught a spy."

"My lieutenants and I held a hearing. He had his say. Refuses to take the oath."

"I heard that much." Robert should have been included in the hearing. That he was not confirmed his suspicions.

"General Clinton's orders are clear. Every man must take the oath and fight for the King. Any man who does not—" Lord Rawdon shrugged.

"The parole means nothing?"

"I guess not."

Robert made a show of examining the paperwork in his lap. He rose and returned the materials to the large flimsy desk in front of his cousin. "Perhaps the men could create a better desk, as well." He fumbled for something to say, to hide his true thoughts. "We may be here for some time."

"An excellent idea."

Before Robert reached his tent, he'd made his decision. He placed several items in his pocket and went to find his horse.

"I'm here to question you," Robert said. It was dark in the small, dirty room. The owners of the tiny cabin had fled long ago, and it was now part of the camp.

"I don't see why." The prisoner's dark eyes were suspicious.

"Can you ride a horse?" Robert had neglected to find out the man's name. It didn't matter now.

The fellow was small, dark, and wiry, and he smelled. His hands were bound—with rope and not with iron, Robert was glad to see.

"Of course I can ride. Everyone in these parts can ride, even my granny."

"There's a horse out behind the house. Not much to look at, but he won't break down easily."

Smelly cocked his head. "What are you trying to get me for? Horse thieving?"

"Spying's a death sentence, and you aren't guilty that I can see." His only crime was refusing to take the oath of loyalty, which was understandable.

"I think you just want to have some fun. Let me run so you can shoot me in the back."

Robert's stomach clenched. He hated this war. He wanted to go home, but the peaceful fields of Leichestershire seemed far away, like someone else's life. "I will take guard duty in an hour." A bottle of Madeira meant no questions asked. "The latch on the back door will be unlocked. The horse ready." He shrugged. "It's that or the gallows."

A glimmer of hope appeared on Smelly's face when Robert passed him a knife. "But why?"

"So you can tell your grandchildren that not all redcoats were evil."

It was dusk when Robert returned to take up the promised guard duty. Just as he reached the house, he heard a commotion in the direction of headquarters. A horse, lathered and blown. Its rider dismounted, yelling.

"Ferguson is dead! His men killed and captured!"

Robert's jaw loosened. *Ferguson?* One of Cornwallis's right-hand men, the aggressive Scot had even invented his own firearm. He led a regiment of capable Loyalists. Surely there was a mistake.

"Crazy wild-eyed mountain men surrounded their position, wouldn't give quarter!"

Chills crept up Robert's spine as he unlocked the back door of the house. He didn't know what this meant for Lord Cornwallis, but he knew it was a wonderful distraction.

Smelly would get away.

40

A few more rolling suns at most,
Shall land me safe on Heaven's coast.
There I shall sing the song of grace,
To Jesus Christ, my hiding place!

—Jehoida Brewer, 1776, found in Major John André's possession at his death

Cold December drizzle threatened the campfires scattered about the grassy knoll. The nearest maple and hickory trees raised bare limbs skyward, but several stubborn sweetgums maintained their rich red foliage. It was getting hard to find firewood; many of the nearest trees had lost their lowest branches, and the shrubs and brush were gone.

Jonathan thrust a few sticks into the fire he shared with a recent arrival and wondered what his mother would do were she the general of this piece-meal army strewn about the hamlet of Charlotte.

She might approve of General Greene's efforts to forage for supplies. The man had been Washington's quartermaster, after all, and knew the importance of every bag of cornmeal.

But she'd cast her eyes disapprovingly over the haphazard camp, with tents and brush arbors scattered in no particular arrangement. She'd make sure latrines were dug properly and no man fouled the stream.

She might take on the filthy language and Sabbath-breaking. But even Abigail Russell wouldn't make headway there. And she'd fail utterly with encouraging the men to wash. He fixed his gaze on the man snoring across the fire, hat over his eyes, seemingly impervious to wet. The man stank, and Jonathan wasn't sure a single bath would make Joseph Brown smell sweet. He'd need several scrubbings to dislodge the dirt, and maybe a few dark teeth pulled by a barber to freshen his breath.

Men were joining them by the day, some of them silent and brutal, fresh from a bloody battle at a place called King's Mountain, where a Loyalist regiment had been soundly defeated. Perhaps defeat was too gentle a word. Invasion by the hated British was one thing; when your neighbors took up arms, it seemed quite another, and the over-mountain men had taken their revenge. Eventually, they'd begun taking prisoners instead of killing them all outright. Jonathan was glad for the victory—the first in a long spell of bad news—but the stories filtering back troubled him.

His stomach growled. He'd eaten this morning, a thin porridge made with cornmeal and a little salt, but it hadn't filled him. He wanted to go hunting, but game was scarce. Even the ubiquitous squirrels seemed to be hiding. And besides, he could tell something was up. He couldn't leave camp now.

General Greene had been meeting with Morgan and the other commanders, and the camp was buzzing, the men wondering what would happen next. A change of location couldn't be too soon, for the farmers around Charlotte had no more victuals to spare.

They'd come here without a single supply wagon, only a few pack mules. Perhaps Morgan was right to travel light, but hungry men were not good fighters. Even Jonathan's horse, Brutus, was probably hungry; the grass was thin and brown.

He pulled his bag of acorns closer and began the painstaking process of shelling them. After soaking, they could be ground into a passable meal or even roasted like chestnuts.

A shadow blocked the wet gray light.

A monster of a man loomed before him. Old dark blood splattered leather leggings, and a fox fur cap—complete with the fox's face and paws—perched on his head, making the tall man seem even taller. Jonathan couldn't make out the color of the shadowed eyes, but the man's brown hair was long, untied, and matted. A brace of rabbits dangled from his belt.

He smelled, too, but the aroma of mingled leather and sweat was the ordinary stink of a woodsman.

"Howdy." Jonathan gestured to the fire, noticing the man's weapon. The long rifle was the cleanest thing about him. "Welcome. Name's Russell."

The mountain man grunted in response and squatted. He drew a knife and began skinning the rabbits. "Name's Harrison."

Brown stirred. Seeing the newcomer, he yelped.

Harrison's mouth twitched into a half smile. "You'uns got salt?"

Jonathan handed him a slender sack from his saddlebag and helped create a spit for the small carcasses. "Ye got a tale to tell?" The man had King's Mountain written all over him.

Harrison stared off into the trees for a few moments, then took off his hat and offered it for them to see. A neat hole pierced the very top. "Ferguson's men were on a hill, thought it a good position. It's no good shooting downhill. Most shots went high." He pulled his long rifle off his shoulder and laid it across his lap. "We surrounded the hill, broke up into twos and threes, and went hunting."

Jonathan shivered hearing the man's cool tone. The blood on the man meant he'd done some of his killing close up. Jonathan rose and tended to Brutus, leading him to water and tethering him nearby. War was a fearful thing. God forbid they become heartless killers.

As dusk descended, the rabbits began to ooze juices into the fire. Jonathan's hunger bit into him, and his mouth filled with saliva.

He heard the familiar gruff voice of Daniel Morgan visiting nearby campfires. Soon the bear-like man approached them.

"A wagonload of supplies came from the valley." Morgan swung a bag of beans into Jonathan's lap. "And Greene made his decision. We're to head out in the morning. We'll take on Tarleton while Greene gives Cornwallis something else to think about."

"What about Colonel Pickens?" Brown asked.

"He's coming, him and a bunch of his angry neighbors." Morgan eyed Harrison. "I can use every rifle. We'll also have some dragoons and some battle-tested men from Washington's army. A good force. I mean to destroy Tarleton."

Jonathan's heart leapt. Morgan had a plan. And Jonathan wouldn't mind having a man like Harrison at his side.

When Morgan left, he hefted the bag of beans. *The valley?* Who was behind this?

"WHAT? SHE WENT WHERE?" John Russell strode across the kitchen and back again.

Jonathan's father had returned to Russell's Ridge, and Ruth was glad to see him safe and well. But now she was faced with the consequences of her choice—well, Hannah's choice. But Ruth had aided her, helped her gather supplies. They'd both knitted wool caps and stockings far into the evening. For a month. Hannah carried her soap and ginseng to the McClures' store and returned with sacks of beans, peas, and meal.

Abigail Russell cleansed her hands and wiped them on her apron, her bread dough forgotten. "She left two weeks ago, but she didn't go alone."

John Russell planted his feet, jaw muscles bunching. "Who'd she go with?"

"Seth Gibson," Ruth said, her voice small. She had to take part of the blame.

Jonathan's father snorted. "Seth Gibson. That ne'er-do-well, horse-racing—"

"Here." His wife handed him a tankard full of ale. "You must be fatigued."

His shoulders sagged a bit as he took the offering. His gaze swung to Ruth. "What do you know?"

Ruth grabbed the broom and clung to it. "She was concerned when Jonathan left with Morgan."

"*Jonathan?*"

Taking turns, Ruth and Abigail recounted the events surrounding Jonathan's return and Morgan's muster.

John Russell pulled out a stool and sat heavily. He did not speak for a few moments. "I dinna ken the ways of the Almighty. He gives, then He takes again."

"John!" Abigail sat and grabbed his hands. "You speak as if he's dead."

"It's a hard thing, to lose one son to war and another, seemingly, to the

Uchee. Now he's back, a son restored from the grave, but he's marching into battle. It is too much for a father's heart." He gazed at his wife, eyes bright. "Or his mother's."

Ruth fled the house and ran smack into William.

"Hey! Who's in the house?"

"Your father! He's back—and he knows about Jonathan—and about Hannah."

"I'm glad he's back safe." William smirked. "Hannah's in trouble now."

"She's in *danger* now, you idiot." Guilt rose in Ruth's heart. She'd helped Hannah every step of the way.

He grinned. "She's tall enough to pass for a man, and she can shoot." The grin vanished. "She's not alone. Gibson will answer to me for her safety."

But it was war, not a dance. Ruth shoved past him and ran to the horse barn, the cold air whipping her face. Once inside, the warmth and smell of the horses calmed her.

Several heads lifted at her approach.

"Ducky, oh Ducky." She ran a hand over Ducat's fine black head and neck. The owner of the Dutch stallion had still not yet been found. Most of the other horses spent their days cropping the last of December's fading grass, but this animal faced a trough with a few remaining wisps of hay. "Jonathan is out there somewhere," she told the horse. "What if he is injured?"

"And ye're right about Hannah," a voice rumbled. William had followed her. "Her disguise won't stop a musket ball. Did ye send bandages?"

"Yes, and a few herbs."

William picked up a curry brush. "I've a thought." He turned. "They'll return through Salem."

She listened to his plan.

DRIZZLE MISTING HIS FACE, Robert navigated the camp and entered Tarleton's tent. A pool of lantern light spilled over a tiny map-strewn table. Both Rawdon and Tarleton were bent over it.

"Shirley." Lord Rawdon beckoned to him. "I suggested we help Ban with reconnoitering."

Tarleton looked up. "Your cousin esteems your horsemanship."

Robert nodded in acknowledgement. No one had suspected him of aiding Smelly in his escape, and plenty of time had elapsed. The faces of the others told him that he was in the clear. "Tell me the plan." He already knew the gist of it—a large detachment under Tarleton was being sent to intercept Morgan. But Lord Rawdon's charge was to stay here in Camden. How could they help?

He drew closer to the camp table. A hand-traced map of South Carolina, the rivers prominent, sprawled over the top. The larger settlements were marked—Charlestown, Camden, Ninety-Six, and across the border in North Carolina, Charlotte.

"Morgan left Charlotte several days ago." Tarleton laid a finger on the map. "Heading in this direction. We will intercept—and smash, no more Morgan." He grinned gaily, and Robert decided that if the man could, he'd leave now instead of at dawn. "Lord Cornwallis is moving here." Tarleton indicated another spot, then tapped his fingers together in a pincer motion. "We will destroy them."

Rawdon raised his brows. "You see why we need decent intelligence."

Robert studied the rivers, frowning. "The Catawba is high. All the crossings will be treacherous."

Tarleton grunted. "Horses can swim."

Swim? Through rushing floodwaters?

Rawdon turned to him. "Robert, we leave at daybreak. We'll take a corporal."

We? "But—"

"My lieutenants will take charge of the Volunteers. I want Morgan."

Robert nodded. "Yes, Colonel." He stepped outside, and the drizzle crescendoed into cold fat pellets of rain, soaking him. It matched his dark mood. Tarleton and Rawdon had just marked out a nearly impossible journey.

Tarleton was insane.

41

Healing and wounding are equally from His hand, and are equally tokens of His love and care over us!
—John Newton

*R*obert had lost track of the date. It was January, he knew that much, but he'd not slept in two days, and every hour was filled with tension. Not the tension of gunfire, but the sinew-straining effort of keeping body and soul together as Tarleton led them over swollen rivers and up muddy banks. They'd headed west, then when a scout had reported Morgan's new position, they'd swung north.

Now the Enoree River lay behind them, and Robert ached for sleep. Since leaving Camden, they had barely stopped to eat, but he'd forgotten his hunger. He'd choose sleep over food. He worried about his horse, not to mention the men. How the infantry could keep up with the cavalry's punishing pace he had no idea. Thankfully, no one had yet drowned on the crossings, the infantrymen clinging to makeshift rafts like rats.

And the rain kept falling. At least they weren't trudging through ice and snow, but the ice-cold drops whipped against his face, found their way under his stock, and dampened his shirt. Tarleton seemed impervious to the elements, and with the force of an iron will, he urged them on, but as the days passed, Robert lost all focus.

Why were they slogging through the Carolina backcountry anyway? There was a plan involving Lord Cornwallis, but how they could coordinate with the general over miles of seemingly impassible terrain he knew not.

The gray morning segued into afternoon. The rain eased into drizzle that thinned into a foggy mist. Robert kneed his horse. He'd lost sight of Lord Rawdon, Corporal Simmons, and the cavalry. Somewhere behind him Fraser's regiment marched inexorably along, tough Highlanders who had never known defeat. Forced by the thorny Carolina landscape to exchange their proud kilts for brown trousers, the Scotsmen certainly knew something about the misery of cold and wet.

The gray faded into dusk. Ahead and to his left, spots of light flickered through the trees. Campfires. He aimed his mount in that direction, glad beyond words—glad they'd halted, and glad someone had managed to start a fire in the wet. Maybe he could sleep.

Lord Rawdon found him first.

"Shirley." His cousin's face was haggard. "Morgan is somewhere over the river." He gestured, indicating the direction. "Get some sleep. We need you to scout his position at dawn."

Robert took care of his horse, then found Rawdon's campfire. He searched the area for more deadfall to add to the coals, his muscles like plum pudding. Once the fire was roaring, he stripped off his coat and set it on propped branches to dry, if that were possible, which he doubted. He warmed himself as best as he could, turning before the flames like a carcass on a spit, first front, then back. Then he rolled up in a blanket and lay feet to the fire.

A dreamless sleep swallowed him.

MORGAN CALLED a halt at Hannah's cowpens. Jonathan wondered who this Hannah was. Certainly, he could imagine cattle here, roaming, grazing, waiting for the next stop in their journey to market. The trees were scattered, their boughs arching wide over a tidy terrain. Both cattle and men had scrubbed the area clear of high grass, low brush, and much of the deadfall.

Jonathan pulled out a whetstone and began to sharpen his tomahawk, dulled from cutting low-hanging branches for firewood. After an hour he was able to warm his hands at a small but bright fire, green oak and maple popping like pine.

He tried to think through Morgan's choice to camp here. Tarleton was so close Jonathan could almost smell him, and yet, there wasn't much cover for riflemen. What was the teamster's plan?

He spotted Harrison's tall form emerging from the nearest cluster of men. Cattle had been scavenged from Tory homesteads, driven here, and slaughtered to feed the hungry men. Harrison went to claim their share and returned to the fire with a foreleg.

Brown peered at their portion. "Not much meat there."

Harrison swung the piece of carcass off his shoulder, revealing a large chunk of flesh adhering to the top of the shank. "This here's good eating."

"Let me add some to the beans." Jonathan sliced off a fatty slice from the edge and plunked it into the skillet, then placed it over the fire. "Brown, d'ye suppose that wagon from the Shenandoah has any ale or cider?" He'd never gotten a good look at the wagon or its driver.

"Sure." Brown grabbed their canteens.

With a large belt knife, Harrison disjointed the foreleg from the meaty part. He thrust the top of the leg into the base of the fire, then drove a sharpened branch through the roast and propped it over the hottest part of the flames.

The smoke from numerous campfires floated over the broad knoll. Soon, the scent of roasting beef filled the air, and Jonathan's belly contracted painfully.

Patience. By full dark they'd have enough food cooked to last several days. No matter what happened tomorrow, they'd still need to eat.

Jonathan lay back and closed his eyes until Brown returned.

"Got some cider—the last of it."

"Who was it?"

"Who was what?"

"The driver of the wagon."

Understanding flooded Brown's face. "Gibson. Man's name was Gibson. And a lad with him."

"Hmm." The Gibsons. Familiar faces joined the names in Jonathan's mind. Ordinary valley lads.

The fat-streaked beef dripped into the fire, provoking even more popping and sparks from the green wood. Harrison sliced into it and stabbed a chunk of meat with a twig.

"Don't mind it rare."

They ate silently until Morgan joined them.

"Pickens and his men have arrived. They'll take this position." He motioned to the open swell of ground nearby. "Riflemen will take position by those trees."

Riflemen included himself and Harrison. Jonathan studied the tree line. The enemy was somewhere on the other side of the Pacolet River, which was no more than a minor hindrance, even in its swollen state. The redcoats would swarm over the river, and through the trees, eating up the ten miles between them in no time. The riflemen would be the first to take the shock of the invading redcoats. And riflemen were no match for Tarleton's cavalry. "D'ye ken whether he'll send in his cavalry first?"

"Probably not, but 'tis no matter. Three shots, and the riflemen fall back and join Pickens's line."

A thoughtful crease appeared between Harrison's brows.

Brown leaned forward. "Where will the rest of the men be?"

Morgan's gaze was fixed on Jonathan as he gestured. "They'll be yonder, just over that swell of ground."

Jonathan's lips parted. He saw it now. The redcoats would chase the militiamen, thinking they were fleeing. Washington's battle-hardened men, the ones who were trained to stand their ground, would be just out of sight.

It was a trap.

ROBERT FOUGHT THE INSISTENT VOICE. He didn't want to open his eyes.

"Sir, Captain."

It was dark, and it was very early, but at least it wasn't raining.

"Captain Shirley." Simmons had shaken him, Robert was sure. "I'm to come with you."

Robert fastened his stock, pulled on his boots, and fumbled with the buttons of his spats. He reached for his canteen and shook it. "Is there any food or drink to be had?" He heaved the saddle onto his horse.

"Sorry, sir. There's nothing. No food. Rations ran out yesterday. Just water." Simmons filled the canteens.

Unbelievable. Tarleton was mad, to push his men without food. "On the way back, we'll look for fiddleheads and such."

"Chestnuts. I saw chestnut trees."

But the reality was they wouldn't have time to scavenge. The rebels were perhaps fifteen miles away. To scout and return would take all day.

They mounted and made their way slowly through the trees, trusting the horses' greater acuity of vision. Once they emerged on the bank of the Pacolet, the quarter moon emerged from the thinning clouds.

Before them, the water gushed and gurgled. Robert could see the far bank twenty feet away, but could not tell how safe the footing was.

"Simmons?"

"With you, sir."

Robert urged the horse forward, and it trudged through the water. At one point the level rose to his stirrups. Not bad.

The opposite bank was muddy and slick. Robert leaned over the horse's withers as it scrambled like a dog to get its footing. Once on the bank, he smelled the smoke of campfires. And roasting beef. Or was that his hungry imagination?

The gray light of dawn suffused the woods. How far was it to the main rebel camp? Certainly they would post sentries nearby.

"Simmons?"

"Sir."

"There are riflemen in these woods. Follow me."

Robert turned his animal to parallel the river. They scouted an hour without seeing anyone. But the smell of smoke was heavier. They were close.

They retraced their steps, and Robert led the way northeast, toward the Broad River. He was acutely aware of the color of his coat, so visible through the trees. But he couldn't take it off. A man out of uniform could be hanged as a spy, like André.

They'd made it perhaps two miles when a rifle barked.

And then another.

"Simmons!"

Robert turned his horse and urged him back toward the Pacolet. He cut a glance over his shoulder. Simmons' mare was at his mount's flank, her eyes showing white.

Then Simmons jerked and his hands let loose of the reins. Robert lunged for the bridle of the mare. "Simmons!"

Simmons fell off the horse, and the mare, terrified by the gunfire, tore loose and galloped away.

Robert's horse reared and screamed, and he grabbed at the mane, desperate for purchase. Then the horse settled into a mad gallop, and it was all Robert could do to keep his seat as branches tore at him.

At least they were going in the right direction. *Poor Simmons.* The best he could hope for was capture. There was a chance they'd treat his injury instead of finishing him off, assuming he wasn't dead already.

Bare limbs plucked at Robert like hands, trying to hold him back, and his strength ebbed as he fought them off.

What was the point, anyway?

He was exhausted and the horse's sides were heaving when they arrived at the Pacolet. The little river was different here, narrower, only fifteen feet across, but the water gushed and tumbled with greater force.

They'd crossed deeper rivers than this. Robert pressed his heels to his mount's ribs, and after a slight hesitation, the animal plunged into the water. They were halfway across, the water splashing Robert's thighs, when the horse stumbled.

Robert was thrown into the muddy, roiling water. He thrashed, trying to regain the surface, wondering why he bothered.

His face found air, and he gasped and drank it in.

I am the way, the truth, and the life.

The verse came from nowhere.

The way. There was a way, whatever that meant. But it meant something good, he was sure, and Robert found the strength to swim to the other side.

The horse remained in the water, head drooping, nostrils red, sides heaving.

"Easy, come on up."

But the horse had difficulty mounting the bank. One foreleg was lame. Robert circled the animal and discovered blood running down its near hindquarters. Just as he'd suspected, the animal had been shot. A bloody froth dribbled from its nose, a result of the panicked run. This poor creature was done for even without the wound.

He laid his hand on his pistol, then reconsidered. The powder was wet, the weapon useless. He pulled out his knife instead, reluctant, but there was no hope for this animal.

He managed to find the great vessel in the drooping neck and summoned his strength. The animal's life blood gushed out, causing the large eyes to flutter and close.

The knees buckled, and the horse collapsed untidily like an abandoned marionette.

He stepped back, his boots splattered red.

I am the way, the truth, and the life.

Death and darkness surrounded him, but somewhere there was hope.

ROBERT MADE it back to camp before dusk.

Lord Rawdon strode up to him. "Where have you been? Never mind, come and make your report."

His cousin didn't even ask about Simmons. They entered Tarleton's tent.

The commander raised his brows. "Report."

Robert gave him a condensed version of his observations, then motioned toward the map on the camp desk. "Morgan is camped well beyond the Pacolet. I believe we can trap him against the Broad River." The Broad River came by its name honestly. Swollen by rain, it would not easily be crossed.

Tarleton scrutinized the map. "I concur. With Morgan's back against the river, he cannot escape."

Obviously, he was not going to wait for Lord Cornwallis.

Rawdon's dark eyes glittered. "We will do to Morgan what was done to Ferguson."

Tarleton gave a narrow smile. "Reveille at two o'clock. We will strike at dawn."

JONATHAN SAW THE STARS. The chill of the night was seeping through his blanket, and he needed to stir the fire, but still he lay, mesmerized by the spectacle through the bare branches above.

The stars glittered unchanging, uncaring. They would remain whether this battle were won or lost, whether this war were won or lost. Like God Himself, they could not be moved by these events.

Did God care about this war?

Jonathan had lost hope for the Cause, partly because of Washington's continual string of losses, setbacks, and stalemates, and partly because of the aching loss of his brother. He'd almost resigned himself to life under tyranny when Morgan had roused himself to fight once again.

God was sovereign over all things, the preachers said. Sovereign over men, rulers, and even those stars. His purposes were certain to stand. Yet those same ministers who preached His sovereignty preached rebellion.

Colonel Pickens was a good Presbyterian like himself. A godly man, so they said. Yet here he was.

Jonathan sat up and added sticks to the fire, mere embers now. He used his tomahawk to chop another sturdy branch from a nearby tree and added the green wood on top, careful not to snuff out the tiny flames.

Tarleton was close. They would fight on the morrow.

He didn't know how to pray. Pray for victory? He wanted it so bad he could taste it.

Lord, hear the cries of Your people. And glorify Yourself despite all our weaknesses, our frailties, and our sins.

Jonathan found Brutus and led him away from the fires and into the woods nearby. A shape loomed before him in a small clearing.

The moonlight illumined the shape of a wagon and several horses picketed nearby.

"Ho," someone grunted sleepily. "Who're you?"

"Russell. Can ye take my horse?"

Brutus nickered, greeting the other animals.

"Say, Russell." It was Seth Gibson, his tousled head recognizable now. "Tomorrow—I want to fight."

"Ye've a musket?"

"Of course—and plenty of ball and powder."

Jonathan explained Morgan's tactics. "After three volleys, Pickens' line will retreat over the knoll where the regulars are. Say, can your brother handle the animals?"

"He's—he's not my brother, but he's real good with horses."

Satisfied, Jonathan returned to the camp.

The moonlight revealed a shape flitting between the campfires. Some of the lads were still awake.

Morgan's gruff voice floated over the grassy space. "You'uns have sweethearts? Make 'em proud. Just two shots, maybe three, then fall back. You'll go home wrapped in glory."

Jonathan stirred the fire and lay down. Wrapped in glory? Maybe. Or maybe gone to glory.

He closed his eyes and waited for the dawn.

42

Boys, get up, Benny's coming!

—General Daniel Morgan, January 17, 1781

*I*n the gray mists of dawn, the green-coated British dragoons burst through the trees, their horses leaping into a full gallop. Jonathan raised his rifle, the weapon fresh-primed.

Get the officers. Morgan's instructions rang in his ears.

Next to him, Harrison's rifle cracked, and a rider fell.

Jonathan chose a well-braided target and squeezed the trigger. *Snap!*

The dragoon lurched in his saddle and tumbled to the ground.

Up and down the line of riflemen the weapons discharged. But still the dragoons galloped on, sabers flashing. Behind them, the woods boiled red with the advance of the infantrymen.

Closer, closer, the charging horses loomed, nostrils flaring.

Jonathan squeezed off one more shot at a green uniform, then joined the others in retreat, running and dodging, as the hooves of the horses drummed the earth behind them.

Then the hoofbeats slowed. He cast a glance behind him and saw

Tarleton. It had to be the man himself, standing in the stirrups, barking out orders, black headgear prominent. They were regrouping.

Over a dozen horses milled about, riderless. They'd slowed Tarleton. It was a tiny victory.

ROBERT CLUTCHED at his cousin's waist as Rawdon's mount splashed through the Pacolet. Before them rode Tarleton's dragoons, and to either side the infantry. Somewhere behind them marched the Highlanders, held in reserve. Ideally the infantry should attack first, along with the three-pound cannon, but the reality was, once Tarleton caught Morgan's scent, the cavalry would outpace the others.

The horse stumbled and Robert almost fell off.

"Patience," growled Rawdon. "Someone will get killed and then you'll get a mount."

It was ignominious, riding behind his cousin like a pack of provisions. But it couldn't be much longer now. They'd defeat Morgan, take the rebels' supplies, and spread out to forage and requisition cattle from the area.

His eyes were gritty. Over the past week he'd slept less than most of the others, scouting for Tarleton. The time of prayer before his eyes closed was strangely refreshing, but reveille came much too early, only the habit of long duty rousing him. Sleep seemed unspeakably sweet and unattainable.

He grasped the hilt of his sword. He couldn't fight riding like this. He was useless until he found a horse.

Ahead, gunfire cracked.

The trees parted. Tarleton's dragoons were before them, regrouping, several loose horses mingled among them.

"Go." Rawdon pointed.

Robert slid off Rawdon's mount and surveyed the loose horses, milling about, agitated. Then he paused. On the ground a dragoon lay face-up, eyes staring, blood thickening around a gaping throat wound.

He recognized the man, one of Tarleton's favorites. An officer. They were targeting officers again.

Robert clutched at his own neck. Without pausing to second-guess himself, he unfastened his gorget and tossed it to the ground.

JONATHAN DIDN'T SEE Harrison but fell into formation with Colonel Pickens's men. Even standing upright they were cloaked from the redcoats by a gentle swell of ground, and Jonathan blessed Morgan's foresight. Who could have imagined that such a seemingly flat piece of ground could hide a whole regiment?

When Tarleton regrouped and pursued he'd have the shock of his life. Instead of a few ragged backwoodsmen, he'd have Pickens to deal with. And beyond here, why, there was another rise and another line of men hiding behind it.

Just three shots. Their orders were to fire a few volleys and fold back.

A cannon barked, and Jonathan recognized the sound of a tiny three-pounder, dangerous despite its size.

He reloaded and primed his rifle. The ground trembled, followed by the thunder of hooves and shouts of men.

Redcoats popped up over the swell, muskets at the ready. Behind Pickens's line, Morgan galloped gaily, shouting encouragement, his hair streaming loose like a madwoman's.

A ragged series of pops sounded up and down the line. Jonathan took careful aim. His hands were slippery despite the cold.

An officer. He didn't see any brass gorgets, so he targeted a soldier at random and pulled the trigger. The man jerked with the impact, but Jonathan didn't wait to watch him fall. He turned slightly, grabbed a home-made cartridge from his pouch, and tore it with his teeth. He poured the powder, followed it with the shot, then shoved the patch in.

The redcoats stopped as one, raised their muskets, and let loose a volley.

Jonathan lost his balance but didn't know why. He managed to hop and slide to the side, his focus on a tall hickory tree that seemed to offer refuge.

His left leg was numb. Then white-hot fire shot up his shin to his groin and he gasped.

As in a dream, he saw Pickens's men fire another round, then turn and run.

A CHESTNUT HORSE SIDLED NEARBY, ears flicking nervously. Robert lunged for the reins, loose and flapping, but the animal proved elusive, leading him on a merry chase. He gave it up and sought another, ignoring the bodies of their previous riders strewn about the field.

A mass of red-coated infantrymen passed him, a wall of gunfire and shouts, following the fleeing rebels. If he didn't find a mount soon, he'd miss the battle.

Not that he cared all that much.

A large blood bay emerged from the trees nearby, an impressive animal with a broad, well-muscled chest. The rider was a rebel wearing the leather jacket so many of them wore. Robert felt for the pistol in his belt. His useless pistol.

He placed his hand on the hilt of his sword and blinked. He knew this horse. And the lad on its back looked strangely familiar.

The lad's hat fell off, revealing coppery hair shining in the sun. This was no lad. It was Hannah Russell, at the edge of the field, dismounting near a tree a stone's throw away.

He was dreaming. He was sleeping on his feet.

He wiped his eyes. No, he was awake. His gut chilled. Why was she here?

He scurried forward but couldn't imagine what he would do or say when he caught up to this woman.

He noticed a man beneath the tree—a wounded rebel?

The battle had moved toward the Broad River, but lead was still flying everywhere. She was in danger.

JONATHAN COLLAPSED UNDER THE TREE, not able to think. Pain clouded his mind. He wondered vaguely about a bandage and tugged the kerchief off his neck.

He needed to tie it snugly around the injury, stop the bleeding. He squinted at his shin.

It was red with blood. His own blood.

He'd been shot. Was his leg broken?

A line of British infantry moved past, hallos and shouts tearing from their throats as they chased Pickens's men. None seemed to notice him in the smoky haze.

A horse emerged from the trees and trotted closer. It was Brutus, and for a moment he was glad—Brutus, his faithful colt.

No, not out here, not with bullets flying. Not where the cavalry could steal him. And who was that riding him, anyway?

Hannah?

He panicked.

ROBERT CLOSED THE DISTANCE RAPIDLY. He did not know what to say; he only knew he had to get Hannah away from danger.

Then he recognized the man lying under the tree.

Hoofbeats sounded from behind, and Hannah turned toward the sound. Her hair had been cut, but the shoulder-length locks had come loose from their tie. She hadn't noticed him yet.

"Captain Shirley, what have we here." Rawdon's deep, sonorous voice sent shivers down Robert's spine. His cousin had approached out of nowhere. "A horse *and* a woman?"

Just twenty feet away, Jonathan Russell lay injured, red soaking one leg. Robert purposely ignored him and grabbed the bay's bridle. "Yes, I suppose I caught a real prize." He led the animal several slow steps away from Russell while Hannah clung to the bridle on the other side.

Rawdon mustn't know he esteemed this woman. Her safety teetered on the edge of a knife.

Thankfully, Rawdon's gaze did not veer toward the tree. His eyes traveled over the stallion, then appraised Hannah.

Robert tensed his gut against the nausea rising in his belly.

"Tarleton will want the horse—or the girl. Or both." His cousin chuckled, an ugly sound. Two steps and his arm had pinned Hannah against his side. Her gaze fell on Robert and she stilled, eyes widening.

Speak of the devil. Tarleton rode up, but his horse was gasping, bloody froth pouring from both nose and mouth.

"Rawdon, a horse?" Tarleton's baritone assumed compliance. "Nice specimen. My mount is lung shot. Too bad." His gaze lingered on Hannah, who kicked Rawdon ineffectually. "A woman? Dressed in breeches? Alas, you must take the girl. I need to call up the Seventy-First. They'll conclude matters here."

Tarleton grabbed the bridle of the horse. In moments, the cavalryman had mastered the snorting, side-stepping animal and galloped away.

Scowling, Hannah thrashed in Rawdon's grip. From the corner of his eye, Robert caught movement. Russell was not dead and would seek to defend his sister if he could.

And then Rawdon would shoot him.

Robert wanted to strike Rawdon, tear Hannah out of his arms. To strike an officer was death—maybe. A mere brawl between fellow officers could be overlooked, but during a battle?

"Lord Rawdon, I have met this woman before." He pitched his voice to match Tarleton's lustful nonchalance. Perhaps Rawdon would mistake his interest for that of a soldier with a cold bed.

Staring at Robert, Hannah's expression changed from shock to rage.

"Oh?" Rawdon secured Hannah's arms behind her back. "I like this one, so feisty."

Hannah had a knife somewhere, but if she used it on Rawdon, he would hurt her—or worse. Robert's heart ached. She hated him and he didn't blame her.

"Fran, you need to share."

He hadn't used his cousin's childhood nickname in years. It was worth a try.

Somewhere beyond the trees, bagpipes sounded. The Highlanders were coming.

WITH FUMBLING FINGERS, Jonathan tied the kerchief around his leg, just below the knee. He sagged back from the effort and wiped red hands on the cold leaf litter thick on the ground.

He scrambled for his rifle, but it was out of sight. What had happened to it?

His hands fell to his waist, and he laid his right hand on his tomahawk. Two redcoats. His sister in danger.

The nearest redcoat grabbed his colt's bridle. Then a green-coated cavalryman galloped up.

It was Tarleton. Jonathan tensed. He slowly levered himself up to a sitting position as the cavalryman exchanged his mount for Brutus.

Jonathan's gaze followed his stallion as Tarleton galloped off. He groaned inside, but Hannah was his first concern.

She was a strong woman, but the redcoat who held her was stronger, and controlled her easily with one arm. Jonathan could hear snippets of conversation. The two men were arguing over her.

He gauged the distance. His mind went back to the Uchee village, to the laughing warriors who sometimes included Jonathan in their contests. His height and reach served him well in footraces and wrestling, but a bow and arrow was harmless in his hands, and the Indians mocked him.

The tomahawk was different. It was a part of him. Every woodsman used it for all kinds of things, including self-defense. From a standing position, he could throw it accurately for at least twenty feet. The Indians regularly hit targets from much farther away but had respected his efforts to improve.

He wasn't standing—couldn't stand. He pushed himself up against the tree with his good leg, the bark digging into his back. He hefted the tomahawk.

Bagpipes sounded from beyond the trees.

The redcoat holding Hannah looked back toward the sound, then adjusted his stance, holding her with his left arm—his right side was open.

Jonathan gripped the handle of the tomahawk and raised it. Time seemed to slow as he gauged the distance to the redcoat, the black brows, the shining gorget, the line of buttons marching down the facings.

He aimed for the head.

Ignoring the pain, he summoned his strength and threw. Then his good knee buckled.

He slid to the ground.

FROM THE CORNER of his eye, Robert saw movement.

Jonathan Russell. But what could he do?

"Find your own woman," Rawdon was saying. "Get my horse, I'm taking her with me. Fraser's men will finish off Morgan."

Robert grabbed the animal's dangling reins, then several things happened all at once.

Rawdon collapsed. An Indian hatchet lay next to his body. Hannah danced away.

Jonathan Russell slumped to the ground. Impossibly, he must have thrown the hatchet.

Robert scurried to his cousin's side and knelt. There was no blood—must have been a glancing blow. Rawdon blinked and struggled to sit up.

Bagpipes echoed through the trees, closer. Fraser would be here in no time.

Robert helped his cousin up. "Rawdon, take your horse." The man was lucky to be alive.

His cousin's unfocused gaze fell on his mount.

Hopefully the advance of the Highlanders would convince his cousin to leave. "I'll see that this woman finds your tent."

Wincing, Rawdon mounted his horse. "See that you do," he spat, and rode off.

Robert sagged in relief. Hannah strode up, her face stormy. She stepped back, holding a pistol.

His pistol. And it was aimed at his chest.

"I surrender." Robert lifted his hands, strangely glad. The pistol was water-logged and useless, but she didn't know that. "I give you my parole."

Stone-faced, Hannah used the pistol to motion him toward the tree where her brother lay. "I want ye to help me. If ye don't, or if ye try to trick me, I will blow your head off."

Robert nodded and moved slowly toward Russell. "My parole is my word of honor. I will not attempt escape. Do you accept it?"

"Accept it." Russell's voice was weak.

"Aye, I accept it." Hannah waved the pistol.

The bagpipes were louder. "The Highlanders are coming," Robert said. "We need to leave here now."

Hannah's eyes widened in alarm. "Pick him up and bring him to the wagon."

Robert knelt and scooped her brother into his arms, discovering at that moment how weak he was. He gritted his teeth and forced his limbs to move. He knew the reputation of Fraser's Highlanders and for the first time, he was terrified of them.

He followed Hannah through a copse of trees to a small clearing, where several horses grazed near a wagon. Robert left Jonathan on the wagon bed and helped Hannah harness the animals, forcing his hands to move quickly. They needed to leave.

"Head northwest." He pointed, hoping the battle would not shift.

"Get back there and see to my brother. There are bandages." She indicated a bag.

Robert stripped off his coat, turned it inside out, and used it for bedding. Hannah slapped the reins on the horses' rumps and the wagon jolted forward. Robert fought to concentrate on Russell's injury as they bounced over the uneven ground. The horses were fresh and the wagon almost empty.

A kerchief was knotted above the wound, red with blood. A clumsy bandage, but it had slowed the bleeding. Russell needed proper care—and a doctor with a needle. For now, Robert would do what he could.

Robert pulled out a knife and discovered Russell's gaze on him. He was calm but glassy eyed. "Take care of my sister, will ya?"

Robert used the knife to cut a bandage to a proper length, wrapped it around Russell's leg, then fastened the whole thing with the leather stock from around his neck. "Take care of her yourself," he said gruffly.

Shouting from the battle nearby penetrated his consciousness. Something was happening.

The Highlanders. They'd struck.

The battle was over.

Robert waited until the sounds receded into the distance and all he could hear was the creaking of the wagon and the jingle of the harness. Then he lay back, closed his eyes, and let sleep take him.

43

I further believe that all must be saved through the merits of Christ.
—Daniel Morgan, letter to a friend

Maggoty Gap, Virginia, January 1781

*R*uth sought for the first line, the first word. Unused to verse, the prospect of forming a simple couplet was daunting, but it distracted her from the saddle's chafing. After two days of travel on horseback even the breeches under her skirt didn't protect her.

On either side of the road south, naked branches rose high over their heads, stark against the white of the powdery snow beneath. But the austere January beauty had begun to gall after the first day. It was cold in the hills.

"We'll follow the stream a while here." William's words created white puffs of air as he rode just ahead on his newly broke filly. His saddlebags bulged with supplies. Her own were filled with bandages and herbs. Canvas tents and jugs of vinegar and whiskey were strapped on a mule following them on a leading rein.

The section of the road through Maggoty Gap had proved to be gentle. Hannah had managed it with the wagon, after all. From here it was an easy trek south to Salem, their goal. Easy except for the cold and the hard saddle.

Ruth's thighs ached, and she longed for the warmth of a fire. She fought to distract herself by composing a poem, a hymn. Her topic was Abraham. She sighed. Composing a logical essay was so much easier.

Abraham left his cherished home, a promised land to seek.

No. Awkward. Abram would work better. It had two syllables and would fit much more easily into the rhythm of verse.

She looked up. William's hair looked so much like Jonathan's. "Are you sure Jonathan will return through Salem?"

William cut a glance over his shoulder. "The only road to the valley goes through Salem. Sooner or later, they'll have news of the militia."

"I'm surprised your father let you go."

"I'm a man full grown. Even so, he'd tan my hide if I stepped a foot beyond Salem." He paused, and for a moment Ruth thought he'd finished speaking. "It's hard for a man who's lost one son already. He knows I willna join Morgan. I'd love to kill redcoats. But my time will come."

Abraham. Nathan's last words were Abraham's vision. *A better country. A heavenly country.*

"Abram left Ur of the Chaldees, by faith he saw a city heavenly," she spoke aloud. "No, no. That does not give me the meter I need."

William slowed his filly, turned, and raised his brows. "A better country, heavenly; a fair abode beyond this veil ..."

"William! You're a poet!"

He smiled sadly. "I've had a long time to think. I do want to fight the redcoats, but Da keeps saying that even if we lose, we are free men in Christ."

Even if we lose. Somehow this consideration did not cheer her. Was it so wrong to hope for life and peace and a home with a husband?

A life without the oppressive presence of redcoats?

Lord, remember Jonathan for good. Please preserve him.

"Drink this," Hannah's voice commanded.

Jonathan managed to prop himself with one arm and reached for the cup with the other. His arm felt so weak. Where was his strength? Where was his rifle?

He spotted his firearm slung over Hannah's shoulder. *Good.*

Slowly, it all came back. The standoff, the tomahawk—and the redcoat.

Robert Shirley lay next to him in the wagon bed, snoring softly. His familiar face was thinner than Jonathan remembered, with hollows under his eyes and a thin white scar on his cheekbone.

And this British officer had just given his parole to Jonathan's *sister*.

Jonathan sipped what tasted like broth and scanned the sky. The shadows were long, pointing east. "Where are we?"

"We're a good distance into North Carolina."

He hadn't slept well in the jolting wagon, pain stabbing his leg like a red-hot poker, his mind floating in a half-wakeful state that felt like a bad dream.

Hannah took his empty cup and refilled it. "Here. I boiled jerky. You lost a lot of blood."

By the time the sun settled behind the trees his thoughts were clearer. "Ye still have the man's pistol?"

"Aye." Hannah raised her brows.

He held out a hand. A suspicion niggled at him. In any case, they'd have to get rid of anything that shouted *redcoat*.

She passed it to him, and it was unexpectedly heavy. The beauty of the wood grain was marred by a film of grime, and the pan was worse.

"I doubt this would fire."

He pulled the mechanism to a half-cock and inspected the pan more closely. "The powder is fouled." Careful not to move his throbbing leg, he ducked his hand into his satchel and pulled out his tools. He cleaned the pan and primed it with fresh powder, then took aim at a tree across the road and pulled the trigger.

A flash and pop made him blink, but the pistol did not fire.

He snorted. "He must've dropped this in the river."

Hannah laid a hand on the wagon's side and stared at the sleeping Shirley. "D'ye think he knew it wouldna fire?"

"A soldier's weapon is his life. Aye, he would have known."

The lines of Shirley's face were peaceful in repose. A bird squawked nearby in the woods, interrupting the quiet.

"I wanted to kill him." Hannah's eyes filled with tears. "I really did. Only for a moment. But … oh Jonnie, I hated him so. I hated the uniform, but more, I hated to see *him* wear it."

"Like he betrayed us."

Hannah nodded. "Did Ruth know?"

"She knew in Boston he was on half pay. But she didn't realize he wasn't truly retired."

Jonathan blinked and sagged back. He was so tired. Should he explain the rest? Shirley's true duplicity? His letter to the earl?

"So why did he surrender to me if he knew I couldna hurt him?"

"I dinna ken." He surveyed their campsite, the modest fire. They should be safe enough. "Han, we need to bury his coat. And the pistol."

He wondered about the results of the battle, but just then it didn't seem important. He slid back into sleep.

ROBERT WOKE to the smell of a fire and a painfully full bladder. He opened his eyes and remained still, taking stock of his situation. Russell lay beside him, wrapped in a wool blanket, and it was nearly full dark. Was it morning? Or evening?

His nose was freezing, but someone had thrown a blanket over him.

Cracks and pops to his left marked the site of the fire. Small sounds indicated activity. A glimpse of fiery red hair.

Hannah?

His body protested as he sat up. How long had he slept? "Miss Russell, may I trouble you for the time?"

She swung a rifle off her shoulder, but she didn't cock it. The fire lit her from behind, casting a golden halo around her head but leaving her features shrouded.

"Time?"

"How long have I slept?" According to his bladder, it had been a while. He wagered he'd slept the rest of the day and all night.

"You slept round the clock. It's now evening."

He gaped at her for a moment, then his need reasserted itself.

"You must excuse me, I require … a tree."

The muzzle of the rifle dipped, and he skirted barren bushes to hide behind the wide trunk of an oak. That rifle was loaded, and she knew how to use it. He couldn't believe she'd kill him now, and in any case, the prospect did not trouble him greatly.

The night before the battle, he'd prayed, prayed to the God of the New

Testament, the words that smote him like fire. Upon waking the promise was his. *The way, the truth, and the life.* It wasn't just an idea, a philosophy, or even a moral teaching.

It was life. And now he had that life.

He returned to the fire and held out his hands to warm them. "Your brother's injury, it needs a physician."

"We'll make Salem tomorrow." Her gaze was fixed on him, her stance rigid.

"I have given you my parole. My word of honor."

"Word of honor? Ye lied to Ruth."

He shook his head. "Not exactly. But I was in Boston under false pretenses. I was sending information to the Earl of Dartmouth."

"Dartmouth? I recognize that name." She squatted by the fire, frowning.

"The Earl of Dartmouth is—or rather, was—the Secretary of the Colonies, and needed information outside of official channels."

"Sounds sneaky to me."

He grabbed a blanket from the wagon, threw it around his shoulders, and sat across from her. "It was … sneaky. Where is my coat?"

"I buried it. Your coat and your pistol."

Both of which would mark him as a British officer. He reached for his neck, but both gorget and military stock were gone.

"Are you going to bury me as well?"

She huffed in frustration. "I canna kill you now, though I had thought to do it. Why did ye surrender to me?"

"You had my pistol."

"A useless pistol."

A few lonely snowflakes fell from the sky.

"Oh." He wrapped his arms around his knees, his stomach troubling him. He couldn't remember when he had last eaten. "I suppose you could call me a coward, but I could not bear it anymore. I couldn't bear the army, couldn't bear my cousin."

"Your cousin?"

"My commander. He's as bad as Tarleton. I wanted to leave the army, but there was no honorable way out."

She seemed to digest this. "So you surrendered to escape."

"In a manner of speaking. I wanted to deliver you from those rascals, but when you grabbed my pistol, I saw my chance."

"What shall I do with ye?"

Robert was silent. His newfound peace did not mean he wanted to die. Major André's face flashed in his mind. He would avoid the gallows if he could. By surrendering to a civilian, he'd side-stepped the necessity of facing Morgan—and perhaps Washington. "You can send me to General Washington, but I might not be exchanged."

"Why not?"

"My correspondence with the earl … Washington hangs spies." He was no longer a spy, but that was no guarantee. That night on the road to Concord condemned him, and if anyone found out, he would be executed.

He couldn't tell her about Concord. Couldn't tell anyone.

Silence fell, and fat snowflakes surrounded them like a veil.

Hannah's gaze was thoughtful as she filled a cup from a kettle over the fire. "Here. I might as well feed you."

"Thank you. I will take the watch. You must be exhausted."

She handed him a chunk of bread and a piece of dried venison. "I willna give ye the rifle. But dinna worry about wolves. They dinna like the fire, just keep it burning bright."

The rock-hard bread tasted sweet in his mouth. The flickering light of the fire cast strange shadows on the barren branches of the woods. He was not a woodsman, but the horses would sense a threat before he could. On top of which, he had a knife, and he could sharpen a stick.

Hannah clambered into the wagon and peered over the edge. "Wake me if a wolf gets close, if ye can see its eyes. I've never yet shot one," she said cheerfully.

Robert cast about for a hefty branch, hopeful. She didn't trust him with the rifle, yet she trusted him to stand guard while she slept.

His heart clenched with gladness. She might hate him, but she trusted him. It was something.

∼

IT SNOWED the night before Ruth and William reached Salem, and they fought all night to keep a fire going. Morning light revealed a thick carpet of white. A single raven croaked out a call in the morning stillness.

Without speaking they saddled the horses and journeyed on. By the time the sun was high a few homesteads were visible, the outskirts of Salem.

The road headed into the heart of the Moravian settlement, where the snow was already beaten to muddy slush. What Moravians believed Ruth knew not, and she studied the structures with interest. The sturdy half-timbered building to her right boasted a steeply pitched tiled roof. Smoke curled out of the two chimneys.

A young man emerged from the structure and greeted them. "*Willkommen.* I am Jakob Ernst. Are you married?"

Ruth stared at him and Jakob blushed.

"That building"—he pointed at the one he'd emerged from—"is for the young men. The single men. Yonder is the one for young women. Sorry about the question, but we often house travelers."

William explained their errand to find Jonathan, and Jakob's face underwent interesting changes of expression.

"We are not allowed to fight, you see. Violence is not right, we must turn the other cheek." He frowned. "Militiamen went south a few months past, was he one of them?" His voice grew softer. "Sometimes we get news of the battles." He glanced to his right, toward a neat building with a porch. "Come, Oma will decide where you will sleep."

"Oma" proved to be Anna Heinz, a vigorous woman just past middle age, judging by the silver streaks visible under the rim of her white linen cap. Her embroidered apron, dusted with flour, encircled a healthy girth. Pottery of every size and color covered the numerous shelves and broad counter. A pottery shop.

"Have you eaten?" was her first question, delivered with a German accent. "Jakob tells me you are not married." Her dimpled face twisted in concern.

The air was filled with the warm aroma of baking bread, and Ruth's stomach gurgled. "William is the brother of my betrothed, who is with General Morgan. Their enlistments should be up soon, and ..."

"But you are not here because of the enlistment."

The perceptive woman saw right through her. "Quite right. I worry—he could be injured."

"Are you continuing south?"

Ruth shook her head. "Have you any news?"

"That fellow Morgan has not returned, nor any of his men." Her face tightened, as if the mere consideration of war troubled her. "You can stay with me. Your *Schwager* will stay in the single men's house across the street."

"*Dankeshôn*," William said.

Oma Heinz smiled broadly. "You are welcome. Now we eat."

"WAKE UP," Oma murmured.

Ruth opened her eyes to the strange room. She sat up and remembered where she was. Oma's house. The woman was a widow but served as a matriarch of this highly structured community. And she was a midwife, Ruth had been happy to learn yesterday. Midwives were sometimes quite competent when it came to illness and injury.

Oma stood in the doorway of the small, simple space. The room was almost austere, relieved only by a colorful braided rug on the floor. "A wagon has arrived." She set down a steaming cup on a tiny table and left abruptly.

Could it be Jonathan? Or someone with news of him?

Ruth jumped up. The floor was cold, but that didn't matter. She reached for her skirt and pulled it on over her chemise, then grabbed her bodice. In a minute she was dressed. She found her cloak and brought the cup of coffee with her as she darted through the house and onto the porch.

The coffee sloshed onto her skirt. She ignored it, blinking against the glare of morning sunlight against the snow.

Hannah stood next to a wagon, bare-headed and still wearing breeches. William's coat seemed to swallow her form. A rifle was slung over her back.

"Ruth!" she said. "Jonathan is injured. We need help."

Sweat marked the flanks of the familiar Russell horses. On the wagon's seat, reins in hand, sat a disheveled man. A familiar man.

It was Robert Shirley.

44

Oh, horrid war, how hast thou blasted the fairest prospects of happiness. Robbed me of parents, sisters and brother, thou art depriving me of the society of my husband, who alone can repair the loss.

—Lucy Knox to her husband Henry, *Letter,* 1781

*R*uth could spare no time for questions. Robert Shirley's presence would have to be explained later. Oma Heinz was already clambering onto the wagon bed, giving rapid-fire orders to all and sundry, mostly in German.

Ruth rounded the wagon. Jonathan lay swathed in a blanket, his face flushed.

"Ruth? Is that you? Or am I dreaming?"

"'Tis me." She laid a hand on his forehead. Definitely fevered, but she had seen worse. "What happened?"

"Couldna dodge fast enough."

Oma tugged away the blanket. Jonathan's left leg was heavily bandaged below the knee. Blood stained the linen.

"Let's get him inside. The men's *haus.*"

William, Robert, and a Moravian youth carried Jonathan into the building. Ruth followed. It was clean, remarkably so for a men's dwelling. Oma directed them to a hearth where a pallet was quickly set up.

She frowned at Ruth. "We do not allow the *schwester*—sisters—in here, but you are to be married, *ja*? We will make an allowance."

Ruth suspected that Oma's word carried great weight. "Yes, thank you. I brought a few things, bandages, herbs, hoping I would not need them." Tears threatened suddenly.

"Och, *liebling,* Stay strong. I will help you."

"I helped the doctors in Philadelphia ..."

"Not the same when it is your own."

William passed them with the saddlebags full of medicinals, and Jakob brought tea.

Ruth examined Jonathan's leg while Oma kneeled on the other side.

"Here, Ruth." William's face was lined in worry as he handed her linen cut for bandages.

"I need my huswif. And a cup. And vinegar."

Oma squinted at Jonathan's face. "He will need laudanum. Or spirits."

"I have laudanum." William brandished a bottle and a spoon.

"Give him two spoonfuls," Ruth said.

Jonathan frowned at the taste but swallowed it obediently. Just beyond him, Robert Shirley leaned against the wall, his eyes closed and his lips moving. Where had he come from? But Ruth had no time to speculate.

"Mr. Shirley, we will need help holding him down," Ruth said.

"His name is Rob Sherman." Jonathan's speech was already thickening. "Sher ... man. From the hills of ... Hillsborough." He grinned at this.

Something was going on. "Rob Sherman, whoever you are, we require your assistance," she said.

"Anything." His voice was the same, but his face thinner, worn.

The bandage was secured by a thick piece of leather. Ruth removed it and realized it was a stock. A military stock.

The redcoats in Boston. She's seen these before. Captain Preston, on that horrible night of the Boston Massacre, had worn a dark stock like this above his shiny gorget.

She tossed it aside with a jerk.

Jonathan's eyelids fluttered shut, and Oma unwound the bandage gently.

"Whoever saw to his leg did well," she murmured when the wound was exposed.

Ruth's heart hammered in her chest. It was as she'd feared. A musket ball had sailed clear through the thickest part of his shin. "Anything broken?"

A broken bone might require amputation.

Oma gently prodded the wound and Jonathan grunted. Blood covered her hands. "This bone"—she pointed to his shin—"*gut ist.* I do not know about the other. But it needs—how do you say—sewing?"

Ruth could see that for herself. "William, clean the needle and thread."

"Jakob, come. Hold down the leg."

Oma grabbed the vinegar, poured some in the cup for William, and poured some in another vessel. She diluted it with warm tea, then splashed it on the injury.

Jonathan groaned loudly but did not appear to wake.

"*Gut.* He sleeps." Oma sat back on her heels. "Now *liebling,* you sew."

The muscles were torn beneath the ravaged skin. She remembered Dr. Rush attending to an injury much like this, sewing the muscles together first, then the skin.

"Anatomy is the first lesson in medicine. You must learn the location of every muscle, every sinew, every vessel." The physician had spoken half to her, half to himself. "Only later does the student delve into the how and the why, for in truth, we can only speculate as to the function of each system—the nervous tissue, the muscles. It is one of God's mysteries, like the great currents of the sea. We see the effects but cannot trace very far beneath the surface."

And four years ago, Ruth had been an eager student, peering over his shoulder, ready with the clamp and the bandages. Now she wavered, wishing a physician would take her place.

But there was nobody else.

She seemed to watch as from a great distance as her trembling fingers stitched the edges of the muscle together.

The white of bone appeared under the muscle.

"Oma, this bone." It was loose—broken.

There were two bones in the lower leg, but Ruth could not remember what Dr. Rush would call the thin companion to the heavier shin bone.

Oma mopped away the blood with a fresh piece of linen. "Keep sewing, the muscles will help the bone come together."

Ruth tried to hurry, as she had no clamps—nor the expertise in using them—and the bleeding continued, flowing out of the wound and over the uninjured skin.

"The blood cleans the wound," Oma whispered, as if reading her mind. "It is *gut*."

After what seemed an eternity, the muscle was repaired, very crudely in Ruth's opinion, and she hoped the ends of the bone would knit properly. Oh, how she wished for a physician—any physician!

She slipped her needle under the skin, frowning at the thin line of yellow fat underneath and the blood weeping from invisible vessels. Jonathan groaned and writhed, Mr. Shirley's hands firm on his shoulders. Ruth's hands paused, trembling. *Jonathan.* How could she do this?

"Almost done," Oma murmured.

A drop of sweat rolled down Ruth's face. She forced her needle into the flesh, in then out, again and again.

She knotted the final strand and looked at Jonathan's face. He slept on, but peacefully.

Oma carefully bandaged his leg. Mr. Shirley sat back, his face shiny with sweat.

Arms embraced her and nearly crushed out her breath.

"Ruth, oh Ruth," Hannah's words were half sobs. "Thank ye. Thank God."

Ruth returned her embrace. "He still needs doctoring. For the fever."

Wishing for a bath, Ruth joined the others in clearing away the soiled bandages and blood.

Jonathan stirred. She could breathe easier now.

IMMENSE BLACK EYEBROWS danced on a face jeering at Jonathan. The ugly redcoat wrapped his arms around Hannah. *No!*

Fire shot down his leg and Jonathan writhed, desperate to save her, but he couldn't move.

His tomahawk. He struggled to lay his hand on it, but his whole body felt paralyzed, inert.

Ruth, Ruth was here. And a Moravian woman. What were they doing to his leg?

Were they going to take it? It was a fear that had niggled at him, the fear of losing his limb. It was a horrifying prospect.

His tomahawk. Where was it?

The pain eased. A familiar pressure. "I … I need to make water," he said.

"A *gut* sign," the Moravian woman said. The next thing he knew, he was using a gourd as a chamber pot.

Robert Shirley assisted him silently and helped him to sit once he'd finished. The man looked scruffy, stubble covering his jaw. Jonathan supposed he looked the same—or worse. His mouth was foul.

The woman was gone. Ruth—Ruth was gone, too.

"Shir—Sherman, is there any ale or cider here?"

Shirley frowned, his brown hair hanging loose about his shoulders. "Here." He passed him a tin cup. "For fever."

Jonathan eyed the contents suspiciously and swallowed half of the bitter brew, knowing he'd catch it from the women if he didn't.

"They must have ale." Shirley braced as if to stand.

The door opened and Ruth burst in, followed by a man as scruffy and dirty as Jonathan felt.

Ruth's face was twisted. "I told him you were injured—"

"He needs to know," the man said. It was Joseph Brown, and his strong scent confirmed his identity. "Russell? That you?"

Jonathan grunted and tried to rise.

"Naw, stay there, I heered you bin shot."

Shirley leaned back against the wall, silent, eyes cast down.

"Tell me. Did Morgan escape?" Jonathan asked. "How many of our lads were taken prisoner?"

"Are you fevered? Hah! We took the entire regiment of Scottish skirt-wearers prisoner, even the feller playing the bagpipes. They tried to turn our flank and we surrounded them. Wept like babes, they did. Morgan kept us from taking revenge, he's a good man all around."

"So … we beat Tarleton?" It was too good to be true.

Brown frowned. "You were there. You saw how many cavalrymen we took down on the very first charge. Tarleton escaped in the end, but we smashed them."

Morgan's plan had worked after all.

If it weren't for his leg, he'd dance a jig. *Thank you, Lord.*

ROBERT STIFFENED and tried to make himself invisible. The escaped partisan he'd once labeled Smelly knew Russell.

He couldn't help hearing the news. What a shock.

Even the feller playing the bagpipes …

The swelling noise he'd heard on the battlefield hadn't been victory—not a British victory. The undefeated 71st regiment captured. Tarleton stymied, his power in South Carolina curtailed.

Tarleton would not take defeat kindly. It wasn't the last the rebels would see of him.

Keeping his face lowered, he surveyed Smelly, hoping the man did not look too closely. He'd done the man a favor, but still—

"Hey, who're you?"

Smelly had abominable manners. Robert looked the man in the eye. "We have not been introduced."

Jonathan gestured to him. "This is Rob Sherman. He saved my life at Cowpens."

But the recognition on Smelly's face was plain. "You remind me of someone," he said carefully. "Name's Joe Brown."

"Pleased." Robert decided that he'd need to speak like these people. Well, perhaps not like Smelly Joe Brown.

Brown settled back on his haunches. "Plenty of folks in the mountains have secrets. You learn not to ask. But some things give you away. Most folks can spot a redcoat from a mile away no matter the color of his clothes."

Jonathan tried to sit up. "Brown—"

"No, I'm just doing him a favor," Smelly said. "He stands out. Even dressed as he is."

Hannah strode in. "Horses are fed. Poor things, I drove them hard." Her gaze fastened on Brown. "Who's this?"

While Jonathan and Brown gave her the details about the battle, Robert relaxed against the wall and simply gazed at her, enjoying the play of expression on her face. First puzzlement, then gladness.

"The entire regiment?" she said. "Captured? Oh, I'd have loved to see it."

Smelly Brown fixed an appraising eye on Hannah, then studied Robert's face. "So, that's how it is." He turned to Hannah. "Teach this man country manners, will you? Or he'll be in danger from Colonel Mathews and every other man in the Shenandoah Valley."

45

Jesus, Thy blood and righteousness,
My beauty are, my glorious dress
'Midst flaming worlds, in these arrayed
With joy shall I lift up my head.
—Nicolaus von Zinzendorf 1739, trans. John Wesley

*J*onathan's leg throbbed painfully, but he wanted no more of the laudanum. He eyed the tempting jug of whiskey on the side of the mule following the wagon, but he pushed that thought away too. He needed to stay alert. Shirley's presence in the wagon bed next to him continually reminded him that not everyone would understand this redcoat who'd surrendered to a waterlogged pistol.

Jonathan wasn't sure *he* understood all the man's motives. But he'd answer for the man, deflect any suspicions, as long as Shirley showed himself honorable.

He cut a glance ahead of the wagon where William and Ruth rode. They were approaching Maggoty Gap, and the road was rougher here.

One of the wagon wheels hit a deep rut, and the vehicle lurched.

Jonathan groaned and closed his eyes against the sudden fire that enveloped his leg.

"Sorry." Hannah's voice floated from the wagon seat where she drove.

"Perhaps I should ride tomorrow." How much worse could it be?

He opened his eyes to see Shirley assessing his bandage. "Miss Haynes would disagree."

"I can feel every jolt."

Shirley did not respond, and Jonathan was grateful. He didn't want false assurances. He knew he was fortunate to keep his leg—though whether he would ever be able to walk without a limp was another matter.

He decided not to think about it. "Shir-Sherman. Will the British look for you?"

Shirley ran a hand over his stubbly jaw. "I cannot be sure. They will look for me on prisoner lists, and if they do not see my name may conclude I was killed. What I am concerned with is what to do next. I cannot go home."

"Canna? Or dinna wish to?"

His expression strained, he lowered his voice. "I suppose it is both. I hoped for so long to escape the bondage I was under, the indignity of what is euphemistically described as intelligence—"

"Spying, ye mean."

"Later, I served as aide-de-camp, but even ordinary service chafed me."

"Burning people's homes not suit ye?" Jonathan couldn't resist the dig.

Robert smiled grimly and pulled out a small water-stained book. "Miss Haynes gave me this New Testament, and it gave me hope."

"I see." Jonathan decided to reserve judgment on anything the man said of a religious nature. His own road to peace had been long and hard. He hoped the man had truly found it. Time would tell.

"I have been turning it over in my mind. Your sister being there, every-thing that happened. It seems providential. If I had surrendered to anyone else, my end might well have been the noose, like Major André."

"Hannah is no soldier and would rather shoot you herself than turn you over."

Shirley chuckled. "Precisely."

Hannah turned her head. "Talking about me?"

"Sherman here needs a home."

She stared at him for a few moments, expressionless, then turned her attention back to the horses.

"That difficult?" Shirley tugged his blanket closer over his shoulders. "I never thought I'd say this, but all I want is a quiet place to live, to work, to use my trade. And I have resources. I may be able to obtain funds with which to start anew."

"But how?" Jonathan studied Hannah's back. He was sure she was listening to every word.

"My godmother. I own a few head of horses worth some money. I could have them sold."

Hannah turned. "What's the name of your godmother?"

"Selina Hastings, the Countess of Huntingdon."

Hannah's mouth dropped open.

Jonathan puzzled over it, and then the pieces fell into place. "Sherman, did ye give my sister's name to this woman?"

Hannah turned again. "She is Whitefield's benefactress."

What a strange coincidence. But then, Da would say there were no such things. Only providences.

ROBERT WOKE to a freezing predawn darkness. A single cardinal chittered and chirped.

Insane bird.

He remained for a minute longer encased in his blanket, which was much too thin for the outdoors. The younger Russell had thoughtfully piled up a bed of leaf litter for him, though it seemed more suitable for a bear than for a person. The women were sheltered in a tiny canvas tent, and the Russell brothers were in the wagon, from which a soft snore issued.

Robert jerked to a sitting position. No one was on watch. The younger Russell had taken second watch, but had apparently succumbed to sleep, and the fire had ebbed to mere embers. He stood and tried to wrap the blanket about him in such a way as to keep him warm but free his hands.

He failed. The breeze found his shirt quite easily. He rebuked himself for minding the cold. He was an Army officer, after all.

Had been an officer. Past tense.

He moved vigorously then, trying to get his blood flowing, scouring the area for twigs and fallen branches. He discovered a hefty piece of deadfall twenty feet away and lugged it to the fire.

He fed the twigs to the embers and waited until the flames grew and popped. He added the larger pieces, then the deadfall. In another quarter hour the fire was radiating warmth.

Gray light suffused the roadside camp and revealed the horses straining at their tethers. Robert moved them to better places to forage and found a rag. The horses wouldn't mind a bit of grooming, and the activity would keep him warm.

"Thanks for the fire," Hannah said behind him.

Robert jumped. "My pleasure."

Her hair was tousled from sleep. Wisps pulled free of her plait, forming a halo around her head.

She stepped closer. "Let me see that." She tugged on the blanket hanging ineffectually around his neck and pulled out a knife.

He knew that knife.

"Hold it up," she commanded.

He held it by the edges, and she quickly cut three slits through the fabric. Then she thrust the blanket over his head.

"See? This middle hole for your head. Now put your hands through the slits."

In a moment, Robert was wearing the blanket, an improvement. "Your knife is sharp." Without thinking, he lifted his hand halfway to his face, where that same knife had sliced his cheekbone.

Hannah's gaze followed the motion. "Had you that scar in Boston?"

Robert's lips parted and he hesitated. "Nay, it was acquired later."

He knew the instant she remembered him.

"Ye were there, at the jail—were ye the jailer?" Conflicting emotions ranged over her face, first puzzlement, then rage, then sorrow.

He shook his head. "I was not the jailer.... I'm sorry."

Hannah's chest heaved. "Sorry?"

"And thankful. Thankful you delivered me from my part in this war."

"What were ye doing there?"

"In Philadelphia? I told Miss Haynes where your brother was being held, and I wanted to make sure she was safe—women are not safe around soldiers."

"British soldiers."

He did not dispute that.

"I cut you?" Her whole form seemed to slump then. "I am sorry for that."

"You did not know who I was."

"You! Ye gave him a stone ... a proper stone with his last words." Hannah wiped her eyes.

"I heard his words, good words. I wish ... I wish none of this had happened."

But it was not entirely true. If none of it had happened, he would not have met this woman.

THE ROAD NARROWED and rocky outcrops threatened the trail. From the back of the wagon, Robert compared this wild wooded land to England but failed to find any similarities.

South Carolina was a swampy jungle, complete with colorful, exotic birds, and now they navigated mountainous terrain. Robert hoped for gentle fields and painted homes, but everything was bigger and wilder here. And homesteads were few and far between.

Was it his imagination? Ahead, the slopes looked gentler.

He turned and found Jonathan Russell's gaze on him.

"We're almost to the valley."

"Is your farm nearby?"

Russell chuckled. "No, we've several days travel ahead." He seemed to consider. "We're two days away—if ye've a good horse and dinna mind a hard ride. We'll take three, I reckon."

Tarleton could travel seventy miles in a day, a feat by any measure. These frontiersmen thought little of such distances.

"I asked my commander once about the size of this country. I had just come to South Carolina, and it had taken forever by ship. The green haze of the coastline stretched on and on.

"He said the size was unimportant, as the main settlements were on the coast. Boston, Philadelphia, Charles Town. And the British Navy cannot be beaten."

Russell snorted. "Maybe. But this is our home. He doesna understand."

Robert said nothing but watched the silent woods. Here and there evergreens interrupted the stark hues of the winter landscape with splotches of color.

"Shir—Sherman. Have ye given thought to how ye'll present yourself? I mean, if they ask about your loyalties."

He took a deep breath. "I do not wish to lie. I will tell them that my first allegiance is to Christ. I will honor local magistrates. If I stood before the King, I would confess my inability to serve him as I ought. I cannot throw off the mantle of loyalty for light reasons."

"None of us did."

Robert studied Russell's face. "I have read Rutherford. I understand the arguments—"

"Ye are now a rebel, *de facto*, as my Grandda would say. And the King would see you as one, if your surrender is not reported."

"'Tis a conundrum, I confess. Yet, I can only hope that Providence will guide me."

"Say *nothing* about it. Have this discussion with none but us. If Tories were killed by their neighbors in the Carolinas, well, I hope that would not happen in the valley, but feelings are high."

"I appreciate your kindness to me."

Russell cocked his head, and Robert heard the faint echo of hoofbeats.

"Hannah, my rifle."

She slipped the weapon off her shoulder and passed it. He eyed the pan and primed the weapon.

"Hannah, slow the horses just a bit."

The animals reduced their pace.

"Shirley, lie down. Ye're tired, aye? Dinna speak."

Robert complied and shut his eyes. If it weren't for the tension, he'd gladly sleep.

It seemed like a very long time before the hoofbeats drew close.

"Ho! Howdy!"

"Is that you, Seth Gibson?" Hannah's voice sounded from above his head.

Robert felt the tension ease, but it did not leave.

"Gibson." Russell's low rumble. "Shoot any redcoats?"

"What happened to you? And who's this?"

Robert felt vulnerable. His knife was no match for a firearm. *Lord, help.*

A peace settled on him. A peace like the one he'd experienced the night before the battle. Somehow it would work out.

He relaxed.

"Rob Sherman. Saved my life at Cowpens. Helped drag me outta there—I dinna remember much. Got shot pretty bad in the leg."

"Valley man? Don't recognize him."

"No, he's one of Tarleton's victims."

"Oh, the poor ba—the poor feller."

"He's exhausted. Dinna mind us, we have to travel slow."

Hannah's voice intruded. "Say, where'd ye get the horse?"

"Found it, reins tangled in the brush. A lot of Tarleton's men got shot off their horses."

Russell's voice. "The spoils of war."

"Maybe Johnson will take me in his mounted militia."

There was a pause, then various invitations, what Robert took for valley manners. Then Gibson took his leave, trotting up the path.

He stayed put and listened to far-off greetings as Gibson caught up to Miss Haynes and the younger Russell. Then nothing.

"He's gone. Harmless. But now the whole valley will know your name, heroism, and the ladies will bake you pies if ye're not careful. Stay on the Ridge and avoid town for a while."

Robert sat up. "Pie sounds delightful."

"My mother will feed you. You look thin."

"As do you."

They traveled in companionable silence for a while, then Hannah stopped the wagon.

"Be right back."

She disappeared behind a tree.

An awkward silence was broken by Russell clearing his throat.

"Sherman, what are your intentions regarding my sister?"

Robert's jaw weakened. "I ... I—"

"I take you for an honorable man. But this is a question my father will ask."

"I can give her nothing—"

"Ridiculous. Ye've horses, ye say, and a strong back." A wistful expression passed over Russell's face.

With his injuries, would this man ever be the same? Robert hoped so, but it gave him an idea.

"Russell, when we arrive, introduce me as a hired man. I will take your place at the plow until you recover."

"As penance?"

A redcoat had shot him. Did Russell think he was only desiring to repay a debt?

"No. Because I want to."

46

The enemy are in the vicinity of Moravian towns and are advancing with great rapidity. Our force is so inferior that every exertion in the State of Virginia is necessary to support us.

— Nathaniel Greene to Thomas Jefferson, letter, Feb. 10 1781

February 1781

*R*obert descended from the wagon and followed the Russells to the meetinghouse. He tried to keep his eyes down, but he was keenly aware of every man in the vicinity.

He was relieved to see that his own simple garments were similar to those of the other men. His neat cuffs and closely trimmed beard contrasted with the ill-kept appearance of some scruffy fellows, but not enough to cause notice.

Ahead, Jonathan Russell hobbled forward with the aid of a crutch. It was the man's first outing after several miserable weeks in bed and Robert was glad of it, partly because he shared a room with him and knew his frustrations intimately.

Nightly worship in the Russell household warmed Robert's heart, and he'd looked forward to the Sabbath—yet, he feared it, too; feared the gazes of the men of the valley, who surely would discern who he truly was. What he truly was.

And so, he'd stayed away until Jonathan could attend.

Once inside, the Russells slid into a pew near the front, and Robert found a place to sit just behind them. Around him, conversation buzzed.

"Jonathan Russell, bless you." An aged woman smiled at him.

"G'morning, Miz McClure."

Robert felt the eyes of many upon him but remained quiet, wishing he could become invisible. He shook himself mentally. He needed to face the people of the valley, find a home here, if it were possible.

The crowd quieted, and a man advanced to the front, using a cane. He didn't seem to be weak or injured; instead, his steps were firm, the end of the instrument gently probing the way to the pulpit.

When the minister faced the congregation, Robert was sure.

The man was blind. The preacher's cloudy blue eyes failed to focus on any one person as he scanned the congregation. But as the man spoke, his handicap seemed to fall away. The scriptures were ready on his tongue.

"In the Seventy-Sixth Psalm, we see the truth of divine Providence, a doctrine that is full and complete in the sacred oracles."

Robert forgot the rebels surrounding him and soaked in the sermon.

"The sovereignty of God extends not only to things which we may think of great importance, and therefore worthy of notice, but also to things small and indifferent. 'Are not two sparrows sold for a farthing,' says our Lord, 'and one of them falleth not to the ground without your Heavenly Father' …"

Sparrows. God ruled over sparrows.

"'Surely the wrath of man shall praise thee; the remainder of wrath shalt thou restrain,' meaning, even the injustice of oppressors shall bring in a tribute of praise to thee …"

Robert curled his fingers over his blistered palms, now slowly settling into calluses. He'd plowed the barley field the week before, a physically demanding experience. He ignored his aches and refocused on the words the minister delivered with such earnestness.

"These words were penned after a great deliverance from the Assyrian army. We face another army, another threat, today—"

The man was a rebel. It was not surprising.

"The ambition of mistaken princes, the cunning and cruelty of oppressive and corrupt rulers, and even the inhumanity of brutal soldiers, however dreadful, shall finally promote the glory of God, and in the meantime, while the storm continues, His mercy and kindness shall serve as a hedge to their rage and fury."

The ambition of mistaken princes ...

King George? The man was stubborn, Robert knew this in his heart of hearts, and Lord Germain was the worst kind of fool. He could recognize that while still remaining loyal. But what did loyalty mean? He would not burn a church if ordered to by King George himself.

Mistaken princes. That much he would acknowledge.

He grappled with the thesis as the minister supported it with point after point. Yes, God was sovereign over all. But this war?

Was everything that happened determined? Preordained, even?

He blinked. God was good—everything he'd read in the New Testament testified to that.

The remainder of wrath thou shalt restrain.

So when a man did evil, God chose whether to allow it, and He allowed it only if there was a good purpose in it—if God would ultimately be glorified.

Tarleton had chosen to destroy Morgan. Well, that hadn't happened. How any of this glorified God Robert had no clue, but he was a mere man, and could not see all ends.

He was barely aware of the minister's concluding comments as his thoughts continued to churn. If these verses were true, he could rest in the dealings of Providence.

Whether the Crown reconquered North America, or whether the rebels established their new nation, or whether—God forbid—a lasting partisan war turned this beautiful land into a canker sore, he could trust in God.

The service ended. In the pew ahead of him, Hannah stood, her red-gold hair gleaming through a net-like binding. She looked at him, and he found his feet automatically.

Gentlemen stood when a lady did.

He followed the Russells out of the building and stood blinking in the sunlight, feeling like he'd had too much Madeira.

Conversation swirled about him.

"Robert Sherman." Jonathan Russell was introducing him to someone.

He focused on the man in front of him—thin to the point of gauntness, but with strong, decided bones. A penetrating gaze took Robert aback. He needed to watch his words.

"Pleased to make your acquaintance, Mr.—" He'd missed the man's name.

"Colonel. Colonel George Mathews." The man extended his hand.

Despite his appearance, the man's grip was firm. He wasn't as old as he looked.

"Militia?"

"Ninth Virginia. Fought at Brandywine and Germantown. And you? You have the look of a soldier."

Robert nodded, giving as much truth as he dared. "Mustered out." Suddenly he remembered the Ninth, and his throat closed. "You served at Germantown. Nathan, Nathan Russell."

"Yes. There were times when I considered the man lucky. Better than a prison ship."

"You—"

He nodded. "Spent two years aboard one of those hulks in New York harbor. Would have died if I hadn't been exchanged."

"I … I have heard of the ships."

"Now there's one in Charles Town harbor, I hear. Redcoats are savages." He followed this statement with a few choice curses under his breath.

A chill crept up Robert's spine. According to the Russells, no Loyalist had been hanged in the valley. But a British spy? What would they do?

"Heard you rescued our Jonathan," the man was saying. "Are you a horseman? Colonel Johnson's always on the lookout for solid men for his mounted militia."

"A cavalry unit?"

"Not exactly. Most folks here are better with a long rifle than a saber. But a mounted militia can move fast."

Robert's chest squeezed. He was being asked to join the rebels, and he would need a good excuse to forbear.

"I'm plowing until Russell has recovered."

Mathews waved a dismissive hand. "Cornwallis is in North Carolina. We know where he's headed, him and that bloody Tarleton."

"Virginia."

"Governor Jefferson moved the capital to Richmond." He pointed vaguely east. "And his home is nearby, just over Rockfish Gap. I'm sending my brother and some men now. But it's not enough." His eyes became unfocused, his mind far away. Then he brought a sharp gaze to Robert's face. "Colonel Johnson needs men who can drop the plow and jump on a horse. Are you with me?"

Robert's breath caught in his throat. He scanned the men and women around him, talking, listening, smiling.

Then the Russells came into his field of vision. Jonathan leaning on a hand carved crutch, talking to Miss Haynes, and beyond them, red-gold hair flashing in the sun. Hannah Russell turned to greet a friend, and her easy laugh spilled out into the crowd.

Robert returned his gaze to Colonel Mathews. "I'll do it. When the time comes, I'll defend this valley with my life."

He was now a traitor. But it didn't feel wrong.

RUTH LEANED on the fence rail and watched the horses. Hannah's chestnut mare, Boudicea, pulled at the grass, a tall black colt at her side. Both were shedding, the thick hair of winter giving way to the sleek coat of spring.

Several more horses grazed on the other side of the fenced pasture, tails swishing.

She turned and pulled her shawl closer. A cloak would have been wiser, but it was spring—almost. The oaks and cottonwoods lining the river were furred with tiny leaves, the promise of new life. At her feet the ground rolled gently, rising slightly, then sloping down to the South River, one of the fat streams that merged to form the Shenandoah.

Ruth had been as far north as the Triple Forks, but could only imagine the curving, splashing Shenandoah heading north to the Potomac and the sea. The men were laconic in their praise. *Good fishing.*

Well, even here there was good fishing. And when the sun touched the western ridges, a spectacular view.

She loved this spot. She couldn't stay to see the sunset, though. Today was Saturday, and even now William was filling the bath with water from the spring. Hannah was looking forward to washing her hair.

Ruth turned back to the fence and saw a figure hobbling down the path.

"Jonathan, what are you doing?"

He grinned, but a flash of pain came and went as he took a few more steps, waving his cane. "Going stir-crazy. And when my sister barged in my cabin and announced it was bath time, I thought it prudent to depart."

"'Thought it prudent?'"

"With Robert as a housemate, can't help picking up his speech."

"Hope he's picking up yours."

Jonathan's face grew more serious. "Aye. He may dress like us, but—"

"He looks different in a beard."

"Even his beard is disciplined. Trims it every Saturday."

Ruth chuckled. "I love this place." She gestured toward the river. "The sunset is beautiful on this little rise."

Jonathan was strangely quiet. When he spoke his voice was rough, hesitant. "I want to build ye a house, Ruth. A home. But I dinna ken ..."

"Today is the anniversary. March fifth."

"The Massacre. And now Cornwallis is pushing north."

"You have done your duty. 'Tis William's turn now."

"He's joined Colonel Johnson's mounted militia—and Robert too. They'll defend the Gap." Jonathan leaned his cane against the fence and sat awkwardly.

Ruth joined him, sitting close and feeling the warmth of his body.

"Ruth, I dinna ken whether I'll ever plow again."

It was a huge and painful admission, and instinctively, she did not try to contradict him. The problem was bigger than plowing. Words would not heal it. Men needed to provide, and farming was Jonathan's trade.

"I heard the Dutch stallion is going home," she said.

"Da's found the owner, but the war—"

"I can imagine. The horse has done his duty, though," she said cheerfully.

"Oh, aye." He turned his head and examined the yearlings. "Yonder are two of his get. Beautiful animals."

"I'm thinking there will be a good demand for quality horseflesh after the war."

Jonathan's face relaxed. "You've a bit of your shopkeeper aunt in you."

Ruth thought back to the years in Boston, helping her family. She'd enjoyed it, and yet they were duties laid upon her by necessity.

She looked at her hands. Boston lay far behind, Philadelphia a torn memory. "Jonathan, I want my own home. Our home, and I think ... I think your hands are as cunning as ever."

His expression softened. "My hands? Och, the knives are a winter's fireside handicraft, not truly a trade."

"Is carpentry a trade? Your father indulges himself that way."

He wrapped an arm about her shoulders. "This place would be a lovely site for a home. When the war is over. We'll build a house, and ye'll sew curtains. And we'll watch the sunset at the end of the day." He turned his gaze south. "See that stretch of ground yonder? I'll clear it and we'll ..." his voice hesitated, as if coming to a decision. "We'll raise horses."

"What about your knives?"

"What about your writing?"

"Papa needs no help. Mr. Sherman will help him with the press once plowing's done, and the apprentice knows how to handle ink." Ruth's ideas were hazy, but she'd abandoned verse in favor of something more practical. "I can write anywhere."

"Robert is sweet on my sister. But I dinna ken whether it would work."

"I think she likes him."

"Before you knew my darkest secrets, well, I couldna think of marriage. I'd feel a traitor, a deceiver. I know Robert is an honest man. He'd eventually have to tell Hannah everything, and—"

"Tell me what?"

Hannah stood behind them, skirts billowing in the breeze.

47

The eyes of all America are upon us, as we play our part posterity will bless or curse us.

—Henry Knox

*R*obert stroked the sleek black head of the stallion for several indulgent minutes, then led him out into the sun. He tied him to a sapling and returned to the heady aroma of warm horse, musty straw, and manure inside the barn.

He grabbed a pitchfork and began to muck out the stall, his shoulders welcoming the exercise. If his godmother could only see him now, laboring like a stable boy. But truth be told, she'd understand better than most.

"Sherman?" Jonathan's voice came from outside.

Robert leaned the pitchfork against the side of the door. Russell was running his hands over the stallion's head and neck, his crutch propped against the sapling.

"May I help you?"

"Hmm. I need to saddle him."

After a month, Russell's leg was still bandaged, but the injury had knitted well. Pain still creased the man's features from time to time, and Robert suspected it was worse than he let on.

He settled a light leather saddle over the horse's back. Russell threaded the cinch strap and pulled it tight.

"Thank ye kindly."

Robert said nothing as Russell led the animal to a stump he used as a mounting block. It would be difficult for a man with a weak left leg to mount a horse, but Robert resolved not to offer help.

Russell planted both feet on the stump and laid his hands on the saddle. He gave a stiff-legged hop and swung his right leg over the horse, grunting once. His smile was triumphant.

"He's a sensible horse, Ducky is," Russell said. "Couldna do this on a high-strung colt."

Ducky. It had taken Robert several weeks to discovered that the animal's name was Ducat, for the Dutch coin, but no one called him that.

Russell circled the animal about, experimentally. "Dinna feel like an invalid up here."

"Jonathan!" Hannah strode down the path toward them, her face a puzzle, seeming to decide whether she approved. "Be careful." Then she caught sight of Robert and her expression hardened.

For several days she'd ignored him. Not that they conversed much, but any ease of manner she'd once had was gone. She was the hostile, pistol-wielding woman once again.

Russell eyed his sister. "Sherman, I'll take this beast down the path."

Robert lifted his brows in response. So he'd be alone with this Amazon. Might as well discover what the problem was. "May I help you?"

She folded her arms and glared at him. "Aye, ye can." She pointed to the tree stump. "Sit."

He obeyed.

"Tell me everything. Your secret."

He inhaled sharply. *Secret?*

"Ye told me ye wrote to an earl. Observations. But then ye said something about Washington hanging you. Are ye a spy?"

"Yes, I mean, it depends." He stared at his hands. He determined to tell her the absolute truth.

"What? How can it depend?"

"Writing letters as I did was not spying. It was deceitful as I was there under false pretenses. But I did no actual spy work until just before those first battles at Lexington and Concord. I scouted out locations of munitions and informed General Gage."

Her eyes were hard but she said nothing.

"If I had worn my uniform, it would not have been spying. But I was dressed as a civilian. Even though my commission was inactive, if I had been captured, I am not sure what would have happened. Possibly the noose."

"Nathan Hale was hanged for less than that."

"Yes, he was a soldier dressed as a civilian. The rest of my intelligence-gathering activities was done in uniform. One of Major André's mistakes was picking up information incognito, wearing civilian clothing."

He paused, his throat too thick to speak. The loss of his friend still hurt.

Hannah squatted. "My father was there."

"Your father?"

"After that spy was captured, my da spoke to him about his soul."

Moisture sprang to Robert's eyes. "And?"

She shrugged. "My father was encouraged, thought the officer died well with hope in Christ."

Robert could not stop the tears that streamed down his face. "Thank you. He was my friend."

"I'm that sorry. I hate this war." She took a deep breath and stood. "But I have to ask. Are ye still loyal to the King?"

He slumped. "I know not. Perhaps. And yet ..." He wiped his face and looked up at her. "If Tarleton comes, I will defend your family with my life."

Hannah's face was unreadable. "I have something for you."

INSIDE THE HOUSE, a sword dominated the Russells' walnut table. A letter lay next to it.

"How?" Robert was stupefied. It was his own officer's sword, as best as he could tell.

"I buried your coat and pistol." Hannah reached for the sword and loosened it from its dark sheath. "But this I slid under the wagon seat. We have a place for weapons, to keep them ready to hand, and besides, I thought I deserved a souvenir, if nothing else."

"It is a British officer's hanger. Recognizable as such."

"We picked it up at Cowpens." Her brows lifted in wry humor. "If anyone asks."

The British lion was cast into the gleaming brass hilt and pommel, the grooved pale leather grip darkened in places by his own sweat. He pulled out the blade from its sheath, and Tarleton's face came to mind. If Robert were to actually fight, he would need weapons, and from horseback, a sword.

This sword was slightly shorter than Tarleton's curved cavalry sword, but it would serve. And Robert knew how to use it.

He returned it to its sheath. "I thank you."

"We received a strange letter." Hannah picked up the missive which lay on the table. "I received it, rather. From your godmother, the countess."

"My godmother?" He swallowed.

"Ye look like someone walked over your grave."

"No, she is a wonderful lady. I write her when I can."

Hannah's mouth twitched. "And ye gave her my name."

Ants could be crawling up his back and he would not be more uncomfortable. "I wished her to pray for you, for your family—"

She raised a dismissive hand. "She writes about Mr. Whitefield's orphanage."

She passed him the letter and he read. The first few sentences were commonplaces, but the next paragraph caught his eye.

The Bethesda Orphanage in Savanna requires Attention I cannot give from afar. I am sorry to say that our Soldiers have used the Grounds in a disrespectful Manner. I need someone I can trust to restore the Property and resolve any Conflicts resulting from the current Unpleasantness.

I wish I might give this Charge to my godson Robert, but what has become of him I know not. His Duty brought him south, but my Grandson reports he is missing, possibly captured. If he is indeed a Prisoner there is Hope, and my Prayers are given daily for his well-being and Release.

If you gain Information of his Whereabouts, will you inform me? In any case, will you join your Prayers to mine?

Yours in Christ, Selina Hastings, Countess of Huntingdon.

"My cousin—my cousin must have mentioned ..." Robert considered. Lord Rawdon wrote voluminously, but most of it was official. A letter to his grandmother had never crossed his cousin's desk. The man was looking for him. "My cousin is the man who ...the man your brother struck with his hatchet."

Hannah's face was comical. *"Him?* And he's your cousin?"

"He's looking for me."

"He willna find you here."

Robert shrugged and thought about the orphanage. "How far is it to Georgia?" He had a vague notion, having traversed the Carolinas.

"Jonathan can tell you more. He was there. That Uchee village is in the mountains of Georgia." She laid a hand on her hip. "Why do you want to know?"

Jonathan woke, sweating. Hannah ... No, Hannah was safe. He drew his hand over his face and sat up. It was the first nightmare in weeks. And come to think of it, the lance-like pain in his leg had moderated to a throb that only bothered him when he did too much.

He was alone in the cabin—Robert must be at his chores. Jonathan pulled on his clothes. The light from the windows accused him—it was late. He grabbed his crutch and made it over to the house for breakfast.

The air was chill and sweet, laden with the soft smells of May. The horses would need exercise. Maybe he could take Ducky all the way to town.

He ducked his head under the lintel. "Good morning, Mother."

She turned from the hearth, one blond lock dangling over her forehead. "You're cheerful."

"Going to town. MacLeod says there's news. Let me know if you need anything."

She glanced at his face without comment while setting day-old cornbread and buttermilk before him.

Finally, she spoke. "I've mint and thyme ready for Betsy."

Jonathan's shoulders relaxed. His mother wasn't a nag, but he was glad to avoid mention of his leg. He crumbled the cornbread in a bowl and poured the buttermilk over it.

The women thought he was pushing himself too quickly after such a grave injury; the men said nothing. They understood.

He made his way to the stable. He managed to saddle the horse and mount without assistance, and he rode all the way to town, thankful for the animal's smooth gait.

Mathews's Tavern was buzzing with activity, a number of horses tied up in front. Perhaps there was news. Cornwallis was now in Virginia, the war creeping up to their doorstep.

He ducked inside, ordered ale and found a place to sit. He eased his aching leg under the table and drew the pewter tankard close. More men entered, and the haze and acrid odor of Virginia leaf thickened. He knew many of them. A number hailed from Rockbridge County; some lived north of the Triple Forks. But some he did not recognize at all.

Rumor passed for news, and everyone desired George Mathews's opinion. All Virginia was in uproar with the invasion of Lord Cornwallis.

His father ducked under the lintel, followed by MacLeod. Jonathan supposed Robert had stayed behind. There was one last field to plow, and besides, the man was shy of gatherings, only attending meetings on the Sabbath. His hands had calluses now, one more element of camouflage. Robert Sherman would never speak the valley idiom. But his British inflections were softening.

He was trying. But Jonathan worried for him. Wondered if he could settle here.

Colonel Mathews was signaling with his pipe at the front of the room. His spare frame still commanded respect, all the more because everyone here knew of his suffering at the hands of the British.

"Latest news. Cornwallis has taken Richmond."

The murmur that rose was subdued, as if the valley men were gathering their strength for battle. Everyone lived in the shadow of the redcoat advance—and Tarleton's raids.

Even children spoke of the war and "nasty Ban."

"The Assembly is now meeting in Charlottesville—"

That was just over the Gap!

"—and Governor Jefferson has gone to his home at Monticello."

How far could Tarleton's men travel in a day?

Neither Charlottesville nor Monticello was safe.

And Charlottesville was a stone's throw away.

Jonathan curled his hands into fists. His leg might be weak, but he still had a strong right arm.

48

We fight, get beat, rise, and fight again.
—General Nathaniel Greene

June 1781

*R*obert inserted the paper and waited until Billy finished inking the type. Then he closed the press, pushed it forward, and cranked the devil's tail. He opened the press and hung the sheet to dry.

They needed fifty broadsheets finished by noon. The war was spilling information—much of it inaccurate, he was sure—but people clamored for news. An ordinary newspaper would not suffice, so Gideon Haynes published single sheet bulletins as often as he could.

And the man was tired.

Robert was glad to help him now that the corn was in the ground. The men at church seemed accepting, so he braved their stares and rode to the print shop in Staunton each morning.

Outside, a horse's hooves clattered. Then another's.

Billy laid down the inking balls and rushed out, the door banging behind him.

"William!" Robert called. "Billy Bob" did not come easily to his lips.

There was a commotion in the dusty street—more horses and a shout. He went to the door. Where was Mr. Haynes? Robert decided to gather as much information as he could for the printer. He'd want to know the news.

The news was almost uniformly bad—Lafayette had been forced to retreat, and now Lord Cornwallis was in control of central Virginia. But at what cost? Was the British Army eating well? He doubted it. And how many had been injured in North Carolina?

He knew the sluggish Cornwallis was given to duty and would press ahead inch by inch despite setbacks. He also knew General Clinton, an unpleasant man. The two generals disagreed over much. If Cornwallis asked for reinforcements, would Clinton even respond?

Only God knew. There was hope for the rebels, though Robert dared not voice it, even to himself.

There were a dozen men in the street. Half he recognized as Staunton men, half were strangers, dressed variably in tradesmen's clothes or fine waistcoats. The strangers' horses were dusty, with red-rimmed nostrils and flanks dark with sweat.

The bobbing head of Gideon Haynes appeared in the middle of the dismounting men, and Robert joined him.

"News?" Mr. Haynes asked the crowd.

"Tarleton!" Struggling to catch his breath, one of the riders wiped sweat from his brow.

"Tarleton's men came to Charlottesville," said a dark-haired fellow in a maroon waistcoat. "We would have been captured if we hadn't been warned. Jack Jouette rode through town hollering about the redcoats."

The speaker led his mount to a water trough, but only let it drink a few seconds before walking it about. Robert offered to cool down the horse.

"Name's Patrick Henry. And I thank you."

Henry! Robert walked the animal in a daze. He recalled writing the earl about a seditious Virginian—this was him! An ordinary fellow—polite, even.

Caesar had his Brutus ... Cornwallis would crow over this prize if he captured him.

Robert brought the horse back to the watering trough and when it finished, returned the animal back to its owner.

Patrick Henry. So, who were these other men? He'd heard the Assembly—the Virginia legislature—was in Charlottesville. The pieces fell together. Tarleton had tried to capture the rebel government. Evidently, he'd failed.

The knot of men was drifting toward the Tavern. Bits and pieces of the discussion met his ears.

"Tarleton will come here!"

This was answered by the low rumble of Colonel Mathews's voice. "The mounted militia must ride out this afternoon."

Another rider trotted into town, face bloody and horse trembling with fatigue. Robert raced to help. A horse could die under such treatment. He laid his hand on the animal's bridle, and the man's long limbs loosed from the saddle. Somehow his knees did not buckle when his feet hit the ground.

Mr. Haynes rushed up. "I'll summon Betsy."

"Jouette!" Several of the strangers gathered round. "Someone get him ale."

Robert led the horse about, giving it brief sips of water. He kept close enough to hear.

Mr. Henry strode up. "Is the governor safe?"

Jouette shrugged off a dirty, tattered militia coat and grinned through the blood. "I went to Monticello first thing. Jefferson should have escaped. Tarleton was right on my tail. Not everyone in Charlottesville got away."

Someone pressed a tankard into his hands, and he drank greedily.

Mr. Henry looked about and seemed to count heads. "I think we've got a quorum, thanks to Mr. Jouette. You saved the government of the Commonwealth of Virginia."

Mrs. Ward emerged from McClure's shop, which she had transformed into an apothecary. "Make room!" She peered at Jouette. "What have you been doing?"

She began to clean the stripes across his face. He looked like he'd been beaten with a whip.

"Couldn't use the main ... road." He gasped. "Ouch! I mainly need to sleep, been riding all night."

The man had ridden cross-country. The marks were from branches he could not dodge in the dark.

"This one needs stitches."

He brushed her off. "I'll be fine, just show me a bed."

Robert brought the horse to the trough again and watched it drink. Tarleton ... Tarleton was on his way.

Colonel Johnson joined him. "Sherman, we muster at noon."

"Yes, sir." His heart thrummed. What had he gotten himself into?

SEEING THE BROADSWORD, Jonathan's breath hitched. "Arch May's claymore."

His sudden decision to join Johnson's militia solidified in his mind. On horseback, his game leg would not hinder him much.

His father placed the sword on the walnut table, its basket hilt gleaming. A wide strap of leather, dark with age and sweat, was wrapped around the base of the blade at the hilt.

"Someone has used it two-handed." Sherman's voice surprised him as he hadn't noticed him come into the kitchen. The man was buckling on his own sword. "See the leather wrapped at the base? Place your left hand there."

Jonathan grasped the hilt with his right hand and lifted the heavy sword. It had to be twice as heavy as Sherman's. Longer, too. He slipped his left around the base of the blade.

The reality of the looming battle flooded him. It wasn't the same as mustering with Morgan and Pickens in South Carolina. This was a defense of his home and those he loved.

Faces swam in his mind—old Maggie McClure, the midwife present at so many births. The carefree Robinson clan. Hard-faced George Mathews. Uncle Roy and Aunt Lizzie, the MacLeods, Betsy Ward and Gideon Haynes.

His mother and father. Hannah and William.

Ruth.

"Come outside." Sherman led the way.

They found an open space away from any obstacles.

"Tarleton is an expert swordsman." Sherman unsheathed his sword and held the point low. "You will have the advantage of reach, but—"

"This thing is heavy." Jonathan lifted it one-handed and swept it through the air. He'd always admired the old Scotsman's blade—the way a child did. But then, he'd been a child when old Arch had been killed by the Shawnee.

Sherman blocked his blade with a clang of steel then stepped forward, locking their weapons together. "Do not let them get close, they can parry with skill. Use the sword as a lance if you must, and use the size and weight of the horse to block and intimidate."

Jonathan sighed and stepped back. He was no cavalryman. Perhaps he should take his rifle instead. He noticed William across the yard, standing with a rifle slung over his shoulder.

Sherman replaced his blade. "Cavalry can run right through the infantry, overwhelm them. We only need to slow Tarleton down, give the riflemen a chance to pick them off."

Slow Tarleton down. Yes, he'd do it. If only he had Brutus ...

"Which horse will ye ride?" His father Asked. Everyone stood outside, watching. MacLeod's forehead puckered in concern. His mother blinked rapidly. Hannah looked peaked for once.

"Ducky."

"A true warhorse," Sherman said.

William's face was grim. "My rifle will be there."

"The Lord bless ye and keep ye." Da's face was white. He embraced William for several seconds, his forearms knotted fiercely against his brother's back.

Then he wrapped his arms around Jonathan. His father's strong frame was thinner, frailer than he expected. It would crush his parents to lose another son.

Oh Lord, may it not be.

His da released him. "MacLeod and I will be at the Gap, with supplies and loaded rifles. No one will get past ye."

"Let's find Johnson and the others."

"Wait." Hannah stepped forward. "My Bodie—Sherman, ye can ride my Bodie."

Sherman's lips parted. "I thank you."

But there was no time to wonder at Hannah.

Jonathan headed for the barn.

ROBERT KEPT his mount at Russell's side as they approached the rest of the militia.

Seth Gibson cantered up on his horse. "Hey, Jonnie Russ! Your horse is a dandy one."

Ducky's black coat gleamed under the noon sun, and so did the sword, lying over the pommel of the saddle.

Colonel Johnson rode up. "Hear me, brave lads! Those with swords go first, rifles follow." He turned his horse and fixed his gaze on them one by one. "Swordsmen, go for Tarleton. Slow him down. He's got both riders and infantrymen, but close to the Gap the road is narrow. I've singled out a number of you to take to the trees and shoot from cover."

"We'll skewer Bloody Ban!" someone shouted.

Cheers rose from the men, but they were quickly subdued. The mood was sober. They were defending their homes and families, and the air crackled with silent energy. A solemn energy.

Robert kept close to Russell as they moved over the Gap, two and three horses abreast, unhurried. The roughest part of the road was here. Presumably the trail widened out below. Robert could only assume that every man here knew this road, knew this ground.

It was twenty miles to Charlottesville. In his mind's eye, Robert saw the green-coated Tarleton, rising in his stirrups, saber flashing. And not just him but dozens of cavalrymen—and an unknown number of foot soldiers.

Red-coated soldiers. His own comrades-in-arms.

A chill coursed through him. What was he doing?

At least Lord Rawdon had remained in Camden. He couldn't imagine writing his godmother.

I regret to inform you that I have slain your grandson ...

No, he was spared that circumstance. But how could he justify riding with the rebels? It was dishonorable.

He was no better than that fool, Benedict Arnold, who had betrayed his own side and proceeded to fight for the other.

Colonel Johnson lifted his sword, signaling the men. Ahead and to the right, Ducat's shiny black rump flashed as Russell nudged him into a trot.

Russell was defending his family.

Defending Hannah. Her tall chestnut carried Robert into battle, a token of favor and trust, like the gift of a damsel to a knight. His heart yearned over her—and all the residents of the valley. What did his own honor matter in the face of danger to those he loved?

He was answerable to the King, true. But he was answerable to his own conscience first—and answerable to God. He knew Tarleton, knew the man, knew his motivations. He had to stop him.

Now Robert understood why the rebels targeted officers.

He would target Tarleton if it cost him his life.

JONATHAN'S LEG HURT. He slipped his left foot out of the stirrup experimentally. Ducky's trot was smooth, and sure enough, he managed well enough with a single stirrup.

The countryside was opening up, wooded hills rising on either side of the road like giant swells of the ocean. Charlottesville was about five miles away—but where was Tarleton?

Colonel Johnson signaled and slowed his mount.

The green of uniforms flashed ahead. And horses churning up dust.

They were coming.

He glanced back and saw men dismount and take their horses into the trees. Riflemen would defend the road.

He tightened his grip on the hilt of the sword resting on the pommel of his saddle. There were only twelve valley men with sabers or swords—and they weren't trained as cavalry.

He swallowed and breathed a prayer for deliverance.

There is no restraint to the Lord to save by many or by few.

Jonathan straightened. The British were in loose formation, the cavalry first, riding in columns, as the road was not wide enough for them to spread out.

With riflemen in the trees, the militia could not be flanked by the redcoats.

Colonel Johnson lifted his saber. "Yell like furies!"

Ducky leapt underneath Jonathan like a well-trained cavalry mount as a cacophony of sound swelled and pulsed.

A jagged yell tore from his own throat. He swung the broadsword into position, bracing the hilt with his left hand, ready to joust like an ancient knight.

The knotted reins jumped loose against Ducky's withers, but the horse never faltered, guided by his knees.

Tarleton's men advanced in a cloud of dust. A blood bay dominated the center—Brutus! And his rider wore the signature black plume.

It was Tarleton himself.

Jonathan tightened his grip on his weapon and aimed for the man.

ROBERT HAD HEARD the screeching yell several times before. Rawdon claimed it was the Highland war cry, but he wasn't so sure. The eerie whooping scream made him think of savages.

But then, he'd never heard Indians on the warpath.

At Germantown, the sound had made his knees weak. Here, it had the opposite effect—his blood pulsed powerfully through his veins.

Robert unsheathed his sword and kept his horse's nose even with Ducky's flank as the horses thundered forward.

Tarleton was in the front with several officers at his horse's flanks. Would the man recognize him?

Possibly. His beard and simple clothing would not form a sufficient disguise.

Russell's mount veered slightly, toward Tarleton.

Robert eyed the cavalryman at Tarleton's side, targeting him. In moments, the two sides clashed, and Robert's sword met the cavalryman's. Underneath him, Bodie danced but did not turn or bolt.

The man's arm was like steel. Robert met each blow with a twist of his sword, all the while aware of Russell's duel with Tarleton, steel clanging, horses pressed together, Ducky's black against Brutus's red.

Robert turned his own mount, bringing Bodie's strength and weight to bear on the other, and managed to bring his sword down on his opponent's shoulder.

He didn't stay to see if the man was disabled. Russell was no match for Tarleton's blade, and Robert needed to help him.

Robert maneuvered the mare around and behind the black stallion, trying to get to his foe from Russell's other side. Tarleton's sword flashed and with a clang, Russell's sword flew from his hands.

There was no doubt. With his next swing, Tarleton would kill his opponent.

Robert tried to get his own sword within reach of Tarleton, but it seemed hopeless.

He would never make it in time.

49

We few, we happy few, we band of brothers;
For he today that sheds his blood with me
Shall be my brother ...
—William Shakespeare, *Henry V*

Jonathan's first strike missed. His blade was easily deflected by Tarleton's saber, and Jonathan fought to stay seated. Muscles burning, he brought up the sword again and again to block the cavalryman's quick parries.

He glimpsed a white bandage wrapped around the man's sword hand.

Tarleton was injured?

Jonathan might have little chance against such a proficient swordsman when hale, but now he took hope.

Sherman was nearby, but he had no time to look. His universe shrank to the man three feet away, mounted on the horse he loved.

Dust and sweat filled his nose. He was vaguely aware that he was shouting with each stroke.

Clang—slip. Screech, clang.

Tarleton's blows slowed. Then he parried into the hilt, locking

Jonathan's weapon low, and twisted. In a moment the shining broadsword was sailing through the air.

Jonathan knew he was dead.

A sword flashed toward Tarleton, but the lunge fell short, and the tip of the blade sliced Brutus's flank instead. The stallion screamed and reared. Coming down, he bucked, jostling Tarleton in the saddle, and for a moment Jonathan thought Tarleton would be thrown.

This was his chance. He drove Ducky close.

Later, he wasn't sure how he accomplished it with his weak leg.

Jonathan leaped from the saddle and grabbed Tarleton, wrestling him off the still-dancing Brutus. They fell to the ground.

Pain stabbed his leg, but he ignored it, grappling for Tarleton's sword arm. Jonathan squeezed the man's wrist until he let loose of the sword. Hooves flashed close to Tarleton's head.

The cavalryman thrashed and kicked. A fire-hot lance of pain disabled Jonathan's leg, and he loosened his hold. Like a greased pig the man was away.

Jonathan scrambled to his feet, ignoring the raging fire in his left leg. Rifles cracked from behind them, horses squealed, men shouted. Brutus pranced before him, nostrils red and flaring, and Jonathan grabbed the reins. Suddenly Sherman was there, helping him into the saddle.

His left leg was nearly useless.

"Where's Ducky?" Jonathan swallowed, his throat thick with dust.

"Gone. Tarleton took him."

His heart sank. He wanted to rain curses on the man but focused his mind on the battle. The cavalry was falling back as the riflemen advanced. The redcoats were beaten.

"We did it. We did it." Jonathan directed his horse away from the line of fire. The valley was safe. His family was safe.

"By the grace of God and the braw warriors of the Shenandoah Valley."

He smiled at Sherman's speech and followed him behind the trees. Now the danger was past, the pain roared in his ears, and he breathed slowly and deliberately.

Finally, he could think again. He studied the former British officer, riding Hannah's mare.

"Robert Sherman, ye have my permission to marry my sister."

Of course, Sherman would need to convince Hannah, but Jonathan wagered he was already halfway there.

"WHAT DID YOU DO?" Ruth studied Jonathan's leg as he lay back on the settee, forearm across his grimy forehead. Her locket lay in the sweaty depression between his collarbones, visible beneath his loosened neckerchief.

"Jumped out of the saddle."

Crazy man. The jagged scar was inflamed, and he could barely walk.

His mother brought warm sassafras and onions, and together they lay the poultice on the scar and wrapped it under a layer of linen. He thanked them, sat up, and Hannah brought him a tankard of ale.

The problem of the strained leg faded before the accomplishment of the militia—driving back Tarleton's men, keeping the valley safe.

The relief was so great, Ruth's limbs felt strangely light. She leaned over and placed a chaste kiss on Jonathan's head. He gave her a tired grin.

She poured cider into a cup for herself and drifted to the table, where the men of Russell's Ridge conversed in low tones.

Out of habit, she took mental note of every detail, then remembered that Sherman was here and would help Papa compose the news. He'd been there, after all.

He was speaking now.

"The British Army is divided. Cornwallis is here in Virginia, his men tired after weeks of campaigning. General Clinton is holed up in New York. If he were to come or send a large detachment to reinforce Cornwallis, the situation would quickly become dire in the tidewater."

"It's already dire." Ian MacLeod set his empty tankard on the table with extra force.

"We are not conquered yet." John Russell steepled his fingers. "They harass us, raid our stores of ammunition, and hunt our governor, but they will never take the Gap. Nor take the hearts of the people of Virginia, save a few Tories here and there."

"What about Washington?" Hannah's eyes were large in her face.

The men looked at her. They all knew the Continental Army was in New Jersey.

"Good question," Uncle Roy said. "But even if he came, would it be enough?"

That was Ruth's own question. Long years of skirmishes and retreats had not made her hopeful.

~

DAYS PASSED, and Ruth winced every time she saw Jonathan maneuver about with his crutch. At least he was up and about, though his jaw clenched in pain time and again.

She busied herself. Helped Papa, helped the others shuck the corn.

One day, trudging up the path after bringing switchel to the men in the fields, Ruth spotted Hannah trotting up on Bodie.

"I've a letter for ye," Hannah said, dismounting. She handed a water-stained missive to Ruth.

She looked at the direction. "'Tis Lucy. Hurry, I'll wait for you."

Ruth walked to the house and waited for Hannah to care for her horse. Sealed with a familiar K, the letter's return was marked Mount Vernon, Virginia. Why was Lucy Knox in Virginia? Had Henry sent her there while he remained in New Jersey?

Hannah bounded around the corner toward the house, cheeks pink with the heat of Indian summer and her exertions. "What does she say?"

Ruth popped open the seal and scanned it. "She describes Mount Vernon —seems to be the Washingtons' home." She kept reading and found what she wanted to know. She read aloud:

You may wonder why I'm here. Harry sent me, as you may have guessed. Last winter my darling children and I were crammed into a drafty farmhouse in Morristown, but that was nothing as I was with my dearest. Then he sent me away. What a horrible thing war is! Eventually Harry fetched me but left me here with Mrs. Washington. He is headed south with His Excellency.

I know little, and Harry tells me less, but he did mention Washington met with a French general, not La Fayette, but a more important man. Harry mentioned the French Navy. But even a brain filled with feathers would discern that if Washington is headed south, so is the French Navy.

"Washington went south," Hannah observed.

Chills crept up Ruth's spine and spread over her body. "I need to tell Papa."

"I need to tell Da."

ALL OF RUSSELL'S Ridge gathered for supper, a hearty conglomeration of leftovers, fresh corn, and ham. Ruth helped serve cider and ale to the tired men. Then she poured herself a tankard full of last year's cider and tasted it. Pungent and sharp, it was probably stronger than the ale.

She sat on a stool next to Hannah, who sat on the floor with her long legs crossed beneath her skirts. The kitchen was full of men, women, and children. The MacLeods' youngest, a lad of ten, joined Hannah on the floor.

They had come to hear Lucy's news, which surprised no one.

"Washington's in Virginia," John Russell said. "General Knox is with him, and presumably they mean to join Greene."

General Greene had fought a losing battle all the way north, Ruth knew. What would happen now?

"The French Navy is out there somewhere," Papa said.

Ruth stood, feeling conspicuous. "Lucy—Mrs. Knox—wrote that Washington met with the French. She thinks the fleet is coming here."

Robert Sherman cleared his throat. "We cannot succeed as long as the British Navy rules the Chesapeake."

Silence fell for a long moment.

"An obvious fact, even to the French." Jonathan's voice.

"Aye, the French Navy is coming to the Chesapeake." John Russell's brows drew together, puckering an old scar. "I think we can hope. We can certainly pray."

Hope broke through Ruth's gloom like a sudden sunrise.

50

From the bottom of my heart I congratulate you upon the arrival of the French fleet.

—The Marquis de Lafayette, letter to George Washington, Sept. 1781

October 1781

Jonathan pumped the lathe with his good leg while shaping the length of walnut wood with a plane. It irked him that he couldn't be outside heaving the logs into place on his new house, but Aunt Betsy scolded him whenever he tried to do anything strenuous.

Not to mention Ruth.

Jonathan stretched his gimpy leg gently. It had been over a month since the skirmish on the road to Charlottesville. The muscles of his lower leg were still stiff but not really painful. Perhaps he'd be able to work on the roof.

A puff of cool air and a creak marked the opening of the cabin door.

It was Robert, sweaty and carrying a jug.

"Want some switchel?"

"Aye, I can take a break." Jonathan left the piece of walnut in the grasp of the lathe. It was the last of four table legs. Soon he'd have a kitchen table to present to Ruth. Something he could do while recovering.

Robert stepped around the lathe and grabbed two cups from a shelf near the hearth. The main room of the cabin was filled with the Russells' wood-working tools and leftover wood. But two single men didn't need a fancy house.

"There's news, Billy Bob rode up from Staunton." Robert poured the switchel. "De Grasse's fleet has anchored at Jamestown."

Jonathan's cup paused on its way to his mouth. "How can you tell me that so calmly? It's great news." The French fleet stationed in the Chesa-peake could change everything. They could keep out the British Navy, for one.

"Washington's on his way to Virginia with his army." Robert drained his cup. "But I know not what Mr. Haynes will print."

The British could read too. Washington and Lafayette, Cornwallis and Tarleton, all thrown together. There would be a battle, and it might deter-mine the war.

His pulse quickened and he glanced up at his rifle over the door.

No, he couldn't go over the Gap to fight. It was William's turn. His brother had left with Colonel Johnson's militia yesterday.

Jonathan sipped the tart liquid.

Robert poured himself more switchel and drank thirstily. He set down the cup. "Come out and see the walls. You will be pleased, I think."

They walked outside but did not get far before Ruth intercepted them.

"Billy Bob brought me news." Ruth's gaze was intense. "Washington has arrived." She gulped a breath. "And the French—and the militia—all at Yorktown."

"Aye, it's all coming together." He cradled her face in his hands. Robert slipped away. "Ye think this is the end, that we have a chance."

She nodded, her eyes bright with tears.

"The roof will be on in a week." He kissed her. "Let's say our vows then."

Her eyes widened. "I'll ... I'll tell Hannah. She'll want to plan the kay ..."

"The ceilidh. Aye, she'll want to do that." He chuckled with joy.

∾

RUTH SMOOTHED her hands over the heavy fabric of the gown. The swirls of red and blue became indistinct as she blinked back tears. This garment had traveled a long way—first from General Arnold to Boston, then from dear Lucy Knox to Philadelphia, then folded carefully in a trunk for the long trip to the valley.

There were long months when Ruth despaired of ever wearing it to her own wedding. There were long nights when she wondered if she ought to give it away, or perhaps air it out and use it as a Sabbath gown.

But somehow both plans never came to fruition. The rich colors of the garment had lain dormant until this moment, when aired and freshly pressed, the gown was ready.

Jonathan was alive, and he had survived the clash with Tarleton's men. Past the cornfields stood a new house, redolent of fresh-cut pine.

She grabbed a handkerchief, but not quickly enough to stop the spill of tears over her cheeks.

She was grateful. Grateful to God. So much had gone wrong, there had been so much pain.

But now—

Joy cometh in the morning.

She scrubbed at her face and reached for her petticoat. Aunt Betsy would wonder what was taking her so long, and she'd probably fuss at her for crying and making her eyes red.

"Ruth?" Hannah's voice sounded from outside the bedroom door.

"Come in."

Hannah slipped inside the room. Coppery curls framed her face. "Ooo! I love the colors. Suits you." She cocked her head. "Now for the hair."

Ruth inhaled. "Yes, well—"

"I've a hair iron. And a ribbon that might match the gown."

Ruth was coaxed into submission, and thirty minutes later Hannah handed her a mirror.

A stranger looked back. Her hair was upswept with curls dangling behind and alongside her cheeks.

Hannah gave an approving smile. "Now for the finishing touch." She handed Ruth a tiny pot of rouge. "Just a dab."

Ruth remembered her mother's dresser, the rouge tucked away discretely. "Yes, just a dab."

Her heart swelled. Yes, she was thankful.

Now, if only she could brave the stairs.

IN THE OLD cabin he shared with Robert, Jonathan was sweating. His waistcoat fit, but the cravat—tied by Robert into a complicated spill of linen —choked him.

It was October, and the day was cool, but his clothing felt too warm.

It was his wedding day.

Nathan. If only …

An ache suffused him, the absence of his brother a palpable thing. Nathan should be here, should be at his side.

Sparrows … one of them shall not fall on the ground without your father.

Strangely comforted, Jonathan tucked the love of his brother inside his heart like a talisman.

"Ready?" Robert's voice was low and steady.

Jonathan took a deep breath. "Aye." He put on his coat, and they left the cabin for the house.

The wedding would be simple, private, signatures on a document. It was the Presbyterian way, to reject the fripperies and solemnities of Rome. But the valley folk affirmed the union of man and wife with a great deal of joy— and that would take place in Staunton.

Robert accompanied him up the path to the house. The heavy oak door seemed strange somehow. Once Jonathan stepped over the threshold of the Russell family home, he would see his bride. He'd been over this threshold innumerable times; it was an anchor of his boyhood, and now it would be the symbol of a new life.

He hesitated, then rapped on the door. First softly, then firmly.

"Behold, the bridegroom cometh," Robert quoted in his ear.

The door opened. His father's eyes looked suspiciously bright, then a grin spread across his face. Beyond him, his mother, Hannah, Aunt Betsy, Mr. Haynes.

Jonathan ducked under the lintel. Where was his bride?

He saw Colonel Mathews then, still thin but hearty, splotches of pink on his cheeks. Was he still sheriff? Jonathan couldn't remember, but supposed he'd been pressed into service as a magistrate.

The marriage document was on the walnut table. But where was the bride?

His father started singing. The tune was all old as time, but the words sailed past Jonathan's head. For there, descending the narrow stairs, was Ruth.

He melted.

She looked up and smiled.

He met her at the last stair-step and took her hands in his.

"Say ye'll never leave me."

"Never."

THE WAGON JOLTED beneath Ruth as they sped to Staunton and the ceilidh. She wiped her eyes, relieved the process was over. A simple signing of a document—how could it be so nerve-wracking? And yet her hands had trembled, and the ink had dripped. Thankfully none had spilled on her gown.

She snatched a glance at Jonathan beside her on the wagon seat.

He had spoiled the perfect lines of his cravat. Of course. It wouldn't stay on long.

The wheels clattered as they crossed the bridge before town. Ahead, wagons, horses, and people filled the streets.

Then she noticed. The people were clustering in front of the courthouse.

"There's news." Jonathan's voice was taut.

The war. Cornwallis. Washington. The reality of the fierce struggle across the Gap intruded.

Had the British smashed Washington? Ruth's stomach curled in fear.

Jonathan drove the horses as near as he could to the courthouse, then slipped off the seat. Ruth started to clamber down, but he darted around the wagon, put his hands around her waist, and lifted.

Heat rushed up Ruth's cheeks as he set her down.

But they were married, weren't they?

Jonathan took her arm and led her as close as possible to someone addressing the crowd.

Her heart lurched at the sight of William near the front—he was whole, smiling—and filthy.

Colonel Johnson was speaking. "Cornwallis has sent his surrender!"

Surrender?

Ruth felt dizzy.

Jonathan scooped her in his arms, and she floated half-aware, until finally she found herself blinking on a chair.

"Here, lass, take some cider." Andrew Lewis's creased face came into focus.

"Jonathan?"

"I'm here. Ye fainted straightway. Canna say as I blame ye."

"Is it real?

He knelt beside her, and his face came into her field of view, hair tousled, cravat unknotted. The scar on his cheekbone had never looked so beautiful. "Aye, it's real. We've won."

51

Some folks will think your husband a negotiator, but it is not to be, it is General Washington at Yorktown who did the substance of the work, the form only belongs to me.

—John Adams, letter to his wife Abigail

November 1781

"They forgot Tarleton." Lucy Knox repinned a lock of her hair that had loosened over the course of the evening. Her hair—piled high in the best formal fashion—could come down soon. She envied Martha Washington, who had managed to look perfect, stylish without being ostentatious. Her hair was curled artfully but without the cushion Lucy used; her gown was fine damask but without gaudy frills; and her garnet earbobs were a perfect touch.

Lucy longed for a new gown. But they had no money.

Henry was sprawled in a chair too small for him, feet propped toward a crackling, hospitable fire. "Washington's secretary forgets nothing."

Lucy scooted a chair close to Harry's and eased her bones into it. Then she kicked off her shoes and propped her aching feet next to his. These chairs were made for midgets. "So, we entertain Lord Cornwallis properly and leave out a single man?" She could guess the reason.

He opened a sleepy eye. "Washington was very correct in every other way."

"But he made his point by omitting Tarleton's invitation." The formal dinner hosted by the victors was a European custom, Harry had explained. It seemed strange to her. One moment Cornwallis was killing people, the next he was eating basted capon and drinking fine wine.

"The food was good," she admitted. "Cornwallis looked like he was sucking on a lemon."

The conversation had been awkward. Harry and Lafayette had helped to ease the tension. The wine helped, too.

"Hmm."

Henry was not going to stay awake long. She felt for the letter in her pocket. "I've a letter from Ruth—remember the Haynes?"

Dear Lucy (she read),

My most solemn and joyous congratulations to your husband for helping to bring this horrific conflict to an end. I have heard that artillery played a significant role in Cornwallis's defeat. I wish I could have been there, seen the armies line up, French and American, and the British marching between them in surrender.

What an amazing course Providence has taken! We are feeble in comparison to the British, yet the Lord has overruled, and surely now the British will concede defeat and recognize our independence. All Virginia rejoices to be free of Cornwallis's men, and Tarleton, of course. Jefferson's home was ransacked, I am sorry to report, his horses stolen, and those too young to ride butchered like pigs.

Our deliverance came none too soon. Please give your dear Harry a warm greeting from an old friend. My gratitude for your service is too deep to express.

And now you must congratulate me. Do you recall a certain chintz gown you gifted me, the one from that blackguard Benedict Arnold? I wore it to my wedding, and to the frolic afterward. It is the custom here, that though the ceremony itself is simple, the cele-bration with family and neighbors is a grand event. Dancing and plenty of ale. It so chanced that the frolic also celebrated Washington's victory. A double joy!

You may recall the groom, Jonathan Russell. I have written both of his trials and exploits at great length, and so I will not bore you further. His leg is stronger, and he no longer uses the crutch, though when he tires he begins to limp. I just make sure he is warm enough—mulled cider in his hands—and say nothing.

Jonathan plans to study metalworking, of which he already comprehends a great deal. Has Henry a book, or know where we might look in Williamsburg, for such a thing?

With affection, Mrs. Ruth Russell

"What? Benedict Arnold?" Henry blinked.

"Have you been sleeping all this time?"

ROCKFISH GAP WAS cold and windy, but Ruth had a thick blanket over her knees, and Jonathan seemed impervious to the weather.

"Mind you," he told her once they'd descended beyond the worst of the wind, "my leg tells me when the weather changes."

Aunt Betsy had occasioned this trip, her frequent complaints about her barren shop shelves giving them the final impetus to leave. Ruth had hopes for embroidery thread for curtains and kitchen supplies for their new home before the snow made the Gap difficult to navigate.

Now that Lord Cornwallis had surrendered to Washington, and the French Navy dominated the Chesapeake, goods would be coming into shops in Williamsburg and Yorktown.

Half-naked trees lined the sides of the rutted road. The heavily laden wagon jolted beneath them, and the two large mules in harness swung their furry ears, relaxing clip clops sounding in her ears. Goods of all sorts filled the wagon bed—whiskey, furs, ginseng, even a hogshead of tobacco. The the neighbor's tobacco would go to a warehouse in Richmond, the rest they'd take all the way to the coast.

She thought of Robert Sherman. At their wedding frolic, Sherman led Hannah out in reel after reel. It was only a matter of time. Williamsburg would have what she needed for the next wedding.

"I've decided what I will write."

Jonathan's brows rose. "For the paper?"

"No." She straightened her lap blanket. "I've taught Billy Bob to read better, and some of the Robinson children."

"And one of the Kerrs, I noticed."

The tone of his voice was approving, so she plunged ahead.

"They know how to write their names—most have been through the primer. And many know their catechism. But they are not prepared for Latin school. I want to write simple readers. Easy books they would learn from after they master the primer and the catechism."

"Sounds wonderful." Jonathan straightened, his hands tightening on the reins. "Ho, what's that?"

He halted the mules and eased himself to the ground. A bit of metal gleamed from the dust. He reached down and picked up a sword half buried in the dirt.

"Jonathan! Is that the one you lost?"

His grin was lopsided. "Aye. Banged up a bit—see?"

The basket hilt was crushed. "Can it be repaired?"

"Of a surety! I did say I was hoping for a book."

After the skirmish near Charlottesville, Jonathan had questioned the blacksmith about metalworking.

"It's a tinker ye want to talk to," the man had said. "Tinkers do all kinds of things. Many do silver too."

Tinkers appeared from time to time in Staunton, but none lived there —yet. Metalworking and fancy leatherwork, studded bridles and harness, all these appealed to Jonathan—and of course, knives in fancy tooled sheaths.

"My cousin Ben knows leather," Jonathan had said. "Uncle Roy taught him everything."

And so it had been decided. Jonathan and Ben would set up shop in the spring.

And with the decision, the strain in Jonathan's face had lifted.

Warm air embraced Ruth as they walked through the door of the shop Henry Knox had recommended. She welcomed the smell of paper and old books.

Jonathan went to the counter. "D'ye have books on tinkering? Metal-working?"

The bookshop owner's face contracted in a frown. Jonathan followed him as the man examined the musty shelves. Ruth cast her eyes over the titles. Some were new, uncut volumes; others were dusty and worn, sold to the shop for a pittance, most probably. Loyalists—Ruth hesitated to use the derogatory term Tory—had either fled or hunkered down now that the tide had turned. Some had sold many of their things before leaving. Some—Patriot and Loyalist both—sold their things simply to eat.

A bell marked the entrance of another customer. Ruth caught a glimpse of red and ducked behind the nearest bookshelf.

A redcoat!

She was trembling. Then warm arms circled her. "Dinna fash," Jonathan murmured into her hair. "He'll no bother ye, he's given his parole."

But they stayed in the shadowed nook until the man left.

"Most of the army is being held prisoner until arrangements are made," he explained. "But the officers can give their parole."

Ruth finally relaxed. "Did you find a book?"

"Nae luck." Jonathan escorted her outside.

"What will we do? I've everything I need, the goods are sold—"

He steered her by her elbow to the wagon. "Yorktown. That fellow said there is a man in Yorktown I should see."

The trip to Yorktown was like a trip to the moon. The armies had ravaged the countryside, tearing down fences for firewood and chopping down trees.

And when they neared the battlefield, evidence of fighting—a dropped musket, a canteen, once even a soiled wig—abounded. The wagon lurched and creaked over a shallow trench that Jonathan claimed was dug by a cannonball. The acrid smell of latrines was discernible despite the heavy marshy scent of the nearby river, and once Ruth caught the putrid whiff of death.

She shivered when they drove past the earthworks, so reminiscent of Boston's, bringing back memories of that long night of treating the injured. She reached for Jonathan's hand, and his warm fingers eased her heart.

A church spire poked above the trees, and soon they were surrounded by fine brick homes, untouched by the battle. Afternoon shadows banded the main thoroughfare of the town, a peaceful sight. Several men came out of a tavern, conversing.

A seagull's rhythmic squawking sang of the sea.

Ruth scanned each side of the street, looking for the shop. A wagon passed them, then a man on a chestnut. Ahead, another man rode toward them on a black horse.

The horse had a distinctive feathery mane. It had to be Ducky.

Jonathan stiffened. "Ye have your pistol?"

She fumbled with her satchel, tucked behind her in the wagon bed. Jonathan drew out the battered sword he'd tucked under the seat.

She handed the pistol to Jonathan, who opened his powder horn and primed the pan.

She studied the man riding Ducky. He was of modest height and erect carriage. The afternoon sun laced his auburn hair with fire.

"Tarleton," Jonathan breathed.

Her heart hammered in her chest. "Jonathan, you said ... he's surrendered!"

"Dinna fret. I'll tie this onto my belt, see if he remembers me."

He jumped down and turned to look at her. "But cover me, if he doesna remember his parole."

The rider was only a few yards away. This was Bloody Ban? His calm features were ordinary, even pleasant.

"Ho, Tarleton! Is that your horse?"

A wary look was quickly replaced by a saucy grin. "I borrowed it from a friend."

Ruth's breath came in short gasps. She tightened her grip on the heavy pistol but did not lift it.

Tarleton's gaze took her in—and the pistol.

Jonathan grasped the bridle. "Hey Ducky, what say we go home." He stroked the animal's head in a seemingly casual manner, but to Ruth his motions seemed calculated, every word, every touch careful.

"I say, would you return the stallion for me?" Tarleton dismounted with the grace of a dancer, then bowed. "A fine animal."

He turned and walked into the nearest tavern.

For a long moment, Jonathan simply watched him leave.

He stroked Ducky's nose and looked at her. "That's the end of Tarleton."

"He didn't seem so horrible."

Seeing the infamous man so obviously defeated didn't give her a feeling of triumph. Just an ache inside, a memory of all they'd suffered.

Jonathan shrugged. "War is horrible. Even though the Cause was just ... it was still horrible."

He tied Ducky onto the back of the wagon. "Before we look for the print shop, I've another place I want to visit."

Ruth looked down at the pistol and studied the wood grain. She took a long, slow breath, slipped it into her pocket, and snaked her arm around her husband's.

Tarleton humbled, unhorsed. A visible sign that the war was truly over. After so long, after such loss. Every morning she woke to the new experience of a warm husband and no more war, having to adjust her mind to a fresh new reality. It was like spring water after days with nothing to drink.

Jonathan urged the mules and they continued on down the street. To their right was a print shop, but they passed that without stopping. They pulled up at a glazier's.

"Why are we here?"

Jonathan smiled impishly and pulled out a coin purse. "Da sold a horse to the Jeffersons. One of Brutus's get. Gave me the money for a wedding gift." He looked at the shop. "I'm going to place an order. For windows."

Tears flooded her eyes. Not many in the valley had glass windows. Not for their first house, anyway.

"Ye spoke of curtains. Ye need nice windows to go with them."

Ruth squeezed his hand. She had a home. She was home.

EPILOGUE

Russell's Ridge, March 1782

*R*obert took a deep, steadying inhale of the chill morning air, the same deep breath he used to calm himself when shouldering a weapon.

It didn't work this time.

He clutched the letter, and the edge of the paper sliced his skin. He sucked at the tiny well of blood.

What would he do if Hannah rejected him?

There was nothing for it. He knocked on the solid oak door before him, and in a breath of time Mrs. Russell opened it. Several silver strands highlighted the golden blond hair fringing her face. Were they new?

The war had changed them all.

"Come in," she said, and Robert found himself escorted to the humble parlor. She returned with a mug of hot coffee.

"Thank you." He sniffed at the steam rising from the hot liquid. Real coffee. A measure of trade had started up again. The British were slowly evacuating the surrendered men, and General Clinton had been recalled.

According to his godmother, Lord Rawdon had left South Carolina before Yorktown due to illness, only to be captured at sea by the French. The process of exchange was slow, but sure. He would be home soon. Robert was consoled that an ocean now separated them. He had no desire to see his cousin again.

News of a treaty appeared now and then in the *Gazette*. The King was resisting the plain truth, and the wheels of diplomacy were grinding very slowly.

But the British had plainly lost. The Army humiliated. First, with Burgoyne, second with Lord Cornwallis. There was no coming back from that.

They had lost. No, they had won, the colonies had won. Every time the thrill of victory surged through him, he felt less strange, less foreign.

More American.

He was no longer Robert Shirley, British officer. He was Robert Sherman—

Hannah Russell stood before him, and Robert's gut balled up tight. He set the mug down and rose.

"Good morning," he said. The letter burned in his hand, the tiny wound throbbing. "I ... I—"

"Sit," she commanded gently.

Her mother had disappeared, and they were alone.

They both sat, and Robert took a steadying breath. He'd made a decision, and he didn't know how to break it to her. She might reject him—should reject him—

"I ... I made Miss Haynes—Mrs. Russell—an offer, she has a project in mind—"

He was fumbling, unable to speak of his true purpose.

"The readers? For children?" Her blue eyes were fixed on him.

"Um ... yes."

"She told me all about it. She's quite excited." Hannah sat patiently, waiting.

"It will take some time. When they are printed, I will bind them." Robert took another breath. His hand twitched, and the paper crackled.

Her eyes fell on the letter.

"I have a letter," he began.

"From your godmother?" Her calm blue gaze settled him. He could live in her eyes.

"Yes—and no. That is to say, I have received a letter from the countess, and she included a letter from the Earl of Dartmouth. He is sending funds—and two fillies."

She cocked her head. "That's good news. And what about the orphanage?"

He swallowed. "There has a been a fire, you see, and—"

"She wants ye to see to it, to put matters right."

His lips parted in surprise.

"I kent all about Whitefield's orphanage. She wrote me over a year ago, you knew that."

Robert studied Hannah's face. She wasn't alarmed at the prospect of his departure. But did that mean she did not care for him at all? His face flushed as he remembered a kiss in the barn.

He thought he knew her. But did he?

"Robert. When you asked me the distance to Georgia, ye weren't being subtle. Ye were thinking about it even then. I know ye're going."

His heart seemed to stop beating.

She smiled. "And your wife will be going too."

"You mean—"

"Aye, ye clot-heid. I'm coming too. And yes, I'll marry you."

AUTHOR'S NOTE

Thank you for coming on this journey with me! If you enjoyed this story, please share your experience on Amazon, Goodreads, or Bookbub. Reviews help both authors and readers! Sign up for my newsletter at www.lynneta gawa.com for updates and discounts.

~

Keep reading for a recipe and a brief glossary of Scots words. But first, the story behind the series. The first of the series, *The Shenandoah Road*, was written to place the reader in the time of the Great Awakening of the 1730s-40s. As I researched and wrote, I had this book in mind as well.

The American Revolution is unique in history. The actions of our Founders were influenced by what they believed. Their worldview was influenced by the scriptures, partly because George Whitefield's preaching had revived believers and saved many souls during the awakening. Churches flourished, especially Baptist and "Methodist" gatherings.

"Give 'em Watts, boys!" shouted Rev. James Caldwell, chaplain of the Continental Army, when the artillery grew low on wadding during the Battle of Connecticut Farms. He carried over stacks of hymn books from the local church to supply the gunners. During the Great Awakening, Isaac Watts's hymns became popular, and later Charles Wesley's poetry crossed the ocean. The hymn book containing Amazing Grace--*Olney Hymns*—was not actually published until 1779. I took liberties, therefore, in giving Nathan Russell that song. But the first of the Countess of Huntingdon's hymn books was published in 1765. Undoubtedly these had found homes in America as well as Britain.

Our Founders were influenced by enlightenment writers such as John Locke. However, the most influential treatise among Scottish Presbyterians was undoubtedly Samuel Rutherford's *Lex, Rex*. He must have influenced non-Presbyterians as well. At any rate, the Founders followed his principles regarding what is allowable under tyranny.

But if you're like me, it's the people who grab your attention. And you can't make some of this stuff up.

Francis, Lord Rawdon was the grandson of Selina Hastings, Countess of Huntingdon. This woman was labeled the "Queen of the Methodists" by one politician for her tireless work to support Whitefield, the Wesleys, and a number of younger ministers. I'm sure she wrestled in prayer for her family members, but few of them followed in her footsteps. I can only imagine that Lord Rawdon was a grief to her mind.

Rawdon served in the British Army with some distinction and a little notoriety. He probably shot Dr. Joseph Warren in the face at the Battle of Bunker's Hill and served as one of Lord Cornwallis's right-hand men in the southern campaign.

He was also a key figure in the execution of a man named Isaac Hayne for "spying" in August 1781. The circumstances were similar to the fictional event I portray in the story (Robert's rescue of "Smelly") and served as a clue to his character. Parliament opened an inquiry, and a member of the House of Lords made comments to which Rawdon objected. He insisted the man make an apology or face him on the "field of honor." The duke said he was sorry. I guess he didn't want to face Rawdon's pistol.

The King, however, was pleased with Rawdon's service and gave him a barony. He became a friend of the Prince of Wales, was once put forward for Prime Minister, and served in India.

I took one notable liberty with Lord Rawdon's service for story purposes. He (most probably) remained at Camden when Lt. Col. Tarleton took a force to meet General Morgan. I doubt he was present at Cowpens.

Banastre "Bloody Ban" Tarleton is more well known in the US than in the UK, though there is a nice portrait of him in the National Gallery. Fans of Mel Gibson's *The Patriot* may recognize him as the inspiration for the character Tavington. In reality, there were several British officers who did stuff like burn churches, and the movie just rolled them into one nefarious villain with a name starting with the letter T. Tarleton may not have been as evil as his reputation. But there is no doubt as to the way people responded to his name, and so he symbolizes British brutality during the war.

In person, Tarleton could be charming. He was the son of a man who made money in the slave trade, and like Major André, he had no social standing. Unlike the major, he was a womanizer who tended to gamble his money away. He was wounded in the hand at the Battle of Guildford Courthouse and lost part of two fingers. I am not sure what happened after he captured several members of the Virginia Assembly in Charlottesville in 1781. We know two things: the Shenandoah Valley militia were assembled at Rockfish Gap to deny him entrance. We also know that he turned back on the road. Was there a skirmish? It was fun to include it for story purposes. We do know that Tarleton was not invited to Washington's dinner, and he really did surrender a "black charger" to an unknown man in Yorktown who claimed to be its owner.

I enjoyed including a Friesen stallion, which would have been an unusual sight, both then and now. But about this time in history, a horse was foaled that would become the first of the "Morgan" breed, one of the first truly American horse breeds. Morgans are thought to be part thoroughbred but they also probably have some Friesen ancestry.

Betsy Ross was not the only one to produce flags during the war. Rebecca Young was widowed after the British took Philadelphia but returned with her family after they left. Her brother helped set her up in business, and she produced quite a lot of goods for General Washington's men: flags, caps, and other odds and ends, including tools to clean firearms, made by her older son, who knew metalworking from his father. For story purposes, I imagined her producing flags from the get-go.

Colonel George Mathews was a hero at Brandywine but was captured with the rest of the Ninth Virginia at Germantown and ended up on a prison ship. The British Army used derelict ships to house prisoners of war. It may have been a reflection of the ambiguity of the prisoners' position—thought to be treasonous criminals rather than true POWs—that lay behind the horrific treatment of these men. But the army was known for brutal discipline of its own members, and even the legal system in Britain for civilians was harsh. When my character Robert notices that only murder carries the death penalty in Boston, he marvels. So it fits with the state of the thinking of the time.

Generally, prisoners did not survive captivity unless they escaped. Thousands perished in these prison ships, more in number than died on the battlefield. George Mathews somehow managed to survive for two years on one of these hulks and was exchanged because he was an officer.

Jack Jouette was Virginia's Paul Revere. He rode forty miles to warn Thomas Jefferson and the Virginia Legislature that Tarleton was coming. I couldn't resist including him, although I am not sure where he went after the ride. In the story I have him cross the Gap into the valley.

The Revolutionary War was won, humanly speaking, by the unlikeliest of men. A large bookshop owner, Henry Knox; a limping, lapsed Quaker, Nathaniel Greene; and a former teamster with sciatica, Daniel Morgan, all served with heart and integrity. George Washington trusted them like no others, and was especially close to the genial Knox, with whom he could relax his normally rigid persona.

Men like Washington and Knox made heartfelt references to the decrees of heaven when speaking of the war. They weren't fatalists, but knew God ruled in the affairs of men. I think we may step back and glorify God as they did when viewing the events that led to the birth of our nation.

My house is now filled with (more) books—biographies, books about specific battles, and general histories. There are a few books I'd like to mention.

John Adams by David McCullough is a classic. Well-written.

Selina: Countess of Huntingdon by Faith Cook. A forgotten founder of Methodism.

The Long Fuse: How England Lost the American Colonies by Don Cook. A unique point of view.

The British Are Coming by Rick Atkinson, great read.

Bunker Hill: A City, A Siege, A Revolution by Nathaniel Philbrick.

Henry Knox: Visionary General of the American Revolution by Mark Puls.

Rush by Stephen Fried.

For a general history, Atkinson's is wonderful—alas, it is the first of a trilogy which he has not yet completed.

A classic general history that reads well is *Patriots: The Men Who Started the American Revolution* by A.J. Langguth.

~

Now, about those words:

There are three languages spoken in Scotland: British English (with a local accent), Scots English (sometimes classified as a dialect of English, sometimes as a separate language), and Scots Gaelic, a totally unrelated language. Some of my characters are either immigrants from Scotland or Northern Ireland or their descendants and would retain many of these linguistic characteristics. Some of their vocabulary vanished over time, but some remains as part of American English—words like malarkey and smidgen.

- clot-heid. Scots English, meaning dunderhead
- ken, kent. Scots English, meaning know
- canna. Scots accent, can't
- dinna. Scots accent, don't
- eejit. Scots English, meaning idiot

~

Now, that recipe!

In the eighteenth century, colonists drank "switchel" in warm weather. It was like a sports drink, full of electrolytes. It's a simple recipe, combining apple cider vinegar, molasses (or another sweetener, like maple syrup), ginger, and water.

You can vary the proportions of vinegar to molasses to suit your taste. A typical recipe might be:

- One half cup apple cider vinegar
- One cup molasses
- One tablespoon powdered ginger
- One gallon water

ACKNOWLEDGMENTS

First, I'd like to thank my Lord and Savior Jesus Christ, who has blessed me and strengthened me in my writing. And my husband, who has continually supported and encouraged me. And my readers, who have made encouraging comments and asked for more stories!

The beautiful cover is a result of the talents of several people. A former student offered to pose (on the condition of anonymity, so we cut her head off). My daughter-in-law Sara took photos, and Jane of JS Design formed the cover image.

I'd like to thank Bob, Natalie, Lynda, and Diane of my ACFW critique group, and Alynda, Teresa, Judy, Kristen, and Dena of my Word Weavers' group. All your input has been invaluable. My beta readers are a joy, and I'm very thankful for Robin Patchen's editorial input. Jayna Baas's suggestions have been invaluable. Thanks to Trudy Cordle for proofreading. And thanks to Vikki Kestell for her kind recommendation.

Soli Deo gloria.

ABOUT THE AUTHOR

Lynne Basham Tagawa is an emerging author of Christian historical fiction who sometimes falls down hobbit holes when pursuing minutiae in her research. She is also prone to using big words and even semi-colons, which clearly went extinct in the last century.

But her true passion is gospel truth and the big ideas that have shaped our country's history. An educator, she hopes her stories feed her readers' hearts and minds without the pain of quizzes and tests.

Not very tech-savvy, she has fried one computer and now pounds away on a laptop. Her grandchildren like to sit with her in church, and her daughter-in-law took the photos that made the cover design possible. Her husband supports her by not complaining about the dust.

You can support her by posting a review! Or by following her on these sites:

Made in the USA
Monee, IL
06 September 2023

42238182R00240